To Naomi, for her boundless enthusiasm for this story.
You made writing it a joy.

TALKING
C(IN)DE

ARIEL TACHNA

Published by
DREAMSPINNER PRESS

5032 Capital Circle SW, Suite 2, PMB# 279, Tallahassee, FL 32305-7886 USA
www.dreamspinnerpress.com

ISBN: 978-1-63533-442-5
Digital ISBN: 978-1-63533-443-2
Library of Congress Control Number: 2016916565
Published March 2017
v. 1.0
Printed in the United States of America

This paper meets the requirements of
ANSI/NISO Z39.48-1992 (Permanence of Paper).

PROLOGUE

"COMMANDER, WE found Newton!"

Timothy Davenport looked up from the mission plan he was studying as Victoria Amato burst into the room, her usually impassive expression hopeful for the first time in four months. His heart beat faster as he waited to hear the details. He didn't glance over at Richard, sure his expression would give too much away. They might be independent of the Navy now, after reaching the point they could no longer deal with a colleague's racist remarks—never directly about Richard but always where Richard could hear them—but the lessons they'd learned about discretion and keeping their relationship under wraps had never worn off.

"Where?" demanded Richard Horn, commander of Strike Force Omega and Tim's longtime lover. Tim set aside the mission plan and moved to Richard's side.

Amato handed the aerial surveillance image to Richard, but her smile was all for Tim. "Eric will be home before you know it, Davenport."

"Knock on wood," Tim replied, the superstitions of old sailors too strong for him to cast aside easily. He might not wear the uniform of a SEAL anymore, but he was no less one at heart. "Thank you, Amato."

"Sir."

She left them alone with the photo and the dossier that accompanied it.

"We can't go in there guns blazing, Richard," Tim said before Richard could speak. "It doesn't matter how desperate we are to get him back. We have to do this right, or he could end up dead before we get there."

"They'd never see us coming," Richard replied. He was right, of course. They'd been on more stealth missions with their teams, both as SEALs and after they created Strike Force Omega, than he cared to count, but this was Eric they were talking about, the third leg of their triangle, their breath of fresh air, their precious, precocious other half, who had been held captive for far too long already in conditions Tim didn't want to imagine. If ever collateral damage had to be minimized, it was now. "We leave in an hour."

"You know we can't do that," Tim said. "Even if we had nothing else in the works, we have to plan this right. This isn't something the two of us can do alone."

"You really want to send someone else after him?" Richard asked.

"Of course I don't," Tim all but shouted. "I love him as much as you do, but that's all the more reason not to throw something together. We only have one chance at this. If we can't pull him out on the first try, we won't get another shot. You saw the same video I did right after he was captured. They'll kill him rather than give us another opportunity."

The anguish on Richard's face reflected the ache in Tim's heart, but Tim didn't back down. He couldn't. This was too important. He hadn't spent twenty years at Richard's side without learning how to bring him around when it really mattered.

"What do you suggest we do?" Richard asked.

Tim let out the breath he was holding. If Richard was asking the question, he was open to the answers, and that was the battle half won.

"We have to move on this before they realize we know and move him or kill him, but the Syria op is set. We're already going to be in the Caspian while we run that mission. You can oversee a second one from the same command post. We'll have to do it quietly since it's not a government-sanctioned rescue op, but nobody's going to complain about us shooting some terrorists to hell."

"You want me to sit on the deck of a fucking aircraft carrier while you go into… where the hell is this, anyway?"

Tim looked at the map. "Turkmenistan."

"While you go into Turkmenistan to rescue Eric."

"No," Tim said. "I'm going to Syria."

"The fuck you are. We're both going to Turkmenistan. We'll deal with Syria when we have Eric back."

"We can't do that, and you know it," Tim said. He cradled Richard's cheeks in his hands and rested their foreheads together. "We can send Amato and her team to get Eric now, or we can wait until we finish in Syria and hope they haven't moved him while we weren't looking. As much as I want to be his knight on a white horse, we can't afford to wait."

"Amato could go to Syria," Richard muttered.

Tim wished she could, but it wasn't that easy. "Without Eric, she doesn't have a sniper, and Taylor won't work with her." He'd never gotten the full story out of either of them, but he suspected Amato had taken it upon herself to teach Taylor a lesson in respect after Eric had finally joined Richard and Tim as their lover. It was just as well that she had. The last time Tim had to teach someone that lesson (a former employee had called Eric a half-breed), he'd quit less than a day later. "That's why I was taking the Syria mission in the first place."

"Damn you for always being right."

Tim kissed him swiftly. "We'll get him back, and we'll help him through the aftermath of whatever they've done to him, and we'll blow them to pieces once he's out of range. Amato will bring him home."

"I hope you're right."

So did Tim.

Chapter 1

Richard Horn had two good things in his life. His hands and his eyes, he called them—Eric Newton and Timothy Davenport—his lovers, his sanity, his support, and his life. The fucking terrorists had taken both of them from him, Eric four months ago in an op gone wrong when Richard was half a world away and could do nothing but plot and plan how to get him back, and Dav mere minutes ago in a hail of bullets no one could hope to survive. Richard would be damned before he let them take anything else.

He stared at the twin data streams from drones in two different parts of the world. The team had managed to evacuate Dav, although the last he heard, he had coded. Richard's heart had stopped right along with it until they'd announced they had a pulse again. How long that would last with a dozen bullet holes in him, Richard didn't know, but if anyone could take those hits and survive, it was Dav. Richard had never met anyone who defied the odds the way Dav did. He'd switched audio channels after they revived him. He couldn't do anything for Dav now, and he had another mission to run, one with no backup if it went sideways.

The UAV hovered over the scene unfolding below, but distance and smoke and dust from a series of explosions—some set by his team, others of unknown origin—made it impossible to make out details. His team could be dead and he wouldn't know it, since they were maintaining radio silence as much as possible. Or they could be pulling Eric out even now. His eyes in the sky weren't any good to him inside the terrorist compound, but he could make sure nothing approached from outside. Or bomb the hell out of them if they did.

"Fuck. Found him."

Victoria Amato had seen more combat than anyone working for them except Richard himself and Dav. If Eric was in bad enough shape that she cursed at the sight of him….

Richard pushed the thought aside. He didn't have time for sentimentality. They still had to get him out of there and home. He spun the drone around to check the perimeter.

"Get the hell out of there. You've got incoming," he snapped.

"On it."

Richard angled the drone to allow him to get off a shot at the convoy headed toward the compound. He hit the shot. Of course he hit the shot. Then a missile from the ground nearly took off his wing. He cursed a blue streak as he dodged and circled up out of range. He'd have to settle for surveillance and warning them of anything incoming. It was all he could do at this point. He prayed to a God he didn't quite believe in that it would be enough. "They've got surface-to-air missiles," he warned the team. "I'm not going to be much good except as eyes in the sky."

"You make a good set of eyes." Richard nearly sagged in relief at the sound of Eric's voice on the comm no matter how broken. Even after months of who the hell knew what kind of torture, he still had the nerve to mouth off at the first opportunity. God, he loved that man, and if the terrorists thought they were taking the one good thing Richard Horn had left, they didn't know a single fucking thing about him. "We'll be your hands."

Davenport was their eyes, usually, but he….

"Don't fuck it up, Newton." He hadn't said it before Eric left for the mission that had landed him in the hands of a particularly sadistic branch of terrorists. He wasn't going to risk not saying it again.

"No, sir."

He circled the drone again, at an altitude out of the range of their known weaponry, and waited. Within moments he saw his team come stumbling out toward the rendezvous point. "Sanders, get them the hell out of there."

"Yes, sir." The Jeep broke cover the moment Richard spoke, rolling across the rocky terrain toward the team, but Sanders swerved almost immediately.

"We're taking fire, sir. Undetermined location."

"Damn it all to hell and back," Richard swore as he steered the drone lower. If he could find the shooter, either he or Eric could take him out. "Someone get Newton a weapon. If I find this son of a bitch, I want him dead."

"You really think he walked out of there unarmed?" Victoria replied. "I brought his M40 with me."

"Find me a target," Eric said.

Richard circled the drone around the field, but he couldn't distinguish the shooter's location. When he flew lower, the UAV came under fire. He saw that installation and fired back.

"Move," he shouted into the comm. "Get to the Jeep and get the hell out of there. I'll cover you."

They scrambled across the field and into the Jeep. Richard shot at anything else that moved until Sanders had them on the way out of the

mountains toward the airstrip where they'd hidden the Blackhawk they flew
in on. If they could get back to that, they'd be safe. He clicked the comm
over to Victoria's headset. She didn't know all his secrets, but she knew
more than anyone else on the rescue team.

"Keep an eye on Newton. Davenport is down, and I don't have an
update. Until I do, Newton is considered a flight risk."

"Yes, sir."

He trailed them from above as they careened down narrow roads
toward the landing strip. Only when they were safely aboard the copter and
in the air did he pull off his headset and hand the controls over. He didn't
even look to see who took his place. It didn't matter. Eric was safe.

"Sir?"

Richard looked up at Margot Heikkinen, his second-in-command.
He'd picked her up from an op with the CIA, more years ago than he cared
to count. She was a treasure trove of information—as long as he didn't ask
where she'd gotten it. "Yes?"

"I heard from the medevac team in Syria. They have Davenport at a
military hospital in Israel. They're still trying to stabilize him for transport
to Landstuhl in Germany."

"He's alive?"

"For the moment, yes." Richard closed his eyes against the relief that
flooded him. It had nearly killed him to turn off the audio channel from the
med team as they fought to save his lover of over twenty years. Only the
necessity of helping the other team save Eric had made him do it.

Shit. He'd told Amato that Dav was down. If she told Eric, the other
third of their triangle and the only other person who kept Richard sane, and
Richard didn't manage to reassure him, they'd be lucky if he ran rather than
self-combusted right there. He grabbed his phone from his belt and texted
the number for the replacement phone for Eric that he'd given the rescue
team, the one message guaranteed to keep Eric from losing his shit until
Richard could get to him.

The phone indicated the message had been delivered, but that didn't
tell him who held the other device. He prayed once more, this time that Eric
had the new phone. He considered texting Amato or one of the others just to
make sure the message got through, but he wasn't ready to let any of them
inside the layers of secrets that protected his heart.

"Get a line open to the hospital in Israel. I want updates every five
minutes." He wanted to get the hell on a plane and fly straight to Israel, but
being there wouldn't change anything for Dav. Not being here for Eric was

out of the question. Yes, it was usually Dav's job, but Richard had let them all down enough already. He'd have to step into those shoes until Dav was well enough to take back over.

ERIC NEWTON collapsed into the cargo hold of the unmarked copter Sanders was currently piloting the hell out of Dodge. He didn't even know where that was at the moment, or where they were going. He felt like death warmed over, and from the looks Victoria kept sending him, he probably looked even worse than he felt. He didn't care, though. He was upright and out of the hands of his captors, and they'd taken out most of the base on their way out. He figured that was a cause for celebration.

He ought to let Tim know he was okay. He'd heard Richard's voice on the comm, so Richard knew, but Tim hadn't said anything, and he hadn't come on the rescue op. That meant he was running another op somewhere else in the world. Better to wait, then, and not disturb him. Richard would find a way to let him know when the time was right.

Superstitious old bastard, he thought with a quirk of his lips as Richard's voice echoed in his head. In four years of battles, Richard had never sent him out without saying those four little words. *Don't fuck it up.*

"Eric?"

Victoria's voice drew Eric's attention from his memories. "Yeah?"

"I'm sorry," she said with more sympathy on her face than he had ever seen her show anyone. "Horn told me Davenport went down. He was leading an op in Syria."

Syria.... His captors had asked him about Syria every time they tortured him. He didn't think he'd said anything, but they'd drugged him with so many different concoctions, and he had large stretches of time with no memories at all. He could have said anything and he wouldn't even know. Tim was down, probably dead because the bastard never did anything halfway, and Eric was responsible. He bent double, fighting the urge to retch on the floor of the chopper. His team would kick his ass.

"What did he say?" Eric asked when he could control the bile rising in his throat. "His exact words."

"Davenport is down and I don't have an update," Victoria repeated.

"Hey, sorry to interrupt, but Horn gave me a phone for you, Newton, and it just buzzed at me. I figured you'd want to see whatever the message was."

Eric almost asked why he would want to see anything with Tim down—wounded for sure, possibly dead—but Westin wouldn't get it.

None of them would except Victoria, because she was the only one who knew about him and Tim. He took the phone. If nothing else, he could text Richard and demand an explanation. He unlocked the phone, keyed to his fingerprints—one of these days he'd ask how Richard did it—and opened the text program. One word stared back at him. *SNAFU.*

He choked out a laugh. "It's a lie. Or a sleight of hand or something. Richard Horn is a motherfucking liar who lies. I ought to know. I coined the phrase." And what a twisted, wonderful memory that was, of Richard inviting Eric to join him and Tim, assuring him it didn't mean anything, that they liked the occasional one-night extra to liven things up. He'd believed it, too, right up until the moment they pulled him between them and held him like they'd never let him go. "He lies like he breathes, but he wouldn't lie about this. Not to me."

"Newton, I know what Davenport means to you, but Horn told me he was down."

"Then it's not as bad as he thought it was or something. Horn texted me this. He wouldn't have sent it if Davenport was dead."

"Situation normal, all fucked-up?" Westin said, peering at the text over Eric's shoulder. "How is that reassuring?"

"Because nothing about our situation is ever anything other than fucked-up. It's the normal part that matters. He calls Davenport his eyes. Do you really think he'd say the situation was normal if Davenport was dead?"

"Why did he text you?" Westin asked.

"Because he'd know hearing Davenport was dead would break me if he didn't," Eric replied honestly. "I know I'm on everyone's shit list for whatever I might have let slip when they drugged and tortured me, but Horn wouldn't want me broken."

"What aren't you telling us?" Westin demanded.

"He and Davenport have been together for years," Victoria answered for him.

"And what, Horn's your go-between?" Westin asked.

"No, he's our third."

Eric wished he could record this moment to share with his lovers. Trey Westin speechless was a sight they'd both appreciate, but they'd have to settle for hearing about it. Westin was good, or they'd never have taken him on after working with him as their military liaison, but he had a serious stick up his ass and a smart mouth to go with it. "I have to get back to wherever we're working from now. I need to see how much damage I did."

"Newton," Westin said, "you don't know that the problems in Syria had anything to do with intel you might have had. You were gone for months. We put contingency plans in place in case they'd broken you."

"I practically wrote our playbook," Eric reminded him. "If I spilled while they had me out of my mind, they know the contingency plans for our contingency plans. I have to assume everything I've ever touched was compromised."

"We'll be back at the aircraft carrier we launched from soon," Victoria said. "We'll figure the rest out from there."

Eric slumped back against the seat and tried to focus on the sound of Richard's voice in his ear and the text on the phone. He wanted to believe he'd been strong enough to resist the torture he'd undergone. He had no memories of spilling their secrets, but the blank spaces haunted him. He'd recognized the early effects of some of the drugs they'd given him. Sodium pentothal, LSD, and mescaline were easy to recognize if not to resist, but then they'd started mixing things together, all while telling him he'd said one thing one day and another the next, when what they reported made no sense half the time and too much sense the rest.

He was lucky not to be in the military anymore. If he were, he'd face court-martial for sure. As it was, he only had to face Richard and Tim.

He held on to hope by dint of the text and Richard's voice in his ear. If Richard hated him, he wouldn't have told Eric not to fuck it up as he escaped. He wouldn't have sent the text about Tim. He would have let Eric find out about it from the team and go insane with grief and guilt.

His phone buzzed again.

Stop thinking and get your ass back here where it belongs.

He choked back a sob. Maybe Richard could forgive him after all.

RICHARD STOOD alone on the deck of the aircraft carrier, having run everyone else off by the simple expedient of assigning them work elsewhere. There was more than enough of it to go around as they tried to figure out what had gone wrong in Syria, and this way he didn't have an audience for Eric's arrival. He hadn't gotten an answer to his texts, but the chopper was on its way here, and Eric was on it.

Amato's muttered, "Fuck," gave Richard nothing to go on as far as what shape Eric would be in when he got off the transport. He was walking, Richard could tell that much from the drone visuals. His hair had gotten long, hardly surprising after four months in captivity. Usually he kept his straight black hair cropped short, not quite a military buzz cut, but almost, a way to cover up his Kiowa heritage. Dav had told him more than once to embrace that side of himself, but Eric had never felt any connection to the tribe, having only known his grandmother, herself of mixed heritage, for a few years before she died. He might look like he could have come from any western novel or TV show, but he was a Georgia boy through and through. Such a contrast to Dav's fair skin, blue eyes, and dirty-blond hair, although not as much as Richard's own brown skin. He'd just stopped thinking of himself and Dav that way when Dav refused to see Richard as "that nigger with the stick up his ass," as several of their fellows in basic training had labeled him. Richard was pretty sure he'd fallen in love on the spot. Dav always said his own generic appearance made him the perfect spy because he could blend in anywhere in North America or Europe, and anywhere else in the world, he was a nondescript American. He would never be bland to Richard, who saw the harnessed power hidden beneath the plain suits Dav wore most of the time, but he had the rest of the world fooled. Eric, though…. Eric would never blend in anywhere. He could never manage to hide the self-assured swagger that had set him apart from all the other soldiers they'd considered recruiting when they brought him in. He was good and he knew it.

The rotors on the copter had barely begun powering down when the hatch opened and Eric limped out. He looked like hell, not surprising, but he was upright and moving on his own, and Richard couldn't ask for more than that. Okay, he *could*, but he was already pushing his luck to get this, so he'd take it. He moved forward to meet Eric halfway, or a little more than halfway since Eric was moving so much slower than usual. He tucked Eric against his chest when they met, holding him tight as he felt the tremors running through him.

"I've got you," he murmured against Eric's hair. He smelled of smoke and dust, explosives and worse, but Richard didn't care. He had Eric in his arms again. The rest of the world could go fuck itself.

When someone cleared his throat, Richard looked up to see the rest of Eric's team watching them. For one awful second, Richard fought the urge to drop his arms and step away, to draw his authority back around him like a cloak, but this was Eric in his arms, Eric who'd had his body and mind pushed beyond the limits of any endurance, who had to live with the knowledge of what he'd suffered, what he might have been forced into revealing. Fuck pulling away. He wasn't leaving Eric without support.

"What are you looking at?" he growled instead.

"Not a thing," Amato replied coolly.

"Newton said Davenport's alive," Westin said, finally regaining his voice. Richard would have preferred he stay speechless.

"At the moment, yes. He coded in transit, but they got his heart restarted. He's at a hospital in Israel. I texted Newton as soon as I realized he had a chance at surviving. This is the first chance I've had to talk to the rest of you."

"He's going to be okay?" Eric asked, and the vulnerability in his voice nearly broke the heart Richard would have denied having if anyone other than his lovers asked.

"He's still in surgery, but as soon as you're fit to travel, we'll fly out and join him, whether that's in Israel or in Germany," Richard said.

Eric nodded.

"Westin, Sanders, help me clear the corridors," Amato ordered before Richard could move or think about how to avoid the rest of Strike Force Omega finding out about his relationship with Eric. It might only delay the inevitable, but he'd take it for now. He'd deal with the rest later.

"Let's go," Sanders said with one of his manic grins that made sane people think twice about being anywhere near him.

"Thank you," Richard said with a nod to each of them as he guided Eric toward the door. He could tell sheer willpower alone was keeping Eric on his feet as they made their way to the lower decks of the aircraft carrier and the infirmary. Fortunately Eric had that in spades.

"I've got you," Richard said, wrapping an arm around Eric's waist. "Just lean on me."

Eric nodded again, his breathing too fast and his eyes glassy. Not drugged, just glazed over like he was in shock.

Richard's earpiece crackled to life. "They're stitching Davenport up now, sir. He'll be in recovery for another hour or two before they move him from surgery to a room in the ICU."

"Prognosis?" Richard demanded. He pulled the earpiece free so Eric could hear as well.

"Guarded. The bleeding is stopped and the bullet wounds stitched up. His heart rate is elevated but steady, and the ventilator is a precaution rather than a necessity. If he makes it through the next twenty-four hours, his chances of survival are good."

"Do whatever it takes," Richard ordered.

"See him?" Eric mumbled.

"Soon," Richard said, worried that Eric was losing track of where they were. "Let's get you checked out first."

Eric pulled out of Richard's hold and took two steps toward the infirmary before his eyes rolled back in his head and he collapsed. Only reflexes honed by years of fighting let Richard catch him before he hit the floor.

"Doctor!"

CHAPTER 2

ERIC CAME to, slowly taking stock of his body before he opened his eyes. He was cold. He could feel the weight of a blanket over his body—where had the blanket come from? They never gave him anything to protect from the cold of the desert nights—but he wasn't generating enough body heat for it to do any good. His hand hurt. Had they broken it? If the motherfuckers had damaged his hand, he'd see them all in hell for it. When he flexed his fingers, he felt the pinch of the IV under his skin. He shuddered at the thought of what drugs they might be pumping into him this time. They'd shot him up so many different times he couldn't keep them all straight anymore, but they'd never used an IV before. His fingers moved at his command, though. They hadn't broken them. They'd threatened so many times, not just with breaking them but with removing them entirely. He shuddered and pushed down the memories that threatened to paralyze him. He could feel the pressure of a mask over his nose and mouth—were they gassing him on top of everything else? But he wasn't restrained. That didn't make sense. His left leg felt heavy, more so than his right, making him wonder if they'd broken it without him realizing.

The weight against Eric's leg shifted, drawing his attention to the end of the bed and the welcome sight of Richard sitting up from where he had rested his head against Eric's knee.

Richard. The rescue. He wasn't in that pit anymore. He was… in Medical on an aircraft carrier somewhere with Richard standing guard. It was an IV in his hand and an oxygen mask on his face, not more torture dreamed up by men more twisted than anyone Eric had ever encountered.

Eric pulled at the oxygen mask with the hand not currently sporting an IV line.

"Not yet," Richard said, catching Eric's hand and holding it tightly in his. "As much as I want to kiss you right now, we're going to call the doctor in to check on you first. You were dangerously dehydrated, half-starved, so sleep-deprived the doctor didn't know how you were still on your feet, and suffering a concussion, not to mention numerous abrasions, burns, and other superficial injuries. I don't know how you fought on the way out like you did, but I watched the fight. You were magnificent." He fixed Eric with the glare that had new recruits trembling in the boots. Never mind that it hadn't fazed Eric even the first time he saw it, much less after four years together. "Don't try to take the mask off and don't get up until I get back."

Eric nodded his agreement, knowing Richard would trust his word. He didn't feel up to moving yet anyway. He wanted the mask gone, but he could wait the few minutes it would take for the doctor to check him out.

Richard returned moments later with a doctor Eric didn't recognize in tow. He didn't know everyone in Strike Force Omega, but it was always easier with a doctor he knew. "Newton, this is Dr. Jameson, on loan from Bethesda. He happened to be there when you collapsed and examined you."

Eric nodded to show he understood and to give his permission for the doctor to examine him again now. The doctor might not see it that way, but Eric knew Richard wouldn't let the man touch him until he gave that nod. They all had their issues, and Eric's problems with strangers touching him were well established, even before he'd spent four months being tortured.

Dr. Jameson took Eric's blood pressure, examined both his pupils, and tested the rebound on the skin of his hand. "You seem to be recovering well. I'll take the mask off so you can talk with Mr. Horn, but if you start feeling light-headed or short of breath at all, put it back on immediately and have someone call me." The doctor reached for the oxygen mask, but Richard beat him to it, saving Eric from the embarrassment of jerking away from the hands that he knew rationally were only there to help him. "You're extremely fit, so there's no reason to think you'll make anything less than a full recovery, but you were far past the point of exhaustion. You need rest, plenty of fluids, and several weeks of square meals before you'll be fit for duty again."

"How long before I can go home?" Eric asked, his voice still rough.

"We'd like to observe you for at least another twelve hours," Dr. Jameson said. "Mr. Horn explained that you aren't fond of the infirmary, so I would suggest you shower and change and see how you feel. If you're steady, you could get some fresh air and come back when you're ready to sleep again. That way you won't feel so trapped. Your actual injuries are each relatively minor, even your concussion. The problem is the cumulative effect of them on top of dehydration, starvation, and exhaustion. You will sleep better in your own bed, I know, but the dehydration and the concussion require monitoring."

"I can send someone to get clothes for you, Newton," Richard said, which Eric translated to raiding the spare clothes they all kept in Richard's quarters on whatever base or boat they were currently using for moments just like this. "You'll feel better if you're clean."

Eric took a moment to look at his skin. Richard was right. He was filthy. "Yeah, a shower would be good."

"You should have someone stay with you while you shower," the doctor added. "You're doing better, but you're likely to feel some shakiness for a while. I can have a nurse come in if you'd like."

"No need," Richard interrupted. "I'll keep an eye on him."

If Dr. Jameson was surprised at the thought of the head of an active paramilitary organization sitting outside the shower of one of his assets, it didn't show on his face. Eric was too tired to care anyway. The doctor nodded and left.

"Did you… did you really let me cry on your shoulder in front of the rest of the team?" Eric asked, his memory of everything since he'd been taken more than a little blurred.

"There were no tears involved," Richard said with a glare. "There might have been hugging."

"In front of the team?"

"You needed me," Richard said. "Nothing else mattered. Westin said you told them about Dav, which means they demanded an explanation. If you managed not to tell them, I'll be really impressed."

"I told them."

Richard cupped Eric's cheek in one big hand. "You've proven yourself a thousand times, Eric. No one who matters questions your right to be here."

"Don't give me that bullshit, Richard," Eric said. "Nobody but you and maybe my team are biased enough *not* to question my right to be here. I've been held prisoner and tortured for months. I don't know how many people are dead because of what they might have gotten out of me. I nearly got Tim killed. They invaded my mind. They took everything I knew and used it against me, against us."

"And yet you're here, Dav isn't dead, and the world isn't in shambles," Richard pointed out. "So either you're not as good as you think you are— don't answer that—or you're a damn lot better than they ever realized."

"What do you mean?" Eric asked suspiciously.

"If you wanted to gut Strike Force Omega, where would you aim?" Richard asked.

"What?" Eric said. "I don't want to do that!"

"I know you don't, Eric, but answer the question anyway? Where would you hit?"

"The house in the Caymans. Everything else is transitory, but that's home."

"Then if the terrorists took everything the way you think they did, why haven't we seen any sign of interest in that direction? I'm not saying nothing was compromised, because we may never know that completely, but we took steps to counteract anything you might have let slip, and we haven't had anything go wrong in a way that could only have come from inside information, so whatever they got from you, they didn't get as deep as you fear."

Eric wanted to believe Richard was telling the truth, but their voices were still fresh in his head, twisting everything insidiously until he didn't know what was real anymore. His drug-induced visions while he was in captivity were usually memories, as if his interrogators had sifted through them for more information, rather than imagined, longed-for scenes. That could mean anything or nothing, though, given all the chemicals they'd pumped into him.

"Stop," Richard ordered, leaning forward and kissing him. He tasted like day-old coffee and breath mints, and somehow that reassured Eric in a way nothing else could, because his dreams, hallucinations—whatever he had lived or relived in that nightmare—hadn't had a taste or smell.

Eric relaxed into the kiss, the familiar softness of Richard's perfectly trimmed goatee welcoming him home. He let the kiss steal his senses. He had no use for them anyway. They'd lied to him for so long now that he didn't know what to trust except for this. The kiss stayed gentle and lazy as Richard traced Eric's lips with his tongue but never invaded. Eric broke away with a soft sob, resting his forehead against Richard's, basking in being there and being alive.

"I'm going to get your clothes. If you aren't still in that bed when I get back, I will kick your ass into the next century. Got it?"

"Yes, sir," Eric said with a mock salute.

Richard caught his hand and squeezed it tight. "I'll be back before you have a chance to miss me."

Eric missed him the moment his back was turned, even before he was out the door.

"DON'T FUCK it up? That's the best you could think of to say to him?"

Richard looked up to see Amato, flanked by Westin and Sanders. "Not your business, Westin."

"Maybe it isn't his, but I can make a case that it's mine," Amato said. "He's the spotter and sniper on my team. His well-being is my business."

Richard raised an eyebrow sardonically. "I appreciate your concern, but how I handle my personal life is not open for comment."

"It is when it affects our teammate," Amato insisted.

"He was dehydrated and exhausted, beaten and bruised, half-starved," Richard said, because they deserved to know that. "The doctor wants to keep him for observation, but after he's had a shower, he'll be allowed visitors. You will not upset him more than you've already done by telling him about Davenport before I could talk to him."

"How were we supposed to know?" Westin demanded.

"You weren't," Richard said. "But he's been through hell, and you will not make it worse, or I will bury you, Westin."

"Sir."

"Not talking to you either, Amato. Sanders didn't know, and Westin wasn't even on the team yet when Newton was taken. I get that. If they thought about it at all, they thought he lost a friend, maybe a handler, but you knew the truth. You knew what Davenport means to him. You don't tell someone they've lost their partner that way."

Amato's eye twitched, an expression that had struck fear into the hearts of lesser men, but she had nearly cost Richard his two good hands. If Eric hadn't gotten his text, he could have gone off the grid. Richard would have tracked him down, but the damage would have been done.

"Sir," she said, her voice tight.

"Do not go in there until I give you approval. Any of you."

He left them standing in the hallway, completely ignoring Westin's continuing protests. Amato would keep him out, or Richard would send them both to Siberia. Amato wouldn't care, but Westin wouldn't last a day.

He let himself into his quarters on the aircraft carrier and dug in the drawer for the extra clothes he'd brought with him when they started planning the rescue op because he refused to acknowledge that Eric might not be coming back. He took a minute and ran his fingers over the weave of Dav's spare suit. He promised himself he'd be taking that to him in no time at all. Eric was waiting for him, though, so he didn't linger.

Heikkinen tried to stop him with a question as he returned to the infirmary, but he brushed her off with orders to show a little initiative and make some decisions herself. She was his second-in-command for a reason. It was time for her to earn her pay.

Eric was, to his relief, exactly where Richard had left him, on his side with his eyes closed.

"Eric," Richard said, setting his hand on Eric's shoulder but letting his voice wake his lover rather than shaking him awake. "Come on, time for a shower."

Eric blinked awake slowly. "Richard?"

"I'm here, Eric," Richard said. "You're safe. Let's get you in the shower. Even if you go back to sleep, you'll feel better if you're clean."

Eric let Richard pull him out of bed, careful of the IV still in Eric's hand. The hospital gown was no impediment, and Richard helped Eric into the bathroom, although Eric drew the line at Richard following him into the shower stall. He settled for leaning against the wall as he listened to Eric shower.

About the time he started worrying, the water shut off and Eric pushed the curtain back. Eric's face still showed signs of exhaustion, dark circles bruising his eyes. Richard ran an assessing gaze over the rest of his lover, taking stock of every cut and contusion on Eric's body. He'd been whipped, burned, cut, and probably waterboarded, although the doctor found no indication of sexual abuse, thank fuck. He needed a haircut to put some order back in his usually short black hair, a shave to get rid of the pitiful excuse for a beard, and about a year's worth of sleep and good food.

"You're still the best thing I've ever seen," Richard said, handing Eric a towel and then his boxers.

"You're full of it," Eric retorted.

Richard almost let it go. He'd listened to a lot of bullshit in his tenure in the SEALs, and more since he'd started working alongside rather than inside the military, but this wasn't about putting up with bullshit. This was about Eric and his self-esteem issues, and Richard had never put up with those. "Stop right there," he said, pushing off the wall and getting in Eric's face. "You think I don't see you, but I do, Eric Peter Newton. I have seen you every moment from the first time I laid eyes on a file with your name on it. You're a smartass high school dropout with no formal education and the best goddamn aim in the world. You're a slob, and you're lazy when you're off duty. You're sarcastic and insubordinate when you're on duty. I'm not blind to your faults. I listened to Dav whine about them for three years before I convinced him being in love with you wasn't being unfaithful to me, so don't think for a minute that I don't see you. You know what else I see?"

Eric glared at him, but he didn't pull away, so Richard took it for permission to continue.

"You're a brilliant strategist. You see situations from an angle the military's best analysts still miss. You can hit any target you choose with any weapon you pick up within seconds of firing it the first time. You throw yourself into every battle like the world depends on it, and you never give up. You're as generous with your time as you are with your heart, and maybe no one but Dav and I see that, but *we* see it every time you reach for both of us instead of just him. You're not perfect, and I'm not pretending you are, but that doesn't make you less than exactly what I want."

CHAPTER 3

THE ABSOLUTE and unwavering certainty in Richard's voice did what all of his captors' demands could not. They broke him.

Eric felt the sob well up from deep inside him. He fought it, hating to show weakness, but Richard was holding him tight, continuing to mutter admonishments and affection in his ear, and Eric's resistance shattered. He was safe in exactly two places in the world: in Tim's arms and in Richard's. Richard stood between him and the rest of the world, his broad shoulders blocking anyone else from seeing the tears he couldn't hold back anymore.

"That's it," Richard murmured. "You're safe. I've got you. Never gonna let you go again."

"Liar," Eric said through the tears that still ran down his cheeks. "As soon as the doctors clear me, you'll have another mission to send me on because you know if you don't, I'll start terrorizing people again."

"You'd rather do that than help Dav through his recovery?" Richard asked seriously. "Because that was going to be your full-time assignment. He's going to need us, Eric. This isn't going to be something he just bounces back from, and with the Pentagon breathing down my neck and the whole world in a panic because of increasing terrorist attacks, a lot of that's going to fall on you, at least during the day. I can only pick and choose so much if we're still going to have jobs when this is over. Think you can handle it?"

Eric nodded as another sob escaped him. He couldn't wrap his head around everything. His capture, the subsequent torture, his rescue, Richard's text, Tim's injury, Richard's faith in him… fuck, he didn't deserve it. He didn't deserve any of it, but then he never had. Richard and Tim had been a gift beyond price from the moment he met them, even before he realized what they were to each other and what they would become to him. They'd taken one look at the little shit he'd been and instead of letting him go to jail where he belonged, they'd given him another option. He'd needed a year to believe they weren't going to jerk the job away from him the first time he screwed up. He'd needed two years to settle with Tim as his permanent handler. By the third year, he'd fallen for Tim so hard he couldn't think of anything else, much to Victoria's amusement. He'd never considered

Richard as anything other than their badass motherfucking commanding officer until he'd made a pass at Tim. Richard had walked in on them kissing (Eric still didn't know how they'd managed that timing) and had told him gently but in no uncertain terms that any relationship with Tim had to include Richard as well.

He'd nearly bolted right then, but Richard had kissed Eric, and that had been the end—or the beginning—of that. Eric hadn't looked back.

Until the terrorists had taken everything that made him who he was and twisted it for their own use. He'd heard what Richard and Westin said about the intel he might or might not have spilled. He even mostly believed it, but that didn't negate the fact that they couldn't ever truly know what damage he had done or who might have died because of him.

Richard kept holding him, letting him cry, until noise in the next room interrupted them.

"Wash your face and get dressed," Richard told him. "I have a few things to say to those idiots who can't follow directions."

Eric scrubbed at his face with the towel, blotting away the tears. He mustered a smile for Richard and started getting dressed.

Richard disappeared through the door, closing it behind him, but the thin layer of wood did nothing to disguise Richard's diatribe.

"I thought I said to wait until I gave approval for you to come in," he started in on the team. "Did I use words that were too big for you?"

"It was taking too long," Sanders said.

"It's all right, sir," Eric said, coming out of the bathroom. "I'm up for a short visit."

Richard didn't look convinced, but he stepped aside and let the team engulf him in hugs and pats on the shoulder and a punch in the ribs from Victoria—much softer than her usual hits. He grunted at that one. She just glared at him unrepentantly.

"Why didn't you tell me?" she demanded, angling her eyes toward Richard.

"I didn't tell you about Tim," Eric said.

"Yes, you did. Not in words, but anyone with eyes could see it."

"I didn't," Sanders said.

"I said anyone with eyes, Sanders," Victoria snapped.

"I didn't tell anyone," Eric said, interrupting their bickering. "You know what kinds of scuttlebutt there was about favoritism already because I only worked with other teams if Davenport approved it and because the complaints about me never seemed to result in any kind of consequences."

"You only disobey the stupid orders," Victoria said at the same time Richard did.

"That's not the point," Eric said, even if the fact that they understood it was what had allowed him more success with Strike Force Omega than he'd had in the Army. His COs there hadn't cared if he thought the orders were stupid, and he hadn't lasted much beyond basic training. "If people had known I was sleeping with the commander as well as with my handler, nobody would ever believe I'd earned anything on my own merits."

"Anyone who says that has never seen you shoot," Victoria said. "Your place on this team is *not* in question. Every single one of us in this room is here because you took a shot at one time or another."

"What she said," Sanders said.

"I owe you my life too many times to count," Victoria added. "I'm not going to say anything." Eric knew the count part was a lie. She kept a tally in her head, but Eric appreciated the sentiment.

"And if we don't care, what does it matter what the scuttlebutt says?" Sanders asked. "Seriously, Newton, there will always be haters who only see what they want to see. People talk. You can argue with them, but it won't change anything. Figure out whose opinions matter to you and forget about the rest. So when are they going to spring you?"

"In the morning, I think," Eric said. "At least that's what it sounded like when the doctor was in here earlier."

"Good. What happens next?"

"He and I leave for Israel, if that's where Davenport is still, or to Landstuhl if he's stable enough to be moved," Richard replied. "He's officially on medical leave to take care of his partner."

"You know that's not actually a thing, right?" Westin asked.

"Who's running this party?" Richard asked, his voice low and cold. If Eric could have mustered the energy to laugh, the expression on Westin's face would have elicited one, but he was flagging again already.

"Out," Richard ordered. He glared until the team had all started toward the door, then turned back to Eric. "Come on, Peaches. Let's get you back in bed."

"Peaches?" Sanders said as someone, Eric didn't see who, pushed him out the door.

Eric let Richard tuck him back in bed, although he refused the oxygen mask. He'd be facing more questions next time he saw the team since they'd heard Richard's name for him. The memory still made him smile. Richard always called Tim "Dav" in private and sometimes even where others could hear him. After Eric had become a fixture in their lives, Richard had decided Eric needed a name too. That had led to a hilarious round of brainstorming. They hadn't come up with a way to shorten either his first or last name, and Eric had vetoed Snipe because it was what he did, not who he was. In the end Tim had suggested Peaches, what with Eric being from Georgia.

"Perfect," Richard had said even as Eric shook his head.

Eric refused to answer to it for the first month, just on principle, but Richard hadn't given up, and Eric couldn't deny the secret thrill he felt every time Richard said it, usually either right before or right after he and Tim had left Eric totally fucked out. Talk about positive reinforcement.

"They're going to ask about that."

Richard shrugged. "They can ask all they want. We don't have to answer."

Eric yawned.

"Get some sleep, Eric. I'll stand watch."

Eric wanted to ask when Richard was going to sleep, but he couldn't keep his eyes open long enough to form the words.

"EXCUSE ME, Amato?"

Victoria looked up from her mess tray to see Westin standing there. She hadn't worked with him directly when he'd been their liaison to the US military, but he'd left enough of an impression on Horn for him to hire Westin after he'd decided not to reenlist. That was almost enough of a recommendation for her. The rest would depend on how he handled the situation with Newton. Victoria had very few loyalties in life, but her loyalty to her team was absolute.

"Yes?"

"I need some advice." He shifted uneasily from one foot to the other.

Victoria pushed out the chair opposite hers with her foot. "Have a seat."

"I… I don't think we should discuss it here," he said, looking around at the other people clustered around the room. "It's… private."

Victoria frowned. If Westin didn't want to discuss this with her here, it was probably about Newton. Victoria wasn't sure she wanted to discuss that anywhere, given the revelations of the past few hours, but Westin was right that the mess was not the place for it.

"Let's go." She deposited her tray on the way out and led Westin to her quarters. He stopped outside the door as she walked in.

"Are you sure it's appropriate for me to—"

"Shut up and get in here," Victoria interrupted, jerking him into the room. She probably ought to appreciate his attempts to be a gentleman, but at the moment, it only added to her irritation. The discomfort on Westin's face increased when she sprawled out on the bed, leaving the room's only chair for him. She looked at him pointedly and waited.

"Newton and Davenport and Horn...."

"Are three of the most dedicated men in this outfit," Victoria said when Westin didn't finish his sentence.

"I didn't mean to imply otherwise. It's just... well, there are fraternization rules for a reason."

"This isn't the military," Victoria said.

"I know that, but there's a command structure. Horn makes decisions about who to send on what missions, and Davenport makes decisions about how to run those missions. It just seems... inappropriate for them to also have such a personal relationship."

"Would we be having this conversation if I were the one they were involved with?"

"Wait, you think this is because they're *gay*? I couldn't care less about that. Some of the best men I served with were that way. I'm worried about the command structure of an organization with very little oversight and more firepower at its command than I'm sure I trust anyone with."

"You didn't seem overly concerned about that when you echoed my assurances of Newton's place on our team."

"You've led the team since I've been a part of it, and I haven't seen anything to make me question your leadership," Westin said. "It doesn't matter who Newton is sleeping with if you're the one sending him into the field. Your judgment isn't clouded by it."

"Neither is Davenport's or Horn's," Victoria assured him. "They respected Newton's judgment before any of this happened, and nothing's changed in the four years Newton and Davenport, and Horn, I guess, have been together. I've served with them, before and after. The only difference is the... tenor of Newton's comments to Davenport compared to everyone else."

"Meaning?"

"Meaning he makes smartass comments to Davenport in a way he doesn't to anyone else," Victoria explained. "Davenport makes them right back. It's their way of flirting, but it never gets in the way of the job. Davenport never leaves anyone behind, so that's not an issue. If anything, he relies on Newton too much, trusting him to get into and out of situations he'd never send anyone else into."

"That's as much an error in judgment as not sending him somewhere because it's dangerous."

Victoria snorted inelegantly. "Davenport doesn't make errors in judgment. If he'd been running the op when Newton got captured, it wouldn't have happened. I realize you don't know Davenport well, and I know what he looks like, but of everyone in Strike Force Omega, he's the one you should be the most afraid of if you ever give him reason to come after you."

"He seems so—"

"Unassuming," Victoria said. "Yes, I know. He's raised it to an art form. He could kill you—any of us, really—without breaking a sweat. He's slick and sneaky and far more deadly than the rest of us combined. He was a SEAL, just like Horn. He just hides it better."

"I'll keep that in mind," Westin said. "This doesn't bother you?"

Victoria shrugged. "Personally I don't have any use for love, but I'm not worried about what will happen in a fight because of them."

"YOU WANTED to see me, sir?" Heikkinen said.

"What's the status of our ongoing ops?" Richard asked as he stepped outside the door to the room where Eric slept.

"You should come to the bridge and check for yourself."

"Is there something going on that's beyond your abilities to handle?" Richard asked, keeping his voice mild. Usually he had Dav there to take someone apart without ever raising his voice, but Dav wasn't talking at the moment, and Richard didn't want to wake Eric. He'd just have to take a page from Dav's book.

"Of course not," Heikkinen said defensively.

"Then give me your report."

Heikkinen rattled off updates on the op in Syria and on the continuing surveillance of the terrorist camp in Turkmenistan where Eric had been held. Richard listened with one ear, the other firmly focused on the room behind him.

"We need to debrief Newton," she said when she finished her report. "We need to know what he may have told them, and we need to know anything he might have observed."

"Not now," Richard said firmly. "For one thing he's asleep and still recovering. For another, we'll get far more useful information from him after he's slept and seen Davenport."

"But, sir—"

"But nothing. This isn't the CIA, Heikkinen. We don't have to debrief within the first few hours." They had contingency plans in place for any kind of security breach, and when they hadn't rescued Eric within the first week of his captivity, they'd scrapped every op he had information on. Despite what Eric was thinking—Richard really had to work on that—he couldn't have compromised the ops they'd run since then because they'd changed every single plan. Anything the terrorists got from him would have been outdated or general information at best. "Make sure to keep a close eye on the rendezvous point in Syria. Our security can't be compromised."

Heikkinen cast a pointed look at the room behind him. "No, we don't want anything compromised."

Richard narrowed his eyes, feeling his temper getting the better of him, but Heikkinen walked away before he could decide the best way to answer her.

THE SOUND of a door opening jarred Eric awake. He sat up as fast as his injuries would allow. He couldn't stop his captors from torturing him, but he could keep them from taking him unaware.

He blinked a couple of times when the world righted itself and resolved to the inside of a military infirmary, lit only by what spilled through the window from the corridor outside.

Right.

The rescue. Richard had sent Victoria and the team to get him out. They hadn't left him there, even though he deserved it after everything he'd spilled. His torturers had taunted him with details he'd given them while he was drugged. Sometimes he could console himself with the fact that even drugged, he'd lied to them or they'd misinterpreted what he'd said, but other times, he couldn't do anything but live with the coiling shame of having been forced into giving up secrets that could cost his comrades—his friends—their lives.

"You okay, Newton?"

Westin. That was Westin's voice. He'd come with Victoria to rescue him. He'd insisted Eric still had a place on the team. He frowned and stared at Westin intently. He wasn't wearing his Army uniform. That was new.

"You're out of uniform."

"You're as observant as ever," Westin said. "I retired soon after you were captured. Horn offered me a job. It seemed like a way to continue fighting."

"You couldn't just stay in the Army?" Eric asked.

"I'd reached a point I wouldn't have been fighting. How are you doing?"

"I've been better," Eric said with a grimace. "But I'm better than I'd be if you guys hadn't come after me. Thanks for that. I'm not sure I said it when we were in the field."

"We had a few other things going on."

Eric's head was starting to pound again. It was probably time for another dose of pain medicine, but he would put that off as long as he could. He'd never liked feeling drugged, but now....

"Was there something you needed? I don't mean to be rude, but I'm not sure how long I can stay awake."

"Amato said something earlier that stuck with me. I figured that of anyone, you'd know best if she was right."

"She was right," Eric said immediately. "Whatever it was, she was right."

Westin laughed. "Oh, it's like that, is it?"

"I'm not stupid. It's always safer to agree with her."

"She said Davenport never left anyone behind. Well, that and a few other things about him, but that was the important part."

Eric smiled. "You can believe what the rumor mills say about him. Even the stuff that's gotten exaggerated was mostly unbelievable when it happened. He's pretty badass."

"You care for him very much."

"Yeah," Eric said. "You aren't weirded out by that, are you? I mean, the military doesn't have much of a track record where same-sex relationships are concerned."

"I don't think it's my place to have an opinion on your private life," Westin replied with so much offended dignity Eric wondered if the guy was for real.

"If it were actually private, I'd agree with you, but I'm pretty sure nothing about Horn, Davenport, and me is private anymore. That's what I get for sleeping with people I work with."

"It isn't just sex, though, is it? I mean, you're not putting yourself and them at risk because you're horny."

Eric nearly choked on his surprise. "No, Westin, that's not why I'm with them. If all I wanted was to get my rocks off, there are plenty of places I can do that without repercussions. I have been in a committed relationship for four years now, and I intend to continue in that relationship for as long as I live, unless they decide to get rid of me. I'm frequently more trouble than I'm worth."

"Did they tell you that?"

Eric resisted the urge to roll his eyes. Westin had a protective streak apparently, although Eric didn't know how he'd ended up on the man's list of people to look after.

"No, they'd kick my ass for comments like that, but it's pretty hard to argue with everything the terrorists got out of me in the past four months."

"We said it before. I'll say it again. There's no proof that anything you might have told them actually impacted any missions," Westin insisted. "Horn knew what you knew and took steps to avoid any issues."

Eric resisted the urge to shout at him. What did he know about it anyway? He glared at Westin, fighting the black swimming around the edges of his vision. It wasn't just the details of specific missions, although that was bad enough. He knew the way Richard and Tim thought, the way they planned. If he wasn't in on the brainstorming sessions, he could predict the way they'd gone with near perfect accuracy. Westin didn't understand. The terrorists had gotten into his head, all the way down to his very soul, and they'd ripped it out and torn it to shreds because what they'd taken from him couldn't be fixed by simple counterintelligence or changing a few mission details. They'd taken everything.

"Whatever." He faked a yawn to get Westin to leave. He couldn't deal with this anymore.

"PEACHES? THAT'S the best they could come up with?"

Eric woke from a light doze to the sound of Amato sneering at him. What was it with his teammates and barging in while he was sleeping? And how did she get all the way to his bed without waking him? "Go 'way and leave me alone."

"Not until you look me in the eye and tell me this is really a good thing," she said.

He opened his eyes enough to glare at her. "It's a good thing."

"You're full of shit, Eric. I've spent seven years working with you. I hear the things Horn says to you. 'Don't fuck it up.' How is that a good thing?"

Looking at it from the outside, Eric could see her point, mostly. Except he was exhausted. And in pain. And Tim wasn't there to curl around him and hold him like he'd never let go.

"He has a reputation to maintain." Eric forced his brain to cooperate. The sooner he answered her question, the sooner she'd leave him to sleep. And when he woke up, he'd be that much closer to well enough for Richard to take him to Tim. He needed to see Tim, even if Tim was unconscious. Maybe then he could put this fucking nightmare behind him. "Not to mention that no one knew about us. He couldn't very well end a premission briefing by telling me he loved me or even to be careful. Nobody blinks an eye at him telling me not to fuck it up. They figure it's a sign of how hard I am to work with in the field, how unpredictable I am, all the shit people say about me. It adds to my rep at the same time it protects him and hides our secret while still letting *me* know he cares."

She shook her head. "Soldiers and their superstitions."

"It hasn't failed us yet," Eric said. "I keep coming home."

"Barely sometimes."

"I'll take it when the alternative is not coming home at all."

If he hadn't been in a hospital bed, she'd have smacked him. He recognized the look in her eyes. As it was, she glared at him. "I never questioned whether being with Davenport was good for you. I've seen how you are when he's around and when he's not. He grounds you. If he were here, I would never have found you alone, even if you were asleep. Where's Horn?"

Eric shrugged. "He can't drop everything because I'm injured. He has missions to run."

"That never stopped Davenport."

Privately Eric agreed, but he had always known he came in second to Richard's work. It had never mattered before because Tim was there (and Tim came in second too). Now, though, Tim wasn't there.

"I'm fine. Or I will be. He'll be here when he can, and that will be enough."

It would have to be.

CHAPTER 4

"TIM!"

Richard stood at the door to Dav's hospital room in Germany and watched in silence as Eric raced to his side, far faster than Richard would have expected him to be capable of moving so soon after his rescue. He should have known not to underestimate how much Eric needed to see Dav.

"He's on a ventilator," Richard reminded Eric. "They'll keep him unconscious until he's well enough to wean him off it."

"How long will that take?" Eric asked, his focus never leaving Dav's slack features.

Richard couldn't see the bandages that had to cover Dav's body beneath the hospital gown and sheets. He had a bandage on his forehead as well, although it wasn't wrapped around his head, so Richard took that as a good sign. In a minute he'd go find a doctor and insist on getting an update, but first he needed a moment to simply look. Dav's chest rose and fell in time with the hiss of the ventilator. It had only been thirty-six hours since he'd watched helplessly as bullets tore into Dav's body. He couldn't expect miracles, no matter how much he wanted to demand them. The fact that Dav was here and not still in Israel meant he'd stabilized enough for the medical transport. They wouldn't have put him on that plane if they'd been worried he'd code along the way. "I don't know. We'll have to ask a doctor."

Eric nodded but never even looked Richard's way. Maybe he ought to go find a doctor. He could play the commanding officer card since no one here knew about how Richard fit into Dav's life. He'd taken a step back into the hall when he heard footsteps approaching. A woman in a white coat came down the hall. "Oh good," she said when she saw Richard. "I was told someone would be coming for Mr. Davenport, but I didn't realize you'd arrived."

"Ma'am," Richard said with a sharp nod. He'd learned more than military jargon at an early age from his father and grandfather, both decorated war heroes. "Richard Horn. I'm Davenport's commander. His partner is already inside."

They'd talked about it after they got together, how they'd present the situation when one of them got hurt. Richard could always get the information he needed by dint of rank, so rather than open themselves up to speculation, Eric and Dav held each other's medical POAs. Usually Dav was the one sitting by Eric's bedside and sending reports on his condition to Richard, but it worked both ways.

"Nice to meet you, Mr. Horn. I'm Captain Smithers. I took over care for Mr. Davenport when he was transferred here from Israel. Shall we go in?"

He nodded and opened the door for her. "Newton, the doctor is here."

Eric startled at the sound of his voice, which set off warning bells in Richard's head. Eric's situational awareness was usually so heightened that nothing startled him. For him to have been surprised now, in an unfamiliar place... he'd have to keep a close eye on him.

"Eric Newton, Captain Smithers," Richard said by way of introduction when Eric stood. "Newton holds the medical POA for Mr. Davenport."

"I'm sorry to meet you under these circumstances, Mr. Newton, but I'm glad you're here," Smithers said.

"What's going on with him?" Eric's voice cracked as he spoke. Richard took a step forward, but Eric cleared his throat and straightened. They weren't alone here and couldn't afford to be outed. They occasionally took contracts from other sources besides the US military, but they couldn't really afford to lose that source of income entirely.

"Multiple GSWs to the legs," Smithers said. "One to the chest, which collapsed his lung before it could be repaired. He's on the ventilator while that heals enough for him to breathe on his own again."

"How long is that going to take?"

"That's a very good question," Smithers replied. "It could be a few days, it could be a couple of weeks. The trauma surgeons drained the air and fluid around his lung when they removed the bullet and patched up the hole, but he'll have to stay on the ventilator until his chest X-ray is clear. We haven't seen any additional problems since he got here, but it's still going to take time."

"When will he wake up?" Eric asked.

"He's unconscious now because we're keeping him that way. It's easier for his body to heal if he stays perfectly still, not to mention that the tube in his throat would be extremely uncomfortable for him if he were conscious. Once we start weaning him off the ventilator, we'll stop the sedation so he can wake up."

Eric nodded, but Richard could see his attention drifting back to Dav. Richard didn't blame him. The only thing that had kept him from tearing off the second Dav went down was the need to know Eric was safe. He heard Dav's voice in his ear the whole time.

There's not a damn thing you can do for me that the doctors aren't already doing. Rescue Eric and bring him home where he belongs.

Richard had done that. He'd gotten Eric out and safe and here to Dav's side.

Where he belonged.

"What's his long-term outlook?" Richard asked when it became clear Eric had lost interest in the conversation.

"He'll live, if that's what you're asking me," Smithers said. "If he was going to die from his injuries, it would have happened before he ever made it to me. He's critical but stable. The longer he goes without developing complications, the more chance he'll have of recovering, but there's a reason he's in the ICU. We need to keep a close eye on him to stay one step ahead of every possible complication. At the moment, his digestive tract, his kidneys, pretty much everything is shut down because of the toxins in his bloodstream from the extensive injuries. Thus the ventilator, the feeding tube, the dialysis. We have him on antibiotics to head off what we can, but it's not going to stop everything."

"I'm glad to hear he's going to live, obviously," Richard said, "but what happens when he wakes up? Will there be long-term issues because of his injuries?"

"Almost certainly. One of the bullets shattered his knee. There wasn't even enough left to repair. They did a replacement while he was out. He's honestly lucky not to have lost the leg. You don't get hurt this way and bounce back overnight. It's not physically possible even if it were mentally possible. He's going to have months of physical therapy ahead of him, possibly years. He may never regain full capacity."

"Thank you for your honesty, Captain," Richard said even as he tried to digest what she'd just told him. They'd always said they'd go down in a blaze of glory, but this changed things. Dav was in extraordinary physical condition for a man of their age, but while that might help, it couldn't fix everything. "Please let either Newton or myself know if there's anything he needs. Anything we can do to help him, consider it done."

"I'll keep that in mind." The pager on her belt vibrated. She glanced at it and thumbed it off, but Richard could see the tension that invested her shoulders. "Do you have any other questions?"

"Not at the moment," Richard replied. He had a thousand questions, but none of them could really be answered except by time.

"Then I'm going to answer this page. I'll check in with you before I go off shift for the night."

He saluted as she left. If he were still in the Navy, he'd probably outrank her, but he'd have saluted anyway. She was taking care of Dav. She deserved his respect.

The moment the door closed behind her, he turned back to look at Eric and Dav. Eric had leaned over Dav to press his forehead against Dav's shoulder, his longer than usual hair spilling over against Dav's skin. Was Dav always that pale, or was the blood loss the cause? Richard wanted to join them and wrap his arms around both his lovers, but Eric didn't even seem aware of him anymore. He'd always known Eric was with him because of Dav. He'd done everything he could to nurture that bond because he saw how much they loved each other, often taking over Dav's responsibilities so he could be there when Eric needed him. He had no one but himself to blame for it. He'd known from the start that Eric wanted Dav, not him. Not really. He'd told himself then that he'd be satisfied with knowing having Eric there made Dav happy. He didn't need Eric's interest for himself too. He'd been satisfied with the times he'd been able to spend with Dav and Eric together, in bed or out of bed. He'd told himself it was enough.

He might have been wrong.

ERIC HATED the smell of antiseptic. He buried his face deeper into Tim's shoulder in search of some hint of his cologne, even of his sweat. Something that smelled like Tim, not like chemicals. He breathed as deeply as he could, but it only brought more of the same and the underlying smell of blood. He almost lifted his head to escape the smell of blood. He'd spent so long surrounded by nothing but the smell of his own blood and shit that he'd started to wonder if he'd ever smell anything else again.

He could hear Richard and the doctor talking behind him, but he couldn't be bothered to listen anymore. He didn't have eyes or ears for anything except Tim. Richard would handle the details. He always did. He'd find out everything Tim would need for his recovery and get it all organized. By the time Tim was conscious again, Richard would have it all mapped out—physical therapists, equipment, whatever he needed. It was what Richard did. He got things done. When Tim woke up, he'd look at it all and remind Eric that was how Richard showed he cared. Eric understood, but it wasn't enough. He needed….

He needed to feel safe. He needed to know he hadn't fucked up the only good thing in his life. He'd already used up his allotment of luck catching Tim's eye and having Richard willing to share. Every day he got to spend with them was icing on the cake. He didn't deserve them and never had, but sometimes when they snuggled him between them and held on tight, he could almost forget he was living on borrowed time. He could almost believe they'd still want him tomorrow or a week from now or a year from now when his PTSD caught up to him and he self-destructed for real.

Richard stroked a hand over Eric's hair. If Tim were awake, he would have urged Eric to the sink and taken scissors to the chaos and a razor to the pitiful excuse for a beard that he'd grown over four months. He'd have kissed and nuzzled and seduced the whole time until at the end of it, Eric would know he was home and safe again. Eric couldn't remember now the details of which mission it had been when they started, only that at the end of it his hands had trembled too much for him to shave himself and Tim had taken over. He'd done it after every bad mission since.

Until now.

Eric wasn't a child to throw a tantrum when he didn't get his way. He could wait for Tim to wake up and carry out their rituals. He could wait for Tim to wrap him up in a cocoon of careful intimacy that would drive out the doubts and questions and chaos in his head. He could leave behind the battle readiness and breathe again.

"I'm going to find General Boling and see about a place for us to stay while Dav is in the hospital. Will you be okay alone for a bit?"

Eric didn't even lift his head. He'd known it was coming. "I'll be fine here with Tim."

Richard squeezed his shoulder and left.

Eric reached for Tim's hand. His skin was cool to the touch, but not clammy, and the contact was reassuring, even if Tim didn't squeeze back the way he usually would have. Richard was doing his best, but Eric had long since resigned himself to nights without Richard's warmth in their house or their bed. He didn't question that Richard loved them, but the job would always demand his time and attention in a way Tim and Eric could sometimes avoid. Tim was the one who had nursed Eric through medical every time he ended up there. Tim was the one who talked him down from the ledge when his nightmares got to be too much. Tim was the one who steadied him, who grounded him, and Tim… Tim was unconscious in Germany after a fucked-up mission he wouldn't have gone on alone if

Eric's team hadn't gone to rescue him. They should have gone with Tim and rescued him later. Eric figured he had an excuse to be a little thrown off-balance.

He pulled a chair over so he could lean more comfortably against Tim. "You gotta wake up, Tim," he said into the sheet. It didn't matter that his voice was muffled. It wasn't like Tim was awake to hear him anyway. "I'm falling apart here, and you aren't around to put me back together."

He took a deep breath to steady himself. They'd obliterated his captors. He hadn't been fully with it when Victoria exploded into his cell and dragged him out, but he'd seen enough as they made their way back outside to know the men who'd tortured him weren't anyone's problem anymore. That did little to erase the sounds of their taunts as they slid knives underneath his fingernails or injected him with drugs to fuck with his mind. He didn't speak Arabic, but a couple of them had spoken enough English to make sure he understood them. They were experts at their jobs, both physical and psychological. They never hurt him so badly that they couldn't start again whenever they were ready, and each time they dumped him back in the hole that was his "home," they told him what they had planned for the next session. They rarely stopped with what they had threatened the time before, but they always, *always*, started with it so that even the times Eric was left alone, he was thinking about what they had in store for him. A day or a week later, he never knew. Sometimes he'd thought the waiting was worse than the torture itself.

He shook himself out of the memories. He was safe. He was with Tim, even if he was unconscious. Tim would wake up. Both the doctor and Richard had told him Tim would wake up. He had to cling to that. Once Tim woke up, things would be better. He'd spike Heikkinen's guns and he'd steady Eric and he'd remind Richard to "take out the earpiece and come to bed already. Eric's all worked up and desperate for you, and are you really going to miss out on that ass?" because that's what he did. Tim just had to hurry up before it all went to hell and there wasn't anything left to come back to. As desperately as Eric loved him, loved them both, really, he wouldn't be the reason everything came tumbling down. He'd done enough damage already.

"Heikkinen is gunning for me, not that I blame her, because I'm the biggest damn security leak we've ever had, but she knows about us now, and I'm afraid if she comes after me, it's going to spill over onto you and Richard. I know how much he loves this job. I don't want to put him in a position where he has to choose between me and the job because I already know what the outcome of that would be."

He'd always known. Richard was always the last to bed and the first out in the morning, always listening on an earpiece or on the phone to a stream of information from around the world. He didn't know what it meant to be unplugged and hadn't in all the time Eric had known him. It made him one hell of a commanding officer. It also made him an absentee partner. Tim shared his passion and was always right in the middle of the action during the day—unless Eric needed him—but when he quit for the day, he quit. And when that happened, he gave Eric his full attention.

"You'd choose me over the job, but that would mean choosing between him and me, and that's not fair to you either. As much as you love me, you loved him first, and I never wanted to mess with that. If I'd known you were involved with someone, I wouldn't have come on to you in the first place. You know that. Every day since then has been more than I could have ever asked for, but people know now, and that changes everything. I can't let it tear you and Richard apart. I love you too much to do that to you. If you wake up and I'm gone, that's why. I won't put either of you in that position. I can't. I owe you too much."

He took a shuddering breath, forcing away the incipient panic at the thought of leaving behind the life he'd finally begun to believe in before an op gone bad had led to months of hell. He couldn't focus on that or he'd lose it for real, and then his worst fears would become reality because of his inability to cope.

He leaned forward and kissed Tim's stubbled cheek softly. It felt strange not to have him respond. Even when he was asleep on the rare mornings Eric got up before he did, Tim always turned his head and kissed him back. At least his skin was warm. He might be unconscious, but he was alive, and if he was alive, then he would recover. He'd wake up in a day or two or a week and go right back to giving Eric hell for being an idiot, all the while making sure Eric knew he wasn't an idiot at all.

CHAPTER 5

THE SOUND of the door opening drew Eric's attention away from Tim. He expected to see someone on the medical staff or Richard. He didn't expect Victoria to walk in. He shouldn't have been surprised. Tim was usually the handler when their team went out, and she and Tim had a deep trust that went beyond friendship. Tim had been born a twin, but his sister had been stillborn. For all that he and Victoria looked nothing alike, he'd told Eric once that he felt a kinship with Victoria, like she was the sister he'd missed all his life, until the day Victoria walked into it. It had never been sexual—Tim didn't swing that way, and Eric was pretty sure Victoria didn't swing at all—but it had been instantaneous and unbreakable.

"How's he doing?"

"He's been better," Eric said with a wry smile. "But the doctor says he'll live."

"That's good news." She nudged his shoulder with her hip. He sighed and gave her the chair. She folded into it in a position that couldn't have been comfortable, for all that she looked perfectly content. "You can sit on the bed while you tell me the rest."

Eric perched on the edge of Tim's bed, resting his fingers on Tim's pulse the whole time. He could hear the quiet beeping of the heart monitor, but he needed to feel the steady beat beneath his hands. After all the months of hallucinations and torture, he needed the confirmation from more than one of his senses. He gave her a quick rundown of the situation. "Did you come by yourself?"

"No, the whole team is here along with the team that was out with Tim in Syria," she said. "Heikkinen wants to debrief you. Westin and Sanders are running interference. They'll be here later, if they can find Horn and foist her off on him. He has the authority to tell her to go to hell if nothing else."

"He went to find us a place to stay," Eric said. "We're gonna be here a while. No matter how much I wish otherwise, Tim isn't just going to bounce back from this."

"Hey." Victoria poked his thigh with her foot, drawing his attention. "Whatever it takes. You know that, right? We're a family, you, me, and Tim."

Eric snorted. With her there dragging him out of the chaos of his thoughts, he could push his doubts aside and tease her. "You realize you have to start including Richard in that list too."

She rolled her eyes at him. "Just because you're both sleeping with him doesn't mean I have to treat him any differently. That isn't why Tim is family."

"I get that, but now that the team knows, it changes things. Maybe we won't have to be quite so careful all the time." Not that he and Tim had ever been hugely demonstrative in front of Victoria, even when it was just the three of them, but he hadn't felt the need to repress the urge to reach for him either. A squeeze of his hand, a quick hug, a touch to his elbow, little gestures that spoke of the intimacy between them without shouting it from the rooftops. He had never been able to do any of that with Richard unless it was just him and Tim or with Tim if anyone other than Victoria was around. It was exhausting.

The door opened again to allow Westin and Sanders to enter. Eric summoned a smile for them, however hollow it felt. He didn't know Westin the way he knew Victoria, but he'd risked his life to rescue Eric at her side, and that had to count for something. The rest would come in time.

"How's it going, Newton?" Sanders asked.

"We're all hanging in there."

"Did you find somewhere to stash Heikkinen?" Victoria asked immediately.

"We ran into Horn outside," Sanders replied. "He took her off our hands. Don't know what he intended to do with her, but she's not on her way here."

"Good." Eric would have to go through it all eventually, but he'd put it off as long as he could without making matters worse. The last thing he wanted was to relive four months of hell.

"What's she think you're going to tell her anyway?" Sanders asked.

"No clue. I don't *remember* telling them anything, so it's not like I can say for sure what intel they have now that they didn't have before they got me," Eric replied. "But you know how she is. Everything by the book, even when doing it that way doesn't actually make sense."

"Sometimes I wonder how she got to be Horn's second. It certainly wasn't because she slept with him."

Everyone laughed, Eric included, because despite the comments Richard and Tim had made early on to suggest they enjoyed the occasional third in their bed, Eric had never seen anything to prove that true.

"I think he wanted her contacts, and the only way to get her at all was to promise her a ranking position," Eric replied. "We try not to talk work in private when we can help it, but he let slip a couple of comments that made me wonder."

"That makes sense, I guess. I heard she was pretty well-placed at the CIA. Nobody seems to know why she left."

"Can't help you with that one," Eric said. "I guess Horn knows, but I've never heard anything official, unofficial, or even gossip. She was already a fixture here when I joined, so that's not any help either. I tell her what she wants to know when she asks and do everything I can to avoid her notice the rest of the time."

"For what it's worth," Westin said, speaking for the first time since they'd arrived, "I told her she wouldn't gain anything by rushing you. I got a good look at the place they were holding you when we came in to bust you out, and there wasn't anything to see. The hole they had you in, the room that was obviously their torture chamber, and a couple of rooms for guards. I don't think anyone stayed there full-time, so unless they said something in your hearing that would be useful, I don't see how she's going to get anything from what you might have seen."

"They kept me blindfolded most of the time when they were moving me," Eric said. "I saw the room they tortured me in and the room they kept me in when they weren't torturing me, and that's it. I might be able to identify a few faces, if you left any of them alive, but I don't know what purpose that would serve."

"Newton!" Richard's bark interrupted them. Eric recognized the tone of voice, though he doubted anyone else did. He wasn't actually angry. He was using it as a way to separate Eric from his team so they could talk privately.

"Sir?"

"Debrief. Now."

He turned on his heel and marched away before Eric could reply. He kept his expression neutral, but his team knew the truth and from the grin on Sanders's face, nobody was fooled.

"Enjoy your dressing-down," Sanders said with a smirk.

"Nobody does a dressing-down like the commander," Eric replied with a smirk of his own. He started out the door but then turned back. "Thank you. All of you. You didn't have to help with Heikkinen."

"Get some rest," Victoria said. "You still look like hell."

Eric felt it. Maybe not as badly as when he'd first escaped, but he wasn't as recovered as he felt he ought to be. "I will," he promised. "I'll see you tomorrow?"

"I'm going to sit with Tim for a few hours," Victoria said.

The last bit of Eric's tension eased with those words. He knew the hospital was safe. He knew the doctors wouldn't let anything happen to Tim. Having Victoria there was better.

"We'll all take a shift," Westin added. "Sleep until you wake up. We won't leave him alone."

Eric smiled through the emotion clogging his throat and headed for the end of the hall where Richard was waiting for him. "You wanted to see me, sir?"

"Let's go."

He followed Richard out of the hospital and into their rental car. Richard drove them to a small bungalow back on base, about ten minutes away. "Sir?" His weakness over the past day aside, he never dropped the formality of their respective positions until Richard dropped it first.

"Our quarters while we're here," Richard explained. He opened the door and gestured for Eric to precede him inside. Once they were alone, Richard turned to study him with the same sharp gaze that made him the most feared man in Strike Force Omega. Of course it had a totally different effect on Eric, since he knew the emotions behind that piercing gaze. He let out a soft sigh. He was safe again.

"You look like shit."

"You and Victoria," Eric said. "Always insulting me."

"Come here," Richard said, his voice softening. Eric moved into his embrace. "I have good news and bad news. Boling said we can stay as long as we need to."

"That is good news," Eric said. "Can we just pretend the bad news doesn't exist?"

"We aren't off the hook for the contracts we signed. We can run them from here, but if we committed to a mission, we still have to run it."

"I'll do whatever it takes," Eric said immediately.

"That wasn't in question, Peaches," Richard said, running his big hands down Eric's arms. Eric had thought he relaxed when the team had joined him in Tim's hospital room, but this was comfort of an entirely different level. "Come on. You're off duty for a few hours."

"God, that sounds like heaven," Eric said. "What about you?" He knew he was begging. He knew it was wishful thinking. Richard had an entire military operation to run. He couldn't drop everything just because Eric was feeling insecure. Tim could, sometimes, but not Richard.

"I went off duty the minute we walked through that door."

Eric looked up sharply. "Really?"

"Really," Richard said. "I nearly lost you. I'm not letting you go now."

Eric let Richard bundle him into the kitchen. "Take a shower," Richard ordered. "I'll get dinner ready."

"Is it dinnertime here already?"

"Who the hell knows? We aren't on European time yet anyway. And they barely fed you, based on the weight you lost while they had you," Richard said. "You've got some missed meals to make up for. Clean up. I'm not taking your sweaty self to bed."

"It wouldn't be the first time," Eric gloated.

"Maybe not, but we're not doing it that way tonight. Shower, food, then we'll see what else you're up for."

THE MINUTE Eric disappeared into the bathroom, Richard slammed his fist against the counter. Had he really been so caught up in work that Eric had to question if he was truly off duty? Sure, Dav teased him about it occasionally, but not because he questioned it. It had always been so easy to let Dav be the one to take care of Eric, since it was clear that Eric preferred it that way. Dav had been the other half of him for so long that it hadn't occurred to him Eric wouldn't realize that Richard was covering for Dav so Dav could be there.

"Fuck," he muttered as he dug in the freezer for whatever might have been left behind by the previous inhabitants. He found a couple of frozen dinners that purported to be schnitzel. It wouldn't be fancy, but hopefully it would be edible. "I tell them not to fuck it up, and I've done worse than they ever have."

No more. Dav was out of commission for the foreseeable future even if the doctors did let him wake up in less than the cautious week Smithers had mentioned. Richard wouldn't be able to take on extra responsibility so Dav could do what he did best. He was going to have to pass on as much responsibility to Heikkinen as he could so he could make sure Eric was recovering. He owed his lovers that much.

He turned on the oven and waited for it to get hot. They couldn't even stock microwavable frozen dinners. They had to pick the kind that only went in the oven. When the oven had finished preheating, he stuck the schnitzel in and set the timer. He didn't know how long Eric would linger in the shower, but this way the food would be closer to being ready when he came out.

"So what's for dinner?" Eric asked, coming into the kitchen twenty minutes later. His hair was still damp from his shower, and he'd pulled on only a loose pair of training pants that barely hung from his hips. Richard thought he looked good enough to eat, even with the unusually long hair and scruff—especially with those—but despite the easy words, when Richard studied his face, he could see the exhaustion, doubt, and unease that lingered along with the more obvious signs of abuse. Eric was a master at holding it together when he had to, but Richard didn't want him to have to this time.

"Nothing fancy, just some frozen schnitzel. I haven't exactly had time to go grocery shopping."

Eric's laugh sounded rusty but real. Richard counted that as progress. "Yeah, yeah. I'll buy that this time, but don't let it happen again."

Richard grinned and held out an arm for Eric to come stand next to him as they waited for the timer to go off. He smelled like Richard's shampoo. He knew it was because Eric didn't have any of his own, but it triggered Richard's possessiveness regardless of the reason.

"You smell good."

"You wanna get laid."

Richard shrugged. "You figured out a long time ago that all you had to do was show up shirtless and I'd be ready to go. That's not news."

Eric looked down at his bare torso. "You're way too easy."

"Nope," Richard said as the timer buzzed. "Nothing but the best for me. If I wanted easy, I'd pick up one of the prostitutes that hang around outside the base."

"You'd eat them alive. They wouldn't last a day."

"Probably not," Richard agreed. "I'd be bored faster than that. Come on, let's eat."

Eric grabbed two plates and set them on the tiny kitchen table. Once Dav was well enough to join them, they'd have to think about a different seating option, because it wasn't going to work comfortably for three.

"How are you feeling?" Richard asked once they were settled. "You're looking better."

"No lingering effects that I can tell," Eric replied. "I'm still tired and achy, but it's already better than it was. Another day or two and you won't be able to tell anything happened."

Richard questioned that, but he didn't challenge Eric over it. Eric was talking to him. Richard wouldn't do anything to discourage him.

"That's good. Your team seems glad to have you back. They work better when you're there."

"They trust me. God knows why, but they do."

Richard knew why. He'd known why the first time he'd seen Eric in action, but he also knew he'd never convince his lover of that. Easier to let time do the talking for him. "Because they need you," he said simply. "You ready to tell me about it?"

"You told me it didn't matter, damn it."

"That's not what I meant," Richard said, biting down on the annoyance that rose up at Eric's deliberate obtuseness. He took a deep breath. Eric didn't need someone yelling at him. He'd get enough of that from everyone else. He didn't need it from Richard.

"Sorry, I'm a little defensive at the moment."

"You don't need to be," Richard said. "I'm the only person here, and I left the commander at the door. I want to help, Eric, but I don't know how. Dav's usually the one who helps you back from a bad mission, not me."

"I guess telling you I need to get drunk off my ass is out."

"If I thought it would work, I might go for it," Richard said with a sharp laugh. "We both deserve a drink after what we've gone through, but it's not going to solve anything. What would Dav do if he were here?"

"Exactly what you're doing," Eric said. "Clean me up, feed me, tuck me in bed. Knock me out if I couldn't sleep and be there if I wake up with nightmares. There's no magic cure. It's just time and knowing he'll be there, no matter what."

"He'll be back as soon as he can, and hopefully I'll be good enough until then."

Eric's smile was soft. "I know, and you will be."

Richard tugged Eric closer so he could put his arm around Eric's shoulders. Eric leaned into him so bonelessly Richard wondered for a minute if he'd fallen asleep sitting up. Then Eric turned his head and nuzzled Richard's neck.

"You said tuck you into bed, not fuck you silly," he scolded. "If you're done eating, you have a date with the sandman."

"Stay with me?" Eric asked.

"All night long," Richard promised. "I'm going to take a shower while you get comfortable, and then I'm not moving unless the doctors call about Dav, and if they do, I'll wake you up so you can go with me."

"And if something else comes up overnight?"

"Heikkinen wants my job. She can have it for the night," Richard said.

"She won't call me if she has to send out my team."

"Maybe she won't, but Amato will, and you know it." Eric might be back to questioning his place on his team, but his team believed in him. Richard just had to be patient until their belief penetrated Eric's thick skull. Given Eric's track record and how long it had taken him to realize Richard and Dav weren't just amusing themselves when they kept inviting Eric into their lives, Richard figured Eric might get there in a year or ten.

Richard left Eric to get settled in the surprisingly generous bed while he went into the bathroom. Eric's dirty clothes lay in an untidy heap on the floor, but it only made Richard smile. Dav was the one with the neatness complex, not Richard. He tossed his own clothes on top of Eric's. They could deal with all of it in the morning.

He turned the water on as hot as he could stand and climbed beneath the spray, letting it beat away the stress and worry of the day. He needed to get Eric to Psych if they would see him here, and then he needed to get the therapists to tell him what Eric needed. He wasn't sure which of those would be the bigger challenge, but he would meet them both because Eric was so obviously hurting despite his assurances that he was coping, and Richard refused to let Eric deal with it alone. He'd lost people after rough missions, and the ones that left no physical wounds were the worst. At least if there were broken bones or bullet wounds, they had an excuse for the time they needed to heal. They had tangible proof of both their injuries and their recovery. The ones that were all mental and emotional were far harder to come back from. While Eric had been dehydrated and exhausted, the physical wounds on his body were minimal compared to the damage done to his mind.

Richard knew he was delaying, and that had the potential to do more damage to Eric's psyche. Eric was already having trouble believing Richard would actually stay with him. Richard didn't want to make it worse. He rinsed off and grabbed a towel. He'd forgotten to bring clean underwear into the bathroom with him because when did he ever bother with that after a shower? But he didn't want to make Eric uncomfortable. After having his mind raped by the terrorists, the last thing Richard wanted was to make him feel in any way pressured now.

There was nothing for it but to walk back into the bedroom, though, because he wasn't putting back on his dirty briefs. Not after he'd finally gotten clean. He wrapped the towel around his waist, ignoring how ridiculous he felt for doing that in their own space when he hadn't even bothered with that kind of modesty the first time Eric had stayed through the night, and went to find clean clothes.

"Going modest on me now?" Eric murmured from the bed.

"Careful, not modest," Richard replied without turning as he pulled on his underwear. "You need to sleep."

Dressed now, he went to the bed and climbed in next to Eric. To his surprise, Eric didn't immediately scoot closer, but Richard refused to be deterred. He pulled Eric into his arms, sighing at the comfort of skin touching skin. He ran careful hands over Eric's back and shoulders. He wanted to assure Eric he was there and wasn't going anywhere, not cause more pain by aggravating any of the healing cuts and bruises on his body.

Eric went limp in his arms, giving Richard hope he was on the right track with his comforting. He couldn't stop himself. He kept returning to Eric's arms. Even before he'd considered bringing Eric into the bed he and Dav shared, he'd loved watching Eric shoot. He practiced with his M40 every day, but his real passion was medieval ranged weapons. His collection of longbows and crossbows rivaled any museum Richard had ever visited, and when he shot them, it was a thing of beauty. Every part of his body got involved as he drew the bowstring back and fired. Whether Eric was firing a single arrow or dozens, Richard found it mesmerizing, and the effort had honed Eric's arms even more than the rest of his impressive body. Now that he had time and no ulterior motive, he lingered over the curves of Eric's arms, following the veins and into the dips of his muscles. He'd lost muscle mass along with weight while in captivity, but Richard knew him. It wouldn't take long before he gained it all back. Eric quivered in his arms, so Richard pulled him closer, carding his fingers through the long, black hair. He traced the other hand over the muscles of Eric's back, nearly as defined as his arms. "I could lie here and just touch you all night."

"Please do," Eric purred. He rocked lazily against Richard's thigh, but Richard could tell his heart wasn't in it.

"Close your eyes, and I will."

Eric shut his eyes, and Richard resumed the soft caresses, lingering where it felt right and moving on anytime Eric got restless. Sometimes he knew why after he realized he was stroking a scar from a bad mission or a bad time from his childhood. Other times, he had no clue what set Eric off, but he moved on without question. He wanted Eric to feel safe and loved, not uneasy because of where Richard was touching him. Finally Eric's breathing evened out and he fell asleep.

ERIC WOKE up several times during the night, no surprise, really, but each time, he caught a whiff of Richard's skin and felt his strong arms, and he felt safe enough to fall back asleep.

CHAPTER 6

"THERE'S NO reason for me to see a doctor," Eric complained the next morning as Richard cracked eggs for breakfast. "I'm not dehydrated anymore, and the rest will just take time to heal."

"You say that, but Dr. Jameson was worried some of those contusions might have been deep enough to bruise bone, and that's not something to take lightly," Richard said as he put breakfast on the table. "Plus, you'll need someone to write you a referral for Psych."

"Like Psych can do anything to help. They're going to ask how I'm feeling. I'm going to tell them I'm fine. They're going to ask questions about the torture. I'm going to tell them it sucked. They're going to diagnose me with PTSD like they always do, and it will be the same as every other time I go to see them."

"Maybe, maybe not," Richard insisted, "but you need to talk to someone, and the military psychologists are the best suited to helping you deal with what you went through."

"They're not going to say anything to help," Eric said bitterly. "You know I deal with stuff my own way."

"I also know Dav never lets you skip after a bad mission. See the doctor today, Eric. We'll deal with the psych stuff after you're well. Don't make me order you to do it."

"Fuck you," Eric said, pushing his plate away. "I'll see the damn doctor, but don't expect me to sleep here tonight. I got enough orders from my captors."

Richard watched Eric leave with helpless frustration. "Fuck," he muttered when Eric slammed the door behind him on his way out. "Wake up, Dav. I'm fucking this up already, and you've only been down for forty-eight hours. I'm not gonna make it through your whole recovery without help."

He wasn't going to solve anything by sitting here. He needed to check with Heikkinen, make sure nothing had changed overnight, and give her orders for the missions they couldn't get out of. He also needed to make nice with General Boling to ensure they had the goodwill to stay for the time they would need for Dav to recover. He cleaned up the remains of their breakfast and headed out. He'd give Eric time to calm down and make it to Dav's room, and then he'd go check on them both.

AN HOUR later Eric left the exam room in the base's clinic. They'd managed to see him promptly, for which he was grateful, but he had enough scrapes and bruises and other assorted injuries to have kept the doctor busy for way too long. As he'd expected, the doctor ordered him to rest, to watch the open cuts for infection, to leave the scabs on the closed cuts alone, and to ice any swelling or painful bruising. The doctor offered a Psych referral, but Eric refused.

Politely, but he refused. He hated talking about the shit in his head. All it ever did was stir it up.

All in all, it had been relatively painless, but he could have been in Tim's room an hour ago.

Still, he shouldn't have snapped at Richard. It was a doctor's visit, not a death sentence. It wasn't Richard's fault Eric didn't feel safe anywhere these days and people touching him, especially unknown people, made it worse. Seeing Tim would steady him, even though Tim would still be unconscious. It would be enough to hold his hand and watch him breathe. Eric could time his own breaths to the ventilator, and that would keep him focused.

The tension in his shoulders and jaw doubled as he entered the hospital, the smell enough to make him want to turn around and walk right back out. If he did that, though, he wouldn't be able to see Tim, and that wasn't an acceptable outcome. Eric had knowingly walked into firefights that could have ended his life without blinking an eye. He could walk into a fucking hospital to see his lover.

He made it past the front desk and onto the ICU floor without anyone stopping him. Probably a good thing since he didn't have much in the way of ID at the moment. He hadn't even questioned how Richard had gotten them around security and onto the base, but he knew better than to ask. He was halfway down the corridor to Tim's room when an alarm blared at the nurses' station. He jumped, every muscle in his body on high alert as he searched for the threat.

Hospital. He was in a hospital, not on a battlefield. The only enemies here were death and disease, and his bullets couldn't fight those, no matter how precisely he aimed them. A team of nurses went running past, down the hall in the direction of Tim's room.

It wasn't Tim. It couldn't be Tim. The doctor, Smith, Smitt, whatever her name was, said he would be fine. He heard shouts, someone yelling for a crash cart, and then another flurry of people ran by. He couldn't see which room they went into, the doors a blur as black danced around the edges of his vision until he could only see straight ahead and even then not clearly. He shook his head. He couldn't panic. He couldn't. If he couldn't see, he couldn't shoot, and if he couldn't shoot, he was nothing.

He stumbled a few steps more, catching himself on the wall. Which room was Tim's? Where was the crash cart? Did they go in Tim's room?

His phone. They were supposed to notify him if anything happened. Victoria said she'd stay the night. She'd call him if Tim were coding, wouldn't she? He fumbled for his phone, but his hands were shaking so badly he couldn't keep hold of it. It fell to the ground with a loud clatter.

He winced and ducked for cover. The sounds came at him from every angle. Where were they? He had to find the enemy locations so he could take them out. They'd get a bead on his team, and he'd already lost too many people. He couldn't lose any more. He'd find them and....

Where was his rifle? He never went into the field without it. He didn't have a weapon. He had to find something. He had to defend himself.

The beeping and shouts grew louder. What new torture had his captors come up with now? He didn't know how much more he could stand, but the alternative was betraying his friends even worse than he already had, and he would never knowingly do that. He wouldn't tell them anything under duress. They'd have to drug him out of his mind and then hope they could get something usable out of the babble. He wouldn't tell them. He wouldn't. He woul—

"Sir? Are you all right? Do you need assistance?"

The sound of the voice—the American accent—shook Eric out of his nightmare. He blinked a couple of times to clear his vision. White vinyl tiles marched through his line of sight, row upon row of spotlessly clean floor, nothing like the dirt and sand of his prison. Right, not in Turkmenistan anymore. Germany. He was in Germany.

"Davenport," he said with cracked glass for a voice. "Is he—?" He couldn't force the words out. Thinking them was bad enough. If he gave them the weight of his voice, it would make them real. He braced his back against the wall, ignoring the pain from the broken and bruised skin there, and pushed to his feet. His knees wobbled precariously, but he knew how to make pain work for him. He clenched his jaw and tightened his abs until his balance returned. "I'm fine. Thank you for checking on me."

The medic looked skeptical, but he didn't press, much to Eric's relief. Instead he watched as Eric started down the hall again. At least the infernal beeping had stopped.

He nearly stumbled again. If the beeping had stopped, the code was over. Whoever was in crisis could be dead now. He forced his feet to move faster until he hit the door to Tim's room. He leaned against it, panting heavily as he raked his gaze over the interior, taking it all in with a single glance that made him such an effective sniper.

Tim lay exactly where Eric had left him, the heart monitor beeping regularly as the ventilator pumped air in and out of Tim's lungs. Victoria sat next to the bed, reading. He sagged against the door.

"Eric?"

"I heard the alarm go off at the nurses' station. I thought it was Tim," Eric explained. "But obviously it's not. I just need a minute for the adrenaline rush to pass."

"Where is Horn?"

"I don't know," Eric replied. "I haven't seen him since I left the house this morning. I had to go by the clinic on base to check on my recovery."

"Don't avoid the question, *pesche*."

He had the sinking suspicion she'd just called him Peaches in Italian. He was never living that down. If he thought that would distract her from whatever idea she'd fixated on, he'd run with it, but playing dumb never worked with her. Not that it ever stopped him from trying. "What are you talking about?"

"I know how you get, and I know Davenport never lets you out of his sight, even if he lets you out of bed, for at least the first forty-eight hours after a bad mission. This was the worst you've ever faced, yet you're here trying to pretend everything is fine. You haven't even shaved yet."

He couldn't. Even if he could steady his hands enough to do it without slitting his throat—not possible now, but it might have been last night with Richard there—doing it himself would be admitting that Tim couldn't. If he waited long enough, Tim would wake up and come into the bathroom, sit him down, and cover his face with lather. He'd find a straight razor somewhere—probably out of Richard's toiletries—because he was talented that way, and he'd erase the stubble from Eric's face, and when he did, he'd take all the stress and terror and pain of the torture with it, and Eric could let it go. If Eric did it himself, if he gave up on that ritual….

No. He couldn't. Nobody would care if he was scruffy for a few more weeks. They didn't have to conform to military standards. He could be as scruffy as he wanted for as long as he wanted.

"You didn't really expect me to spend time shaving when Tim is lying in a hospital bed, did you?"

"I expected you to take care of yourself, knowing I was here looking out for him," Victoria said. "Or if you couldn't do that, I expected Horn to take care of you."

Eric had hoped…. It didn't matter what he'd hoped. He knew Richard cared about what happened to him, if only because it would upset Tim if anything happened to Eric. They had a good time in bed together, the three of them. He knew Tim and Richard had sex without him, and he could live with that. They'd been together a long time. And he and Tim had sex sometimes when Richard wasn't there, stuck late at work or pulled away on a mission that didn't involve them. He'd thought about having sex with just Richard on a few occasions, but it always seemed to work better when Tim was there too. Like last night. Richard had held him as he fell asleep, which was good, but it didn't ground him in his body the same way. It didn't empty his mind and leave him relaxed enough to forget for a while. It didn't bring him *home*.

He was a mess, covered in bruises and cuts. At the end of a bad mission, he usually joked that he'd had worse, but he couldn't say that this time. He'd had bad missions, but none of them had ever compared to this one. He could see why Richard wouldn't want him right now. He wasn't anywhere near his best, even if the pain had dulled to manageable. Hopefully Richard's interest would return when Eric was a little less battered and they were both a little more assured of Tim's recovery. Eric could live without sex. After four years, though, he found it harder to live without intimacy.

A nurse came in, interrupting his thoughts. "Sorry to bother you, but I need to change Mr. Davenport's dressings."

"Do we need to leave?" Eric would leave if he had to, but he'd just gotten here, and his grip on reality still felt tenuous at best. Seeing Tim might not work as well as making love with him, but it was better than nothing.

"No, just stay back so I can work."

Victoria rose and offered Eric her chair. "I need to get some sleep anyway. I'll be back later to check on you."

Eric nodded and took the seat, well out of the way of the nurse. He didn't want to keep her from doing her job, but he needed to see the extent of Tim's injuries. The doctor had given the rundown of his condition and prognosis, but only in general terms. Multiple GSWs, she'd said, but that didn't tell Eric how many or where, beyond the one that affected his lung.

He flinched when the nurse pulled the sheet back to reveal bandages over the bulk of Tim's lower body. He counted as they changed the bandages, noting each place a surgical scar overlaid a pucker. Twelve. Twelve fucking bullets. Bile rose in his throat at the thought. He knew what a single bullet could do to a human body. He was a sniper. He could make a kill shot in half-a-dozen different places. Fortunately none of the holes marring Tim's body had been kill shots, but that didn't make the trauma any easier to bear. He was lucky to be alive.

Eric had known that, but the realization hit him again hard. He closed his eyes and tipped his head back, taking deep breaths to calm himself. Tim was here. He was safe. He would recover. He repeated the words like a mantra. If he said them enough times, he might even believe them.

The sound of the door opening again startled Eric back to battle readiness. He didn't have his rifle, but he wasn't helpless even without it. If they thought he'd go down easily, they had another think coming.

"Eric?"

Richard's voice broke through the fight-or-flight response, and Eric slumped back into the chair. Richard looked almost as haggard as Eric felt, but Eric pushed down the desire to comfort him. The nurse was still in the room, for one thing, but even more than that, Eric wasn't ready to forgive Richard for threatening to order him to see a doctor that morning. Tim would kick his ass and tell him he was acting like a two-year-old pitching a temper tantrum, but the tone of Richard's voice had been a slap in the face. Richard had said he left the commander outside, that he was only the lover in the house, but that had been the commander's voice, not the lover's, and the sense of betrayal hadn't left Eric yet.

"They're changing his dressings," Eric said by way of acknowledgment.

Richard found a second chair from somewhere and drew it up next to Eric's. They didn't touch while the nurse was in the room, but when everything was finally adjusted and the nurse left, Richard reached for Eric's hand. "I'm sorry," he said. "I always tell you not to fuck it up, and this time I'm the one doing it."

Eric shrugged. "I know you were trying to help." Even in the midst of his hurt, he hadn't really doubted that, just the way Richard had gone about it.

"Doing a piss-poor job of it," Richard muttered.

Eric took a deep breath, trying to settle himself. His emotions were all over the place, completely out of his control, and he hated that. He hated being out of control, body or mind. The psychologists said it was a normal symptom of PTSD and something he had to learn to cope with. He hated them for it most days, but it had helped him learn to identify when he was acting irrationally and to rein it in sometimes. He took another deep breath and forcibly let go of his anger. He'd learned one other lesson amid all the bullshit. As hard as this was on him, he wasn't the only one suffering. He was entitled to feel a little raw and rough around the edges at the end of a bad mission, but they were too. He knew his lovers. Richard and Tim had surely been frantic with worry while he was held captive. Richard had to watch helplessly as Tim went down, not even able to go to him right away because of the op to rescue Eric. Eric was legitimately hurting to see Tim in the hospital bed, but Richard was too. Guilt was the only emotion Eric felt in regard to Tim that Richard didn't.

"Yeah, well, I didn't do any better being supportive of you."

"You're the one they tortured for months."

"And you're the one who nearly lost everything," Eric replied. "When they had me, I was in survival mode. I didn't think about anything but keeping my mouth shut and conserving my energy for whatever they came up with next. I couldn't hope for rescue. I couldn't do anything but stay alive one more day. You, though—you had to live with whatever went wrong that led to me being captured and whatever it took to find me again. And then you had to deal with Tim going down. I'm broken. I've always been broken, so that's nothing new. This is just another bump in the road for me."

"I don't want you to be broken anymore," Richard said. "I want you to feel safe and to be able to trust Dav and me and then maybe your team. I want you to be whole again."

Eric smiled sadly. "I don't know if that's possible at this point. You don't get over the kinds of things that've happened to me. You just learn to live with them. And we're still active in the field. Things are going to keep happening. I'm always going to be broken."

"Then I guess I'll have to keep helping Dav pick up the pieces."

"God, this is so fucked-up," Eric said with a rusty laugh. "I'm fucked six ways to Sunday, Tim took a dozen bullets, and you're stuck with us. Somehow I don't think you signed up for this."

Richard grabbed Eric's chin and forced Eric's eyes to meet his. "You don't get to decide what I signed up for, you hear me, Eric? I've been doing this shit longer than you've been alive, and I've seen every goddamn thing you can imagine and some you can't, even after this clusterfuck. You think Dav and I aren't broken too? We were so fucking broken it took you coming along to keep us sane."

"Then you really are fucked," Eric said, "if I'm the sane one."

"That's not what I said," Richard growled, and damn if the sound didn't make Eric's cock hard after four years of hearing it in the bedroom as well as in the briefing room. "I didn't say you were the sane one. I said you were the one who kept us sane, just like I'd like to think we're what keeps you sane. So I'm going to keep taking care of you, and we're both going to take care of Dav, and I hope maybe you'll take care of me too. I know I wasn't your choice, not the way Dav was, but I love you. It gutted me to know you were being held prisoner. I would have given anything to be in your place, would have given them anything to have you back if I'd thought they would actually give you back unharmed. You're not some fucking afterthought. You're my two good hands, and I'd be as fucked without you as I would be without Dav."

Eric surged forward and kissed Richard. It was the only thing he could think to do, the only way he could come up with to counter Richard's comment. He grabbed Richard's face as he deepened the kiss, determined to show Richard he didn't feel that way, that he wanted Richard, that he loved Richard too. Richard's hands closed around his wrists as he took control of the kiss, but the feeling of being trapped was more than Eric could stand. He tore his hands away and pulled back, panting hard.

"Don't…." It took Eric a moment to stop the panic enough to speak. "Don't hold my wrists."

Richard looked at him sharply. "Did they—"

"No," Eric said, "but the psychologists say any new trauma stirs back up all the old ones, and one of the triggers when the PTSD flares up is being tied up or held down or somehow not able to move." His worst nightmare was waking up with his wrists tied.

"How the hell did I not know this?" Richard demanded.

"Because most of the time I keep it under control," Eric said. "Victoria and Tim know, and they do their best to make sure I don't wake up restrained. We don't play those kinds of games in the bedroom. It's just never come up."

"And yet Amato knows about it," Richard said. "It's obviously 'come up' often enough."

"She knows because she and Tim found me in Vladivostok." He didn't need to give Richard details of that op. Richard had read the file of how Eric had been held by a splinter group of a Russian arms syndicate and tortured before he'd been rescued. He'd counted it as his worst mission until this one. Eric had made his move on Tim shortly after he was cleared for duty post op. "They were with me when I came awake on the plane. The medics had restrained me because I was thrashing and they were worried I'd pull out my IV. I didn't deal with it well. Tim got me calmed down enough for Victoria to release me, and they've been careful to keep it from happening since then. I asked Tim to keep that detail out of the report. I don't think anyone would take advantage of the knowledge, but I didn't want to take the chance."

"I can understand not putting it in the report, but we've been together for four years, Eric."

"I told you a long time ago that I wasn't good at relationships."

Richard sighed. "If I don't hold your wrists, can I kiss you again? Because that's what I was trying to do when everything went sideways."

"You can hold anything you want other than that," Eric said, leaning forward again.

The kiss was awkward with the hard plastic chairs and no way to get closer to each other, not like on a bed or a couch, but it brought all the sensation of home and comfort and safety. Eric sighed into it, letting Richard control the kiss, letting go not because it was stolen from him but because he gave it freely to one of the three people in the world he trusted without hesitation.

CHAPTER 7

THE SOUND of someone knocking at the door startled them apart. Richard didn't let go of Eric's hand, but he did sit back in the chair. Most of Strike Force Omega knew about them now, but that didn't mean he wanted them to walk in on him kissing Eric. Some things were meant to be private. And if it was someone from the base, not one of his team, then it was even less something they needed to see.

"Come in," he called.

The soldier who poked his head through the door couldn't have been more than nineteen, by Richard's best estimate. He looked as nervous as a raw recruit on his first day of basic training. Richard kept his expression stern. He had a reputation to maintain, and the kid needed to toughen up if he couldn't even handle walking into a hospital room. "Yes?"

"Excuse me, sir, but General Boling sent me to find you." The airman rocked back and forth from one foot to another as he spoke. "He said he was sorry to disturb you but that it was urgent."

"Where is he?" Richard asked. Next to him, Eric flinched, but Richard let it pass for the moment. He'd take care of Eric when the airman left.

"In his office, sir. I'll take you there."

"I know where his office is," Richard snapped. He'd left it less than half an hour ago.

"I'm sorry, sir, but he gave me orders to escort you to his office."

"Then you can wait outside until I'm done checking on my operatives," Richard replied, biting back the urge to give the soldier a dressing-down he'd never forget. It wasn't his fault Boling chose this moment to be a demanding asshole.

"Sir." The private stepped outside.

As soon as the door closed behind him, Richard turned back to Eric. "I'm sorry. I thought I'd satisfied Boling earlier. Will you be all right here while I go see what bug he's got up his ass this time?"

Eric nodded. Richard hated to leave him, because his posture suggested he was less at ease than his nod implied, but they were at least somewhat at Boling's mercy until Dav was well enough to leave the hospital. It would be useful to stay on base for rehab as well, but they could manage that elsewhere if they had to. Getting him transferred to a different ICU in his current state wouldn't be as simple. "I'll be back as soon as I can."

"We'll be here," Eric replied.

Richard cursed under his breath as he bent to kiss Eric again before leaving the room. The airman stood at parade rest outside the door. Richard would give him credit for form if he were feeling more charitable. As it was, he stalked right past him toward his car so he could drive back to base and to Boling's office. The kid could keep up. Richard was going there and back as fast as he could without sacrificing his dignity and authority.

"What's so important it couldn't wait?" he demanded when he walked into Boling's office a few minutes later. "I was trying to check on Davenport."

"General Collins at the Pentagon would like to speak with you," Boling said. "I put the conference call on mute while I was waiting for you to get here."

Richard probably should have been glad Collins hadn't heard his outburst, but he couldn't be bothered to care. He refused to be bullied into anything by anyone. He'd play by their rules as long as they understood that he chose to, not that he had to.

"Let's get this over with."

He took a seat on the opposite side of the desk from Boling as Boling turned the monitor on his desk around and turned the speakers and microphone back on.

"General Collins, you wanted to speak with me?" Richard asked.

"What's this I hear about you running an unsanctioned op at the same time you were overseeing the op in Syria?" Collins asked.

"My people achieved their objective in Syria," Richard ground out. "At the cost of serious injury to one of the team. I don't see how rescuing one of my operatives who was captured on one of your ops when *your* team failed to protect him is any of your concern." He'd be facing court-martial if he'd spoken to one of his Navy superiors that way, but that was one of the reasons he'd gotten out. He had gotten tired of curbing his tongue. As it was, he took their money and ran his ops his way, as long as he achieved their objectives. If they didn't like it, he was sure another of their allies could find a use for his services.

"I don't appreciate your attitude, Horn."

"And I don't appreciate my people paying the price for your people's mistakes. Was there anything else, General?"

"I want the reports from the debrief of the operative you rescued," Collins said. "I should have had those already."

Richard saw red. The fucking bastard, thinking he had any right to demand anything of Eric after their errors cost him four months of torture. More than anything, he wanted to deny Collins any right to Eric's debrief. If Dav weren't in a military hospital, Richard would tell him to fuck off, but if Collins ordered Boling to break ties with them, Dav would be up shit creek. No, he'd have to play nice and give him access to it eventually, especially since Eric was on a government op when he was captured. He didn't have to hurry it up, though. He'd do the debrief when it wouldn't make things worse for Eric. He bit back his angry retort and forced himself to give a measured reply.

"Mr. Newton is still being debriefed. He was in no physical or mental state to give a report immediately after his liberation. I will forward the report to you when completing it does not further compromise the health of my operative. The Syria debrief—on the operation that is within your purview—is being completed as we speak and will be turned in to General Boling today. I'm sure he will make sure you receive a copy of it."

Collins's face twisted in disgruntlement, but Richard was used to it. Most of the people he worked with at the Pentagon still remembered what it meant to be in the field and listened when he talked, but Collins was a stuffed shirt of the worst degree. Richard took great pleasure in pissing him off.

"Watch it, Horn. You're skating close to the line."

"Sir."

"Dismissed," Collins said, like his orders meant something to Richard. Richard didn't bother to salute as he rose from the chair and left Boling's office. He had to find Heikkinen and make sure she had finished the Syria report. She always knew just how to phrase things to make the higher-ups happy. The faster he found her, the faster he could get back to Eric and Dav, where he belonged.

ERIC MANAGED to sit at Tim's bedside for about twenty minutes before the walls started closing in around him. If he'd been anywhere near home or had planned to be in Germany, he'd have his tablet or a book or something to pass the time. As it was, he had nothing to occupy his mind except the dark thoughts that never completely left him. At any other time, he would have planned better, could have thought through his options, but his brain still felt completely offline. If he stayed, he'd have another meltdown like earlier. He'd been lucky with that one. He'd come out of it without striking out at anyone, and the orderly who'd found him hadn't clicked to the fact that he was dissociating. He might not be as lucky next time. He had to keep it together or he'd end up in the psych ward, and then he wouldn't be able to help Tim through his recovery. Since that was unacceptable, he'd just have to find a way to cope until Tim was well enough to help him in return.

He debated leaving a note for Richard, telling him where he was going, but seven years of moving in the shadows had made him leery of leaving traces anyone else might find. Richard surely knew him well enough to guess that if Eric wasn't at Tim's side, he had gone to the shooting range. Of course, that assumed someone at the range had a rifle he could check out and practice with, because he wasn't sure what happened to his rifle after they left the compound where he'd been held captive. He'd had it when he got on the copter, but everything else after that was a blur. He was slipping. He had to do better than that or Richard wouldn't trust him out in the field again. Eric could deal—had dealt—with a lot of things, but losing his place on the team wasn't something he knew how to face.

He'd hoped Richard would spend the day with him, keeping his mind occupied even if all they did was hold vigil at Tim's bedside together. He hadn't expected it for himself, but he'd hoped that Tim and Richard's relationship would be enough to keep Richard there. He should have known better.

As soon as the thought crossed his mind, he knew it was unfair. Ignoring a summons from a general wasn't done lightly. Tim's condition hadn't changed overnight. However much Eric wanted Richard there, having him there didn't change anything about Tim's situation. Nothing to justify ignoring the general's request. That didn't keep Eric from wishing Richard had blown him off anyway. He supposed he was lucky Richard even asked instead of simply leaving when the airman first showed up.

He leaned over Tim and kissed his forehead tenderly, brushing his blond hair away from the bandage. "I have to go shoot for a while, but I'll come back later. Get well while I'm gone, okay? I love you."

It took him a few minutes to remember where the shooting range was once he got back to base. It had been a while since they'd been on the base in Germany. Once he gave his name and affiliation, though, the sergeant in charge of the shooting range was happy to show him the rifles they had for target practice and get him set up. They didn't have anything particularly unusual, which was what Eric really wanted, but some of the rifles were models he was less familiar with. With his thoughts as scattered as they were, he needed the challenge of mastering an unfamiliar rifle or pistol, something to make him focus. At home he had a whole armory of old muskets, rifles, longbows, crossbows, and more, plenty to keep him challenged, but they were in the Caymans, and he wouldn't be there anytime soon, at least not until Tim was well enough to leave the hospital. He and Tim might convince Richard that Tim would do better completing his rehab at home rather than in Germany or at a base in the US, but even that was a long shot. Richard would argue that they put Strike Force Omega at risk by bringing in a physical therapist and by running ops from there.

Because he had the time, he took the rifle apart and reassembled it. It was completely standard, with none of the personal modifications every sniper he'd ever known had made to guarantee their rifle functioned the way they expected it to. Still, it would do for today. He wasn't prepping for a mission. He was challenging his ability to master an unfamiliar rifle in as short a time as possible.

When he'd learned all the secrets he could from examining it, he took his position at the firing line and sighted down the barrel. The barrel drifted just slightly to the left. He compensated and fired a single shot. When he pulled the target in to check, the bullet hole was barely a fraction of an inch off center. If he'd been shooting at a mark, it would have been a kill shot with no problem, but he wasn't in the field, and on the range, nothing short of dead center was acceptable. He returned the target to its place and aimed again, keeping in mind where the first shot had ended up. When he fired again, it took out the center exactly. He pulled the trigger again, several times in rapid succession. The rifle wasn't a machine gun, designed to spray bullets across a wide area, but he still prided himself on being able to take out multiple targets quickly without sacrificing his accuracy. This range wasn't equipped for that kind of practice, but it would do for now.

RICHARD FINISHED his quick skim of the Syria report and looked up at Heikkinen. "Good. Get this to Boling today so Collins stops riding my ass for it."

"Yes, sir," she said.

"Is there anything else? I need to get back to Davenport and Newton."

"The planning for our upcoming missions is progressing as expected. We still need to complete Newton's debrief," Heikkinen said.

"We had this discussion already. We'll debrief when he's recovered," Richard replied.

"Respectfully, sir, the longer we wait, the more we risk him forgetting."

"You don't 'forget' four months of torture."

"I don't give a damn about the details of what they did to him," Heikkinen said. "I don't even really care what he told them because we have protocols in place to handle that. I want to know what he learned about them while he was there."

"He doesn't speak Arabic or Farsi, so I doubt he overheard anything useful," Richard reminded her.

"But if they interrogated him, then they spoke at least some English in order to ask him questions. We need to know what they asked him. That information could potentially reveal as much about their plans as any intelligence currently available to us."

As much as Richard refused to pressure Eric, this was why he kept Heikkinen around. Her background with the CIA gave her a different attitude toward intelligence than anyone else in Strike Force Omega. When she sat down to debrief Eric, she'd pull every scrap of useful information from him. Not yet, though. Even Richard could see he was still too tightly strung to sit through that kind of debrief.

"Soon," he said because she was waiting for an answer. "Not today, probably not tomorrow, but maybe Friday." That gave him two more days to figure out how to help ground Eric. Dav had talked in general terms about helping Eric back from bad missions. Richard wished now that he'd pressed for more details instead of simply taking on Dav's responsibilities so Dav could be there for Eric. He hadn't anticipated a time when Dav would be unavailable. He should have known better.

"The longer we wait, the harder it will be for him to remember and the less useful it will be because they will have had more time to change their plans too," Heikkinen warned.

"I said Friday," he snapped as he rose from his chair and headed for the door. He had to get out of there before he said something he'd regret. Like telling her to leave. She might drive him batshit crazy sometimes, but she was good at her job, and he needed her. Just not right now.

"Sir."

Richard kept walking. She'd acknowledged his orders. The rest would wait. He stalked to his car and drove back to the hospital, but Eric wasn't in Dav's room when he got there. He slammed his fist against the wall. He'd known he shouldn't have left, but Eric hadn't given him anything he could have used to refuse. And now he wasn't there.

"Where did he go, Dav?" he asked, knowing he wouldn't get an answer. The silence that followed his question drove home just how far they still had to go. He needed to find Smithers and see if there had been any improvement and if she thought Dav could come off the ventilator sooner rather than later. He needed advice, and Dav was the only one who could give it to him. Then he needed to find Eric and figure out what the hell he was doing wrong, because he could feel everything spiraling out of control.

One thing was certain. After the exchange earlier when Richard had reached for Eric's wrists, he'd have to be careful to let Eric be in control of their interactions. He wanted to help, but he couldn't impose on Eric in any way. The last thing he wanted to do was trigger Eric's PTSD by ordering him around. He wouldn't have a choice in professional situations, but he could sure as hell avoid making that mistake again in private.

Smithers came in before Richard could go looking for her.

"How is he?" he asked with a wave toward Dav's bed.

"Remarkably well, given the extent of his injuries. His chest has stayed clear, his heartbeat is regular. All signs point to him making a significant recovery in time."

"How soon can you wean him off the ventilator?"

"The longer he stays asleep, the better," Smithers insisted.

"Yes, I know, but the longer he stays asleep, the worse the situation he's going to come back to," Richard replied. "He's the glue that holds us together."

"Even if he's off the ventilator, he's not going to be doing anything but sleeping for a while," Smithers warned.

"I know, but at least he'll be able to tell me what the hell I'm doing wrong and how to fix it."

"Not for at least another couple of days," Smithers said when Richard glared at her. "He survived severe trauma. His recovery is going to be complicated enough. I don't want to jeopardize that by rushing. The good news is his digestion has kicked back in. That's a sign that his body is healing. It's not the one you're looking for, I know, but it's a concrete step in the right direction."

"Thank you, Doctor. Keep me posted, please." It wasn't the answer Richard wanted, but it was better than none at all, and honestly better than he'd expected. Now to find Eric and see what he could do about that situation.

"I will."

Richard left the hospital and got in the car, still trying to decide where Eric might have gone. Back to their temporary quarters was a possibility, but Richard didn't think it was a likely one. Given how Eric filled his time when they had any to spare, he had probably gone to the firing range. It would give him something to occupy his mind and hands while he waited. Richard might not know as much about his lover as he really should after four years, but he knew Eric didn't tolerate being idle. With no real access to entertainment at the moment, the firing range was his best option.

He crossed the base and entered the range to see Eric in the far lane. Richard stopped to watch, blown away again by the sheer beauty of the man in front of him. He'd always seen it, of course—it was his job to notice things—but now he could simply stand there and stare. Eric fired shot after shot, his concentration unwavering. Richard didn't have to see the target to know every one hit dead center. Eric never missed, certainly not on a range like this where everything was controlled.

Eric stopped after a few minutes to brush his hair out of his eyes. Richard had never known him to wear it this long, but that was Eric's call to make. Even from that distance, Richard could see the ease in Eric's body that hadn't been there last night or this morning, not even in Dav's room. Here, where he was in control, Eric had relaxed.

Maybe not the complete relaxation that came from firing his bows, but enough.

That gave Richard an idea. He didn't know how complicated it would be to bring any of Eric's arsenal to Germany, but he could probably find something nearby that would suit. Even if it ended up being a duplicate of something Eric already had, it would still give him a bow to work with while they were here. The recoil of a rifle might require some muscle to absorb, but it was nothing compared to the draw weight of Eric's bows. Richard could shoot most of the compounds, but the medieval longbows Eric had collected and restored had draw weights of well over a hundred pounds. Richard didn't know if he could find anything like that here, but he could certainly look. Anything to give Eric a way to keep the calm Richard saw in him now.

He'd start looking immediately, and in the meantime, he'd just have to ensure Eric had control of as much as possible in his life until the wariness in his eyes faded and the tension in his body eased.

CHAPTER 8

SEVERAL HOURS later, Richard admitted defeat for the day. The laws concerning weapons in Germany would have required both him and Eric to have a license in order to purchase a bow. Not only would that ruin the surprise, but he hoped they wouldn't still be in Germany by the time that paperwork was complete. He'd have to find another way to get what he needed, because he could see how tense Eric was when he found him sitting in Dav's room again shortly before dinner.

"Hey, Peaches," he said with what he hoped would be a reassuring grin. "Did the doc tell you the good news? Dav's food tube was clear this morning, which means his stomach is back in the game. His body is trying to resume all its normal functions."

"Does that mean they'll let him wake up soon?" Eric asked.

"It's not his lungs just yet, but she said it was an expected first step and a good sign that it had happened this quickly," Richard replied. "How quickly they can take him off the ventilator will depend on how he continues to heal. I know it's hard, but we don't want to compromise his long-term recovery by rushing now."

"No, of course not," Eric agreed, but his voice sounded dull to Richard's ears. Damn, he'd hoped going to the range had helped more than this. He really needed to find Eric a bow.

"Do you want dinner?" Richard asked when his stomach rumbled. "We still don't have anything at the house, but we could go to the mess until we can get into town to buy groceries." He'd been too focused on the idea of finding Eric a bow to think of more practical matters. Dav would have a field day with that. Richard would make sure not to tell him when he woke up.

"That's fine." Eric shrugged and stood up.

"Hey, what's up?" Richard caught Eric in his arms, watching carefully for any sign that Eric wanted free. He would let go if so, but until then, he needed the reassurance of the embrace, even if Eric didn't.

Eric shrugged again. "I'm not used to having nothing to do. I know there will be plenty to do once Tim starts rehab, but I almost wish we'd get a mission so I'd have something to do besides sit and stare at the walls."

"There are things we could do," Richard said. "At some point we have to debrief. Heikkinen is chomping at the bit. I put her off a few days, but we can't put it off forever."

Eric snorted. "Not exactly how I want to fill my time."

"I know, but it has to be done. Are you up for a new mission?"

Eric started to say yes automatically. Richard could read it in his body, but he stopped before the word came out of his mouth. "Physically I'm not a hundred percent, but I'm field ready. It will take time to build back up the muscle I lost from lack of nutrition and lack of movement."

"You can use the gym on base if you want to work out," Richard reminded him. "I don't know how elaborate the facilities are, but it's better than nothing. There might even be something here at the hospital if you need a break during the day and don't want to drive back to base."

"I know. It's just…."

"Not the same," Richard finished when Eric trailed off. Part of that feeling had to come from Richard being the one trying to help him rather than Dav, but they'd just have to make the best of it. "You ready to get out of here for the night? We can get something to eat, maybe watch a little TV, whatever you want to do."

"Dinner would be good," Eric said, "and maybe a beer or two, if we can find some."

"We can get some on the way back to base," Richard said.

TWENTY MINUTES later, they made it home, beer in hand. They'd decided they both needed to clean up before going to the mess for dinner.

"Beer or shower first?" Richard asked.

"Both," Eric said.

"Go on. I'll bring it to you."

"Thanks."

Eric disappeared into the little bathroom off the living area while Richard dealt with the beer. He stuck the rest of the six-pack in the fridge and cracked open one for Eric.

Walking into the bathroom, he stopped for a moment to appreciate the view as Eric bent over to adjust the water in the tub. His jeans pulled tight across his ass at that angle, giving Richard all kinds of delicious ideas, but the discussion about control loomed large in his mind. He gave Eric's ass a good grope as silent invitation but didn't press beyond that. "Take your shower. I'll be waiting when you're done."

"Okay," Eric said. His voice sounded a little off, but he didn't say anything else, so Richard let it go. He didn't want Eric to feel pressured.

ERIC CLIMBED into the shower and waited for the door to close. "Fuck," he muttered. Richard's hand on his ass had raised his hopes, but then Richard had disappeared, leaving Eric alone with his spiraling thoughts. He'd let himself hope when Richard kept coming to find him instead of leaving him alone, but he missed Tim, who always knew what to do or say to make Eric feel better. Richard was trying. Eric knew he was trying, but it just wasn't the same. Tim would have known what Eric needed without words, would have wrapped him up in such a cocoon of love and caring that Eric's doubts would fade away. Richard apparently hadn't learned Tim's tricks, however much Eric needed him to have done so.

Tim always made the same thing when they were hiding in safe houses or recovering from an op. He'd pull out whatever meat they had and mix it with vegetables for a wonderful hot stew that tasted of love and safety, even if the ingredients were never the same twice, and then once they'd eaten, Tim would wrap Eric up in his arms and make long, slow love to him until he couldn't breathe, until his brain shut off and all the doubts went away, and he *knew* in his very marrow that Tim loved him and wouldn't ever let him go.

Dinner would have to wait until Tim was out of the hospital since making stew himself or asking Richard to make it wouldn't have the same effect, but at least he could rely on Richard to fuck him into the mattress. Richard hadn't passed up a chance to get at Eric's ass in four years, unless Tim got there first, of course. If it wasn't the slow, sweet lovemaking that was a balm to Eric's soul, it would still be better than nothing.

He finished his shower and toweled off, then pulled on a pair of sweats and a T-shirt for dinner. He figured Richard would have him out of them about a minute after dinner was over, but that would be good. A round of sweaty, mindless sex to put the taunting sense of betrayal out of his head. And then maybe he'd make it through the night without nightmares again. Richard's arms around him had helped last night. Hopefully he'd go two for two tonight.

"Feeling better?" Richard asked when Eric joined him in the living room. He clinked his beer bottle against Eric's and gave him a quick kiss, but it was a careful one, not a "prelude to fucking Eric boneless" one. Then again, they hadn't eaten yet.

He was a sniper. He could be patient.

"Clean, anyway," he answered because it was true.

"Is there anything I can do to help?"

There were plenty of things, but if Eric had to ask for them, they wouldn't help. They helped not because of the actual gestures but because Eric knew what those gestures meant. Tim putting a bowl of stew in front of him meant they were safe, for the moment at least, and they were together and Tim was taking care of him as he always did. Tim bringing him to bed and worshipping his body meant Tim loved him and wouldn't let him go, no matter how badly the op had gone. Tim shaving him meant Eric could let go and put his life in the hands of one of the few people he could trust not to turn the razor on him for a buck or two or just the hell of it. Eric could ask Richard to do those things, but it wouldn't mean anything if he did.

"Beer is good," Eric said. "Food is good. It'll just take time."

"We have time," Richard said. "At least as long as Dav is in the hospital, we have nothing but time."

Of course that was part of the problem. Eric could play the waiting game in the field, when adrenaline kept every nerve on edge and the necessity of watching out for his team put his senses on high alert, no matter how long he sat in his nest, waiting for the shot that would put a terrorist out of commission or save the life of one of his friends. Once he was back on base, that patience disappeared.

"If sitting at the hospital gets to be too much, there are other things you can do while we're waiting," Richard offered. "Even if you don't go out on any ops so you can be here when Dav wakes up, you can still help plan them. It might not keep your body busy, but it'll keep your mind active."

Richard knew him that well, Eric grumbled silently.

"Sorry," he said. "I'm bad company tonight."

"I'm not here to be entertained," Richard said. "I'm here because I love you and want to be with you. Remember?"

"Yeah," Eric said. The doorbell interrupted them. Richard went to answer it, leaving Eric to try to push down his doubts. He'd worried about Eric while the terrorists had him; he'd stayed with Eric when he was in Medical; he'd held Eric through the night last night, keeping the nightmares at bay. Maybe Richard didn't know Eric the way Tim did, but he *was* trying. Tim hadn't always known what to do either.

"We have company," Richard said, coming back with Victoria, Westin, and Sanders in tow.

"We came to get you for dinner," Sanders said. "We hadn't seen you and figured you had to take a break to eat."

There went his hope for a quiet dinner with Richard followed by a long, sweaty fuck. They'd be lucky to ditch the rest of the team before midnight.

"Sure." Eric hoped Richard would put his foot down and get rid of them, but he only nodded and rested his hand on Eric's arm to guide him toward the door. Well, fuck.

He followed the rest of the team out the door, trying to push past the unease of having the one post-op ritual he'd hoped to carry out delayed. He'd had missions where he didn't get them right away, because it wasn't safe, because he was in Medical or Tim was, because they didn't have access to a razor, just because, but he'd never had his body and mind stolen from him the way the terrorists had done with their drugs and their lies and their torture, and that was fucking with his ability to think rationally about the situation in ways he was afraid to consider.

RICHARD SAT next to Eric in the mess, where he'd positioned himself with his back to a wall. Richard hoped his presence on the other side provided an extra layer of security. With Amato, Sanders, and Westin across the table, Eric was as safe and surrounded as they could make him. That didn't seem to do anything for Eric's tension, though. Richard wondered if they'd made a mistake coming out. He should have offered the team a beer and then sent them on their way. Not that they had anything to eat in the house since he'd gone looking for bows instead of grocery shopping, but whatever he could have scrounged up would have been better than watching Eric withdraw into himself again.

"Any new ops in the works for us, boss?" Sanders asked.

Richard could have kicked his ass to Syria and back, with the way Eric flinched at the question. "Not yet. Heikkinen is running the ones we already had in the pipeline, but those were already assigned to other teams. We're still analyzing what went wrong with Davenport's mission. That's two missions in a short time with unacceptable costs. I'm not committing to anything new until I know for sure Collins and his cronies aren't sending us on suicide missions. Our function has always been to take the missions they can't, but I have no interest in taking the missions they won't."

"We're with you on that," Amato chimed in. Westin looked distinctly uncomfortable.

"Did you have something to share with the class, Westin?"

"Not sure, to tell you the truth," Westin said. "Nobody ever said anything directly when I was still with the Army and coordinating with you, but a couple of things seem odd in retrospect. Who are you working with now?"

"Today I got yelled at by Collins directly," Richard said with a dry laugh. "He wanted the Syria report and the debrief from Eric. I told him to go to hell."

"Really?" Westin asked.

"Not quite, but I told him he'd have it when we were done with it, and not a minute sooner. I'm not jumping through his hoops any more than necessary to keep Dav safe in the hospital."

"Delay as long as you can," Westin said. "Let me talk to my buddies who are still in. This feels off to me."

"I'm sure we can convince him that Eric isn't stable enough to debrief yet," Richard said.

Eric laughed bitterly. "I can play the victim. Just let me know when to stop."

Richard bit back a curse. He had no doubt Eric could play any role they asked of him. He'd never questioned what Richard and Dav had asked him to do in the field. This, though, hit far too close to home.

"No playing necessary," Richard assured him. "We'll do the debrief and analyze the data like always. We'll just wait to share that with anyone else until we make sure Collins isn't playing us. They got you captured. I'm not letting them profit from it. Not until I'm sure how they intend to use it."

Damn, he needed Dav to wake up. He was the one who was good at this spy shit. Heikkinen had it in her blood, but Richard was only partially convinced of her loyalty. Normally Dav kept her in check, but that would fall to Richard now, like everything else with Dav out for the foreseeable future. He looked over at Eric, who sat hunched over almost double, and wondered how the hell he was supposed to keep all the balls in the air without fucking something up.

Eric had wanted to come out with the team, so Richard had encouraged him despite his inclination to kick them out. He'd done his best not to give in to his usual imperious tendencies and simply snap orders. He was *trying*, damn it, and he didn't like the feeling of having failed before he ever got out of the gate.

They finally finished eating and rose as one to head back out into the falling night. At least it was late enough in April that it wasn't freezing at night. They hadn't exactly planned a trip this far north when they'd left on their most recent missions. Sanders and Westin fell in step beside Eric, but Amato headed them off. "Sanders, you're on hospital duty tonight. Westin will relieve you in the morning until Eric or Horn can get there."

Sanders shot her a half-assed salute, but he detoured toward the parking lot.

"Westin, I want to know everything you suspect or even think you might have heard. Nobody abuses my team," Amato said.

Westin looked at Richard for confirmation, but Amato's loyalty wasn't in question. Richard could let her pick Westin's brain tonight, and then he and Heikkinen could go over his intel tomorrow. If they needed to follow up on anything, they could take care of it then.

That left him alone with Eric as they reached their base housing.

"It's still early," Richard said when they went inside. "Anything in particular you want to do tonight?"

Eric shrugged. "Just being here is good."

Richard moved to the couch, trying to give Eric the space to decide what he wanted to do. Richard wanted nothing more than to whisk Eric off to bed and keep him there, preferably moaning and coming for about a week, but he couldn't do that to Eric. He wouldn't take the choices out of his hands. The terrorists had done that. Richard wouldn't do the same. He couldn't even suggest it because Eric was still too biddable. When he was back to his usual snarky self, when Richard could trust him to say no if he didn't want something, then he'd make the suggestion.

Eric joined him on the couch after a long minute. He grabbed the remote and flipped channels until he found a soccer game. Tossing the remote on the table, he leaned back against the cushions, close enough that Richard felt safe putting an arm around Eric's shoulders. He didn't pull him closer, not wanting Eric to feel crowded, but enough to issue the invitation if Eric wanted to take him up on it. Within moments, Eric had fallen asleep.

Richard did pull him closer then, settling him so his head rested comfortably against Richard's chest. Richard closed his eyes and drifted as well, wrapped up in the scent of Eric's shampoo and the warmth of his body.

He woke suddenly a couple of hours later when Eric cried out and thrashed in his arms. "Easy," Richard said, not shaking Eric, but trying to wake him gently. "You're safe, Eric. I'm here. Come on, wake up now."

Eric jerked away from Richard's hands, so he didn't try that again. "Come on, Peaches. It's just a nightmare. Snap out of it," Richard urged, hoping the sound of his voice would be enough to bring Eric back to him. Eric's eyes opened, but Richard could tell Eric didn't see him, lost in whatever nightmare was currently haunting him. That blank expression would figure in Richard's own nightmares until the day he died, right alongside watching Dav bleed out and hearing the medics call it.

The nickname seemed to break Eric out of his dreams. Richard filed that away for future reference. "You okay?" Richard asked when Eric's eyes focused on him.

"Yeah, just a bad dream," Eric said hoarsely.

"You want to talk about it?"

Eric shook his head.

"You want to go to bed?" Richard suggested. "We'll be more comfortable there."

Eric nodded this time, so Richard led him into the bedroom and tucked him into bed, climbing in beside him and hoping they were done with nightmares for the night.

CHAPTER 9

WHEN THEY finished breakfast the next morning, Richard turned to Eric.

"Do you feel up to starting the debrief today?"

Eric couldn't stop his flinch at the thought of having to relive the four months of hell, but it had to be done. "As much as I don't want to do it, having it hanging over my head is worse. Tell me what time to meet Heikkinen and where. We'll start it, even if we can't finish. If Collins is using us, we need to figure it out."

"That isn't all she'll focus on in her debrief," Richard warned. "She thinks we can learn something from the kinds of questions they asked you. It won't just be what went wrong that resulted in you getting captured. She's going to want to know it all."

Fuck, what Eric would have given to have even a few minutes with Tim to steady himself before the debrief. He ran his shaky hand over the scraggly beard that was all he could grow even after four months. He couldn't shave himself given the state he was in, even if doing so wouldn't feel like he was giving up on Tim's recovery, so it was a moot point. He'd just have to wait for Tim to wake up and get well enough to do it for him. Unfortunately he couldn't wait for Tim to wake up and complete any of their rituals before debriefing. He'd have to find a way to keep it together. And maybe get very, very drunk tonight.

"I'll deal with it. Like pulling off a Band-Aid. Do it hard and fast and get it over with."

"Do you want me to go with you?" Richard asked.

Eric was tempted to say yes. Richard would put a stop to the debrief if it got to be too much, but if he was there, Eric wouldn't be able to stop worrying about how Richard would react to everything he said. The thought of Richard or Tim being tortured, of being helpless, and of then having to hear about it later made him want to puke. He couldn't do that to Richard when it wouldn't make any difference except to his own balance. Richard had more important things to do with his day.

"I'll deal with it." Richard got such an odd look on his face at Eric's words that Eric reached across the table and squeezed his hand. "Thank you for offering, though."

"I will always offer when I can," Richard assured him.

If it wasn't the assurance Eric wanted, he had no one but himself to blame. He'd always known he came in after work on Richard's priority list. He rose and put his dishes in the sink. He couldn't sit across the table from Richard for much longer and not break. He wanted—*needed*—so desperately for Richard to declare it a day off, to lock the rest of the world outside, and to put him first for a while. It wouldn't happen. Not even in his wildest dreams could it happen, but if Eric didn't get out of the house now, he was going to beg for it anyway. This way he wouldn't have to hear a rejection.

"I'll probably go to the range or the hospital after I finish with Heikkinen. I'll see you later."

He made it to the door before Richard called his name. Eric turned back to meet Richard's dark gaze. "Don't fuck it up."

Eric smiled at the familiar admonishment and walked out the door. He had no real idea where to find Heikkinen. He'd been too focused on Tim to even ask where the rest of his team was housed, much less the others in the organization he spent less time with.

"Eric!" The sound of Victoria's voice from farther down the row of barracks housing startled him. Eric couldn't stop his reflexive flinch, although he hoped she was far enough away not to notice.

He should have known better.

Victoria laid a gentle hand on his arm. "You're on edge this morning. Did Tim take a turn for the worse?"

"Not that I've heard," Eric replied. "I'm just not used to having nothing to do. Usually Tim is the one waiting on me to recover, not the other way around. And I have to debrief with Heikkinen today, assuming I can find her."

"Are you up for that?"

Eric shrugged. "Putting it off won't change anything, not with Tim in the hospital. He can't exactly welcome me home while he's unconscious."

Victoria looked at him sharply. "You have more than one lover. Horn could do all the things Tim usually does. I know we all had dinner together last night, but he could have made you stew the night before. I know he owns a razor."

"We're in borrowed housing, and we've spent all our time at the hospital," Eric replied. "It's not like there's stuff just lying around to make stew. Besides, he's not much of a cook. Tim or I do most of the cooking when we're all home."

Victoria pursed her lips, her expression so thunderous Eric flinched away automatically. "I'm not upset with you, sweetheart, but I'll be having words with Horn the next time I see him."

"Victoria, don't," Eric said, relaxing a little. If she was still using endearments with him, he wasn't in too much trouble. "Everything is fine."

"He didn't make you stew. It's *stew*, not haute cuisine. I can guarantee he could find whatever he needed on post. I will come to the hospital at four to collect you, and *I* will give you stew since your lover didn't bother."

"Victoria, he didn't know, okay? Tim is the one who always makes the stew, and most of the time, Richard isn't even there. He's doing his best."

"His best isn't good enough."

"I'll come with you at four," Eric said because it was easier than arguing with her. "We'll get through this. Tim's digestive tract started working again yesterday, and that'll get better each day. Everything will be fine once he's back on his feet."

She didn't look convinced, but she let it go. "I'll take you to Heikkinen. Do you want company?"

"No, I'll be fine."

"Wrong answer," Victoria said. "You had to go through the torture alone. You don't have to be alone for the debrief."

"Victoria."

"Eric," she mimicked, giving him the stink-eye as she spoke. "If you won't take care of yourself, and if your idiot lover won't do it, then I will."

"Lay off," Eric said. "He's doing the best he can. We didn't exactly have contingency plans for Tim nearly dying on us, okay?"

"They're your lovers. You shouldn't need contingency plans. Let's go."

Eric let her drag him across the base to a house not too different than the one he was sharing with Richard. "Boling let Heikkinen set up here. It's private and has enough space for a functional office."

Eric followed her up the sidewalk to the entrance. He wasn't sure letting her stay was a good idea, but he'd never convince her to leave. She was stubborn that way, and he loved her for it. Heikkinen opened the door at Victoria's knock.

"I'm here for my debrief if you have time this morning," he said before Victoria could say anything.

"Come in," Heikkinen said. She looked at Victoria in surprise when she followed Eric inside. "What are you doing here, Amato?"

"Supporting my friend," Victoria said in a tone that brooked no argument.

"She'd hear everything I told you eventually anyway," Eric added when he saw the stubborn look on Heikkinen's face. "I don't keep secrets from her."

"Very well. Do you want something to drink before we get started? Coffee? Tea? Water?"

"Just water. I get jittery if I drink too much caffeine, and I already had a cup of coffee with breakfast," Eric said.

Heikkinen brought a glass of water to the kitchen table and gestured for Eric to sit down. "I'm going to record this so that I can focus on asking questions now and drawing conclusions later without having to call you back because my notes were incomplete. I can't swear I won't call you back if I think of more questions later, but this will decrease the likelihood of having to go over the same thing twice."

It was the same speech she gave at the beginning of every debrief, but he'd done enough with her to know she genuinely meant it and did her best to make them as painless as possible for everyone involved.

ERIC'S VOICE cracked as he tried to answer Heikkinen's question. He took another sip of water, but it didn't help.

"That's enough." Victoria reached over and clicked off the recorder. "You've been at it for four hours. That'll give you enough to analyze for days. If you need more, you can ask him then."

"We aren't finished yet," Heikkinen protested.

"Yes, we are." Victoria's tone sent a chill down Eric's spine. He shook his head, trying to force himself out of the memories and back to the present.

"It's okay, Victoria. I just need a bathroom break and I can keep going."

"I said we're done," Victoria insisted. "You don't have the self-preservation of a pea. We're going to the hospital to check on Tim, and then we're going to have stew. Everything else can wait until tomorrow."

"Peas don't have brains," Eric replied.

"You just proved my point." She stood up and grabbed the back of Eric's chair, forcing him to stand or be dumped on his ass. "If you have more questions, write them down. You can ask him the day after tomorrow."

"This is highly irregular. I'll be speaking to the commander about it."

"Please do," Victoria said.

Eric heard the implied *He'll side with me* in her voice. He only hoped she was right.

He followed her out of the house and into the midday sun. He blinked a few times, wishing he had his sunglasses. His captors had kept him in near or complete darkness for the entire time they'd had him, and the glare made it impossible to see for a moment. His heart beat faster as he squinted, trying to get the world to come back into focus.

"Newton!"

His attention snapped to Victoria, but her face blurred as he blinked rapidly.

"Here." She shoved her sunglasses onto his face. They didn't fit right, but they shielded his eyes. He tried to slow his breathing as his vision settled down, but adrenaline raced through him, leaving his hands shaking and his body fighting to run. He flinched away from her hand on his back. "Eric. Breathe!"

He shook his head. He was hyperventilating, but he couldn't get his lungs under control.

"Put your hand on my back," Victoria ordered. "Feel my breath."

Eric fumbled blindly for her. His hand found something solid, only for her elbow to meet his ribs. "My back, idiot. Not my boobs."

He snorted despite the panic that had yet to recede. "I'm gay, remember?"

"Doesn't mean I want you groping me." She moved his hand to her ribcage. "Now, with me."

He focused on the slow rise and fall of her ribs and measured his breath to hers.

His lungs burned and he gasped in a breath before she'd finished the first exhale, but she simply patted his hand and continued to breathe evenly. He focused again and breathed in as deeply and slowly as he could. That was better. That was what she wanted. He exhaled with her and then inhaled again. Slowly his pulse settled and breathing at her pace became less of a chore. He didn't know how long they stood that way before he felt safe to drop his hand and step away. "Thank you."

"What brought it on?"

He might have wondered that she recognized what was happening as quickly as she had, except they all had things they wanted to forget. "The sun was too bright. I couldn't see, and for a second I was back there instead of here."

"Keep the sunglasses, then. I have an extra pair somewhere."

"I'm not sure they're quite my style."

"Ass."

He turned to peer over his shoulder. "And quite a nice one too."

"Eric, stop," she said gently. "You don't have to hide from me. I know what it feels like to fall apart, and I know what it feels like to have no control over what happens to you. You don't have to pretend with me."

"It's how I keep it together."

"I know, but at what cost?"

He shrugged. He could give her a flippant answer that she'd see right through, but he didn't have anything else. "Do you have a car? Could you take me to the hospital?"

"Yeah, let's go."

She walked with him all the way up to Tim's room but stopped at the door. "I'll be back at four," Victoria reminded him. "Don't make me track you down."

"I'll be right here," Eric promised. "Tim spent enough days and nights sitting by my bed. I won't do less for him."

ERIC SLUMPED back into the chair in relief when the doctor left. Digestive tract yesterday, kidney function today…. Tim's body was coming back online. If his chest X-ray was clear, they'd start weaning him off the ventilator in a day or two. He would still have a lot of recovery ahead, including physical therapy for the damage to his knee done by one of the bullets, but he'd be awake and talking. He'd be okay.

Almost immediately the door swung open again and Westin walked in. "Amato said something about making stew for dinner. You know anything about that?"

"Yeah," Eric said. "It's a tradition with Tim. We'd get back to the safe house after a mission, and he'd make stew out of whatever was in the cabinets." It went back further than that, to the gang he ran with for a while and even to his mother, but he hadn't shared those memories with anyone but Tim. He might share them someday, but not with Westin first.

"Sounds like a good tradition," Westin said. "You gonna join us?"

"Victoria isn't giving me a lot of choice," Eric said, "but yeah, I'll be there. She said she'd pick me up at four."

"Good. She's been worried about you."

"Sorry I haven't been around more, but well, with Tim—"

"No, no," Westin interrupted. "I get needing to be here with Davenport and home with Horn. God, I can't believe I just said that, but you've got to take care of yourself too. We can invite Horn if you want."

"I don't know what he has planned," Eric said. "I haven't seen him since I left the house this morning. He said something last night about trying to figure out if Collins has been playing us. I don't know if he'll be done in time for dinner."

"Well, text him and invite him, at least," Westin said. "I hate to drop in and run, but Heikkinen said something about wanting to go over mission specs with me to make sure we weren't walking into another trap. I don't want to keep her waiting."

Eric summoned a smile and waved Westin away. "You told me what a bastard he could be. You didn't tell me he was a marshmallow."

Tim didn't stir.

"IT'S FOUR o'clock, Eric."

Eric looked up toward the door. Victoria leaned against the frame, dressed casually. "Already?"

"Already. Let's go."

"I should wait for the doctor to come back. She was running some tests, and depending on the results, it could be as early as tomorrow when they wake Tim up."

Victoria shook her head. "You should come with me and let me make you stew. Even if the tests are 100 percent positive, it won't change anything tonight, and you need to let me take care of you. Tim'll be okay here until Horn gets here or until you make it back, whether that's tonight or tomorrow."

He looked back at Tim, unconscious and unmoving. He probably didn't know Eric was there, but even if he did, he'd take Victoria's side. "Okay, let's go."

She took him back to the house he and Richard were sharing. "The team is in the barracks, nowhere to cook, so we'll do it here. That way if Horn ever gets his head out of his ass and comes home, he can join us."

"Ease up, Vic," Eric said. "You're acting like he's done something wrong. He's doing his job, the same as he always does."

"I don't know whether you're stupid or just self-sacrificing," she muttered. "But I'm done. I won't say anything else because you're clearly not listening."

Eric didn't know how to explain that it wasn't stupidity or self-sacrifice. It was just the way their relationship worked. Richard loved Tim enough to let Eric join them. He cared about Eric enough to worry about him, but his passions were his work and Tim, in that order. Eric had known that from the first. He accepted it and he lived with it. "Stew?"

"Yeah," Westin said, coming into the kitchen area. "Is this some special recipe Davenport uses?"

"Something like that," Victoria said as she went to the stove and stirred the huge pot. Eric would have wondered how she got inside, but it wasn't worth asking the question. She probably wouldn't answer him anyway.

Westin followed her, clearly intent on investigating, but she turned on him with the wooden spoon still in her hand, and he thought better of it, deviating to the fridge. "You want a beer, Newton? Or something stronger?"

"A beer would be good," Eric said. He figured he'd better avoid anything stronger. He'd already lost it once today, and hard alcohol made his episodes worse.

Westin grabbed two from the fridge and tossed one in Eric's direction. Eric caught it easily, popped open the cap, and took a healthy swig. It tasted so good going down that he took another gulp.

"Drinking hard, there," Sanders said when Eric finished the second swallow. "Everything okay?"

"You mean besides spending the morning with Heikkinen trying to figure out if I somehow gave the terrorists information that nearly killed my boyfriend?" Eric replied with a hard laugh. "Sure, everything's fucking awesome."

"Oh, are we having a pity party?" Sanders asked. "Hold on, if we're doing that, I need something stronger than beer."

"Fuck off," Eric said with a groan.

"No, no," Sanders said. "This'll be good. Team bonding. We can get drunk and talk about how much our lives suck, because I bet we've all got stories to tell, each one worse than the last. What do you say, Amato? Are you in?"

"Sanders, can it," Victoria ordered.

"Okay, the scary lady is out. Westin, what about you? You spent twenty years in the Army. I bet you've seen some shit."

"I get it," Eric interrupted. "I know I'm not the only one who's had a rough time. I've never thought I was the only one, so don't give me that shit, but at the same time, I *have* had a rough time, and I'm entitled to a little comfort food with the one person willing to give it to me right now, okay?"

"I know why Davenport isn't giving it to you since he's sort of out of it at the moment," Westin said, "but what about Horn? What's his excuse?"

Eric wished he knew the answer to that himself.

"He had to deal with Collins today."

"That's today," Westin said. "What about—?"

"Westin, shut the fuck up," Victoria interrupted. "It's none of your business, and if you undo all my hard work trying to make Newton feel better, you'll regret ever leaving the Army."

Westin backed off, raising his hands placatingly. "Shutting up now. So how long until it's ready?"

"In an hour," Victoria said. "In the meantime, don't you have a report to get to Heikkinen? Unless you turned it in without me noticing?"

Westin blanched and disappeared out the front door.

"Thanks," Eric said. "He's a little overwhelming without a buffer."

"You get used to him," Victoria replied with a shrug. "When you're feeling a little more like yourself, I'm pretty sure you'll like him, actually. He's not a bad guy, underneath all the bluster."

"You crushing on Westin?" Eric teased.

"Don't tempt me, Newton. I can kick your ass on a good day. Right now you look like you couldn't fight a strong wind. I'd wipe the floor with you."

Eric laughed. This was what he needed, to be treated normally, not like something broken or breakable. "God, I love you."

"Love is a weakness," Victoria retorted, but Eric heard the fondness in her voice.

Eric finished his beer and set the bottle aside. He'd have another one with dinner, but he really didn't want to end up so drunk he had another flashback or fell asleep on the couch. Maybe if he could actually stay awake, Richard would get around to making love to him tonight.

When Richard hadn't arrived home an hour later as Victoria started serving up the stew, Eric refused to give up hope. Richard had worked late more than once, only to stumble into bed and fall on Eric and Tim like a starving man.

"Where's Horn?" Victoria asked when she put a bowl in front of Eric.

"I don't know," Eric said. He hadn't texted Richard as Westin had suggested. He hadn't wanted to impose.

"I saw him at Heikkinen's as I was dropping off my report," Westin said. "I asked if he wanted to join us, but he said he'd been dealing with the Pentagon's antics all day and that he was going to the hospital to see Tim. Because he needed a bit of peace and quiet."

"Somehow I don't think he used the word 'antics,'" Eric said, trying to hide the feeling of rejection. He knew what a pain in the ass the Pentagon was for Richard. He'd spent more than one evening listening to him rant about their idiocy and then helping him work out his frustrations, but Tim had always been there too, and it seemed that even unconscious, Tim's company was preferable to Eric's.

"No, it wasn't," Westin said, "but my mama would wash my mouth out with soap if she heard me cuss in front of a lady."

"Your mother isn't here, and I'm hardly likely to be offended," Victoria said, "when I teach the boys new words on a regular basis. Knowing Horn, I imagine it was something along the lines of fucking bullshit."

The look of discomfort on Westin's face almost made Richard's absence worth it. "Excuse me a minute," Eric said to Victoria and Westin before moving to the other side of the room so he could text Richard in private.

We have dinner. You could come join us.

I'm going to sit with Dav for a while.

Eric winced but forced himself not to take it personally. *Do you want me to come back to the hospital?*

Almost immediately his phone buzzed with a reply. *No, enjoy yourself. I can watch over Dav. You need to spend time with your team.*

Eric wanted to tell Richard that was the wrong answer, but he'd left himself open for a rejection by phrasing his offer as a question in the first place. *If you're sure.*

I'm sure. Have a good time.

Eric waited for a moment longer. To his relief, his phone buzzed once more. *Don't fuck it up.*

"Anyone know if we've got any good stuff? I could use a real drink."

CHAPTER 10

ERIC WOKE up the next morning alone in bed with a mouth that tasted like puke and a skull that felt six sizes too small for his brain. He groaned and rolled to one side, grateful his stomach didn't protest too strongly. He stumbled out of bed and into the bathroom, where he filled a glass and took a tentative sip of water. When that stayed down, he drank a little more and stared at himself in the mirror. God, he looked like shit. Red-rimmed, bloodshot eyes with circles so dark they looked like he'd been in a fight, sallow skin, deep lines around his mouth, and that damn scruff he couldn't get rid of until Tim woke up. No wonder Richard didn't want him.

He turned the water on in the tub and drank a little more while he waited for the tap to run hot. He'd shower and see what he could scrounge up for breakfast, and then he'd hope he could find Richard and see what the doctor had said last night.

The hot water scalded his skin, but it also cleared his head. He tried to remember if Richard had even come home last night, but his memories were fuzzy at best. Someone had dumped him into bed, but that didn't mean it was Richard. It could have been Westin or Sanders. Amato would have left his sorry ass on the couch or the floor or wherever he passed out.

What the hell had he been thinking, getting that drunk last night? Even if Richard had come home eventually, Eric wouldn't have gotten the fucking he wanted. He hadn't been in any shape for it, and now he had no one but himself to blame for waking up alone.

He scrubbed his hair roughly and then soaped up his body. His scrawny body that didn't have any of its usual muscle mass or tone. Maybe after he ate—if he could keep anything down—he'd go for a run. Richard had said he could use the gym on base if he wanted to lift weights—he'd never pull a bow this way. Or maybe he could get Victoria to spar with him. He'd get his ass handed to him in no time, as out of shape as he was, but it would let him know what his starting point was so he'd know how far he had to go to get back into his usual shape. He didn't know when Richard would have another mission for the team, but he refused to be a liability when that happened. He had to be able to keep up. Or he had to go before he did any more damage than he'd already done.

The moment the thought crossed his mind, he couldn't get rid of it. He'd made a promise to himself when he aged out of the foster care system that he would never stay where he wasn't wanted. Even before he'd started seeing Tim and Richard, he'd known they wanted him for his shooting, and that had been enough. Now, though, he couldn't go back to that. If Richard was really done with him, he couldn't stay. He couldn't pretend to be satisfied with the professional attention when he knew what it felt like to sleep in their arms, to kiss them and make love with them and love them. No, if Richard was done with him, he had to leave before it destroyed what little sense of self he had left.

Lingering in the shower wouldn't get him any closer to field ready, and stay or go, he had to be ready, so he turned off the water and dried off. Dressed in sweats and a T-shirt, he headed into the kitchen, hoping he would find Richard there. It was only eight, early enough that Richard might still be lingering over breakfast.

Victoria was the only one sitting at the table.

"Have you seen Richard?"

"No. He came in last night after you passed out, but I haven't seen him this morning," she replied.

Eric didn't sigh. "Maybe he's gone to the hospital."

"Maybe. What are you doing this morning?"

"Breakfast, then maybe a run or some weights. Unless you want to spar with me."

"It'll be good practice for you."

That's what Eric was worried about. He opened the fridge to find a container of eggs. That would give him protein for breakfast to ease the hangover. "Do you want eggs?"

"I had breakfast at the mess, but I'll have a cup of coffee if you're making any."

Eric checked the coffeepot, but it was empty and cold. If Richard had made some for himself that morning, it was hours ago.

He started a fresh pot and cracked eggs into a bowl to scramble. The coffeepot hissed and sizzled as water heated up and moved through the pipes, dripping through the beans to fill the air with the scent of heaven. Eric waited for the stove to get hot and cursed the Air Force for buying the cheapest stove available. At home he'd have had the eggs ready in the time it took the burner to heat up here. Finally, though, he had his breakfast ready. He poured a cup of coffee for Victoria and one for himself and dug in, hoping the food would settle his stomach instead of making it worse.

They sat in silence while he ate. He washed the dishes quickly and turned back to Victoria. "I'm ready when you are."

"Let's go."

She led him to the base's gym, which included a mat set aside for hand-to-hand training. He stripped off his shoes and socks and waited for her to do the same. She was no less lethal without them, but he figured it at least gave him a fighting chance.

She took him down in less than two minutes.

Eric looked up at her from his spot flat on his back on the floor and groaned.

"What the fuck, Newton?" she demanded. "I haven't taken you down that easily in years, maybe ever."

"Guess I'm not as recovered as I thought I was," he offered. He wasn't about to tell her he was distracted by his worry over his lovers and their unraveling relationship.

"Obviously not," Victoria agreed, "but you've been hurt before and fought better. What's going on?"

Eric shrugged. "Nothing."

"I'd noticed," Victoria said, her eyes narrowing in a way that had Eric flinching beneath her without her even lifting a finger. "Kind of hard for anything to go on when you pass out before he gets home."

"Kind of hard for anything to go on when Tim's in the hospital and Richard stayed there instead of coming home for dinner," Eric muttered.

He got a smack to the side of the head for his pains.

"Yesterday I was angry at Horn because you were hurting and he wasn't taking care of you. Now I'm wondering if I should be angry at you too."

"How do you figure that?" Eric asked, but he already knew the answer. He should have expected it, really. After everything he'd done, he didn't deserve anything less than their anger and derision.

"Why didn't Horn make you stew, Eric? Why didn't he know what you needed after a rough mission? For that matter, even if he didn't know, why didn't you tell him?"

Eric flinched again, not even needing the smack of her hand to feel the reproof. "It doesn't mean anything if I have to ask for it."

Three people in his life had done things for him without him having to ask: his mother, Victoria, and Tim. With everyone else, attention had been "earned" and had always come at a price: the smack of his father's hand, being given extra chores if he acted out in his foster homes, lies, betrayal, the list went on. Richard tried. Eric knew he did, but Richard's first love would always be Strike Force Omega. Even when Eric was off on solo missions with some other handler, not that it had happened often recently, when he'd talk to Tim about it later, he'd hear about Richard's late nights at headquarters, never about what Richard and Tim did alone without him. Eric had never minded that too much because he had Tim with him and Richard's attention when he was around. It had seemed like a fair enough exchange for what he got in return.

"That's the biggest pile of bullshit you've ever tried to hand me," Victoria said. "Are you trying to push him away?"

"He can't take the risk of being with me," Eric protested. "I can't do that to him. Strike Force Omega is his life. I'd never win if he has to choose between it and me, and I wouldn't want to win. We need him because the options if he leaves are no option at all. Can you imagine Heikkinen in charge?"

At least Victoria seemed to share his opinion of that option, if the pinched expression on her face was anything to go by. "Did he tell you this?"

Eric shook his head. Richard hadn't needed to tell him. Eric had figured it out easily enough on his own. "He told Westin he was dealing with the Pentagon and their bullshit yesterday, and then he didn't want to join us for dinner. He didn't need to tell me."

"Maybe he was just too tired to put up with Sanders's antics on top of the Pentagon's bullshit," Victoria countered. "Sanders is a lot to take on even a good day. Maybe he just wanted to have a quiet night in with his lover."

How Eric wished that were true, but he'd asked Richard to come for dinner, asked and been rebuffed. "He said he was going to stay at the hospital with Tim. He told me to have a good time."

Victoria rolled her eyes, and Eric could all but hear her thought about the stupidity of men. "And that somehow translated to getting drunk off your ass and passing out before he even got home? Eric, I don't pretend to understand love. I never have, but if I can see that you're screwing this up, then you know it's bad."

"Yeah, that's me," Eric said. She wasn't telling him anything he didn't already know. He'd been screwing up from the minute the terrorists had taken him. He just needed her to accept it so he could get the hell out of there before he made it any worse. The team would want to come after him, but Victoria was the only one who would be able to find him if he really didn't want to be found. "A screwup. They're better off without me."

"That's not what I meant," Victoria said, smacking him again. "I didn't know about Horn until a few days ago, but Tim has never considered himself better off without you. He called me in when you were captured. I saw him and how much he was hurting, knowing terrorists had you. I saw Horn's reaction when we came back to the carrier after we rescued you. He didn't act like you were a liability. He stood between you and the world while you were unconscious. He put his reputation on the line when Heikkinen tried to turn it into a pissing match. Yes, I was angry with him yesterday, and maybe I'm still angry at him for letting this drag on, but I'm just as angry at you because you're being obtuse."

"If you're going to insult me, I'm leaving," Eric said, trying to roll out from under her, but Victoria wasn't having any of it. She pinned him more firmly.

"I'm not insulting you. I'm kicking your ass for acting like an idiot and asking for an explanation. Give me one good reason I shouldn't call Horn and have him come pick you up and take you home right now."

Because Eric wouldn't be able to go through with his plan if she did.

"I… I can't, Victoria. I betrayed him. I nearly killed Tim. I still don't know everything I might have given away to the terrorists. They deserve someone they can trust."

Victoria smacked him sharply on the chest. "That's the poorest fucking excuse for self-pity I've ever heard. Get your ass in the shower, and don't even think about leaving the gym. I beat sense back into you once. I'll keep doing it as long as it takes."

Eric collapsed back against the floor and wondered how long it would take him to find a way to sneak past her. He'd wanted to wait until he knew Tim was really going to be okay, but he couldn't wait if Victoria had decided to interfere. He couldn't let Richard and Tim take the fall for his stupidity.

THE CLATTERING of free weights falling startled Eric onto high alert.

Gotta go, gotta run, gotta go, gotta go.

Eric shot upright, panting. He was safe. He was sitting on the floor of the gym at Ramstein. Victoria had left him there when she went to take a shower. It was just someone lifting weights.

Gotta go.

He took a deep breath, trying to steady himself. He didn't need to bolt like a scared rabbit, no matter what the voices in his head said. He had to leave. He'd decided that already. But he had to plan it out and do it carefully. Running like this wouldn't solve anything because he wasn't prepared. He didn't even have his real passport, much less a fake one that would let him disappear.

Gotta run, gotta go, gotta go.

He shook his head, trying to clear the panicked voice from his mind, but it had its claws in him deep.

Gotta run, gotta go, gotta go, gotta run!

Eric looked down at his shaking hands. Even if he was going to run, he couldn't do it like this. He wasn't entirely sure he could stand with his body trembling the way it was. He took another deep breath and focused on the one memory that had centered him for the past four years: his first night with Richard and Tim.

For a moment Tim's voice in his head drowned out the one telling him to run as Tim explained firmly that he and Richard were together, that if Eric wanted to be with Tim, he had to be willing to be with Richard as well. Eric hadn't had a chance to answer because suddenly Richard was there, echoing the offer and kissing Eric like he'd dreamed of it for years.

He loves Tim enough to accept anything Tim wants, even being with you.

No, Richard had wanted to be with him. He'd wanted to kiss him, and Eric had kissed back because how could he not, even as he flailed for his bearings in this suddenly changed world. Then Tim had stepped up behind him, sandwiching Eric between him and Richard, steadying Eric with the simple touch of his hand and his lips at Eric's ear, whispering how he'd imagined the three of them together, and Eric had been lost.

Gotta go. They don't want you. They never wanted you.

He struggled to find the thread of the memory. No matter what they felt now, they *had* wanted him. Nothing could make him doubt that. They'd gone to Richard and Tim's quarters, Eric wasn't sure how even then, and they'd gotten him undressed. He'd made love enough times with them since then to know they'd slipped little touches in for each other, but that night he hadn't seen it. That night, he'd felt like the sole focus of their attention, and it lit him up like nothing ever had before. He'd tried to explore their bodies in return, but they'd been too intent.

Intent on fucking you. Intent on using you. Gotta run. Get out while you can.

He didn't want out. He wanted his lovers. He wanted to be back in that bed, them on their sides, Eric ensconced firmly between them, taking turns fucking him, Tim behind him thrusting a few times, then slipping free to make room for Richard to press into him from the front, then Tim driving inside again, each change in angle sending Eric through the roof, until he swore he couldn't take it anymore. Richard hadn't been able to either. The next time Tim had pulled out to let Richard drive him crazy, Richard hadn't stopped, rutting into him until they'd both come like geysers. Eric had tried to apologize to Tim, but Tim had just chuckled and rolled them all so Eric lay prone on top of Richard. He'd proceeded to fuck Eric down onto Richard's lax body until he'd come as well.

Using you. Gotta go. Gotta run.

No, it hadn't been like that. It hadn't made Eric feel used. Instead it had made him feel like the most desirable man in the world. Richard had kept touching and kissing anywhere he could reach, whispering praise into his ear. Tim wasn't silent either, telling Eric how long he'd imagined having him there, kissing his neck, his shoulders, running his hands over Eric's ass, talking about all the things he'd do, they'd do next time, and Eric had known beyond a shadow of a doubt that whatever this was building between them, it wasn't casual and it wasn't a one-night thing, no matter what they'd implied to get him there.

Gotta go, gotta run, gotta go, gotta go, gotta go*!*

Eric grabbed his head, trying to make the voice stop. This wasn't right. This wasn't him. He didn't act this way. He couldn't—Bile rose in his throat, everything he'd eaten for breakfast clawing its way back up. He curled on his side, trying to keep it together.

"Victoria!"

CHAPTER 11

THE SOUND of her name shouted in such distress brought Victoria out of the locker room at a dead run. Eric lay on the floor, curled in a fetal position, rocking fitfully.

"Eric, what's wrong?" she asked as she checked his pulse. He flinched away from her hands, so he was conscious and aware enough to know someone had touched him.

"What's going on?" Westin asked, appearing at her side. She might have been annoyed not to see him coming, because no one snuck up on her if she could help it, if she hadn't been so glad to see someone she knew well enough to mostly trust.

"Gotta go, gotta go, gotta run. Can't go, have to stay. Can't… can't."

"Find Horn," Victoria ordered. "I don't know what happened, but Eric's falling apart. I don't care what you have to say to the commander. Hell, kidnap him for all I care, but get him here. Now. And if you see Sanders, send him too."

Westin took off toward the locker room. When he reappeared a few seconds later, he had his phone in hand. Victoria turned her attention back to Eric, trying to find a way to help him. She didn't know what the hell Eric and Horn were thinking, but she'd already given Eric a piece of her mind today. Horn was next. As soon as he showed his fucking face.

WESTIN TEXTED Sanders first because he knew his teammate was in the barracks. Horn could be anywhere. As soon as Sanders texted back that he was on his way, Westin pulled up Horn's contact number on his phone.

"This better be important, Westin." Horn's voice sounded as impatient as always.

"You tell me," Westin snarked back. "Your boyfriend is having a meltdown on the floor of the gym. Amato seems to think having you here would help, so you can come voluntarily, or I can make you come. Either way—"

"Don't make threats, Westin. I'm on my way back to base. I'll be there in ten. Don't let Eric leave and don't let him hurt himself."

Westin didn't bother answering. He had some Valium in his bag that his psych had given him for his PTSD. He'd never taken it, refusing to be ruled by his diagnosis, but he'd see what Victoria thought about giving Eric one.

Westin passed Sanders on his way back to the barracks. "I'm getting something that might help. Tell Amato that Horn is on his way."

Sanders snapped an offhanded salute by way of reply.

Westin made it back to the room and dug the pills out of his bag. Back at the gym, he approached the team with far more discretion than he would normally bother displaying. He might refuse to acknowledge all but the most irrefutable signs of his own trauma, but he had enough sensitivity not to want to trigger anyone else's, especially such a recent one.

Sanders and Amato sat on either side of Eric, not quite touching him, but close enough that they could if they needed to. Making sure he was within Eric's line of sight, Westin approached the group and nudged Amato to move directly in front of Eric so he could take her spot on Eric's left.

"Horn's on his way," Westin repeated in case Eric needed the reminder. To his dismay, Eric didn't even seem to hear him.

Westin handed Victoria the prescription bottle. "They're probably expired, but not by a whole lot. I know he won't take one from me, but he might from you."

"Not until Horn gets here," Victoria said. "He needs to see this. I don't know how we got to this point, but he needs to see how bad it is so he realizes something has to change."

"You think this is Horn's fault?" Sanders asked.

Victoria shook her head. "I know this is the terrorists' fault, but I suspect neither Horn nor Eric realized how bad it really was. I didn't, and of all of us, I should have."

"Why is that?" Westin asked.

"It's classified," Victoria answered automatically.

"Aren't we beyond that?" Westin asked. "I mean, seriously. We're practically living together. We will be fighting together. The more we know about each other's triggers, the less likely we are to set somebody off. None of us need that kind of stress in our lives."

Victoria looked at him for a long moment. "I grew up in a cult. Think David Koresh, only about a hundred times worse. We were so brainwashed that we would have believed the sky was made of shit if he'd said it. I have two or three memories that I can identify absolutely as real. Everything else is… questionable. I know what it is to be unmade, to have nothing of my own will or my own self. I've been where Eric is. I thought he was moving past it, but I was obviously wrong."

"How do we help him?" Sanders asked.

Victoria sighed. "We ground him. In the team, in his relationship with Horn and Davenport, in whatever we can to help him remember who he is and what he stands for. I thought fighting his way out helped. Maybe it did help for the time it was going on, but it wasn't enough."

"Eric," Sanders said earnestly. "You know you're not alone, right? There are people here who care about you."

Eric didn't react to Sanders's overture at all, continuing to rock back and forth with his head in his hands. The muttering from before had stopped, but he gave every appearance of not hearing anything outside his own head.

"Give him the Valium," Westin said. "Horn said he'd be here in ten minutes. It's already been at least five. It won't knock him out that fast, and maybe when he wakes up, he'll be a little more himself again."

"I don't know if he'll take it from me," Victoria said, "but I'll try."

She shook a pill out into her hand and offered it to Eric. If he saw her, he gave no indication, continuing the same compulsive rocking. "Eric, sweetheart," she urged. "I need you to take this."

No reaction.

"Eric. Please. You're scaring us. You need to take this so you can calm down and sleep. Richard will be here soon. We'll keep watch until he gets here."

Eric perked up a little at Richard's name, but he didn't take the pill from her hand, and when a quick glance around the room didn't reveal Richard anywhere in sight, he buried his head in his hands again and returned to rocking.

"I think we're going to have to wait for Horn."

RICHARD CURSED up a storm as a taxi cut him off. Landstuhl only had about nine thousand people, and every damn one of them was on the road right now. Fuck them all. Didn't they understand this was an emergency? Richard might not know what the meltdown entailed, but Westin wouldn't have called if it hadn't been serious.

"Stupidass motherfuckers," he shouted as he swerved to avoid an accident with a delivery truck that pulled out into his lane.

"Hold on, Eric," he said, though he knew Eric couldn't hear him. "I'm coming as fast as I can."

He cursed the necessary checks at the entrance to Ramstein and then sped through the base as fast as he could. He pulled up in front of the gym and left the car double-parked. If he got a ticket he'd pay the fucking thing. It was just money.

He burst into the gym at an all-out run. Sanders, Westin, and Amato sat in a loose circle, not touching Eric but surrounding him, protecting him. He took a moment to be grateful they'd kept watch until he could get here, then his focus shifted entirely to Eric.

"How long has this been going on?" Richard asked.

"We called you as soon as we realized it had started," Westin said, "so however long it took for you to get here, plus the few minutes it took Amato to realize something was wrong before I joined her."

"Has he said anything?" Richard asked, approaching the group and staying clearly in Eric's line of sight.

"Not since we first got here," Amato reported. "When I first came up, he was muttering, 'Gotta go, gotta run, can't go,' like he was arguing with himself. Look, Commander, with all due respect, I don't know what is going on between the two of you right now, but you're fucking this up."

"I've got eyes, Amato. I can see that," Richard snapped. "You can yell at me later, after we get him help."

"Here," Westin said, handing Richard a bottle of pills. "They're a little out of date, but they'll knock him out if you can get one or two down his throat."

Richard frowned at the bottle of Valium. That really wasn't the route he wanted to go after Eric had already had all his choices taken away from him once, but he pocketed them just in case. Kneeling down in front of Eric, he touched his lover's cheek.

"Eric?" he said. "What's going on?"

Eric stared at him blankly.

Well, fuck. If that wasn't going to work, he'd have to try it another way.

"Talk to me, Newton," he ordered. He didn't know if it would work for him, but it always worked for Dav.

That elicited a couple of blinks, then Eric's eyes focused, and he gulped a couple of times. Richard couldn't wait any longer. He grabbed Eric's shoulders and pulled him into a tight embrace.

"You're here," Eric said, his voice so broken Richard wanted to hunt the terrorists down and kill any of them Amato and the others had missed himself for putting Eric through this, except he suspected at least part of the blame fell on him as well.

"I'm here, Peaches," Richard whispered into Eric's hair. He could hear the rest of the team backing off, giving them some degree of privacy without actually leaving. "I should have been here sooner."

"I'm fucked-up," Eric said.

"It's okay. We can work with that," Richard assured him. "Whatever it takes, okay? But you have to tell us what's going on. Me or Victoria or Dav once he's better. It doesn't matter who, but you have to tell someone."

"Gotta go," Eric whispered. "I keep hearing that in my head. Gotta go, gotta run. I don't want to go, Richard, but I can't shut it up."

"You had a panic attack," Richard said, although he wasn't sure that was an apt description. "Westin brought you something to help you calm down, but you have to take it or it won't help. Can you do that for me?"

"It'll make me sleep," Eric whined.

"Maybe, but you need to sleep," Richard said. "You're still exhausted. I won't let you out of my sight until you wake up, no matter what happens."

"Even if we get a mission?"

"Especially if we get a mission," Richard said. "If something were to happen, I'm pretty sure I could set up a command post right here, and I'm even more sure your teammates would step up to deal with it."

"Damn straight," Westin said from across the room.

Richard glared at him, but it seemed to give Eric the reassurance he needed because he nodded. "Just one. I don't want to be too out of it."

Richard got a pill out and handed it to Eric. Before he could even ask, Sanders handed him a bottle of water. He nodded his thanks and passed it to Eric.

"Maybe we should go somewhere more comfortable before he actually passes out," Westin suggested. Normally one wouldn't be enough to knock him out, but given how exhausted and weak he still was from the torture, Richard wouldn't be surprised if it did. "Not that we couldn't carry him if necessary, but I think Eric would like it better if he knew where he was going to wake up before he passed out, wouldn't you, Eric?"

"Yeah," Eric said.

"On your feet, then," Richard said. "The car is out front. We'll get you back to the house so you can sleep, and the rest of us will keep watch in the front room."

Richard kept his arm around Eric's waist as he stood unsteadily and helped him toward the door. The other three hovered behind them.

Richard met their gazes and nodded his thanks, but then Eric stumbled against him, and Richard turned his focus back where it belonged. Getting him into the car was a bit of a trick. Getting him out of it when they got to the house was worse, but Eric let Victoria help him too, so they managed to manhandle him inside and into the bedroom. He left the others to their own devices. He'd worry about them later.

Eric all but collapsed onto the bed, exhaustion and the drug clearly taking effect. "Rest," Richard said. He helped Eric undress enough to be comfortable and tucked the comforter around Eric's shoulders. "I'll be here. I won't go any farther than the other room."

Eric nodded. "Love you."

Richard leaned over and kissed Eric softly. "I love you too. Now get some sleep, and then we're going to figure this thing out. I won't let you go."

Eric smiled once more before drifting off.

ONCE RICHARD was sure Eric was asleep, he shifted off the bed and walked back into the other room where the rest of the team waited for him. He pulled the door almost shut, enough to keep their conversation from disturbing Eric, but not so much that he couldn't hear if Eric woke up.

Richard took a seat across from them where he could still see through the crack in the door. "Anybody know what the fuck caused that?"

"I have a few ideas," Westin said, and Richard could already tell he wasn't going to like them, but Amato cut him off.

"I took him to the gym to spar," she said. Her voice wasn't any kinder than Westin's, but at least it was neutral rather than snarky. "When you didn't come home for dinner last night, he got stupid drunk. He woke up alone this morning. I fed him breakfast and convinced him to go to the gym with me. He hasn't been training."

"He was dangerously dehydrated and half-starved," Richard interrupted. "I told him to take it easy for a couple of days."

"When we finished a round this morning, when it became clear he wasn't recovered at all, I asked him about it," Amato continued as if Richard hadn't spoken. "We argued."

"What about?" Richard asked.

"You," Amato said. "He has this idea that you'll pick work over him. I told him he was being an idiot and that I was going to find you and bring you here. I went into the locker room to shower and change so I could find you and drag your sorry ass back to help him, but before I could get changed, I heard him scream my name. I came back out into the gym to see the end of his panic attack."

"That tells me what happened, not why you think it happened," Richard said.

Amato leaned forward, her eyes glittering dangerously. "Do you know what Eric's biggest fear is, Horn?"

"Losing control, or having it taken from him," Richard said immediately. "He nearly had a meltdown when I held his wrists a couple of days ago."

"You really don't know him at all, do you?" Amato said with a sigh. "Okay, here's your first lesson in Eric Newton. No, he doesn't like being restrained, but he can deal with it if you don't catch him off guard, just like he can deal with pain and torture and all the other shit that happens sometimes when you work in the shadows like we do. There's one thing— *one thing*, Horn—that he can't deal with, and that's being abandoned. From where he's sitting right now, you've dropped him like a hot potato. You're lucky he hasn't run already."

"What do you mean, run?" Westin asked.

"Disappear," Sanders said. "Go off the grid. He'd know how. I imagine he has access to everything he'd need to set up a cover identity—false IDs, bank accounts, everything."

"He has everything set up," Amato confirmed. "He did it years ago, before I ever joined up with the team, under the name Frank Porter. He hadn't mentioned it since he and Tim, and you, I guess," she said with a nod toward Richard, "got together, but that's what he was muttering when the panic attack hit. Gotta go, gotta run."

"Fuck," Richard said softly as the full implications of everything she had said sunk in. He'd nearly lost Eric out of sheer stupidity.

"Yes, that would be a good start," Amato said. "Or it would have been, because I'm going to bet you took him home, tucked him into bed, and waited for him to make the first move."

"How did you…?"

"Because if you'd taken him home and made him feel wanted, we wouldn't be having this problem," she said.

It galled him to admit she was right.

"I'm going to need some help," he said, the words tasting like ash in his mouth. "What I'm about to tell you is so classified I shouldn't know about it, but I can't do this on my own, not with Dav laid up too."

He met each of their eyes in turn, wishing more than ever Dav were here to help manage this group of miscreants. Dav did the good-cop shtick so much better than Richard had ever dreamed of doing, but his usual bad-cop routine wouldn't fly with this bunch. Not now. "The Pentagon is out for blood, preferably Eric's, but it would settle for any of ours. Heikkinen sent them the Syria report before I approved it"—and yes it was the one he eventually approved, but she hadn't waited for him before she sent it in—"and I don't trust her for a second not to do the same thing with Eric's debrief. They're unhappy we're here in Ramstein and even more unhappy to get stuck with Dav's medical bills on an op they should never have authorized from what I can tell. If I so much as flinch, Eric and Dav will pay for it, and I can't let that happen."

Amato opened her mouth to interrupt.

"But," Richard went on, waving her to silence, "I obviously can't keep doing what I've been doing because if I do, Eric will run or self-destruct, and I can't let that happen either."

"What do you need from us?" Sanders asked.

"I don't even know," Richard admitted.

"Let me look into the Pentagon issue," Westin offered. "You'd have to give me access to all your communication with them, but I'm probably your best bet at deciphering military double-speak. And if worse comes to worst, I have a few favors I could call in."

Richard nodded. Westin had gone to bat for them, back when Eric had first disappeared, sending them the video from his captors that had been their only lead at the time. "I need a way to access our systems securely. Everything is on our servers in the Caymans, but if I access them through the military's network, they could hack us, and then we'd really be in trouble. Normally I'd ask Heikkinen to take care of it, but I'm not entirely sure I trust her now."

"It'll take me a day or two, but I can make that happen," Amato said. "It's not my best skill, but I learned enough I can do it without the military's knowledge."

"Good. I can't take Eric with me into meetings and still look after him the way he clearly needs. If I can work from here, I can keep up with the things that have to come from me and watch him as well."

"You don't think he's going to wake up and be okay, do you?" Sanders asked.

"No," Richard said. "I hope he is, but I'm working on the assumption that he won't be, because I've already made the mistake of thinking he was okay once. I'm not about to fuck it up a second time. What do you think, Amato? You seem to have a better handle on him right now than I do." He'd be fixing that, now that he realized it, but for the moment, he'd take what he could get.

"Do you know what he asked me when he came to?" Amato said by way of an answer. "He asked me if I knew what it was like to be unmade. You know that I do. So trust me when I say I know as well what it takes to remake yourself after that. I didn't have anyone to rely on when that happened until Eric found me and brought me here. If I could be enough for him, I'd do whatever it took in a heartbeat. I owe him that much and more, but I'm not what he needs, so I'm going to do the next best thing and give him what he needs. I think this is the best solution you'll find, short of taking a leave of absence and dragging him off somewhere private for the next month or so."

"You don't have to do this alone, Commander," Sanders added. "Eric's our teammate. Maybe we can't give him what you would, but we can do our best to help you so you can do what you need to do."

"You just have to tell us what that is," Westin added.

Richard studied their faces, Sanders so earnest, Westin as blasé as ever but with that freakish light in his eyes when he saw a problem he wanted to solve, and Amato... he had never seen her as open as she was in that moment, her eyes pleading with him to give her back her best friend.

"Okay, we have a plan. Let's put it in play."

CHAPTER 12

RICHARD GLANCED at the half-open door for the fifth time in two minutes and gave up pretending he had any interest in anything but Eric, asleep in the dark room. The rest of the team had left. No one had to know if he quit pretending to work when all he wanted was to hold Eric until he woke up and then hold him some more.

Fuck it. Eric's team would be more upset to find him not in the bedroom, and Heikkinen was the only other person likely to come looking. She would knock and look elsewhere if he didn't answer. He didn't have time for her today and even less time for Boling and the Pentagon. The hospital would call rather than knock if something changed with Dav. He didn't have to sit in the living room.

He walked into the bedroom and stripped down to his underwear. Dav teased him sometimes about the white briefs being the only thing Richard had kept from the SEALs, but when Richard had suggested trying some other kind, Dav had overruled that, insisting the white cloth against his skin was too good a contrast to pass up. Since Eric had agreed, the one time it came up in his hearing, Richard hadn't switched. Anything to make his lovers happy.

Hadn't that come back to bite him in the ass. He'd done everything he could think of to make Eric happy over the past few days, only to find out he'd been doing it all wrong. Dav would give him hell for that when he woke up, although Richard intended to fix those mistakes sooner than that. He'd fucked up, waiting until Eric was in the middle of a crisis to figure out what made him tick, but he couldn't change that now. All he could do was move forward. He'd been making the best of FUBAR situations since SEAL training. He could handle this one.

He thought about the package in the trunk of the car, the reason he'd left this morning, planning to get back before lunch and surprise Eric with it. He'd go get it later, when he didn't have to worry about what might happen if Eric woke up alone. If he never saw that blank look on Eric's face again, it would be too soon.

He climbed in bed and settled as best he could around Eric so that when he woke, he would have as much contact as possible to ground him. He slid one arm under Eric's neck. Even in a drugged sleep, Eric rolled toward him and buried his face in the crook of Richard's neck. The scraggly beard itched where Eric's position pushed it against Richard's collarbone. He'd have to ask Eric about that when he woke up. He couldn't ever remember Eric going more than a few hours postmission without getting rid of any scruff that had grown while he was in the field.

Fuck. He'd seen how Eric's hands shook. He probably couldn't shave easily.

"I am a fucking idiot, Peaches," Richard said into the silence. He'd say it again when Eric woke up, and as many times as it took to convince Eric it hadn't been intentional, just ignorance. Not that ignorance was an excuse either, not after four years. He should have insisted on learning all of Eric's rituals the same way he knew Dav's, but he hadn't imagined Dav not being there. He'd gotten so deep in the habit of handling the job so Dav could take care of Eric that he hadn't known what to do when Eric needed *him*.

Eric shifted against him. Richard tilted his head so he could see Eric's face. His eyes were still closed, but his body was starting to shift restlessly beneath the covers. Richard had watched him wake up from sedatives often enough to recognize the signs of him trying to fight off the Valium. He loosened his grip so Eric wouldn't wake up feeling confined but kept their bodies pressed together for comfort. As if Eric had needed just that in order to focus enough to wake up, his eyes opened, the green-brown prisms a welcome sight.

"How are you feeling?"

"Bleary," Eric answered after a moment.

"You want some coffee?"

"Not yet. I'm not sure my stomach can handle it," Eric said. "Is the team still here?"

"No, they're all out taking care of things. Would tea be better?" Richard offered.

"Maybe," Eric said, sitting up slowly.

"Easy," Richard said, sitting up next to him to help support him. "Between the hangover, the panic attack, and the Valium, you need to take it slow."

"I know my own limits," Eric grumbled.

"I know you do, but I nearly lost you because you pushed yourself too hard. I'm not making that mistake again." He pulled Eric against him and kissed the top of his head. "I've made a lot of mistakes I'm not going to repeat."

"Like what?"

Eric sounded curious rather than upset, so Richard took that as a win. "Like giving you a reason to wonder if I wanted you. I know I'm a poor substitute for Dav, but that doesn't mean I care less than he does. I just… don't know the right way to show it."

"There's no right way," Eric said. "Just be with me."

The words eased the last of Richard's concerns about what Eric needed from him. Eric had told him enough about his family and his life before he'd joined Strike Force Omega, not to mention what Richard had read in his file, for Richard to believe Amato's assertion about Eric's fears, but he'd still needed to hear it for himself. "I'm not going anywhere."

"Promise?" Eric asked.

"Promise." Richard sealed the deal with a soft kiss. "I'm sorry if I made you think I was."

Eric shrugged and scratched at his chest absently. "Damn, I need a shower."

"Tea first," Richard said. "You can take a shower when I'm not worried you'll fall over or pass out again from the Valium."

Eric huffed. "You could join me."

"Oh, I'm planning on it," Richard said, the thought of all that wet, slick skin enough to have him wondering if they could skip tea and go straight to the shower, but not talking had gotten them in this situation in the first place. "After tea."

"You're the one who has to smell me."

Richard chuckled. "I've seen you after missions where you were covered in blood and shit. A little sweat isn't going to turn me off, Peaches. Come on. Let's find some tea."

Eric pulled on a T-shirt and sweats, hiding his beautiful chest and legs, but Richard didn't point out that they were alone. If Eric wasn't comfortable walking around in his boxers in the house, Richard wasn't going to push it. He'd enjoy peeling them off Eric later. He followed Eric out into the living area without bothering to dress. He kept the curtains pulled, so he didn't have to worry about anyone but Eric seeing him.

Richard dug through the cabinets until he found some pitiful-looking tea bags. He had to make a trip to the post on base soon. He put the kettle on to boil and sat down across the table from Eric to wait for it to heat up. "Westin has volunteered to do some poking around and see if he can find proof that Collins fucked us over with you, with Dav's op in Syria, with maybe more than that over the past months. Amato is working on getting me a secure connection so I can work from here instead of having to use

Boling's servers, and Sanders said he'd run interference with Heikkinen. That will free me up from all but the most urgent problems. I don't know if being here earlier would have staved off your panic attack, but at least I'll be here if you have another one."

"About that," Eric said.

"Just a minute," Richard said. "Tea's ready."

Richard poured two cups of tea, adding sugar to Eric's just the way he liked it. "Okay," he said as he sat back down, "talk to me."

Eric took a sip and sat silently for a minute before beginning.

"I have a lot of fucked-up voices in my head," he said slowly. "I still hear my dad yelling that I was a mistake, one of the foster fathers saying I'd never amount to anything with my attitude, the gang members saying I was worthless because I wouldn't help them steal. I've learned to ignore them because I have proof they're lies."

Knowing Eric's childhood had been shitty didn't blunt the pain of hearing him talk about it so matter-of-factly, but Richard didn't interrupt. Eric was speaking slowly but deliberately, and Richard was determined to hear him out. He clenched his hands around the mug and waited.

"Then there are the other voices," Eric continued. "The ones that aren't any one person or tied to any one event. They're the real bitches because they're me, my instincts. They tell me to protect my heart, to always be ready to run. They tell me not to trust anyone because no one has ever been worthy of it. They tell me no one will ever love me enough to stay because even my mother left me."

"Eric—"

Eric shook his head, so Richard subsided into silence again, even as the words ripped at his heart. He'd added to that pain this week, even if he hadn't meant to. "I ignore them too, most of the time. You and Tim have given me that, but I couldn't ignore them today." He reached across the table to peel Richard's fingers off the mug and twist them with his own. "This is going to sound stupid after I've just told you that I always struggle with those voices, but what happened today wasn't the same as usual. The voice was the same, the words were the same, but usually, I just ignore them or I think about you and Tim and they go away. They didn't go away this time. The more I tried to ignore them, the louder they got until I couldn't think beyond the need to run."

"Any idea why they were so much worse this time?" Richard asked. "Or how we can keep it from getting this bad again?"

"I don't know. It was completely irrational. I knew it was completely irrational, but I couldn't stop it. Sitting here right now, looking at you, touching you, I can identify other moments of irrationality over the past couple of days. Not that bad, but getting drunk last night would be a good example. With you right here, I *know* that was stupid and that you would have been happy to see me, but last night I was completely convinced you were done with me."

"No," Richard said, tugging on Eric's hand until he stood and came around the table, "never." He pulled Eric onto his lap and kissed him hard. "I thought I was giving you what you needed."

"What did you think I needed?" Eric asked, relaxing into Richard's arms like he wasn't ever going to move.

"You freaked out when I grabbed your wrists. You survived months of torture," Richard said. "I thought you needed to be in control of yourself and us. I thought I needed to let you make the first move so you wouldn't feel like you had no choice but to accept whatever move I made. So when you showed an interest in dinner with the team, sparring with Amato, whatever, I encouraged you to do it. It killed me not to come home and not be able to do more than sleep next to you last night, but if it was what you needed, if you needed them instead of me, I was going to give it to you, no matter what it cost me. I'm so sorry I made you doubt yourself or your place in my life."

Eric kissed him this time, the contact so desperate and hungry that Richard nearly gave in and pushed him back on the table. Eric tongue-fucked his mouth, and Richard let him, sucking on the invading muscle, deep and wet and dirty. Eric moaned and shifted on Richard's lap, his ass rubbing against Richard's awakening cock.

"Fuck," Richard said, breaking the kiss. "Your lips are as dangerous as your aim."

That got a laugh, which wasn't exactly what Richard had been going for, but it was better than the serious, haunted look Eric had been wearing since he'd woken up. "You should laugh more often."

Eric shrugged. "I haven't had a lot of reason to laugh recently."

"We're going to do something about that," Richard said. "We're going to figure out what you really need instead of me assuming I know, and you assuming I don't want you, and we're going to fix this."

"Is that an order, sir?"

"If that's what it takes," Richard replied.

"Kinky bastard," Eric said with a grin. "Abusing your authority for personal gain."

Richard almost quipped back about protecting his assets, but he remembered Amato's offhand comment about Eric thinking he would choose this job if it came to it. "I protect what's mine," he said instead, "and last time I checked, you'd put one of your dog tags on my chain. I'd say that damn well makes you mine."

"Don't let me forget it," Eric pleaded, all cockiness fading as he buried his head in the crook of Richard's neck.

Richard tightened his grip around Eric's waist with one arm, bringing his other hand up to cradle the back of Eric's head.

They sat there for a long time, but Richard wasn't about to break the embrace. If Eric needed to sit there and be held, Richard would sit there as long as it took. Finally Eric lifted his head and met Richard's eyes.

"I don't think I should be alone for a while," he said, his voice as timid as Richard had ever heard it. "Being around people makes it easier to ignore the doubts."

"I'm not going anywhere," Richard promised, "and if something comes up that I absolutely have to deal with in person, we'll get you to the hospital to stay with Dav or get your teammates here or something. Whatever it takes, Eric. We just have to figure out what that is."

Eric reached across the table and retrieved his mug. "I…. This is going to sound so stupid."

"Stop," Richard said. "Nothing that helps you will sound stupid, okay? Dav knows these things without being told, so I always made sure he could be there when you needed him, except no amount of taking on extra work now will make him wake up faster, so you're stuck with me instead. And I don't know what the hell I'm doing."

"Is that why you were never around when I needed you?" Eric asked.

"You needed Dav, so I made sure he could be there," Richard said, surprised to hear the bitterness in his own voice. "Maybe I couldn't do anything to help you directly, but I could give you that much."

Eric was silent for so long that Richard started to worry he'd fucked up again.

"You really thought I didn't want you there?" Eric asked finally.

"I never thought you didn't want me," Richard said. "But you never needed me the way you needed Dav. If it hadn't been for Dav, you never would have looked at me twice."

"Would you have looked at me twice if he hadn't been interested?" Eric replied.

"I don't know," Richard said. "But you stopped being an afterthought for me the moment you took us both on. I'm sorry I didn't find a way to make you understand that. Dav is used to the way I do things, to knowing what I'm doing and why without me having to explain anything. You fit into our lives so seamlessly that it never occurred to me you wouldn't read me the same way."

"Maybe it's time we both stopped talking in code," Eric said. "We've made so many assumptions about each other, and look where it's landed us."

"I'm game if you are," Richard said.

CHAPTER 13

ERIC TOOK one final sip of his tea and pushed the cup aside. "I'm game." He shifted on Richard's lap in a way that would have been provocative if Richard had thought it was intentional. Then he rubbed his cheek against Richard's shoulder, the tufts of his beard rasping pleasantly against Richard's skin.

"What's with the beard? You've never worn one before," he asked as he stroked Eric's cheek.

Eric held his hand out so Richard could see the way it trembled. "I'm fine in the field or on the shooting range. Training takes over, instinct kicks in, and I'm steady as a rock. If I tried to shave myself now, I'd end up slitting my throat by mistake."

Richard had suspected as much. He took the shaking hand in his and lifted it to his mouth. He kissed each knuckle in turn before sucking on Eric's fingers. "If Dav were here, he'd know that. Would he help you shave?"

Eric nodded.

"Do you trust me to do it for you?"

Eric nodded again.

"Then let's go in the bathroom. My razor is in there." He wasn't completely sure coming at Eric's throat with a straight razor was a good idea, but it was all he had and pretty much all Dav used too, especially on missions. If it made Eric uncomfortable, he'd buy a safety razor when he went to get food.

Eric stood immediately and let Richard lead him back into the bedroom. He pulled Eric close for a moment and ran his hands up and down Eric's arms. Later, he'd show Eric the surprise he'd picked up that morning, but for now, he'd focus on what Eric needed. "Take your T-shirt off. No reason to get it wet and covered in shaving cream."

Eric roused enough to flash Richard a flirtatious grin. "You just want to get me naked."

"Eventually," Richard replied because Eric was right. First things first, though, and first thing was to shave Eric and get him into the shower. The smell of sweat might not turn Richard off, but he'd take Eric fresh from the shower any day. He grabbed the hem of Eric's shirt and lifted. Eric raised his arms so Richard could pull the shirt off and toss it away. God,

Eric was gorgeous. Richard could stand there and look at him for hours, all bronze skin pulled tight over solid muscle. Maybe a little less muscle than usual, but that didn't make him less mouthwatering. He pulled Eric back into his arms, relishing the contact of smooth skin against smooth skin, and let his hands wander over Eric's back and belly. If he lingered for a moment to tweak one brown nipple, then the other, who could blame him? Eric gasped and rubbed against Richard's hip, letting him feel his growing erection. Richard snickered. "I'm guessing that means Dav fucks you after he helps you shave."

Eric shook his head. "Sometimes, but that's all for you."

Richard shook his head at the folly of two fortysomething men trying to keep up with someone like Eric, but it didn't stop the thrill at knowing Eric wanted him too. Eric always responded when Richard touched him, but Dav was always there too. Richard couldn't think of a single time he'd made love to Eric without Dav right beside him. Or behind him. Or beneath him. Or....

Not important. He was supposed to be focusing on getting rid of Eric's beard so they could shower and Richard could fuck his brains out. What they'd done or not done in the past didn't matter now.

"Bathroom," he ordered, "or I'm going to end up fucking you against the wall."

"You say that like it's a bad thing." Eric took a step back and dropped his sweats to the floor, leaving him in just his boxers. He reached for those as well, but Richard stopped him.

"It's not, and if that's what you want, I'm sure we can figure it out after we get rid of that thing you call a beard."

Eric's breath hitched, and when Richard looked at him more closely, his pupils were blown and his cock tented the front of his shorts. He grinned and stalked toward Eric, pleased as hell that *he* was the one who'd gotten Eric that worked up. "Bathroom. Now."

Eric backed into the bathroom and sat down on the toilet lid. Richard dug through his shaving kit to find his shaving cream and razor and a towel. "Is this okay?" he asked, showing Eric the razor. "It's all I have."

"I know. I've seen you shave before. Tim uses something similar when he shaves me." Eric leaned against the toilet tank and tipped his chin up so his face and neck were presented to be shaved.

Richard stared at him for a moment. Damn, he'd gotten lucky. Eric should have run for the hills after all Richard's mistakes this week. Instead he sat there with his eyes closed and his neck bared, completely at ease with the thought of Richard putting a straight razor to his throat. He reached for the shaving cream and squirted some into his palm. His hand trembled as he spread it along Eric's jaw. Fuck. At this rate he wouldn't be able to shave Eric either.

Eric didn't even flinch from the shock of the foam against his face.

"Don't move."

"Wasn't planning on it," Eric said, his lips twitching into the barest hint of a smile. Richard braced his hands on either side of Eric's shoulders and bent over him to kiss the expression from his lips, shaving foam be damned. He'd wash it off later.

"Mmm. Keep doing that."

"When you're not covered with shaving cream," Richard said as he wiped it off his mouth. "It doesn't taste good."

Eric chuckled. "I guess I can wait that long."

Richard was stalling, and if he didn't get his ass in gear, Eric would call him on it, which wouldn't help either of them. He wanted Eric to feel safe and loved, not wonder what Richard's hang-up was. He cupped Eric's jaw in his left hand to hold his head steady and set the razor to the edge of the opposite ear. The razor rasped against Eric's skin as Richard drew it down the angular line of his jaw. He wiped it clean on the towel and repeated the process a little higher on his cheek.

Eric leaned a little more heavily into Richard's hand, tension Richard hadn't even realized was still there easing as the razor scraped its way down his cheek.

He was a motherfucking idiot not to have seen it until now. He knew what Eric looked like completely relaxed, but he'd been so caught up in work that he hadn't paid attention enough to see that he wasn't there, wasn't even close.

Now he was. God, what had he done?

Eric's eyes blinked open. "Richard?"

"I'm here, Peaches. Just cleaning the razor."

He wiped the shaving cream off the blade and finished that cheek with three more lingering stripes. He wet a washcloth in warm water and wiped away the remaining foam and whiskers. He had Eric's chin and upper lip, his other cheek, and his throat still to do, but that would have to wait for a moment. He needed another kiss, and not a foamy one this time.

"That's not the razor," Eric observed.

"Smartass." Richard straddled Eric's thighs and kissed him deeply. Eric moaned and tangled their tongues together. As the kiss continued, he reached around and squeezed Richard's ass. Richard broke the kiss and swatted at his hands. "Shaving first."

Eric popped the waistband of Richard's briefs. "Take those off and when you're done shaving me, I can stay right where I am and blow you."

It was a tempting thought, but Richard was supposed to be making Eric feel wanted, not the other way around. Then again, given the way Eric leaned so trustingly into his hands, maybe he'd already achieved that objective.

He pushed back to standing and kicked out of his underwear because Eric had asked. They'd discuss the rest after he finished getting rid of the beard. Eric licked his lips, and Richard seriously reconsidered for a moment. Eric was positively wicked with his tongue.

He shook himself. Later. After he'd taken care of Eric, Eric could take care of him.

He spread shaving cream over Eric's other cheek, noticing as he did how Eric's eyes drooped closed the moment Richard touched him. And when Richard cupped his shaven cheek to support his head, Eric went completely limp. Richard made sure to take as much time and care with the second side. He wanted Eric to feel safe. He wanted Eric to feel loved. They'd said it he didn't know how many times, all three of them in various combinations, but words were easy. If all Eric had needed was words, he wouldn't have fallen apart this morning. He needed to believe all the way to his bones that Richard would be there, no matter what.

When Richard wiped his cheek clean and reached for the shaving cream again, Eric caught his wrist and held it immobile. With a saucy wink that sent heat sizzling along Richard's nerves, he leaned forward and licked the tip of Richard's dick.

"Fuck!"

Eric nudged Richard backward and stood. He gave a sexy little shimmy and slithered out of his boxers. "Should I turn around?" he teased.

"You should sit your ass back down and let me finish what I started," Richard growled.

Eric subsided back to sitting with a playful grin around his lips, leaving Richard blindsided by the change in his demeanor from something as simple as a few swipes of a razor across his skin.

Except it was so much more than that. It was home and safety and security and finding that with someone who wouldn't ever let him down. That's what he'd always worked so hard to allow Dav to give Eric, contenting himself with doing his part in the background. Now, though....

"Dav and I may have to arm wrestle to see who gets to shave you next time."

Eric grinned up at him, sharp and hungry. "I have two cheeks. You can each do one."

"Or he can work late so I can be here with you to pay me back for all the times I covered for him," Richard said. "He owes me. If you don't mind me being the one taking care of you."

Eric snorted. "Do I look like I mind?"

Blown pupils, hard cock, laughing eyes, and that smile that flirted around the corners of his mouth…. No one seeing him would question whether he wanted to be right where he was, but that didn't change the fact that Eric had always gravitated toward Dav first.

"No, but that doesn't mean you'd still want me when you could have Dav."

"Isn't the whole point that I have you both?" Eric asked seriously. "That I don't have to choose?"

Richard couldn't answer. He didn't have the words. Now wasn't the time for words anyway. He cupped Eric's cheek again and smeared shaving cream on his chin and upper lip. Eric held perfectly still as Richard scraped away the whiskers and wiped his face clean.

"Almost done. Just your neck left to do."

"You didn't answer me." Eric didn't move, didn't even open his eyes, as Richard spread shaving cream down his neck and over the bump of his Adam's apple.

"No, you don't have to choose," Richard said as he began work on the last bit of stubble on Eric's skin.

"Good, because I never wanted to."

Richard resisted the urge to ask Eric for clarification or additional reassurance. He needed to focus on Eric right now. Only one of them was allowed to be out of commission at a time, especially since Dav was completely down for the count for a while longer. He finished the last stripe of beard and took a minute to clean the razor and put it away properly. He desperately wanted the lovemaking that would follow when he was done, but he needed a moment to breathe first.

He got everything put away and turned to see Eric watching him intently. He opened his arms in invitation. Faster than he could blink, he had a hundred and eighty pounds of sniper against his chest, holding tight and pressing against him like the slightest distance between them would bring the world to an end. "I've got you," he murmured against Eric's hair. "Not letting go."

Eric dug his fingers into Richard's back, his ragged nails catching on Richard's skin.

"Shower?" Richard asked.

"Not unless you're coming in with me," Eric said, then licked his way into Richard's mouth in a way that should have been obscene, except it felt too damn good to be anything of the sort. Richard broke away to turn the water on full to heat up. As soon as it was warm enough, he switched it to spray and pulled Eric into the tub with him.

Almost immediately, Eric pushed Richard against the cool tiles. Richard let him have control for the moment, enjoying the proof that Eric wanted to be there with him. The water pounded down on them, hot and plentiful, as Eric ran his hands over every inch of Richard's body he could touch. Richard returned the favor, learning Eric's body all over again, both the things that were the same—the sensitive hollow at the base of his spine above the swell of his ass—and the things that had changed—the crisscross of scars on his back from the torture. He couldn't dwell on that. Eric had survived long enough to be rescued. The scars might not get any better than they were now, but they were proof of how strong Eric was, and Richard wouldn't let him forget it.

"Damn it," Eric said, drawing Richard's attention. "No condoms."

Richard flipped them around so Eric was pinned chest to the wall. "I don't need condoms to make you scream."

Eric's head fell forward against the tiles as Richard reached around to circle his cock with one hand, providing a channel for Eric to thrust into. Eric reached back to return the favor, but Richard batted his hand away.

"Later," Richard said. He kept his grip steady as he pushed up against Eric's ass, his cock slotting into Eric's crease and bumping his balls. Eric groaned, making Richard toy with the idea of showering quickly and getting out so they could find condoms and lube, but he wasn't sure he'd have the patience for the kind of preparation Eric would need after so long. Instead he pressed against Eric even more tightly. "Keep your legs together."

Eric looked over his shoulder in confusion, but Richard kept his feet braced on either side of Eric's, caging him in, and thrust into the space between his thighs, right against his balls.

Eric shifted to brace himself better on the wall and started rocking back to meet Richard's thrusts. Need hit him like a tidal wave, and his knees nearly buckled. They were together, making love, and it felt right.

Wanting to make Eric feel as good as he felt, Richard worked his hand in time with his hips until they were moving perfectly in sync with each other. Richard's eyes rolled back in his head as his hand tightened on Eric's cock, and he came with a harsh grunt.

"God, that's almost as good as your tight ass," Richard groaned. "You are so fucking perfect."

Eric shook his head in automatic denial, but Richard was having none of it. He sped up his strokes on Eric's cock. "Don't give me that shit," he growled. "I get to decide what's perfect for me, not you. I've found it twice in my life. Once in the SEALs and once when you joined Dav and me four years ago. You are what I want, issues and all, Eric Newton, and don't you forget it!"

Richard bit sharply at the juncture of Eric's shoulder and neck—just above the collar of his uniform. Fuck it. Let everyone see—and that was enough to set Eric off. He shuddered through the throes of his orgasm, Richard stroking every drop from him until he rested limply against the wall.

Richard continued to nibble on his neck, holding them both steady as they came down from the endorphin rush. Eventually Eric turned in his arms and pulled Richard against his chest. He tilted his head up for a kiss, which Richard gave willingly, finally feeling like he had done *something* right where Eric was concerned.

CHAPTER 14

ERIC LEANED limply against the wall as Richard washed them both. Getting rid of the beard—and all it represented—had steadied him, and the sex had hollowed him out in the best possible way. For the first time since Victoria pulled him out of hell, he actually felt like he could relax all the way to the core. He was with Richard, and he was safe.

And if he was lucky, he'd convince Richard to take him to bed, and then maybe they'd both get lucky again.

Eric roused enough when Richard turned the soapy cloth on himself to pull it out of his hands and return the favor.

Richard was all hard muscle covered in smooth, mahogany skin, and Eric couldn't get enough of touching it. His captors had excelled at sensory deprivation, leaving him starved for anything that wasn't pain. To be able to touch now, to feel Richard's skin like satin beneath his fingertips, lit a spark in the frozen tundra of his broken soul. He leaned closer to its warmth, fanning it until it was a blaze within him. He was home. He was safe. Richard had taken care of him and wanted him still, even as utterly destroyed as he was.

A sob welled in his chest, but he pushed it down ruthlessly. He could let go of the fear and the pain and the doubt, of all the horrors of his captivity and the sinking knowledge that he'd never be found. They *had* found him. Richard and Tim had moved heaven and earth to figure out where he was being held and to get him out. They had come for him, and no power on earth would keep them from always coming for him.

In the darkness of that cell, as the weeks dragged on into months, he had worried that only Tim cared, and that alone, he might not be enough to find Eric, but together, nothing short of death could stop them, and he wasn't entirely sure they wouldn't chew death up and spit it out too, just for the hell of it.

"Eric?"

Richard's voice, deep and warm like molasses—a comparison Richard would probably laugh at since his father's military career had taken them all over the world except the Deep South—brought Eric back to the present and the hot, hard body still pressed against his.

Maybe he wasn't quite as grounded in reality as he'd thought.

"I'm here. Everything's just a little fuzzy around the edges still. I think it's the Valium."

"We can go back to bed if you want to sleep some more," Richard offered.

"Or we can go back to bed and do other things," Eric replied with a jaunty smile.

Richard laughed. "One round wasn't enough for you, Peaches?"

"Is it ever?"

"Give an old man a break. Usually there are two of us to keep up with you," Richard teased.

"You're not old." He gave Richard a once-over from head to toe. No one would mistake him for a young man. His face showed the wear and worry of too many battles, but the breadth of his shoulders and the tree trunks he called thighs didn't belong to an "old man," no matter what Richard might say.

Richard laughed and kissed him, a light, playful buss that still sparked along Eric's nerves. He could say it was because he was touch starved, but it went beyond that. He stepped back into Richard's arms, plastering their bodies together.

Richard reached behind himself and turned off the water. "Bed. Now."

Eric shivered at the thought. Richard wrapped him in a towel and rubbed, and his skin tingled with lightning, every hair standing on end as he arched into the contact.

"Damn, you're so responsive," Richard muttered. Eric moaned and leaned harder into Richard's hands.

When they were both as dry as they were likely to get, Richard propelled Eric out of the bathroom and onto the bed. Eric fell back against the sheets and pulled Richard down on top of him. He gasped and arched into the pressure, his thoughts spinning out of control.

"Hey, look at me," Richard said.

Eric tried to make his eyes focus on Richard's face, but it swam in and out of his vision fuzzily.

Richard shook his head and slithered down so he was more next to Eric than on top of him. Eric moaned as skin rubbed against skin. He reached for Richard, but Richard caught his hands. He should have been scared, but this was Richard. Richard wouldn't hurt him.

"No, I won't hurt you, but if you're babbling like this after just one Valium, you've either still got alcohol in your system or you're less recovered than we thought," Richard said. He turned Eric onto his side and spooned up behind him. "We're going to stay here and sleep it off. I will be here when you wake up, and then we'll see how you feel and what we want to do next."

"Promise?" Eric's voice sounded distant in his own ears.

Richard kissed his neck right where he'd bitten before. "Yes, I promise. Rest, Peaches. I'm on watch."

The last knot of tension in Eric's belly dissolved. If Richard was on watch, he could let go completely.

WARMTH PENETRATED Eric's foggy brain. He stayed where he was, not moving at all, as he waited for his situational awareness to return. He took a slow breath, not wanting to let anyone watching realize he was awake yet. The longer they thought he was unaware, the better.

The spicy scent of Richard's skin filled his nostrils, chasing away the building tension.

He was in bed with Richard. He was safe.

He'd had a panic attack. Richard had stayed with him. Had the shower been a dream? No, they were naked. He could feel Richard's skin against his all the way down his back. He rubbed his cheek against the sheet. Yes, Richard had shaved him, showered with him, and made love to him. He remembered now.

"Back with me?"

"Getting there," Eric replied. "Everything's a little fuzzy, but I think it's all there."

"What do you remember?"

"Talking, you shaving me, taking a shower, you getting me off. I don't actually remember coming to bed, though."

"We stumbled in here and fell asleep. Nothing worth remembering." Richard pressed a kiss to Eric's neck, triggering the memory of a bite where it would show. Warmth flooded through him at the thought that Richard wanted him and didn't care who knew it. He rubbed against Richard, feeling the beginning of an erection against his ass. Time for round two.

Richard rocked forward to meet him, slotting his cock perfectly between Eric's asscheeks. Everything about them fit right now, and it drove Eric wild.

"Fuck," he groaned. "Tell me you have supplies somewhere close. I'm not going to make it much longer without you fucking me."

"You're in luck," Richard drawled in his ear, inflaming Eric even more. "But we already did hard and fast in the shower. Now that the edge is off, we're going to take our time and enjoy it."

"I always enjoy it," Eric protested.

"We're still going to take our time."

Eric groaned and buried his face in the pillow. The round in the shower might have taken the edge off his panic, but it hadn't come close to sating his need to be held tight and fucked into the mattress. He knew that tone of voice, though. Richard was an easygoing lover most of the time, willing to go along with whatever Tim or Eric suggested, but every once in a while, the commander in him came out and nothing would do but that his lovers fall in line and let him run the op. It usually strained Eric's patience and control, but it always blew his mind, and right now, as good as a quick fuck would feel, losing his mind would feel even better.

Richard nipped at the side of Eric's neck, his mustache and goatee adding a hint of softness to offset the teeth. Eric tipped his head, silently asking for more attention. He'd take another hickey if Richard was in the mood or more of the sweet tenderness if that was what he was offering. Whichever he chose, the attention was a balm to Eric's spirit.

His senses floated, leaving him awash with the soft touches Richard spread over his upper body, his arms, his chest, a quick tweak to his nipple followed by long smooth strokes over his stomach. Before he reached Eric's cock, he rolled him onto his back, a manic light in his eyes that made Eric tense in anticipation.

"What are you planning?"

"Nothing much. Just kissing every inch of you," Richard said.

"Every inch?"

Richard grinned, the expression in his eyes making Eric's stomach roll in anticipation. "Every last fucking inch."

Richard started with Eric's forehead, brushing his lips over the creases and worry lines that never completely faded these days. Eric would fret about it, but it never seemed to bother his lovers, so he didn't let it bother him either. He didn't need to be eye candy for anyone but them.

"Dav always says he can tell how a mission went or how badly you're hurt by the number and depth of the lines in your forehead," Richard said. He traced the creases on Eric's forehead. "It's been a really shitty few months, hasn't it?"

"That bad?" Eric tried to joke.

"Not for much longer," Richard promised before kissing Eric's lips again. "I'm taking care of you now."

Richard was certainly doing that. Eric relaxed into the contact, relishing the fact that he was here with Richard after all the doubts and mistakes. He hadn't fucked it up, even if that had more to do with his team kicking ass and Richard loving him enough to forgive him. He pushed at Richard's elbows, trying to get Richard to rest his full weight against his body. He wanted to feel the drag of Richard's chest against his, the pressure of his hips, the full contact of body to body.

"Little hard to kiss you all over if I can't move," Richard teased.

Eric shrugged. "Then kiss me where you can and do other things instead. I don't care what you do, just that you're here with me."

"I'm here," Richard said, "and even when I'm not, it's because I have to be somewhere else, not because I want to get away from you."

"Keep reminding me of that," Eric said. "I, um, I tend to forget."

"I realize that now," Richard said. He tilted Eric's head forward so he could kiss his eyelids, his beard catching on Eric's eyelashes. "You see so well at a distance. It makes you an asset in the field, not just for your aim, but for all the details you see that other people miss. Just don't forget to look at what's right in front of you too."

Eric squirmed at the compliment. Richard and Tim always said, "Good job," after an op, occasionally even citing particular elements that had gone well thanks to Eric, but this kind of praise was different, and it made him uncomfortable. "It's nothing special," he said.

"Yes, it is," Richard said. "Now stop arguing."

"Less talk, more sex," Eric suggested.

"Are the compliments making you uncomfortable?" Richard asked seriously. "I'm not trying to do that. I'm trying to convince you I see you and pay attention to the details, not just the big picture."

Eric didn't know how to reply to that, so he avoided the topic entirely by sliding his hand down Richard's back and over his ass. Richard reacted predictably, grinding down against Eric's groin. "Much better."

"Fine," Richard huffed, "but don't think I've forgotten. I'll just list one or two things every time we make love until I get to everything I love about you."

"That shouldn't take long," Eric joked.

"Only the rest of our lives," Richard retorted. "Because with every day that passes, I discover something new."

"Sorry, it was a bad joke."

"Yes, it was," Richard said, "but we're not going to worry about it now. You wanted sex. I'm going to give it to you."

It wasn't the sex, Eric wanted to say. It was the attention. It was all that goddamn fucking focus that Richard gave to their ops turned on him and nothing else. Then again, he was only human. He wasn't about to turn down sex!

Richard arched and rolled to the side to retrieve lube and condoms from where he'd stashed them. Eric paused for a moment just to look. He'd seen Richard naked before, of course, but the sight never failed to make his breath catch. Richard Horn fully dressed was a badass motherfucker. Ask anybody who'd ever gone up against him. Richard Horn undressed was Eric Newton's wet dream (well, one of them anyway) in the flesh. He reached for Richard, desperate to touch, only to have his hand captured in one of Richard's larger ones and lifted to his lips. Richard traced the length of his fingers before sucking each one into his mouth, his beard tickling the juncture of Eric's fingers. Eric swore he could feel it all the way to his cock, but even more than the contact, it was the look on Richard's face, like he wanted to be exactly where he was and couldn't imagine being anywhere else or doing anything other than precisely what he was doing right now. He lingered over the much-reduced calluses on Eric's hands from his bowstring, and Eric could almost hear the words he didn't say about what Eric's hands represented.

Finished with that hand, Richard reached for the other one and repeated the process.

"You're gonna kill me," Eric groaned.

"No, just make love to you until you collapse and then hold you until you wake up," Richard said. He moved up Eric's arm to the sensitive skin at the bend of his elbow. Eric shivered as a gasp escaped him when Richard's facial hair tickled and aroused his flesh.

"You like that," Richard said with a grin. "You're usually in too much of rush for us to take advantage of it, though."

"Yeah, I like it," Eric said, the words breaking on a moan as Richard traced the creases in his skin with his tongue, "but if it's that or fucking, I tend to go with fucking."

"It's never either or," Richard said. "We won't get bored with you if you don't immediately put out."

"It's not that," Eric said, and for once it wasn't his stupid insecurities getting in the way. "I just want you so much that I don't want to wait."

"You have me," Richard promised, "and we'll get Dav back soon."

"I still don't want to wait."

Richard grinned. "I'll make it worth your while." He trailed his lips up Eric's bicep to his shoulder and collarbone. Eric rolled to his back, giving Richard full access to his body. Richard took full advantage, lifting over him and bracing himself on one arm while stroking Eric's chest with the other. He found one nipple with his mouth, the other with his hand, winning another moan from Eric. "Don't hold back, Peaches. Let me know what feels good."

"Not holding back," Eric gasped when Richard nipped at his skin lightly. "Fuck! I'm gonna come before you ever get around to fucking me."

Richard coasted his hand over Eric's cock so lightly Eric swore he felt more the movement of air at its passage than Richard's hand itself. It shot lightning through him. "Damn it, Richard!"

"You want me to stop?" Richard teased.

Eric grabbed Richard's hand and pressed it to his erection. "I want you to touch me."

Richard slid his hand up and down Eric's shaft a couple of times before releasing it and reaching between his legs to play with his balls. As he did, he kissed his way down Eric's chest, taking his time but with a clear goal in mind.

When Richard reached the tip of Eric's cock where it bumped against his belly, he stopped and looked up. He burrowed his fingers deeper into Eric's crease, bumping his hole. "I did promise to kiss every inch of you."

Eric shook his head. "Later. Just… suck me, please?"

Richard complied immediately, drawing the head of Eric's cock into his mouth, and Eric was lost. Everything after that was heat and wet and rough hair and suction and abso-fucking-lutely perfect. He undulated on the bed, reaching for the pinnacle, but it remained elusive until Richard sucked a finger into his mouth next to Eric's dick and then pressed the moist digit to Eric's entrance again.

That set him off, his body spasming as his release went on and on for what seemed like forever, all the tension and fear and worry of the past months spooling out of him until he was hollowed out. Richard lifted his head, wiping the corner of his mouth on the sheet before leaning up to kiss Eric, and the hollow was filled, love and security and everything he never managed to believe he deserved rushing in to wrap around his heart.

He felt tears prickle under his eyelids. He blinked them back, so trained to show no emotion that he didn't think twice about containing them, but Richard saw it anyway, kissing him again, more deeply this time. "Believe me now?"

"Yeah," Eric said, "but you can convince me again anytime you want."

"I'm looking forward to it already."

Eric couldn't resist. He grabbed Richard's head and pulled him into another kiss, a deep one this time, chasing his own taste on Richard's tongue even as he ignored the whisker burn beginning to make itself felt against his newly shaved skin. Richard's cock prodded at his hip, so he slid his hand around it, jacking Richard lazily. He'd return the favor in a minute, when he could break away from the sheer delight of Richard's mouth. Richard certainly wasn't protesting, if the way he thrust into Eric's hand and kissed him even harder was any indication.

Eventually the need to return the care Richard had bestowed on him pushed Eric to break the kiss. "What can I do for you?"

"You don't have to do anything."

"I know that, but you're a sexy bastard, and you just made me feel incredible. I want to make you feel just as good. What do you want?"

"Anything you do will feel good."

Eric pushed up on one elbow and shoved Richard's shoulder. "That wasn't what I asked. What. Do. You. Want?" He punctuated each word with a poke to Richard's sternum.

Richard's brown eyes dilated fully, his gaze so intense Eric thought he might get hard again just from the way Richard was watching him. "Your tongue in my ass."

Unadulterated lust shot through Eric again. "Then turn over so I can reach you."

Richard rolled onto his hands and knees, giving Eric a target for his attention. He bent immediately, hands on Richard's ass to part the cheeks so he could reach his goal. Richard smelled so good—he always did, but it was different now, with desire high between them, the smell of musk thick in the air as Eric licked his way around the puckered entrance. He sucked and tongued the sensitive skin, loving the sounds that poured from Richard's throat—gasps and moans and curses interspersed with Eric's name in a heady litany that had Eric half-hard again just hearing it.

He kept at it, licking and thrusting and doing everything he could to drive Richard to the brink. When he felt the telltale signs of Richard's imminent release, he pulled back.

"Why the fuck are you stopping?" Richard demanded.

Eric shoved Richard's hips, toppling him onto his back and straddling him. He grabbed the lube and a condom from where Richard had dropped them and rolled the latex over Richard's cock. A squirt of lube and a quick caress coated the condom. He reared up and impaled himself without further preparation. It burned, but he wanted that, wanted the proof that he was here with Richard, alive and safe and loved.

He rode Richard hard, unmindful of his own pleasure. He just wanted to feel Richard come undone beneath him and know that his hands, his mouth, his ass had done that. As wound up as he'd gotten Richard with the rimming, it didn't take but a few thrusts for him to feel the rush of heat inside him. Eric kept rocking through the aftershocks until Richard reached up and stopped his movements. He collapsed forward onto Richard's broad chest and simply breathed deep, letting the scents of home and sex wrap him in a cocoon of safety.

CHAPTER 15

RICHARD HELD Eric tightly, determined not to let go until Eric was ready for him to, but eventually he'd have to deal with the condom. Not yet, though. Right now he had more important things to focus on, like kissing the top of Eric's head and making sure he was comfortable. Eric didn't show any signs of moving anytime soon, so Richard resigned himself to being sticky. He shifted Eric's weight—still less than it should have been—to rest more comfortably on his chest and simply breathed.

Peace.

He hadn't known a lot of it in his life, with all the moving around they'd done as the Navy shipped his father from one base to another. He'd seen more of the world by the time he was eighteen than most people saw in their entire lives, and that was before he'd joined up and shipped out himself. He'd seen action in both wars in Iraq as well as in the intervening war on terrorism. When he'd left the Navy, he'd continued to work with military operations. No, he'd never lived a peaceful life. He fucked as hard as he fought, and his connection with Dav had been the only thing that kept him sane through much of his adult life. There had been moments of beauty amid the horrors they had seen—their commitment ceremony on a beach in Tahiti with the sea they both loved as their only witness; the first time they'd watched Eric fire his bow; the baptism of Dav's niece with his family including Richard into the fold as if they couldn't imagine him not being there—as well as smaller moments of quiet contentment, but they were few and far between.

Even with Dav still unconscious in the hospital, Richard knew this moment would be forever added to that list of precious memories. Eric had slotted into their lives easily, but Richard had always been so sure Eric was really just there for Dav. He hadn't felt that way today, even with his own blundering through a routine Dav would have known. Eric hadn't looked at him like a substitute. Eric had looked at him like a knight in shining armor come to save him.

Eric shifted against his chest and lifted his head. "If I sleep any more now, I won't sleep tonight."

"Then get your scrawny ass out of bed." Richard gave Eric's butt an appreciative squeeze to soften his words. "You need to eat anyway."

"You were all over my scrawny ass an hour ago," Eric retorted.

"And I'll be all over it again every chance I get," Richard replied. "But you still need to eat. And I have something for you."

"Presents?" Eric asked, sitting up with an eager look on his face.

Richard swatted his hip. "Yes, but only after you let me clean up and we eat something."

Eric leaned into Richard's hand, reminding Richard again how much care Eric still needed. He knew how to give it to him now, though. No more making things worse out of ignorance. "Do you want another shower?"

"Will you fuck me against the wall again?"

Richard snorted. "As much as I love you, Peaches, I don't know if I can get it up again that fast. But if anyone can make me, it'll be you. Or we can take a quick shower, eat, get your present, and go check on Dav. And then tonight, I'll fuck you as long and as hard as you want."

Eric's eyes glazed over at his words. Richard licked his lips in anticipation.

"I'll lay you out and spend an hour just playing with your ass. Rub over your hole until you're begging me to stick my fingers in you. I could spend another hour stretching you out until you're sloppy loose for me. You'd be so desperate you'd take anything I gave you. I could stick my whole hand inside you and you'd still want more."

Eric's whole body went pliant as Richard spoke, like he was already anticipating Richard's touch. Fuck, he wanted Eric again. It was too soon for him to get hard again, but if he spent as much time prepping Eric as he'd just promised, he'd be ready. And if he wasn't—yeah, right, but if—he'd suck Eric off again. Eric never complained about a mouth on his dick. Hell, he never complained about a hand on his dick, but Richard wanted more than that too. He wanted to bury himself in Eric's body, just crawl inside and never come out.

"Food can wait." The rasp in Eric's voice nearly undid all of Richard's good intentions, but while the lines on Eric's forehead had eased with sleep and sex, the gauntness remained.

"I'm not going anywhere. We have time to eat before we come back and make love again."

Eric's stomach rumbled in agreement.

"Fine," Eric grumbled, "but just for that, I'm fucking you when we get back."

If that was what Eric wanted, Richard would go on all fours with his ass in the air in a heartbeat.

For now, though, Eric needed food, and that meant getting showered and going to the mess because Richard didn't think they had anything left in the house to eat.

"Are you joining me in the shower?" Richard asked as he toppled Eric off him onto the mattress.

"I don't need a shower to go heat up leftover stew from last night. Victoria made enough to feed twenty people, and there were only four of us eating," Eric said. "I can just pull on a pair of shorts."

Richard had forgotten about the stew. One more thing to be grateful to Amato for. "Heat up enough for both of us. I'll rinse off and join you in a few minutes. I need more than just underwear if I'm going to get your present out of the car."

Eric nodded and rolled out of bed. Richard followed his progress across the room. He'd felt the healing scars on Eric's back earlier. The scabs didn't appear to continue lower than his waist, but he had bruises on his ass and legs, deep black and blue slashes visible even against his tawny skin. They looked like cane marks, the legacy of a torture session Richard hadn't been fast enough to avert. He could hear his grandfather's admonishing voice still. *"We counted our victories by the bombers that came home. They all came home."* He'd brought Eric home, with Dav's help and the help of Eric's team, but it had taken far too long, and Eric had paid the price.

As if sensing his gaze, Eric turned back around. "Shit happens. You learned that a long time ago. You can't take responsibility for what other people did, or you'll go crazy with it."

"They beat you," Richard said helplessly.

"They did. And they burned me and cut me and stuck files under my fingernails and turned me into a human pin cushion and a hundred other things, each worse than the last. There were days I tried to provoke them in the hopes they'd kill me because it would be better than living another day with their sadism. There were days I cried with the pain and wondered if I'd ever be free again. I know you did everything you could to get me back because I'm standing here, free again. I also know you'd have taken every single moment of that torture to spare me if you could have. And *that* is what got me through the worst of it. I curled up in a ball because it gets fucking cold in the desert at night and dreamed that you and Dav were there with me, holding me tight and taking all the pain away. Call it hallucinations. Call it proof my brain is completely fucked. But I could feel your hands on me, comforting me, and it kept me together long enough for you to get there and pull me out."

"Then God bless your fucked-up brain." He climbed out of bed and crossed to where Eric was standing. "I hate every fucking thing they did to you. I hate that you suffered even a minute, but I'm glad that you're safe and that thinking of Dav and me kept you sane." He bent to kiss Eric, groaning when the movement brought their bodies into contact again. How the hell was Eric hard again already? Maybe he really would feed him and then bring him back to bed for a few more hours to play. He had to do *something* to wear him out.

He almost swatted Eric out of habit to send him out to the kitchen to heat up stew for himself, but the memory of the bruises held him back. He gave him a gentle nudge instead. "I'll be out in a minute."

Eric caught his hand. "Don't treat me differently because of what they did. If you do, then they win."

"I'm not treating you differently because they beat you. I'm choosing not to inflict pain on you by giving you a love tap on an already bruised ass. It's not the same thing."

"It is to me," Eric said. He pulled out of Richard's arms, grabbed a pair of boxers, and disappeared into the other room.

"Well, fuck." Richard almost went after him, but he needed to pull himself together first. He went into the bathroom and rinsed off quickly while trying to figure out how to explain his reticence in a way Eric would accept. He wasn't any closer to a solution when he pulled on a pair of loose jeans and walked into the kitchen. "The stew smells good."

"I heated up two bowls. Yours is on the counter."

Richard got his bowl and joined Eric at the table. He took a couple of bites and then set down his spoon. "You said they were sadists. They got off on hurting you."

"Yeah. Sometimes literally. One of them in particular liked to jerk off when he was done and spray all over me. Then he'd toss a bucket of cold water in my face to hide the evidence."

Richard shuddered at the image. "I'm not a sadist. I don't mind getting a little rough in bed. I've even played at spanking once or twice—beyond a simple swat or two, I mean—but that was a long time ago with a partner who needed that kind of thing to get off himself. But it doesn't do anything for me personally. So when I see bruises on you—doesn't matter where they come from—I'm going to be careful with that spot until it heals because I don't like hurting you. I do the same thing to Dav if he's got cuts or bruises.

I'm not treating you different because you were tortured. I'm being careful right now because you have bruises and I don't want to hurt you. When they're healed, it'll be different. I'll go right back to swatting you like I always have."

"I get what you're saying," Eric said slowly, "and if I'd, I don't know, sparred with Victoria and took a bad fall and had bruises or something like that, we wouldn't even be having this conversation. But this is different. Even if it hurts, I need to feel like I'm not broken. They took four fucking months of my life. I need to know they didn't take anything else."

Richard understood what Eric was saying, but not how to act on it. "They didn't. Not where I'm concerned. I will do everything I can to prove that to you, but you may have to tell me how. Or at least tell me when I'm doing something that makes you feel that way. I don't have all the little routines with you that Dav does to be able to say, 'Look, I'm doing the same things I always do,' so I'm going to need you to talk to me. I can tell you all day long that I don't see you any differently, but it doesn't matter what I say if you feel different."

"Thanks," Eric said. "I'll tell you if it happens again." He ate the rest of his stew and pushed his bowl aside. "You said something about presents."

"Present. Just one," Richard replied. "Let me finish eating and I'll go get it."

Eric fidgeted on his chair as Richard finished up the last of his stew. "I'll be right back."

He went out to the car and opened the trunk to pull out the carefully wrapped package he'd picked up early that morning. The antiques dealer hadn't known what to do with the odd piece of wood in his back storage room, but Richard had recognized it for what it was immediately. He carried it back inside and handed it to Eric.

Eric unwrapped it with no care for the paper and froze when he saw what was inside. "Is this…?" He ran his hands lovingly along the curve of the wood. "This is yew. This is a real longbow, not a modern re-creation."

"The man I bought it from said he acquired it in an estate sale near Verdun. The family didn't know where it came from. He wasn't an expert on medieval weaponry, so he didn't even have a guess about when it was made."

"Neither do I yet, but it's amazing. It'll need some restoration before I can shoot with it, but I can do that too," Eric said, awe clear in his voice.

"I take it you like it?" Richard teased.

"I love it." He lifted the bow as if it were strung and ready to have an arrow set to the string. Then he set it aside and looked down at his arms.

"The bow isn't the only thing that'll need some restoring before I can shoot it. I'd never manage the draw on it right now."

"You know where the gym is. You were there this morning. You can lift weights there until we get home, and then you can practice with the lighter bows. And before you say it, they didn't take that from you. You can get that muscle back," Richard said.

"Maybe tomorrow," Eric said. "I have more important things to do today."

"Like what?"

"You," Eric said with a grin. "I have to thank you properly for my gift. If you're up for it."

"Oh, I'm up for it, but let's go see Dav first. The bed will still be here when we get back, but visiting hours will be over. And no, before you think it, I'm not picking him over you. I figured you'd want to see him too."

ERIC PUSHED down the instinctive reaction that tried to rise to the surface. Richard had spent the night at his side even if he was too drunk to appreciate it, had gotten up this morning to buy him an antique bow, and had spent the rest of the morning and early afternoon taking care of him. He'd shaved him, showered with him, made love to him twice, held him as he slept, and eaten a late lunch with him. And he'd promised to be there when Eric needed him tonight and tomorrow and going forward.

But he loved Tim too, as Eric did. Eric wasn't so far gone in his own fucked-up brain to ask Richard to deny that or to neglect Tim when Eric wasn't in crisis. Maybe Tim wouldn't know they were there, but maybe he would. Maybe they'd get to the hospital and the doctor would be ready to take the ventilator out. Or if not that, the doctor might have an update, anything to give them an idea of when Tim would be back with them, mentally if not physically. They could do that and then come back tonight and make love again. Or not. They could have dinner and take a closer look at the bow so Eric could see what restoring it would entail. They could go to the gym, to run or lift weights or spar. He could ask Richard to cut his hair. They could be together tonight, with the peace of mind of having checked on Tim.

"Yes, I'd like to go by the hospital. The last time I was there, the doctor was hoping the ventilator could come out in a few days. If nothing else, we want to be there when they do that—or right after—so Tim won't wake up to strangers."

"We won't let that happen," Richard said. "We'll be there when he needs us, just like he's always there when we need him. Just like I'll be there if you need me."

"I don't know how to be the supportive one," Eric admitted, feeling incredibly selfish as he said it. "You've never seemed to need it—either one of you—and now that you do, it makes me feel pretty fucking self-absorbed."

"Stop," Richard said. He kissed Eric deeply, sweeping his tongue between Eric's lips so he couldn't speak. Eric clung to him, a plant sucking in moisture after a long drought. Richard lingered over the caress, running his hands up and down Eric's back, like he knew how much Eric needed the contact to steady him, like he knew how fucking needy Eric had gotten. When had that happened?

It didn't matter. Maybe he always had been. Maybe it was the lingering effects of the torture he'd endured. Maybe it was Tim's absence that had him so thrown off. Regardless, he was desperate for it. If he hadn't just said they should go see Tim—and he *would* feel better for seeing him—he'd try to lure Richard back to bed again. He could probably do it too, but what would that say about him if he did?

Richard finally broke the kiss, although he kept Eric folded tightly against him. "Do you want a shower before we go?"

"Do you care if I walk around smelling like sex and your aftershave?" Eric asked.

Richard grinned, a sharp, feral expression that had need coiling in Eric's gut again. "I'm never going to complain about that. And it might help Tim wake up. They say smells connect to the brain on the deepest level, and if anything smells like home, it would be that."

"Then I just need to put some clothes on." Eric pulled away reluctantly, but Richard didn't let him go far, instead following him into the bedroom. He only had one more clean pair of fatigues, he discovered when he opened the bag of his clothes that Richard brought from home for him to have postrescue. "I'll need to do laundry at some point. I'm almost out of things to wear."

"There's bound to be a laundromat in town," Richard said. "I should probably do some too. We can worry about that after we've seen Dav."

The normalcy of it—worrying about clean clothes instead of whether Tim would recover or whether Eric would have another panic attack—steadied him. He pulled on a pair of pants and a T-shirt and smiled at Richard. "Let's go see how our hero's doing."

CHAPTER 16

TIM'S ROOM was empty of doctors and nurses when they arrived, but Eric figured that was a good sign. If something was wrong, the room would be bustling. While he would prefer for Tim to wake up, the peaceful hiss of the ventilator was reassuring in its own way. And hopefully the ventilator would be a thing of the past soon enough.

Eric took two steps into the room before remembering that he hadn't come alone and that Richard had even more invested in this than he did, if only because of the years he and Tim had together. He turned back to find Richard right on his heels.

"Go on," Richard said. "I'm right here. He had enough space in his heart to envision us all together. There's enough space at his bedside too."

"We don't deserve him, do we?" Eric asked as he dragged one of the plastic chairs to the foot of the bed, leaving space for Richard at Tim's head.

"Probably not," Richard said, "but he'd tell us it isn't about what we deserve anyway. What's that quote he's always spouting about life and death?"

"Many that live deserve death. Some that die deserve life," Eric said.

"That's it. I never really understood what that had to do with everything else we deserve, but he's said it since basic training," Richard said.

"Have you still not read *The Lord of the Rings*?" Eric asked. "How have you been his lover for twenty years and not read them?"

"I've been a little busy," Richard retorted, although he smiled as he said it. "You know, being a SEAL and then running all of our ops. Plus making sure Dav had the time he needed to take care of you when your ass landed in the hospital."

"That's what we're going to do while he's recovering," Eric declared. "We're going to read his favorite books."

"If it really means that much to you," Richard said.

"It'll mean that much to him. He started reading them to me after my first bad op. You remember? I tore my ACL and was laid up for weeks. He sat at my bedside when I came out of surgery and read out loud. Eventually I could focus well enough to read on my own, but even then, he sat with me and we'd read a few chapters and then talk about it. It kept me sane through that recovery. His is going to be so much longer and harder."

"Do you have a copy?" Richard asked.

"I have print copies at home, but it's on my Kindle too, except I don't know where that is. I didn't take it with me when we left for the mission that resulted in me being captured, so it may be at home, unless Tim thought to stick it in with the rest of my gear for when you finally found me. I honestly haven't looked."

"If it's on your Kindle, we can download it to another device," Richard said. "Even the replacement phone I got you. We can do that tonight so it'll be ready when he's awake enough to know what we're reading."

"Another little piece of home," Eric said with a nod. He rubbed his hand automatically over his face, letting the comfort of being clean-shaven wash over him again. He caught Richard's gaze and smiled, a little shy, a little self-deprecating. It was a silly ritual, but it grounded him. And now Richard was a part of that too.

"All you ever have to do is ask." Richard's voice was heavy with promise, the same dark need that drove Eric whenever he thought of either of his lovers.

"You don't have to wait for me to ask," Eric replied. "You can shave me anytime you want."

"Anywhere I want?" Richard crowded into Eric's space.

Eric had a sudden flash of lying on the bed with his legs spread as Richard drew the straight razor over his balls. He swallowed hard. "Anywhere you want."

The door opened behind him, breaking the moment, but Richard didn't step back. Eric released a shaky breath. They'd maintained the fiction of a professional relationship—and only barely that—for so long that he'd automatically braced himself for Richard's withdrawal behind that façade, but it hadn't happened. He wasn't hiding how close they were standing.

"Commander Horn, Mr. Newton. Just the men I was hoping to see," Smithers said as she walked in the door. "Mr. Davenport is exceeding our expectations left and right. Unless something regresses during the night, we'll take his breathing tube out in the morning and wean him off the drugs keeping him unconscious. We've already lowered the dose to make sure his body would take over and he'd breathe on his own. At this point it's just a precaution, but we want to observe him for a few more hours."

"That's wonderful news," Richard said. Eric couldn't do anything but nod his agreement. He knew taking Tim off the ventilator was only the first step, not the last, but he'd told himself repeatedly not to get his hopes up even for that step, that it could still be days or even weeks, and that those delays wouldn't mean Tim would die. They would just mean he was still healing. To hear that he would be off the ventilator and possibly awake as early as tomorrow….

He couldn't even begin to make sense of the words. He took a step closer to the bed, away from Richard and the doctor. Tim's hand felt warmer in his when he curled his fingers around Tim's lax ones. It had to be his imagination, but when he'd held Tim's hand before, it had felt stiff and cold, like Tim was one step away from dying. Now it felt like he was just asleep, like if Eric shook him a bit he'd wake up. He studied Tim's face, searching for differences. Was his skin really less sallow beneath his light tan, or was that Eric projecting now that they had encouraging news from the doctor? The bandages were all still there except the one on his forehead, protecting surgical sutures to close the wounds where bullets had torn into his flesh and scalpels had followed to allow the doctors to repair the damage. Those hadn't disappeared just because Smithers hoped to take Tim off the ventilator. He was still weeks or months away from returning to duty, but he *seemed* less sick to Eric.

"Eric?"

Richard's voice drew him out of his perusal.

"What?"

"The doctor left. She said we could stay as long as we wanted, regardless of visiting hours, but she also said we don't have to. They won't do anything before morning, no matter how well he's doing. We can stay for a while and then do some shopping so we have food at the house, if you want," Richard said. "And you have to decide what you need to work on your bow."

Eric nodded, but the words only barely registered in his brain. He'd made plans for tonight. Richard had promised to do all kinds of amazing, wicked things to him, but that was before they'd talked to the doctor, before they knew Tim was going to wake up tomorrow. How could he think about anything else?

He stopped the automatic demurral before it could slip out. He'd made so many mistakes where Richard was concerned. As much as he wanted to drop everything and stay at Tim's side, he'd managed to make Richard feel secondary for the past four years without meaning to. Then it had been in ignorance, but he knew now. He couldn't fall back into the same bad habits.

He and Richard had only started to connect on their own. If he did it now, he wouldn't have the same excuse.

"Sure, we can do whatever you want," Eric said.

Richard shook his head. "I can't read your mind the way Dav does. Talk to me, Eric. What's going on in your head?"

"I...." Eric struggled to gather his thoughts, but they raced around in circles, refusing to be put in order. How the hell did Tim manage to juggle both of them? He slumped into the chair by the foot of Tim's bed and scrubbed at his face. "A part of me wants to be here with Tim. I want to find a blanket, pillow my head on his leg, and not move until he opens his eyes again. Even if he doesn't say anything. Even if he's still so far out of it on pain medicine that he can't do anything but blink at us, I want to be here."

"There's nothing wrong with wanting to be with your lover when he's in the hospital," Richard said. "I've spent my share of time in here since he was admitted too."

"But I don't want you to feel like you're less important," Eric said. "I don't want to brush you aside. You went to the trouble of finding me an *antique English longbow*. That deserves some kind of recognition."

"You already said thank you," Richard replied. "That's recognition."

"I was going to do better than that. I was going to blow you at least, even if you ended up on top before the night was over. You made all these promises, you know."

"And I will keep every fucking one of them," Richard said, "but I don't have to keep them tonight. The reason we work, the three of us, is that we've always adjusted to take care of whoever needs it most. And okay, that's been you more often than not because of the three of us, you have the most dangerous job, but you remember the time I got the flu and you and Dav took care of me. Or the time Dav had the concussion and was loopy from pain meds for days. This morning, with the panic attack, you needed something I could give you, and I did, and we made plans to keep giving you what you need, but plans can change. What you need now is to be here for Dav. What you've missed is that I need the same thing. Not because I don't want you too but because Dav's need is the most acute. Unless you're going to have another panic attack if I don't take you home and keep all those promises."

Eric chuckled despite himself. "If you never keep them, I might have an issue, but I can wait a day or two. This is going to sound stupid, but if we went home and fucked tonight, it would feel...."

"Like we were neglecting him," Richard finished. "And you're right, it would. He'd probably kick us both in the ass for thinking such a thing, but you're right." He glanced at his watch. "It's four o'clock now. Let's keep him company for a bit, and then we can get groceries, make dinner, download your books, and try to sleep. In the morning we can get here early and that way we'll be here the moment he wakes up."

"That sounds like a good plan," Eric said.

"Then that's what we'll do, and if it turns out not to be a good plan, we'll do what we always do."

Eric grinned. "Improvise."

"There's no one better at it than you."

"I KNOW all of Tim's stories," Eric said when they had got back to the house with their arms loaded down with groceries. "I don't know any of yours."

Richard looked up in surprise from the groceries he was putting in the cabinets. They hadn't found as much variety as they'd find at home, but it would be better than mess food or frozen dinners. "What are you talking about? My stories aren't any different from Dav's since I feature in most of them."

"But they're all seen through his eyes," Eric replied. He emptied the last of the grocery bags and leaned against the counter, his long, lean body on unconscious display. Richard might have thought Eric had changed his mind about fucking tonight, but for all that Richard could get turned on just looking at him, Eric wasn't being intentionally provocative. Richard had seen provocative on him often enough to know the difference. It didn't stop Richard from taking the time to admire, though. "I want to hear your stories, even if they're the same events. I want to see them through your eyes."

"What do you want to know?"

"It doesn't matter," Eric replied with a shrug. "I just want to share it with you."

"Think about it while we make dinner, and I'll tell you anything you decide on," Richard offered. Dav was the better storyteller, with a tale for every situation, sometimes funny, sometimes serious, but always spot-on with what fit the mood of the moment. Another of those things Richard left to him whenever he could.

Tonight he couldn't.

They fixed dinner quickly, nothing fancy, just pan-fried chicken breasts and steamed vegetables, but it was fresh and they'd made it together, and that landed it high on Richard's list of favorite meals in recent memory.

"I need a shower," Eric announced after they'd finished washing up. "Join me?"

Richard almost said no. He'd showered twice already today and didn't really need a third one, but Eric had asked. "Sure."

Eric stripped as unselfconsciously as ever as he walked into the bedroom, leaving behind a trail of clothes. Richard followed, although he didn't strip down until he was in the bathroom. Easier to clean up behind himself later, not that Dav was there to fuss about their mess. He stopped short at the sight of the bruises on Eric's body on clear view as he bent over the tub, but Richard swallowed hard around the dread and swatted Eric's ass lightly. "Careful there, Peaches. I'll get ideas."

Eric straightened and smirked at Richard over his shoulder, but while the expression was warm, it didn't glitter with heat as it did when Eric was looking for sex. Richard crowded up behind him and wrapped his arms tightly around Eric's waist. "You doing okay?"

"I can't stop thinking that tomorrow night, Tim could be awake," Eric said. "I have to remind myself that taking him off the ventilator doesn't mean he'll wake up immediately. It could be days still. Hell, it could be weeks still."

"It could be, and it could be an hour," Richard said. "We just have to go in tomorrow and see what happens. Dav has a history of metabolizing meds quickly. When he's had to have surgery, he's always come to on the fast end of their estimates."

They climbed into the tub and turned the shower on, dousing them both in warm water. Richard reached for the washcloth, but Eric grabbed it first and worked up a lather. "You gonna do that yourself?"

"No, I'm going to do it for you," Eric said. "You've spent all day taking care of me. Let me return the favor."

"You don't have to do that," Richard said automatically.

"I *want* to," Eric replied. "No obligation involved, I promise."

Richard stood still and let Eric run the cloth over his body. Eric had done this before—although Dav had always been there—but it had never felt quite like this. Always before it had been as much foreplay as it had been anything else. Not that Richard had been complaining. He would never complain about Eric's hands on his body, for any reason. It wasn't foreplay tonight. It wasn't light and teasing, accompanied by Eric's devilish smile and Dav's perfect deadpan. It didn't have any of the urgency of their earlier shower. And yet the weight of the moment pressed down on him. This wasn't foreplay. This was intimacy so far beyond sex that Richard didn't have the words for it. Even when Eric dropped the cloth and ran soapy hands over Richard's dick and between his legs to his balls, it wasn't sexual. It could have been. Half of Richard's brain insisted it should have been, but it wasn't. When Eric was done, Richard returned the favor, taking care to keep his touch tender, loving, rather than arousing. Eric leaned against him trustingly, his cock somewhere less than half-hard, proof that Richard was striking the right note between them.

Another night he might have worried he was losing his touch, but not tonight. They didn't need sex tonight. Not even making love. Their bodies might be here in this shower, but Richard knew Eric's heart and thoughts were still at the hospital, the same as his own. The comfort they took in each other gave them both the strength to survive the waiting. They still had a long way to go to making things right between the two of them, but worry for Dav wasn't making things worse, and Richard would be grateful for small blessings.

Richard turned the water off when they were done and grabbed a towel to dry Eric off. Eric let him, a continuation of the same weighted silence, but he took the towel from Richard's hands when Richard would have turned it on himself. As much comfort as he took from caring for Eric, he didn't deny Eric the same comfort in return. When they were dry, they walked back into the bedroom. Eric started toward his duffel, out of habit, Richard suspected, because he stopped the second Richard caught his hand.

"Come to bed. I don't want anything between us tonight, not even your shorts."

Eric followed him into bed and burrowed into his arms. Richard let the feel of smooth skin and solid bone settle into him, a reminder that no matter what happened with Dav, tomorrow or any day after, Richard wasn't alone. The best, the worst, or anything in between, Eric would be right there at his side, supporting him even as he leaned on Richard for support in turn.

"Tell me about the first time you saw Tim."

"The first time I saw him or the first time I noticed him?" Richard asked.

"Both."

Richard cast his thoughts back, trying to remember the first time he'd laid eyes on Timothy Davenport. "It must have been on the way to basic training. We were in the same unit from the first. I was the only black man in our unit, and a lot of the others took that as permission to make comments. They didn't bother to ask where I was from or what my background was. They assumed I was a poor punk from the ghetto. It probably wouldn't have made any difference if they knew Grandpa was a Red Tail and that Dad got a Purple Heart in Vietnam. They didn't care that I'd gotten better grades than they had or that I was already being considered as officer material because of my entrance tests. They saw the color of my skin and nothing more. A group of them had started my way, and I could tell it was going to end badly. I'm good in a fight—was even then—but there's only so much you can do when you're outnumbered like that. Before it could go to shit, this guy plopped down next to me and introduced himself. Henry James. Stupidest motherfucker ever born, but he was as loyal as the day is long, and he'd decided to sit with me because I looked like I didn't know anyone either.

"I still don't know whether Dav put him up to it—he says he didn't, but I don't really believe him—or if he just took advantage of the opening James gave him, but he headed off the idiots. I didn't meet him then. I didn't actually know his name until roll call, but even then I couldn't look around to put the face and name together. I finally met him for real about a week later. James introduced us in the mess."

"What happened to James?" Eric asked. "I don't think I've heard either of you mention him before now."

"He was killed on our first deployment as SEALs," Richard said. "Jumped between Dav and a grenade. The actual mission hadn't even started yet, but nowhere in Iraq was safe in those days. 'Loyal as the day is long.' That's what we said at his funeral—his parents asked us to speak—and that's what they put on his headstone." He shook his head at the memory.

"Were you together by then?"

"Not officially. Hell, not even unofficially. It was before DADT, and even during DADT, we had to be careful not to get caught. It's one of the reasons we left the Navy. No one to tell us we couldn't be together. No one to yell about being gay or about fraternizing or about turning our couple into a trio. The only people who have any say in our relationship are us."

"But you knew by then?"

"I think a part of me always knew," Richard admitted. "Maybe all he had in mind in stopping the fight was avoiding the whole unit getting latrine duty for the first week at basic training, but he stopped it anyway. He saved me from a beating, from getting the reputation as a troublemaker, and from fucking up the officer track I was on. Half of the idiots washed out of basic training and the other half ended up at the bottom of the heap. And James, Dav, and I went on to SEAL training."

"When did the rest of you know?"

"The first time I saw him kick ass in hand-to-hand," Richard said. "I knew him by then. We ate together anytime we could. I knew he was more than just a pretty, unassuming face. I knew he wouldn't have made it as far as he had if there wasn't more to him than that, but I hadn't seen what was beneath the mask he wears. Then I walked in as he was taking apart one of those same idiots who still hadn't stopped making racist comments where the CO couldn't hear them. He didn't even break a sweat as he wiped the floor with the guy. And when he was done, he leaned down and whispered something in the fucker's ear. I wasn't supposed to hear it, but I was closer than he realized. He said, 'If you ever call him a nigger again, this will seem like child's play. He's a far better man than you will ever be, and don't you forget it.' When he stood up, he met my eyes and smiled like we were about to have tea or something. Like he hadn't just beaten a man into the ground because he'd insulted me. I was lost and haven't looked back."

Eric chuckled. "That sounds exactly like him. Pretty much the only difference between your story and mine is that he was wearing a suit instead of a uniform when he wiped the floor with the guy who called me a half-breed."

"I know." Richard kissed the top of Eric's head. "He told me about it that night. He told me the last time he'd been that angry was in basic training. I teased him about trading me in for a younger model, only to watch him turn bright red. I decided right then I needed to find out as much about you as I could. If I was going to share his interest with someone, it had damn well better be someone worthy of him."

"I don't know why you didn't just kill me and hide the body," Eric muttered.

"Because he wasn't interested in replacing me," Richard said. "He was as interested in you and me being together as he was in being with you. And he wouldn't have acted on any of it, no matter how much you flirted with him, if I hadn't been willing to go along with his idea. By the time you made your move, I was already halfway in love with you just from watching you from a distance. When the chance finally came for something more, I jumped at it."

"I don't suppose I'll ever understand why, but I'm sure as hell glad you did," Eric replied.

Richard tipped his chin up and kissed Eric properly. "None of that, or I'm going to start asking why you saddled yourself with an old bastard like me." He didn't have to wonder why Eric fell in love with Dav.

"You're not old."

"And you're not stupid," Richard replied. "And all three of us are fucked-up in one way or another, so I'd say that makes us even."

Eric subsided against Richard's shoulder again. "We should try to get some sleep. Tomorrow is going to be a long day."

"I love you," Eric murmured.

"Love you too, Peaches."

CHAPTER 17

"GOOD MORNING, Mr. Newton, Commander Horn," Dr. Smithers said when she saw Eric and Richard the next morning. Was it only Saturday? Not even a week since he'd been rescued. It felt like so much longer than that. "The night nurses reported more instances of Mr. Davenport breathing over the vent. We'll begin decreasing the propofol drip after we've changed his bandages this morning. Give the nurses a few more minutes, and then you can go see him."

Eric paced the hall outside Tim's hospital room as he waited for the nurses to finish. He had thought about arguing with Smithers's insistence that they wait outside—he'd seen wounds and Tim naked before—but he knew her type. She wouldn't budge, and Richard didn't have any authority here. Not enough to overrule her anyway.

Eric envied Richard at the moment. He was sitting in one of the chairs along the corridor looking like he didn't have a care in the world as he checked e-mails on his phone. Eric knew part of that was an act, Richard's public persona of unflappable control. They'd spent the night talking, huddled together under the blankets as the hours dragged on. Eric didn't remember falling asleep, but he'd woken up this morning, so at some point exhaustion had won. Even so, Richard hadn't looked any more rested as they made coffee and eggs. To see him now, though, Eric would never guess if he hadn't been there. Richard showed no sign of bleariness, no sign of impatience, no sign of worry.

Eric, on the other hand, was a fucking mess. Everything had progressed overnight exactly as expected and decreasing the drugs to let Tim breathe on his own was standard procedure, nothing to worry about, but that was Tim on the other side of the wall. Until he opened his eyes, Eric wouldn't be able to settle.

The nurse opened the door after what seemed like forever. "You can come in now."

Eric knew nothing had changed since the night before—nothing visible, at least—but he barreled inside anyway. He had to see for himself. Richard followed one step behind him, as Eric took his place at Tim's bedside. The ventilator still hissed regularly, but it seemed to Eric to be softer than before. Was that good? Did it mean they'd turned it down so Tim could breathe more on his own?

"Hey," Richard said, nudging his shoulder, "no panicking on me. If they didn't think he was ready, they wouldn't be decreasing the meds he's on. They want him to get well too."

"Not as much as I do," Eric said. He let go of Tim's hand and reached for Richard. "I feel like I'm five again, begging someone to tell me Santa is real."

"I can't bring Santa back for you, but I can promise you this: he's getting better. Listen to his breathing. Sometimes he takes breaths on his own. Do you hear it?"

Eric concentrated on the rhythm of Tim's breath. In and out, one, in and out, two, in and out, three, in and ou—in. "He did it. I heard it."

"Yes, he did."

Eric gripped Richard's hand tighter. "He's going to wake up."

"He is. You downloaded his books last night. Read to him. It'll help bring him home."

Eric flipped through the apps on his phone until he found what he was looking for. He didn't read out loud as well as Tim did, but that wasn't the point. "In a hole in the ground…."

LUNCH CAME and went without either of them moving from Tim's bedside. Victoria showed up shortly after one with a bag of sandwiches.

"Here. You won't do Davenport any good if you starve," she said as she shoved the bag at Eric. "There's a bench outside. You should go sit on it and eat."

"Thanks," Eric said, "but we can eat in here. They're weaning him off the drugs."

"You need a break."

"I'll take a break when Tim wakes up," Eric replied.

"Horn, make him take a break," Victoria said. Eric flipped her off, but Richard just shook his head.

"I'm not making him go anywhere, and neither am I."

"You're being ridiculous. He's on strong drugs, and they just lowered the dose. He's not going to wake up while you're outside eating lunch, and even if he did, they wouldn't let you stay while they dealt with the tube down his throat. You both know that."

"It's not just about him waking up," Eric said. "It's about being here no matter what happens."

"Idiots," she said with a shake of her head as she left.

"Do you think she's right?" Eric asked.

"About which part?" Richard replied.

"Any of it."

"She's right that Dav probably isn't going to wake up in the next hour or two, and she's right that if he does, they'll kick us out while they calm him down and deal with the ventilator. There's a reason they have him sedated. I don't think that means we should leave, though. I want to be here too. Not because I expect him to wake up if we leave for a bit but because I don't want to leave until he does."

"I'm glad it's not just me."

"It's not just you."

"WE'VE SEEN a rising occurrence of breathing over the vent over the course of the day," Smithers said when she checked in at the end of her shift. "We've decreased the drip again. He's still not expected to wake before morning—his kidneys are recovering, but it takes time to metabolize the drugs in his system—but we're going to dial back the ventilator. His heart rate, blood oxygen levels, and blood pressure are all within safe limits. As long as that continues during the night, we should be able to extubate him in the morning."

"We aren't leaving," Richard declared.

"I didn't expect you to. I don't have any empty cots, though. I'm sorry."

"We've slept in worse conditions. If you had an extra pillow or two, we could use those, but if not, we'll make do."

"I'll see what I can find," Smithers offered.

She fiddled with the dials on the ventilator. Richard could hear the change in rhythm immediately. Instead of a steady in and out, it hissed and then stopped. Richard held his own breath as he waited for Dav's body to catch up. Would he take the breath on his own, unprompted by the machine? He'd been breathing out of sync with it off and on all afternoon, but this was different. His chest rose and fell.

Smithers nodded. "Good. Try to get some rest. Tomorrow could be an exciting day."

"He's breathing on his own," Eric whispered after she left.

"He is," Richard said. He pulled Eric into his arms and held on. He hadn't let himself voice the fears that had haunted him since Dav went down. He'd had to be strong for Eric, for the team, even for Dav himself. He couldn't let things go to shit because the love of his life was in the hospital. Dav would never forgive him if he did, but he'd been scared. Now, though…. Dav was breathing on his own, every other breath coming without the aid of the machine. They were decreasing the sedation. He was going to come out of it, and when he did, Richard would be there to talk to him, to ask his advice on the situation with Collins and for help with Eric. Things between them were better since Eric's panic attack, but Richard didn't believe for a minute that they were done with his issues. Even when a mission had gone like clockwork, Eric sometimes came back off-balance. Numerous times Dav had called him saying he wasn't going to be in a meeting because Eric needed him. Richard had simply taken up the slack because that's what he and Dav did, but that had to change now too. For one thing Dav wasn't going to be in any shape to take care of himself for a while, much less Eric, but even once he was, Richard didn't want to go back to playing second fiddle. He wanted to be part of whatever Eric needed, of grounding him and making him feel safe and loved. He hadn't realized how desperately until he got the chance to actually do it. He'd nearly screwed it up, but at least he was involved.

A nurse came in with pillows and blankets. "It's not much, but it'll help you be a little less uncomfortable, I hope."

"It'll be fine. Thank you."

Eric set the pillow on the mattress near Dav's knees and leaned forward, resting his head against Dav's leg. Richard smiled through his worries and brushed his hand down the back of Eric's head. The long strands of black hair clung to his fingers, making his smile widen. He spread the blanket over Eric's shoulders and settled on the other chair next to him. Eric turned his head and gave Richard a small smile, nothing like his usual wicked grin. Richard leaned in and kissed him tenderly. He hadn't been able to bring back Eric's normal smile—not yet, anyway—but he could assure him he wasn't facing whatever came alone. Whether Dav woke up first thing in the morning or never—fuck, let him wake up—or in an hour or a month or a year, Richard would stand at Eric's side every step of the way. If it came to it, Heikkinen could run their ops for a while. Hell, she could take over for good. He and Dav had enough saved up to live on. They'd get bored long before they ran out of money.

Eric snuffled into the pillow, not quite a snore, not a moan, but not quite a peaceful sound either. It drew Richard's thoughts away from all the different possible futures and back to the present. He rested his hand on Eric's nape, hoping the contact would ease whatever was troubling his sleep. He stretched out his other hand to touch Dav's wrist above the IV line. His skin was cool to the touch, but it warmed up quickly enough beneath Richard's fingers. His pulse thumped reassuringly, duh-dum, duh-dum, duh-dum. His chest rose and fell, about one breath for every three beats of his heart. The steadiness of it lulled Richard toward sleep. If something were wrong, everything wouldn't be so even. They'd take Dav off the ventilator tomorrow, and then he'd wake up.

RICHARD STIRRED during the night when Eric stood up. "You okay?"

"Gotta piss." Eric's voice was rough with sleep, but he stumbled in the direction of the door to the restroom. Richard figured it was there for families because Dav wouldn't still be in ICU when he was well enough to use it. A few moments later, the toilet flushed and Richard heard water running in the sink. Eric opened the door, backlit for a moment by the light in the bathroom, but while Richard could see his silhouette, he couldn't make out Eric's expression. "I'd say come back to bed, but it's not much of a bed."

"I've slept on worse," Eric said.

"Yeah? Where's the worst place you've ever slept?" He was maybe opening a can of worms by asking, but if Eric would tell him, Richard would know him a little better, and that would make it worth any horrors he had to hear. Eric came back to the chair and pulled the blanket around his shoulders again but didn't immediately put his head back on the pillow.

"The hole where they kept me before you sent Amato after me was pretty bad, but I think the worst was the stakeout in Vladivostok. It was November, so it was already miserably cold. I was in a nest on the top of a warehouse. I was dressed as warmly as I could be and still be able to do my job, but I'd been up there for hours. Victoria had the dangerous part of that mission, actually meeting with the contact, but I had to cover the spot. I dozed off while I was waiting for the signal that they were moving in. It's probably a good thing she signaled when she did. Falling asleep out in that kind of weather is a good way to not wake up. And before you say anything, Tim already tore me a new one for not asking for backup when I realized how cold I'd gotten. The problem with hypothermia is that it fucks with your rational thinking even before it screws with the rest of your body."

Richard remembered that mission. It was the first time Eric hadn't come home on schedule. Dav had been frantic. They'd never left a man behind, and Dav refused to do it then. The fact that they didn't know where

Eric was to bring him home only made it worse. Dav had torn the city apart searching for him. Richard hadn't been there when they found him, but he'd never seen Dav as angry as he was when he finally came home. Richard had realized that night just how serious Dav was about his interest in Eric. His emotions had gone far beyond care for a comrade in arms. "That was the clusterfuck that made me realize how serious Dav was about you."

"Then it was worth every minute of it," Eric replied. "I'd go through it all again as long as I knew you and Tim were waiting for me on the other end."

"We always will be," Richard replied. Eric leaned against Richard's shoulder and propped his feet up on the bed. Richard shifted a little so Eric leaned against him more comfortably and closed his eyes again. He had Eric, warm and heavy in one arm, and Dav within reach of the other. The chair might be about as uncomfortable as they came, but Richard couldn't have cared less, not with both his lovers alive and at hand again.

"WE'RE GOING ahead with the extubation this morning," Smithers said after she checked Tim's chart the next morning. "All of his vitals are on the good side of normal range. We're going to leave the chest tube for now, but with the ventilation tube removed, there will be no reason to keep him sedated. We'll leave the morphine drip to manage his pain, but he'll be able to wake and sleep on his own. Of course he'll still sleep far more than he'll be awake for the near future. His body has a lot of healing left to do. We're still monitoring for infection, but the fact that his kidneys and digestive tract are functioning again and that he's able to breathe on his own are huge steps forward."

"Yeah, but he'll be able to wake up and tell us he's healing," Eric said.

"Yes, he will. And I'm sure he'll have a few other things to say. I know his type. He'll complain about every single restriction we place on him, even the ones that are so obvious he shouldn't be able to argue with them. It will be up to the two of you to make sure he doesn't set his recovery back by pushing harder than he should."

"What makes you think he'll listen to us?" Richard joked.

Smithers smiled. "Because you want him well enough to go home with no restrictions, and the more he follows my instructions, the sooner that will happen. Every torn stitch, every strained muscle is one more day he has to stay under our care."

"We'll do our best," Eric said.

"I know you will. Now, if you'll step outside, we'll get the tube taken out, and then you can come back in and sit with him until he wakes up."

Eric reached for Richard's hand without thinking as they stepped out of the room. Richard squeezed it gently and kept hold of it when Eric realized where they were and who might see and started to pull away.

"Like I told you two nights ago, part of the point of leaving the Navy was so no one could tell us not to be together. Maybe we haven't advertised it up until now, and maybe we don't want to 'advertise' it even now, but there is *no* reason for me not to hold your hand right now. It's as much a comfort for me as it is for you."

Eric's breath whooshed out of him in relief. He hadn't really believed Richard would want to go back to pretending they weren't together, but it eased something in his heart to hear it so plainly.

The minutes dragged as they waited for Smithers to come back out and tell them they could see Tim. Only Richard's hand in his kept Eric from pacing as he had done the previous morning. Had it only been twenty-four hours since they'd come in to the hospital to hear that they were weaning Tim off the ventilator? Time felt skewed since his rescue, speeding up and slowing down without warning. He leaned more heavily into Richard's side, trying to stay grounded in the present. He suspected he'd drifted, though, because the door opening startled him to full alertness.

"You can come back in."

The first thing Eric noticed when he walked into the room was how quiet it was without the constant hiss of the ventilator. Tim still had way too many wires and tubes attached to his body for Eric's peace of mind, but they were all monitors now rather than things to keep him alive.

"We removed Mr. Davenport from the ventilator, and he's breathing on his own now," Smithers said.

"How long until he wakes up?" Eric asked hoarsely. "He hates being drugged into unconsciousness. You'd think he wouldn't know, but he always does somehow."

"We've stopped the propofol completely," Smithers replied. "Depending on how fast his body can metabolize what is left in his system, he could wake up in a matter of hours or it could be longer. You can stay, but please don't get in the way of the nurses if they need to tend to him for any reason."

Eric nodded. He'd been through this drill enough times to know how it worked. He moved to the side of the bed away from Tim's IV and took his hand, settling in to wait. It could be ten minutes or ten hours or ten days, but he wasn't moving from that spot until he saw Tim's blue eyes open. Even if they closed again immediately, he wanted to see them, to have the reassurance that Tim still loved him. He'd only need one glance at those blue eyes to know that Tim didn't blame him for the clusterfuck of an op that had landed him here. Richard had told him he couldn't be to blame, but he wouldn't believe it for real until he'd heard Tim say it. After all, Tim was the one who'd landed in the hospital, nearly dead.

"Thank you," Richard said. "We'll stay with him."

"When he starts to wake up, have someone notify me," Smithers said. "We know what kind of physical damage was done, but we won't be able to assess if there's any brain damage until he wakes up."

Eric's heart clenched in his chest. Brain damage.

He'd been so focused on Tim's physical recovery that he hadn't even considered the possibility he could have other issues as well. "Is that likely? He didn't have any head trauma."

"Correct, but he coded at least once before they got him to the hospital in Israel and stabilized. It was only for a short time, and they performed CPR the whole time, but anytime the heart stops, it deprives the brain of oxygen, and that can cause damage in very little time. The speed of his physical recovery is a good sign, but I can't rule anything out until we can assess him properly. And I can't do that until he wakes up."

"We'll have someone call you right away," Richard said.

Smithers left the room. The moment the door closed behind her, Eric reached for Richard. "Don't borrow trouble," Richard ordered. "Just because it's a possibility doesn't mean it'll happen. Dav has been defying the odds for years."

"That just means it's due to catch up with him," Eric said.

"Hey." Richard nudged Eric's chin so he looked up. "None of that. If it happens, we'll deal with it, but until it does, we're going to focus on what we do know. He's off the ventilator, and they're no longer keeping him unconscious. He's going to wake up and he's going to be fine. And then he's going to kick our asses for worrying about him."

"If he's well enough to kick my ass, I'll bend over and let him do it," Eric said with a watery laugh.

"If you bend over, kicking your ass won't be what he's thinking about," Richard replied.

"Heh. I'd rather he fuck me anyway."

Richard smiled and bent to kiss Eric. "We'll get back to that. It won't be this month, even if he wakes up today, but we'll get there. Before you know it, he'll be back to ordering us around."

"I can't wait."

"Me either."

Richard settled back in the second chair, close enough that Eric could feel the heat from his body, and held vigil at Eric's side.

CHAPTER 18

ERIC STARTLED awake and looked around wildly before he remembered they were still at the hospital waiting for Tim to wake up. "Did I fall asleep?"

"Not really," Richard said. "You were dozing a bit, so I gave you something to lean on, but I wouldn't say you were asleep. Just resting your eyes. We had a long night with not a lot of sleep."

Eric shook his head. In other words, he'd fallen asleep. He scooted closer to Richard, ignoring the discomfort of sitting partially across two chairs. He could live with a little discomfort if it got him closer to Richard.

Richard smiled down at him and kissed him. Eric sighed into it, letting Richard control the kiss, letting go not because control was stolen from him but because he gave it freely to one of the three people in the world he trusted without hesitation.

Hoarse coughing caught Eric's attention, and he broke the kiss, looking toward where Tim slept. Only Tim wasn't sleeping anymore. His eyes had opened, unfocused, drugged still, but open.

Guilt swamped Eric. He was supposed to be holding vigil at Tim's bedside, not making out with Richard. He'd already landed Tim in that bed, and now he wasn't even doing his part to help him get out of it. He tensed in Richard's arms, trying to fight the narrowing of his vision that always preceded a panic attack. He couldn't do this now. He needed to focus on Tim, not on anything else. He couldn't melt down and add more for Richard to worry about. Tim was alive and awake.

He jumped to his feet. If he sat here, he'd lose it. He'd fall to pieces while the doctor checked for brain damage or whatever else might be wrong. He had to get out of here. He'd come back later, when he could keep it together and be strong for Tim. They didn't have time to take care of him.

Gotta run.

No, he wasn't running, damn the stupid fucking voices in his head. He was just going to….

The nurses. They were supposed to tell the nurses when Tim woke up. He wasn't running, he was getting the nurses. That was it. He wasn't running. He didn't want to run from the men he loved. They loved him and wanted him there.

"Eric?" Richard's voice penetrated the fog that had paralyzed his brain.

"I… I'll get the nurses."

"THE FUCK?" Richard muttered as Eric fled. He wanted to go after him because Eric's voice hadn't been steady. He probably would tell the nurses Dav was awake, but that wasn't why he left. Richard might not read Eric as well as Dav did, but even he could read that much. Before he could do that, though, he had to check on Dav.

Dav tried to speak, but his coughing returned. Richard gave him a couple of ice chips from the cup the nurses had left for when he woke up and waited for Dav's coughing to ease.

"Eric?" Dav's voice cracked on the word, but it was *his* voice. Drugged, a little vacant—completely to be expected—but his. He might not have all his memories. He might have motor issues to relearn beyond the immediate damage to the muscles in his legs, but he knew who they were. They could work with everything else.

"Yes, we got him back," Richard said, figuring that was what Dav was asking. "Amato and her team kicked terrorist ass and pulled him out right after you went down in Syria. He's a little worse for the wear, but we've got our Peaches back."

"Beautiful together." The words slurred together as Dav struggled to speak, but Richard understood what he meant. Dav had always enjoyed watching Eric and Richard together. He never failed to join in, but more than once, he'd started their lovemaking by sitting back and watching Eric and Richard drive each other wild.

"He's a mess," Richard admitted. "I'm trying to be there for him, but I feel like I'm stumbling through basic again, as raw and stupid as they come."

Dav's eyes cleared a little, and he smiled. "Love him."

"I do," Richard said. "You know I do."

Dav shook his head. "Show him that."

"I'm trying, but it seems like I fuck it up worse each time I try." He'd been a little more successful over the past forty-eight hours. He'd thought it was helping until Eric ran out just now. "You always told me you took care of him, but you never told me how."

"Don't give up."

"Never," Richard promised, although specifics would have been useful. Still, Dav had just woken up. Richard would keep stumbling along on his own until Dav could give him more. "I didn't give up on him when the terrorists had him. I'm sure as hell not giving up on him now."

"Don't let him forget it."

"Mr. Davenport, back with us, I see." The doctor's arrival put an end to the moment. Richard took a step back, looking behind the medical staff for Eric, but he was nowhere to be seen.

"Dav?" Richard said. He didn't want to leave Dav alone with the doctors when he'd just woken up, but the need to check on Eric was growing with each passing second. Something hadn't been right with him when he ran.

"Find him. Bring him back."

Richard nodded, Dav's words the permission he'd needed, and headed for the door.

"Richard."

Richard paused and looked back.

"Don't fuck it up."

Richard laughed because he knew Dav would expect it, but for the first time in more years of missions than he cared to count, he wasn't confident of his battle plan or his chances of success, especially when he didn't see Eric in the corridor outside Dav's room.

At home, he'd know where to look for Eric. He'd be on the range or he'd have found his way up to the roof. He was a sniper, he always said. He needed to be up high with wide-open sight lines. Here in Germany, it was a little more complicated. Eric couldn't exactly climb up to the hospital roof, not easily or quickly anyway, but the grounds sported some good-sized trees. They'd give Eric the height he craved, if not the open view of the sky.

He'd feel like a real idiot if Eric had just gone to the restroom or something, but his gut told him this was more than just a break. Eric's eyes had glazed over, far too similar to the expression he'd worn when Richard arrived at the gym to find him collapsed on the floor.

He stepped out of the hospital's main entrance and scanned the surrounding area. If Eric truly didn't want to be found, Richard wouldn't catch even a glimpse of him, but Richard hoped Eric hadn't gone to ground somewhere. After a minute, he caught sight of a sniper-shaped shadow hidden among the branches of the biggest tree in the area. With a muttered imprecation against reckless assets who couldn't sulk somewhere comfortable, he walked over to the tree and started climbing.

"You freaked Dav out, running like that," Richard said when he reached the closest branch to Eric that he trusted to hold his weight. "You want to tell me what happened?"

"He nearly died, and instead of focusing on him like I should have been when he woke up, I was kissing you," Eric said. "I'm a selfish asshole, and now he knows it."

"That's not what he thought, and if you'll stop and think about it for a minute, you'll know that," Richard said. Panic attacks weren't rational, he reminded himself. And however irrational Eric's might seem from the outside, that didn't make this one less real. "His first concern was that we'd gotten you back. You were still being held hostage the last time he was conscious. You know what the second thing he said to me after I assured him you were ours again was?"

Eric shook his head.

"He told me we were beautiful together. Whatever you're worried that he felt at waking up that way, you're wrong," Richard said. "He's not upset. He was happy to see us, although he'd be happier if you came back."

Eric sighed. "Stupid fucking panic attacks. I can't seem to do anything right. I don't know why you two put up with me."

Richard bopped Eric on the ankle. "We've had this discussion, in the past few days no less. You do plenty of things right, we 'put up' with you because we love you, and you've got to get over this ridiculous idea that we're going to stop caring about you just because something doesn't go exactly the way you want it to."

"Let's just go see Tim," Eric said. He vaulted down out of the tree, leaving Richard to scramble down much less gracefully.

"In a minute," Richard replied, catching Eric's hand before he could head back toward the hospital. "I need another kiss first." He pulled Eric close and kissed him hard and fast. Eric gasped into the contact, so Richard let it linger longer than he'd planned. When he finally pulled back to breathe, Eric's hazel eyes had gone glassy, and his lips were parted for more, a most satisfactory expression as far as Richard was concerned. "You back with me now?"

"I think so," Eric said. "The walls started closing in around me, and I couldn't breathe. I had to get out."

"Because we were kissing when Dav woke up?" The reaction seemed a little extreme to him, but he had his own irrational triggers. They just hadn't been set off by the current situation the way Eric's had been. He took a deep breath and reminded himself not to take the panic attack personally. Eric had relied on Dav for so long and was still learning to rely on him.

"Stupid, isn't it?" Eric said.

"Not if it triggered you," Richard insisted. "I know Dav isn't ever going to complain about us being together when it was his idea in the first place, but flashbacks, panic attacks, and the like are different for each person. So if that set you off, I need to know it so we can be more careful." He couldn't imagine not kissing Eric because Dav was around, but they could come up with some kind of guidelines that would give everyone what they needed.

"No," Eric said resolutely. "I mean, yes, that's what set me off, but it wasn't because he saw us kissing. It's…. I can't even explain it in a way that makes sense."

"Then explain it in a way that doesn't make sense," Richard replied. "Or if you don't want to do that, then tell me what I need to do to keep it from happening again."

"You know how when we run an op, we have to analyze a constantly changing situation and assess where the priority is at each moment?" Eric began. Richard nodded encouragingly. "When we came to the hospital yesterday morning and pretty much since then, the priority has been Tim and what he'd need when he woke up. Not because kissing you is unimportant, but because at this moment it wasn't the most important."

"Like how we spent the night telling stories about Dav instead of fucking each other's brains out," Richard said. "I get that."

"Except that I lost sight of that and stopped paying attention to Tim," Eric said.

Richard could almost see the logic in that. Almost.

"You do realize this isn't an op, right? It's not a life-or-death situation. And even if it were, Dav would never be upset at us comforting each other through it."

"Yeah, but when you kiss me, all thought of anything else goes straight out the window," Eric muttered.

At any other time, Eric's words would have puffed Richard's ego, but Eric hadn't sounded happy about it. "Okay. What happens now?"

"What do you mean?"

"It's going to be a while before Dav is well enough to have sex with us again," Richard said. "He can probably manage some kissing pretty quickly, but not much beyond that. If this means you don't want me touching you until he can join us again, I need you to tell me that." It would hurt like hell if that's what Eric meant, but Richard would live with it. Not happily, but he'd live with it.

"What? No! Fuck, no. Damn it, this is why I ran. Why I should have run sooner. No matter what I do, I always end up doing the wrong thing."

"Stop," Richard ordered, grabbing the fraying strands of his temper with both hands. He wouldn't help anything by letting loose the hurt and anger that Eric had roused. "No running allowed. If that's not what you meant, then tell me what you did mean."

"I don't know," Eric said. "I didn't know this would set me off until it did. I don't know how to juggle everything. I love you both desperately, but I can't seem to find a way to pay attention to one of you without feeling like I'm neglecting the other one. If I'm paying attention to you, I'm not paying attention to Tim. I want to pay attention to you, but I don't want to ignore him."

"If I walked back into the hospital room with you now and kissed Dav, if I asked him how he was feeling and held his hand while he answered me, would you feel ignored?" Richard asked.

"Not as long as I was there and could talk to him too and hold his other hand," Eric said. "It would bother me if you tried to keep me out for some reason, but only then."

"Then give Dav and me the same credit," Richard requested. "Yes, we were kissing when Dav opened his eyes, but as soon as we realized he was awake, we moved to include him. Not in the kiss, but in our awareness. He didn't feel ignored because we were kissing. He was happy to see us together. I'm not going to feel ignored because you're spending time with him as long as you don't shut me out to do it. We're trying to do a very difficult thing here, the three of us together, and Dav being injured only makes it harder. Don't complicate it more than it needs to be, okay?"

"Somehow I think that's easier said than done," Eric said wryly.

Richard snorted. "You're worth the effort. *We're* worth the effort. Try not to run from us. We can deal with anything but that."

Eric swallowed hard, his Adam's apple bobbing in his throat. "No more running."

"Then let's go check on Dav. The doctor should be done with her tests by now."

ERIC'S HANDS weren't any steadier when he walked back into Tim's room than they had been when he fled, but Richard's hand clasped his firmly, and that gave him the courage to go back in and face Tim's reaction. The doctor wasn't in the room, and Tim's eyes were closed. Eric kicked himself mentally for missing the chance to talk to Tim, but he'd woken up once. He'd wake up again.

"He wasn't angry at me?" Eric asked.

"Not at all," Richard replied. "Why would he be?"

"It's probably my fault he's in that bed in the first place."

"No, it's probably not," Richard said. "Nothing in that mission had been planned before you were captured, so even if it was the same organization and they got wind of it and made the connection to you—all of which is stretching coincidence if you stop and think about it—but even if all that happened, you couldn't have told them anything because you didn't know anything about that op. I know they fucked with your head, but I need you to trust me."

"You'd say that just to stop me from freaking out," Eric said.

"No, I really wouldn't," Richard said. "I've yelled at you for enough things over the years for you to know that I don't go easy on anyone when they've fucked up. Maybe I wouldn't bring it up right now because we just got you back and I'm so damn grateful you're alive, but I wouldn't lie to you."

Eric studied Richard's face, his dark eyes as serious as Eric had ever seen them. He'd said more than once that Richard lied like he breathed, but Eric knew his tells now—the way he clenched his left hand, thumb on the inside of his fist, the way he stood perfectly still, not even twitching when usually he was too full of restless energy to sit, much less stand still. Yes, Eric knew his tells, but Richard's hands hung loosely at his side, his fingers tapping against his thigh. Whether he was right or not, he believed what he had said. Eric took a deep, shuddering breath and tried to let go of the guilt.

"And they would lie," he said, thinking of all the things his torturers had said. Enough of it had been true that he'd started questioning the rest, but his team had come for him, with Richard spearheading the mission even as he oversaw Tim's mission. Richard and Tim hadn't given up on him, and if it hadn't been for the Syria mission, they would have been on the ground with the rest of the team. He had doubted it while he was being held captive, but not anymore. He couldn't.

"Yes, they would. Anything to break you."

"They came damn close."

"But you're safe now, and they're dead. And Dav is recovering. It will take time, but things will go back to normal soon."

Tim shifted on the bed, drawing Eric's attention. Eric kissed Richard quickly because he wouldn't make Richard feel like he was less important, then moved to Tim's side. Richard went to the other side of the bed and took Tim's hand. Eric mimicked him because he couldn't think of a better way for Tim to wake up than with his lovers on either side of him holding his hands.

Tim blinked awake slowly. "'ric?" he slurred.

"Yes, I'm here," Eric said. "We're both here."

Tim turned from studying Eric to look at Richard. "You didn't fuck it up."

Richard laughed, deep and throaty and the best thing Eric had heard in a long time. "No, I didn't."

Tim looked back at Eric, his blue eyes a little glazed, but not confused. "Good."

CHAPTER 19

"YOU OKAY?" Dav asked.

Eric laughed, the sound raw but real, a balm to Richard's heart. "I'm not the one in the hospital bed full of gunshot wounds."

Dav tried to shrug but broke off with a wince.

"You've still got tubes in you," Richard said. "Stay still."

"Talk to me, Eric," Dav ordered.

"I'm… here," Eric said after a moment. "The team pulled me out. Richard told you that already. Victoria fed me stew and Richard helped me shave and I'm recovering. I have about twenty pounds of muscle to put back on and a hell of a lot of stamina to build back up before I'm back at peak condition again, but I can handle that."

The details weren't new to Richard, but the ease with which Eric reported them drove home to Richard how far he and Eric still had to go. He ignored the spurt of jealousy. Dav and Eric had had years to build up that rapport, even before Eric became their lover. He couldn't expect to have the same rapport in a matter of days, and it was his own damn fault he hadn't developed it sooner.

"And the rest?"

"The panic attacks are back. Not surprising, really, given everything I went through and the fact that I came back to you being down. Not exactly a recipe for an easy transition home."

Dav's hazy gaze moved to Richard. "Don't leave him alone."

"I figured that out," Richard said. "Amato showed me the error of my ways."

"How long have I been out?"

"A week," Richard said. "Given I thought you bled out at one point, it's nothing short of extraordinary."

"Prognosis?"

"Did the doctor talk to you when she was in before?" Eric asked.

"Mostly asked questions. Everything's a little fuzzy." He held up his hands like he expected to see them covered in fur. Dav had always had interesting reactions to morphine.

"You haven't grown a fur coat," Richard said. "The last we talked to her, she expected you to recover physically, although your knee is fucked. They did surgery, but you'll always know when it's going to rain. That's the worst of it now that you're off the ventilator. You've got muscle damage in both legs from the bullets, but that will heal. PT will be a bitch, though."

Dav nodded, although Richard wasn't sure he'd remember any more of this conversation than he did of the conversation with the doctor. It didn't matter. They could repeat it again when the doctors had decreased the dose of morphine. Dav might not remember it, but he was asking all the right questions, using their code, making Eric talk to him. He had a long road ahead of him, but brain damage wasn't a complication they needed to worry about. He didn't need Smithers to tell him that.

"We'll be right beside you through it," Eric said. "No matter how long it takes."

Dav studied Eric closely. "When did you last sleep?"

"I dozed during the night," Eric said.

"Not what I asked."

"Yesterday morning," Richard replied. "He had a panic attack two days ago. We got him calmed down and ended up napping for a while before we came to the hospital. Yesterday when they told us they were going to start weaning you off the sedatives so they could take you off the ventilator, we couldn't leave. We wanted to be here when you woke up."

"I'm not going to be awake for long," Dav said. "You know morphine knocks me out."

"Let them manage your pain for a few more days," Richard insisted. "Then you can start refusing it if you want. Let your body heal as much as you can so you don't push yourself into a relapse. Neither one of us would deal with that well."

"We want you well enough to come home," Eric added. "Soon."

"A few more days," Dav agreed, "but if I'm here sleeping, you have to go home and sleep too. No more sleeping here."

"As long as you don't get worse," Eric said.

"Fair enough. I'm not going to get worse. I want to fall asleep in your arms again."

"Just fall asleep?" Eric teased with a leer.

"All I'll be able to do for a while," Dav said, "but I can watch."

Richard shivered at the thought of making love to Eric with Dav egging them on. He knew exactly how that would go. Dav would start out watching, but before long he'd make a suggestion, then another one, and the next thing they knew, Dav would be orchestrating the whole thing, and it would be fucking amazing. "Not the thing to say when you're stuck in here for God knows how long."

"You don't need me to fuck each other silly," Dav said.

"No, he's proven that already," Eric drawled. Richard reached across Dav's body with his free hand and squeezed Eric's. Dav wormed his hand free of Richard's grasp and rested it on top of their clasped hands.

"Good. Go home and prove it again. You can tell me about it tomorrow."

Eric snorted. "Going to critique our technique?"

Dav's grin bloomed across his face, slow and sly and far too tempting. Eric thought the same, apparently, because he leaned forward and kissed Dav gently. When he leaned back, Richard took his turn. After a week of fearing he might never get this chance again, he was hard-pressed not to deepen the kiss, but he didn't want to set off any alarms and have the doctor decide Dav needed to go back on the ventilator. He wanted him to get well.

"Give him a prostate massage before you fuck him," Dav told Richard when Richard ended the kiss. The tone was conspiratorial, like he was sharing a secret, but he'd lost all sense of volume control with the drugs, because the words were well above a whisper. "You can make him come twice that way. If you really take your time, you can even get him worked up a third time. He's young. He can take it."

Eric moaned softly, drawing Dav's attention. He flushed red, the sight tickling Richard. The fact that Dav's suggestion coincided so completely with the promises he'd made to Eric before they came to the hospital reassured him. He might not know everything Dav did to comfort Eric or stave off a panic attack, but he had this part down pat. "You weren't supposed to hear that," Dav told him.

"Too late," Eric said. "And what am I supposed to do to him? I can't just lie there and not do something to return the favor."

"Fucking you is more than enough reward for me." Richard's voice sounded rough in his own ears. If they kept talking, Dav was going to get a show now, and that wasn't a good idea for any number of reasons.

"It is a lovely ass," Dav agreed before turning back to Eric. "You could rim him. He likes that."

"I know." Eric winked at Richard and licked his lips. Oh, Eric was asking for it. Richard was going to tease him until he was begging for it. "Got any other suggestions?"

Dav tugged on Eric's hand until he bent down enough for Dav to whisper in his ear. Fortunately for Richard, his sense of volume hadn't improved in the past few minutes. "His nipples," Dav told Eric. "You want to break his control? Play with his nipples."

Nope, Dav hadn't lost any of his memories or his orneriness. He'd told Richard to stay in control and take Eric apart multiple times and then handed Eric the key to making control impossible. From the way Dav grinned at Richard, he knew exactly what he'd done. Smug fucker. Richard would get him back, though. He'd take Eric home, and he'd do everything Dav had suggested and more, even if it took him all night, and then tomorrow he'd tell Dav about it in great detail.

Then they'd see who was grinning at who.

"You sure you're okay with us leaving?" Eric asked.

Dav yawned. "Gonna sleep now." The slur was all the proof Richard needed of how close to sleep Dav really was. He prided himself on speaking clearly and concisely. "Love you both."

His eyelids drooped closed. Eric bent over and kissed him gently. Dav smiled but didn't open his eyes, so Richard kissed him in turn and drew Eric away from the bed. "He'll be asleep before we make it to the end of the hallway."

"And we have some orders to follow." Eric's voice was low and sharp, tempting Richard to push him against the wall and take him right there. Dav wouldn't mind if he woke up, but the nurses might have something to say if they walked in on them. They could be back on base in ten minutes with all the privacy they desired, not to mention condoms and lube.

Richard made himself focus on the road rather than on Eric as he drove them back to base. Eric practically vibrated next to him, all harnessed energy and desperate need. Richard could practically taste the desire rolling off him in waves. He'd put money on Eric being rock-hard beneath his pants. He almost reached over to check, but if he did that, he wouldn't stop, and they still had to pass through base security. Better not to do that with Eric's pants unzipped and Richard's hand shoved down the front.

He showed their IDs at the base checkpoint and drove the rest of the way to their house on autopilot. Dav's encouragement was all he'd needed to abandon any lingering doubts about the best way to take care of Eric. Even drugged as he was, Dav would have told him if something else would have been better. Eric had admitted they hadn't slept, had told Dav about the panic attack—not to mention the one Dav saw the beginning of when he woke up the first time. Dav knew what state Eric was in. If Richard should have been taking him to the range or to the gym or to talk with someone in Psych, Dav would have said that instead of giving them sex advice. He parked the car and pulled Eric to him to kiss him with as much tongue and teeth as he could manage. With the adrenaline coursing through them both from the relief of Dav waking up, Richard bet he could get Eric off before they ever got inside.

A tap on the window broke Richard's concentration. He turned with a snarl for whoever dared to interrupt them. Amato and Westin stood outside the car. "Fuck."

He rolled down the window and glared at Amato and Westin. "What do you want?"

"To see how Davenport is and to report back on the jobs you gave us," Amato said, her arms crossed in a way that dared him to make something of it.

Their timing couldn't have been any worse. He needed to hear what they had to say. He had an organization to run, and he couldn't do that without them, especially with Dav still in the hospital, but he could already feel Eric withdrawing. Fuck that. He'd made that mistake before. He wasn't making it again. "Davenport is off the ventilator. He woke up for a few minutes. He sent us home to sleep since we didn't get much last night. If anything can't wait until tomorrow, report it to Heikkinen. Otherwise come by tomorrow at ten, and we'll discuss it then."

"But, Commander—"

"Tomorrow, Westin, or else take it up with Heikkinen."

"Sir," Amato said with a swift salute that was totally spoiled by the smirk she sent him. Damn her. This was why he didn't tell people about his personal life. They thought it gave them rights.

At least she grabbed Westin's arm and took him with her when she left. He turned back to Eric, who had slumped back into the passenger seat, his arms wrapped tightly around his waist. Fuck. "They're gone."

Eric jerked slightly and looked over at Richard, his eyes glazed. "What?"

"They're gone. I told them to come back tomorrow at ten. I'll have to meet with them then. I can't put that off forever, but I can take you to the hospital first if you want to sit with Dav while I talk to them."

"I don't…. What?"

"You with me, Peaches?" Richard asked, growing concerned.

Eric blinked a couple of times. "Where are Amato and Westin?"

"I told them to come back tomorrow." He climbed out of the car and went around to tug Eric out and into his arms. "Let's go inside."

Eric followed him inside docilely. When the door closed behind them, Eric stopped and shook his head, a smile starting to spread across his face. "You told them to come back tomorrow."

"Yes. I had more important things to do this afternoon. Dav gave us some pretty specific orders. I'm not going to be the one to tell him we didn't listen."

Eric's smile fell. Shit. He'd misunderstood.

"And even if he hadn't, I told you I wasn't going to put work first when you needed me," Richard said. "Dav's orders or not, there's nowhere else I want to be than right here with you. I owe you a long, slow fingerfuck."

CHAPTER 20

ERIC TOOK a deep breath to dispel the shakes that had come over him when Victoria and Westin showed up. He'd been so sure of what would happen next. Richard would make excuses and tell Eric he had to talk to them. After all, he'd given them jobs to do and had to take their report, and the job always came first. If he knew anything about Richard, it was that. Only that hadn't happened. He'd sent Victoria and Westin away, and he'd done it so he could spend time with Eric. The reasons why—Tim's orders or his own promise—didn't matter. He'd chosen Eric over work.

"Yes, we have to follow orders. We can't let Tim down." He stepped into Richard's space and pulled his head down for a kiss. If it bordered on desperate, he blamed it on the worry and fear of the past day and the relief of Tim finally waking up, not on the almost panic attack in the car. If he didn't acknowledge that, it hadn't happened.

Richard returned his kiss with just as much fire. Eric opened his mouth and welcomed Richard inside. Richard kissed into his mouth, taking possession of every last inch, licking and biting and sucking at Eric's lips and tongue. Eric moaned into Richard's mouth and gave back as good as he got. He wouldn't be able to break Richard's control. Most of the time Tim couldn't even do that unless Richard consciously gave in, but he'd give it his best shot. He couldn't just lie there and let Richard do all the work. He'd been selfish enough already.

With Tim's advice in mind, he slid his hands beneath Richard's shirt and up over his firm belly. Richard's arms tightened around him, but Eric kept enough space between them to spread his fingers over Richard's smooth chest. Richard jerked beneath the touch, bucking his hips against Eric's. Damn, this was going to be fun.

He kneaded the hard muscle, making sure his palms stayed against Richard's nipples the whole time.

"Brat." Eric knew that tone of voice. It was the same one Richard used in briefings when Eric had done something equal parts stupidly risky and surprisingly effective. In briefings it made him smirk with satisfaction at a job well done, no matter how risky. Now it reached all the way down into his soul and settled him. He had made Richard sound that way with nothing more than a light touch. What could he make Richard sound like if he really applied himself?

"But I'm your brat," Eric said. "Yours and Tim's."

"You are, and by the time I'm done with you, you'll never forget it again."

Never sounded just about perfect to Eric. Richard's constant presence had silenced the voices in his head with two minor exceptions. If Richard could drive them out the rest of the way so Eric would be free of them, he'd do anything Richard wanted. Not that he wouldn't anyway, but he'd pay any price to be free of the doubts that never completely left him.

Richard propelled Eric into the bedroom. Eric tugged his shirt over his head and unbuckled his belt as he went so that when Richard spun him around again, it was easy to push his pants and boxers down to his knees. He toed off his shoes and stripped the rest of the way.

"Eager much?" Richard teased.

"After everything you and Tim promised me? Hell yes." Eric reached for Richard's shirt. "You're wearing too much clothing."

Richard grinned, his eyes glittering as he raked his gaze over Eric's body. Eric stood still, letting Richard look his fill. He had little in the way of body modesty at the best of times. With the echo of Tim's voice making salacious suggestions still fresh in his mind and Richard's kisses having promised follow-through, this hardly qualified.

"Do something about it."

That was all the permission Eric needed. He stripped Richard efficiently. He could linger later, when he had all that beautiful skin on display. For now, he needed Richard out of his clothes and on the bed.

Richard let Eric topple him onto the bed—at his fittest Eric *might* be able to beat Richard in hand-to-hand, but he was nowhere near top form right now—but the moment Richard hit the mattress, he rolled Eric beneath him. Eric contemplated wrestling for the upper hand, for the fun of it since he would lose, but he didn't want Richard to question his willingness for even a second. Another time, when his panic attacks were under control again, he'd give Richard a good fight for control.

Eric reached for Richard with one hand, pulling him down into a kiss. With the other, he returned to teasing Richard's nipples. Richard hissed into the kiss, making Eric grin. Never let it be said his aim was anything less than extraordinary.

"I'm going to wish Dav had kept his mouth shut," Richard grumbled.

Eric tweaked one taut nub and grinned even wider when Richard bucked helplessly against him. "I'm not."

"We'll see if you're singing the same tune when I get my fingers inside you."

Eric shifted enough to get one leg free from Richard's weight and lifted it up and to the side, the best he could do with Richard lying half on top of him. "I'm waiting."

Richard barked out a laugh. "Insatiable."

"You wouldn't have me any other way."

"No, I wouldn't," Richard agreed. He bent to kiss Eric again, as slow this time as it had been wild before, though no less deep and claiming. Eric sank into the kiss. He still wanted Richard's fingers up his ass, and he still wanted to see just how wild attention to his nipples could drive Richard, but this came first because Tim might have told them to fuck each other's brains out, but even Eric didn't need to be told that what Tim really meant was to love each other with everything they had.

He scraped his nails across Richard's nape, just to feel the shudder that went through him. Deciding he liked that reaction, he tried again, across one of Richard's nipples this time. That got him not only a full-body shudder but also a bitten-off curse.

Richard caught his hand and nipped at the tips of his fingers. "My turn."

He stretched across the bed, pinning Eric completely. A week ago, maybe even a day ago, Eric would have squirmed beneath him, needing to escape, but now the contact only turned him on more. He was as safe with Richard as he was anywhere and safer than most places outside Richard's arms. He snuggled down into the mattress and nipped at the curve of Richard's shoulder where it pressed against him.

Richard rocked back on his heels, the tube of slick in his hand. Eric almost protested the loss of Richard's weight, but this way he could tempt Richard even more. He moved the leg that had been trapped beneath Richard to the other side of Richard's body, opening himself as wide as he could for Richard's pleasure. He considered rolling over and offering his ass that way, but if he did that, he couldn't make Richard feel good in return. No, this would just have to do for now.

Then again, Richard was eyeing him like he was a particularly tasty treat, so he probably didn't have anything to worry about.

Richard coated his fingers and set the tube aside. He cupped Eric's balls with one hand, lifting them out of the way even as he rolled them in his palm, and rubbed the fingers of his other hand into Eric's crack. "Slow or fast?"

Eric arched into the dual caress. Fuck, Richard knew his body too well. He opened his mouth to try to answer, but Richard circled his entrance, teasing a moan from him instead. He swallowed hard to clear his throat and tried again. "Tim would say slow."

"I know he would. And you'd answer fast, and we'd end up compromising somewhere in the middle." Richard flexed his fingers against Eric, not enough to penetrate, but enough to make Eric wish he would. "Dav's not here to dictate the pace tonight, so you tell me. Slow or fast?"

"Fast the first time," Eric gasped. "To take the edge off. Then you can go as slow as you want."

Richard's pupils dilated, and he inhaled sharply. "Dav did say you could handle it."

Tim's faith in his stamina was overinflated, but Eric wasn't about to say that now, not with Richard leering down at him. He pulled his knees to his chest to tilt his hips up, every inch of him on display.

Richard studied him for a second longer, then drove one thick finger deep into Eric's body. Oh, fuck, it stung. He wanted more. He needed more. He needed Richard to—

His vision whited out as Richard found his sweet spot and prodded it. He let out a hoarse shout and thrashed on the bed. "Fuck, more. Richard!"

Richard crooked his finger, dialing the maddening pressure up even higher. Fuck. He'd said fast, but he hadn't expected it to be this fast. He hadn't gone from zero to light speed like this since he was a teenager. Richard pulled back long enough to add a second finger. Eric barely registered the stretch, too eager for another touch to his prostate. He let go of one of his legs to reach for Richard, needing the connection, but Richard grabbed his hand and put it back on his knee. "Stay just like that. Spread wide open and begging for it."

"Kiss me?" Eric pleaded. He'd keep his hands where Richard asked him to because he wanted what Richard was giving him, but he needed something. Richard bent immediately, taking possession of Eric's mouth the same way he'd taken possession of Eric's ass—deep and hard and thorough. Need bubbled through him, threatening to burst out of him. His skin felt tight, like it had shrunk or else like the magnitude of his desire had stretched him to his limits.

"You talk about the shit voices in your head," Richard said against his ear as he worked Eric to the point of delirium. "Next time they start, think of this moment, right now. My voice in your ear. Me making you feel good. And remember what I tell you. You belong here, with Dav and me.

You are wanted here. You are loved. You are what we need." He pegged Eric's prostate again, harder and faster, until Eric was sobbing with need. "Remember it. This is the voice in your head now. Mine. Just mine and Dav's. We want you. We love you. We need you."

Eric dug his fingers into his shins, holding them in place and grounding himself. This wasn't a delusion. This was real. Richard was here with him, saying those things. Richard *meant* those things. Eric buried the words down deep in his soul where they could take root. "Yes," he begged. "Say it again."

"Every beautiful, amazing inch of you," Richard said. "Right here with us, loving us, loved by us, watching out for us. I watched you last night, keeping guard even in your sleep." He twisted his fingers inside Eric to press down with his knuckles. Eric came with a hoarse shout, wave after wave of release slamming through him, tossing him around until his only connection with reality was Richard's voice continuing to whisper in his ear.

CHAPTER 21

RICHARD WOKE slowly, letting consciousness seep back in, a rare luxury unless they were home in the Caymans. His chest was pleasantly sore, testament to just how thoroughly Eric had followed Dav's orders last night. Then again, Eric hadn't woken up once after they finally fell asleep, so Richard had obviously done his job right too.

Job. He sighed and pried his eyelids open. Eight thirty. He had time still before Amato and Westin showed up. He wanted nothing more than to tell them to go away again, but he'd put their reports on hold for two days already, between staying at the hospital with Dav and then last night with Eric. They'd accept it if he put them off again, but he could only be selfish and put his personal concerns first for so long before it had an effect on the people under his command. They'd driven many things home to him in the SEALs but few more deeply than his responsibility for those under his command. If he neglected that duty when he could shoulder it, he had no business calling himself a SEAL, even a former one, ever again. It wouldn't take long to hear what they had to say, and then he could go to the hospital and check on Dav. And Dav would understand. Honestly Dav would be more upset at him for delaying the meeting more than he already had than he would be if Richard came a couple of hours later than Eric.

He only hoped Eric would understand that Richard had to do this. It wasn't a question of choosing work over them. It was a matter of taking care of the people who relied on him—all of them. Eric and Dav could take care of each other for a few hours while Richard took care of everyone else.

And yes, fuck it, that was how they'd ended up in this mess in the first place, but with Dav still in the hospital, there was no one else. Heikkinen could deal with the day-to-day business, but if the Pentagon was playing them, Richard needed to handle it, and Amato's task of getting him secure access to their servers was specific to Richard. He certainly couldn't send that to Heikkinen.

Eric shifted against him, not quite waking up but stirring. Richard snuggled down under the blankets and pulled Eric's head onto his shoulder. He could spend a few more minutes with Eric before he had to get up and go back to being the commander. He kissed the top of Eric's head and took a deep breath. The scent of his shampoo and the musk from their lovemaking wafted up, reawakening the morning wood that thoughts of work had killed. He stroked Eric's hair with one hand and circled the other around his growing erection. He could wake Eric up, but if he did that, the day had to start. He could just lie here and bask in the moment of peace and jerk off lazily. They were both so covered in spunk that a little more wouldn't make any difference.

He closed his eyes and filled his thoughts with memories from the night before: the bite of Eric's teeth on his nipples; the way Eric moaned each time Richard scraped across his prostate; the way he begged—and begged and begged—for Richard to hurry up and fuck him already. Richard gave in eventually, but he'd taken Dav's advice and made Eric wait for it until neither of them could stand it.

The heat of Eric's hand on his startled Richard back to the present moment.

"Need a hand with that?" Eric's accent came out the strongest when he was tired or when he'd just woken up, a soft Georgia drawl that Richard loved.

"Have I ever said no to your hand on my dick?"

"Once or twice," Eric replied, "but it was usually because you wanted your dick in my ass instead."

"That could be arranged this morning," Richard said, but he made no move to roll on top of Eric or even to reach for the lube. They'd done that last night. This morning, a hand job fit better. He shifted enough so he could get a grip on Eric's cock as well. He jacked Eric slowly, matching his movement to the rhythm of Eric's hand on him.

Eric turned his head and nuzzled Richard's chest. The contact didn't demand anything, but the brush of Eric's skin against Richard's overly sensitive nipples made him gasp. "I'm going to wish Dav hadn't told you that, aren't I?"

"I don't know. You weren't complaining last night."

He wasn't complaining now either. Very little turned him on like a hand or mouth on his nipples, even as tender as they were from Eric's attentions last night. "How quickly do you want this to be over? Because if you keep that up, I'm not going to last long."

"I like the sound of that. You're always so in control. I like knowing I can make that crack."

Richard wouldn't regret the times he'd pinned Eric to the bed and fucked him into oblivion over the past few days. They'd both needed the assurance that Eric was home and safe, and Eric had needed to know

Richard wanted him that badly, but now that they'd put those doubts to rest, he could cede control to Eric and let him take him apart at the seams. He could share his tender underbelly. Eric needed that side of him as much as he needed Richard to be in charge, and he needed to see it not just when Dav was around.

"You should have seen me when you were missing," Richard murmured. "Cracked was an understatement."

"Not quite the way I want to make you lose control," Eric replied.

"Then find a better way." Richard bucked into Eric's hand, inviting a more vigorous caress. When Eric tightened his grip and sped up his strokes, Richard didn't even try to hold back the moan that bubbled up inside him. He spent so much of his time as the stoic, badass commander that relaxing the façade wasn't easy, but he'd make the effort for Eric, the same way he made it for Dav.

Promising himself he'd take care of Eric later, he lay back and let Eric do as he pleased, not censoring his reaction or slowing down the swell of arousal in any way. At any other time, he would have been embarrassed by how quickly Eric reduced him to begging with strong, sure strokes and a twist at the end to tease the head of Richard's cock and the constant nuzzles against his nipples, but today, that was the point. He grabbed Eric's head and pulled him up for a kiss, deep and hungry. Eric met him and then delved in to Richard's mouth, taking control of the kiss too. Richard groaned and came hard enough to see stars. He took a moment to catch his breath, then batted Eric's hand away from his own cock. "My turn."

"It won't take much."

Richard grinned and stroked Eric a couple of times until he came in turn. Eric collapsed against him and lay there panting. Richard let the peace of the morning suffuse him for a little longer. Eventually Eric lifted his head. "You have to meet with Westin and Victoria this morning, don't you?"

"I wish I didn't, but I shouldn't put it off any longer."

"Do you want me to stay with you?" Eric asked.

Richard wanted nothing more, but he wouldn't ask that of Eric. "That's up to you, but one of us should go check on Dav. I have to take this meeting, but there's no reason for you to wait for me. Westin is chasing down information from the Pentagon—I'm not convinced they're playing straight with us—and Amato is trying to set up a secure connection to our servers without passing through military channels. Nothing earth-shattering."

"Are you sure? I'll stay if you want."

"I know you would." Richard doubted many things, but he didn't doubt Eric's loyalty. "But I'm sure. If Westin finds anything interesting, I'll tell you and Dav about it later, and you can help me make sense of it. I won't keep any secrets from either of you."

"You won't feel like I'm picking Tim over you?"

"Not at all. Remember that conversation we had yesterday about priorities? You just took amazing care of me. I can handle a few hours without you while I deal with business and you check on Dav. You don't feel like I'm picking work over you, do you?"

Eric shook his head. "You made your priorities pretty damn clear last night."

"This is why there are three of us," Richard said. "It's too much for any two of us to handle, but all three of us? We can handle whatever comes. I can stay here and deal with work because I know you're at the hospital with Dav, and as soon as I'm done, I'll be there to check on you both. And another time, maybe it'll be you or Dav who has to deal with work, but however it plays out, at the end of the day, the job is done and we're all okay, and that's what makes us strong."

"Just as long as you're not the only one who ever gets stuck at work. It's not fair to you, and it's not fair to us if we don't get to see you too."

Richard tilted Eric's chin up to kiss him. "I won't make that mistake again."

TIM LOOKED up when the door opened. He hoped it wasn't Jamie, his physical therapist, coming back to torture him again. He didn't know if he could take another round today, even if she was still the one doing all the work.

Eric stuck his head around the corner and grinned when he saw Tim was awake. Tim returned the smile without hesitation, but he focused on the way Eric walked as he crossed the room, cataloguing the ease of movement.

Eric walked in different ways, depending on the circumstances, and Tim had learned to read them even before they became lovers. He had the focused, deadly stalk that he used in the field, not a wasted movement anywhere, every muscle tense and ready to sprint, a big cat hunting its prey. He had the jaunty, carefree stroll that was reserved for long walks on the beach at home, loose-limbed and relaxed. He had the tired drag of feet after long missions, when countless hours in a sniper's nest had caught up with him and he had no reserves left. And he had the sexy swagger that came out just before or for a few hours after a bout of mind-numbing sex. That was Tim's favorite walk of all because he and Richard had put that swagger in Eric's hips.

To Tim's relief, Eric *swaggered* as he crossed the room, a self-satisfied smile on his face.

"Good night?" Tim asked, not that he needed the confirmation, but he wouldn't complain about getting it.

"Oh, yeah," Eric drawled, the Georgia boy coming out strong in his voice as he spoke. "But you knew that already. You sent us home with orders."

"I had to make sure Richard took care of you right," Tim said, "since I couldn't be there to welcome you home."

Eric's expression darkened for a moment. "You're here now. That's all that matters. And Richard did take care of me. Last night and before that." He ran a hand over his smooth cheeks.

Tim could imagine Richard, straight razor in hand, scraping away the remnants of Eric's captivity. As enticing an image as it was, he regretted not being there to do it himself. He studied Eric's face, seeing the circles beneath his eyes. He might have swaggered into the room, but he wasn't back at peak yet, no matter how well Richard fucked him last night. "Talk to me, Eric."

Eric smiled at the familiar command. Tim had started saying it when he was supervising Eric in the field, and it had become one more little piece of their lexicon, a reminder to Eric that he could confide in Tim, no matter what. In the field, a precise and accurate assessment of the situation was critical to minimize damage and maximize their effectiveness. It had carried over into their private lives, for which Tim was grateful. When all else failed, if he could get Eric to talk to him, he could find a solution for the problem.

"I'm coping," Eric said slowly. "Not terribly well, but I'm trying. I came back to the news you'd nearly died on an op I may have compromised. Before you say it, everyone has told me I couldn't have been the reason it went to hell because it wasn't planned before I was captured, but I'm still not sure they didn't use whatever I might have said against you. I'm having flashbacks and panic attacks, which isn't any real surprise. I've lost twenty pounds, all of it muscle, and can't seem to find the time to start working out to get it back. I'm still bruised, and some of the scars will probably never fade. All in all, it's been a pretty sucky week."

None of that was unexpected, although Tim wouldn't ever wish for any of it to be true. Still, it gave him a baseline. "Are you sleeping?"

"I am now. Richard and I had a bit of a rough start. But my fucked-up subconscious has accepted that I'm safe with him, so other than the night we spent here two nights ago, the last few nights have been better."

"How long have I been out?" Tim felt like he'd asked that already, but the drugs made his memories blurry, and if he'd asked, he couldn't remember the answer.

"A week."

"Do I want to know why the first few nights weren't good?"

"Probably not," Eric said.

"That wasn't the answer I was looking for."

"Yeah, but you aren't going to like the answer I give any better than that one," Eric said.

Tim frowned, but he still had too much pain medicine lingering in his system to suss out what Eric meant. He could ask and Eric would tell him, but judging from the set of his shoulders, it wouldn't be a pleasant conversation. Better to wait for Richard to get here so he could help with any fallout. Speaking of…. "Where is Richard this morning?"

"He'll be here soon. He gave Victoria and Westin jobs to do a couple of days ago and had to take their reports. He'll be here as soon as that's done. He wants to see you."

"I never doubted that," Tim said. "He'll always put duty to his troops over his personal needs. It's part of who he is. It's one of the things I've always loved about him."

Eric looked at him oddly, another thing to add to the growing list of things he couldn't make sense of at the moment. "When you're better, we should talk about that, because some of the problems of the past week might have been avoided if he weren't always the one to work late."

"What do you mean?"

"When you're better," Eric repeated. "I don't want the doctor coming in and yelling at me for raising your blood pressure or whatever. I want you to get well so you can get out of here and come home and we can figure out what happens next."

"Worrying about what you aren't telling me is far worse for my health than whatever you might say," Tim said.

"It's nothing bad. Just… did you know Richard thought I didn't want him the same way I want you?"

Tim blinked a couple of times. He knew he was still foggy, but had Eric really just said—"Why would he think that?"

"I don't know, and he doesn't think it now. But then, I thought the job was more important to him than I was, because he was always working when I needed you both. He told me he stayed at work so you could be with me because it was more important for you to be there than him, but I didn't know that until this week." Eric shuddered visibly. "We made him think he wasn't as important to me as you are. We can't ever do that again."

Tim sank back against the pillows supporting him and ran the conversation back over in his mind. What the hell had happened while he was unconscious to have Eric and Richard thinking such things? Whatever it was, he couldn't get well fast enough, because fixing this from a bed in ICU was beyond even his abilities.

CHAPTER 22

RICHARD'S ARRIVAL distracted Tim from the questions running through his mind. He wasn't sure Richard could give him any clearer answers—who knew what passed for logic in Eric's head sometimes—but given Eric's concerns, Richard would have to be part of any solution. And Tim would be damned if he didn't find a solution to Eric's current mental funk. He still hadn't gotten a straight answer from the doctor about how long it would take him to be back at work, but until he was, he needed Eric and Richard in top form. He needed to be able to rely on them the way they usually relied on him, but Eric was still recovering too, and now he found out there were issues between Eric and Richard.

In a word, fuck.

Richard was harder to read than Eric, no matter how long Tim had known him, but for once, he wasn't trying to hide anything. He was angry. Absolutely fucking pissed off.

"I'd ask how the meeting went, but I don't think I want to know," Tim said mildly.

"Stupid motherfuckers at the Pentagon," Richard ground out. It was a familiar refrain. From the beginning, Richard had had a love-hate relationship with the commanding officers from the Pentagon. By definition, Strike Force Omega took the jobs the Pentagon couldn't do. The ones that needed that step away from the US military, either because they were in areas where they couldn't operate openly or because they were so risky where public opinion was concerned that they needed deniability. Tim had seen enough of the gritty underbelly of human society in the SEALs to accept the need for teams that could operate in that muck without dragging anyone official into it. They'd created Strike Team Omega precisely to take those missions. They'd had a decent working relationship founded on mutual respect with their current contact's predecessor. Tim wouldn't go so far as to say they trusted the man, but they'd believed he had enough respect for them not to lie to their faces. Then he'd retired, and the man who took over his position—Collins—had rubbed them the wrong way from day one.

"What did Collins do this time?"

Richard tossed a dossier on Tim's knees. "That's what Westin put together. If even a single piece of it is accurate, Collins sent Eric into a trap and nearly killed you. The problem is I can't prove any of it. Collins will deny it, and even if he didn't, what the hell are we supposed to do if it's true?"

"I'll read it later. Tell me what he said," Tim said as Eric grabbed the file and started flipping through it. Tim would read it, as promised, but it wasn't the words on the page that mattered. He needed Richard's impression of the messenger. Tim knew Westin, of course. He even liked the man. He was definitely a cut above any other Pentagon liaison they'd had, and if Westin was helping them, then he wasn't in league with Collins.

Richard ran a hand over his close-cropped black hair and paced the room, a caged animal looking for any way to escape. If anyone other than Eric had been in the room with them, Tim would have schooled his expression to blandness, but Eric wouldn't care how turned on Richard's harnessed power made him. It had the same effect on Eric.

"He believes every word in here," Richard said after a moment. "That doesn't make them true, but he trusts his sources."

"That's worth something," Tim said. "He's not an idiot. He's not going to feed us false information knowingly. If he trusts the people who gave him the information, there's a decent chance it's accurate."

"The problem is that none of it's conclusive. As a collection of information, it's damning, but there's no smoking gun."

"If there were, we'd have realized there was a problem a long time ago."

Eric closed the folder. "What happens now?"

"Nothing," Richard said, waving aside Eric's spluttered protest. "Nothing yet, anyway. As damning as it is, it's not enough. We lay low for now. Dav's injuries give us an excuse. We accept the occasional milk run, nothing we wouldn't have given to Heikkinen before this. Enough to keep the communication channels open and money trickling in, but nothing that commits us to anything dangerous. And we watch, we listen, and we look for corroboration. We need a smoking gun if we're going to march into Washington and demand that things change."

"We watch, we listen, and we heal," Tim agreed. He looked from Richard to Eric and back. "And not just me. From the sound of what Eric was saying before you arrived, I'm not the only one hurting."

Richard turned a tormented gaze on Eric, making Tim curse under his breath. "Not Eric," Tim specified. "You."

"I'm fine."

"Really?" Tim pressed. "You didn't spend the past four months worrying about Eric only to watch me get shot as you were trying to rescue him, and then have to manage his recovery as well as mine all while dealing with doubts about Collins? Because I'm thinking of the three of us, you have the most cause for a breakdown right about now."

"I don't have time for a breakdown," Richard said.

"Like breakdowns care about things like that," Tim replied. "You gonna tell me what's going on?"

"Not if you're slurring like that," Richard said. "You're still drugged. You won't remember this tomorrow."

"I'm not that drugged," Tim said. "I haven't had any morphine since last night. I'm tired, but I'm not drugged."

"Then you should be," Richard replied. "Yesterday you were still unconscious. You need your pain meds."

"Not your call to make," Tim replied easily. "You're trying to change the subject, and it's not going to work. What's going on?"

"What isn't going on?" Richard asked. "Eric was captured on what should have been a routine recon op. You were shot on what was sold to us as a basic in and out, blow up a bunch of buildings mission. I've fucked up all but the last three days, and the only reason I didn't fuck that up is because Amato knows my lover better than I do. And on top of everything else, I'm still not entirely sure this isn't a bid on Heikkinen's part to replace me."

Tim took a moment to digest all of that, but it was too much at once. "Maybe I am too loopy for this still."

Eric crossed the room and wrapped his arms around Richard. "You concentrate on getting well," he told Tim. "I can take care of Richard for a little while."

"I'm not going to forget this. Whatever the problem is, we're going to solve it. All three of us. I refuse to let anything tear us apart," Tim said.

"It won't," Richard said. "If anything it'll make us stronger. Isn't that what you always say? We're stronger together than we could ever be in any other combination?"

It was exactly what he said, but something felt off, and he hated not knowing what had changed. "You're still going to talk to me because something is not right."

The door opened, and the doctor came in. Richard and Eric separated, although not enough to pretend they hadn't been embracing before she entered. "Ah, good, you're both here and Mr. Davenport is awake. I can update you all at once."

Tim might have protested her timing, but really they could all use a break. "How long until I can go home?" Tim asked.

"Let's walk before you run, Mr. Davenport," the doctor said with a smile. "You still have a drainage tube in your chest, and your physical therapist still has to move your legs to work the muscles."

"I didn't expect the answer to be tomorrow," Tim replied, "but a ballpark figure would be appreciated."

"Nothing I told you would be anything more than a guess at best. We've clamped the chest tube that was draining air and fluid around your collapsed lung. If your X-rays stay clear, we will remove the tube tomorrow and can downgrade you to a regular room instead of ICU. If they don't stay clear, we'll unclamp it and try again in a few days. You are incredibly fit, even given your service record, and your recovery has stayed at the top end of the curve, but that doesn't mean we can afford to rush it. You have a long, hard road ahead of you even if every step goes as well as the first few have. It's going to be weeks before you can walk at all, months before you'll be able to leave behind the walker. You may always have a limp, and even if you manage not to need a cane, you will have aches and stiffness you never had before. You can't take multiple gunshot wounds to the legs and have a knee completely blown out without long-term effects."

Tim had been peripherally aware of most of the list the doctor rattled off at him, although hearing it laid out so bluntly was disheartening. He took a deep breath, glanced at Eric and Richard for strength, and asked again, "How long before I can go home? Best case."

"A week, ten days, best case," the doctor said with a put-upon sigh. "If you have someone who can help you in and out of bed and into a wheelchair and if you are close enough to come in for daily PT sessions."

"We have a house on Ramstein," Richard said, "and we can arrange for one or both of us to be there round the clock if necessary. We can't provide skilled nursing, but we can bring him back here as often as you—or anyone else—needs to see him."

"I will keep that in mind," the doctor said. "But I won't be bullied into signing release orders until I'm convinced it won't do Mr. Davenport more harm than good."

"Sleeping in a real bed can't do anything but good for me." Sleeping in his lovers' arms couldn't do anything but good for him, but Tim wasn't sure how much the doctor suspected, and even if she'd guessed, there was suspecting and then there was knowing. They might not be military anymore, but he saw no reason to make their lives more complicated.

"Somehow I don't think it's the bed you're concerned about," she said with a pointed glance toward Eric and Richard. "I'll just remind you that doctor-patient confidentiality applies even in the military."

That took care of anything she suspected, but Tim wouldn't out them without talking to Richard and Eric about it first. They'd always been careful to be discreet, although that seemed to have slipped somewhat while Tim was unconscious. Another thing he needed to figure out before he went back to work. If the old rules no longer applied, he wanted to go in prepared. Don't Ask, Don't Tell might be a thing of the past, but attitudes often changed more slowly than regulations, especially in the old guard. "I'm sorry, Doctor. I don't remember your name. I was a little out of it yesterday when we met."

"Smithers," she said as she checked the morphine levels on his pump. "When was the last time you had any pain medication?"

"Last night before I went to sleep," Tim said. "I can't concentrate when I use it, so I don't unless I need to sleep."

Smithers frowned at him and pressed the button. "You need to sleep. You need to heal. Pain takes a toll on the body independent of the injuries that cause the pain. You say you want to go home, but if you aren't going to manage your pain so you can heal, it will take longer."

"Is there something else I could take?" Tim asked. "Something that won't leave me feeling so out of it?"

"Nothing that will be as effective with fewer side effects for the moment," Smithers replied, "but if you continue to improve, we can look at other options in a few days. Gentlemen, Mr. Davenport needs his rest. You can stay, but don't disturb him."

"We won't," Eric said, not that Tim would have let them leave. He hadn't seen Eric in four months. He wasn't letting him out of his sight until he had no other choice.

"I'll rest better knowing they're here," Tim told Smithers. She didn't look convinced, but she finished checking his vitals and left them alone.

Tim could feel the morphine kicking in, both from the decrease in the pain that hadn't gone away since he regained consciousness the day before and from the way everything around him seemed to blur, like he was underwater. He reached for Eric and Richard, needing the touch of their hands to ground him. They came to either side of the bed and twined their fingers with his. He smiled woozily as they reached across the bed and completed the circle.

He closed his eyes because the room was spinning, and let the sound of their quiet conversation lull him. They sounded at ease with each other, he realized after a few minutes. If someone had asked him an hour ago, he wouldn't have said they were uncomfortable around each other after the first few weeks of adjustment when they'd first gotten together, but hearing them now, he could tell a difference. Had he kept them apart without intending to? He'd had such grand plans for their triad, and in more ways than he could count, the past four years had proven that he'd underestimated how good they could be together. Now, though, he wondered if there were fault lines he couldn't see. He tried to force his eyes open, but his eyelids had gotten heavy. He was warm, and Eric and Richard were holding his hands, and really, he couldn't do anything about his concerns now except watch and listen and learn for the future.

Chapter 23

"I'm no intelligence expert, but this looks off to me," Eric said after Dav had fallen asleep from the morphine.

"Tell me what you see." Richard had learned to rely on Eric's grasp of strategy in the field even before they were lovers. Eric had a gift for seeing ways in and out of situations or of turning situations to their advantage that had saved their asses more than once, but that was mission based. How best to take out a target with minimal collateral damage. How best to stage a rescue—or a coup—and get the hell out of Dodge. How best to neutralize an enemy position with the least risk to the infiltrating team. Give him a situation and a goal, and he had ten different plans fully formed in a matter of minutes.

This wasn't mission work. This was intelligence gathering in its purest—or most bastardized—form. He'd always turned to Heikkinen for that and to Dav if Heikkinen wasn't around. He could call her in on this now, and would when he had a better grasp of it himself, but this had the potential of being too big to trust to anyone but his lovers until he knew what it meant and what he intended to do about it.

"Lots of little things," Eric said, flipping through the pages. "Here, for example. This says the installation in Syria is military, but these photos show women and children. Now, I'm no expert on the guerrilla tactics of all the different jihadists—and even religious fanatics have to eat—but that doesn't look purely military to me."

"No, it doesn't."

"So you think they played down the possibility of civilians in order to convince us to take the op."

"The thought had occurred."

Eric tapped his finger against the photo. "Okay, devil's advocate time. We know the Daesh has captured and enslaved women as sex slaves. Depending on how long they've been held, those could be children of rape."

"Would they keep those children on a military outpost, though?"

"They'd be considered unclean because they were born bastards, and they'd be completely isolated from any outside influences. They could raise them as child soldiers and use them as suicide bombers in a few years. Some of them look like they're about to be old enough."

Richard shuddered at the matter-of-fact tone of Eric's voice. None of what he had said was wrong or even far-fetched, but fighting this kind of horror was the reason Richard had joined the Navy, the SEALs, and eventually founded Strike Force Omega. No child deserved to be the victim of that kind of indoctrination. "Okay, suppose you're right. Yes, there are women and children, but it's still a military training camp. The children are child soldiers, and the women are either volunteers or sex slaves. How does it impact the op?"

"What was the objective?" Eric asked. "I don't recognize this one."

"That was Dav's op in Syria, the one that nearly got him killed."

Eric's frown deepened. "You think they sent him into a trap?"

"I don't know. I'd like to think it wasn't an actual trap. The mission objective was to assassinate a Daesh leader and do as much damage to the installation as possible."

"The assassination part wouldn't be affected by the second photo. A good sniper can take out a single man on a crowded street and never touch anyone else."

"Yeah, well, you weren't around to ask for help," Richard joked. Eric grinned at him, a much better reaction than the other times his captivity had come up.

"Who did you send in my place?"

"We didn't. We weren't worried about collateral damage. We were trying to cause it. The plan was to get in unnoticed, plant explosives in as many of the buildings as possible, and then take out as many enemy combatants in the ensuing chaos as we could."

"Not a bad plan. What went wrong?"

"That's really a question for Dav. One minute everything was going according to plan. The next the team was taking fire and Dav went down. Heikkinen debriefed with the rest of the team, and they all reported nothing unusual, nothing out of place, nothing to warn them of any impending problems."

Eric shook his head. "Something went wrong. Somebody stepped on a cat or kicked over a bucket or something. Even if it was just a guard running late or early on his route around the camp. Unless it was booby-trapped, but why would they do that if they didn't know we were coming? Did they get the guy they were after?"

"No, they hadn't gotten far enough into the compound to find him when they had to retreat."

"So we don't even know if he was there."

"If he wasn't, why send us in? Why give us that objective?"

"To stir up trouble."

"That's an awfully big leap from a photo of women and children in the compound. You're going to have to give me more than that if you want to sell me on the idea."

"It was a guess," Eric replied. "You said why would they do it. I gave you an answer. Maybe not the right answer. Just an answer."

"An answer isn't enough for me to renegotiate our contract with the Pentagon. It has to be *the* answer with proof."

"Then let's see what else Westin got for us. Proof of my answer might not be in there, but maybe proof of an answer is."

"I DON'T know how intelligence people do it," Eric said an hour later. "None of this is proof of anything, not really. It's all suggestive but that's it."

"They make predictions," Richard replied. "They look at everything that is or could be suggested by what they have to go on, and they draw the best possible conclusion they can based on it."

"Give me solid field strategy any day. This would drive me insane."

"You say that, but they aren't as different as you think they are. You've spent enough time in the field to have a sense of what things mean. And a different perspective is always a good thing."

"The problem I'm seeing is that if we didn't have any of this information as we were planning the ops, then we were going in half-blind. If they didn't have it to give to us, fine. We always go in at least a little blind unless there's someone on the inside because things change from the time surveillance pictures are taken to the time our boots hit the ground. That's why we never go in with just one plan. But if they're withholding information from us, that's different. That's setting us up to fail. That's setting us up to get captured or killed."

And that was the piece that was totally unacceptable to Richard. His teams took risks. That was part of the job. To send them in without the most complete information available was unethical.

"Then that's the conversation we need to have with Collins," Richard said.

"Good luck with that."

"Don't think you're getting out of it. You're as much a part of this as Dav and I are."

Eric shook his head. "Oh no, you're not putting that on me. I don't do military bigwigs."

"You're part of this team. I let you forget it once. Or maybe I forgot it. I'm not doing that again. I'm used to relying on you in the field, but for all your complaints, you've made good suggestions today too. If Dav doesn't recover enough to take missions again, you'll have to step up and do his job in the field."

"You wouldn't do that to me, would you?" Eric whined.

Richard laughed. "You'll be brilliant at it."

"Only if Tim can't. I never wanted a leadership role."

"You should have thought about that before you made yourself indispensable to the leaders."

"Indispensable?"

Richard swallowed hard. He'd told Eric he loved him. He'd told him how hard it was, knowing he was captured and being tortured, hoping he was alive but never knowing for sure. He hadn't told him the rest.

"The voices in my head are different than the ones in yours, but I have them too." He rose from the chairs they'd been sitting on to pace Dav's hospital room. "My grandfather trained in Tuskegee. He flew with the Red Tails during World War Two. He didn't talk about it much, but the one thing he would say was that they never lost a bomber. If they flew out on a protection detail, the planes they were escorting flew home. Maybe the fighters didn't, but the plane they were protecting sure as hell did. You can imagine what my grandfather's voice in my head had to say about you getting captured and it taking us four months to find you."

"And then Tim got shot."

"That didn't make the voices worse, though, because even when I thought he'd died, the team was bringing him home. We didn't bring you home. For four fucking months, we didn't bring you home."

It had eaten at him, a canker sore on his mind and heart, making everything painful. He couldn't eat without worrying if Eric had food, couldn't sleep without hoping Eric was allowed to rest, couldn't shower without imagining the squalor of a small cell. "I think the only reason Dav put up with me was because he was hurting too much at losing you to tell me to fuck the hell off. I spent the whole time you were gone in a fury. If it weren't for Dav smoothing things over, you wouldn't have had an organization to come back to."

"I don't give a fuck about the organization. I only care about you and Tim. Is there anything I can do to make things better? After everything you did to help me."

"You already did. You walked off that plane into my arms and you let me hold you until I believed you were safe again." The nightmares still came and probably always would, but they weren't new. They just had a new variation on the theme. Waking to Eric safe in bed next to him took much of the venom out of their bite.

"We need to get Tim home. As glad as I am that we cleared up the misunderstandings these past few days, there's still this hole where Tim is supposed to be."

"Not long now, I hope. And until then, we can spend our days here with him. Amato worked her tech magic so I can access what I need to without going through the servers on base. We'll keep combing through this, figure out what questions still need answers. We'll put together a plan of action, and when Dav is up and about again, we'll go to Washington and get this straightened out."

"I still think you'd be better off going without me, but if you want me there, I'll be there," Eric grumbled. "Just don't complain when I fuck it up because I don't know all the military protocol."

"If that's the reason it gets fucked up, nothing we could say would make any difference anyway," Richard replied. "It's nearly noon. I don't know how much morphine Smithers gave Dav, but he should be out for at least another hour. Let's find something to eat. We can discuss the rest when he wakes up."

WHEN TIM woke, he found Eric and Richard in exactly the same spots they'd been in when he fell asleep. "Did you move at all?"

"We went out to have lunch and everything," Eric said. "You should be proud of us."

Tim rolled his eyes at them. "Should've gone home."

"Nah, we wanted to be here with you. It's been too long since we've all been together. If you can't come home yet, then we'll stay here with you as much as we can. Somebody has to make sure you follow doctor's orders, and we all know it won't be Eric."

"Hey! I'm not that bad."

"Yes, you are," Richard and Tim said at the same time. Eric pulled his hands away and pouted at them. Tim reached for him, but Richard was faster—not to mention better able to move. Tim watched with growing fascination as Richard wrapped his arms around Eric and murmured something Tim couldn't hear in his ear. Whatever Richard had said, it worked because Eric positively melted in his arms. Tim tried to remember the last time he'd seen Eric cede ground, even teasing ground, that quickly. He'd have to ask Richard what he said later, and that left him feeling once again like the world had shifted without him.

"I could lie here and watch the two of you together all day," Tim said because he had to lead up to the questions burning his tongue or he wouldn't get any answers, much less the real ones.

"Until you get clearance to get out of that bed, that's all you're going to do, unless you want to see what you make of this dossier," Richard said without letting go of Eric. "We've gone through some of it, but you were on the ground in Syria. You have a perspective we don't."

"Is anything in there going to change the next twenty-four hours?" Tim asked.

"No, I've already told Collins we aren't taking any big missions again until you're well enough to help coordinate them. He wasn't happy, but being able to choose our own missions was one of the reasons we went independent." Tim studied Richard's expression and the way Eric seemed to shrink into his arms.

"Is he trying to manipulate us into taking missions we'd refuse otherwise?" Tim asked.

"It's certainly a possibility. Or else his intelligence apparatus sucks."

"Paper pushers who wouldn't know field experience if it bit them in the ass and so don't know how to actually judge what we need to know," Tim mused. "It's still a problem, just a different one."

"And either one is a problem for later," Richard said.

Wasn't that interesting? Richard never voluntarily changed the subject when he had a problem to solve. It took an act of God to divert him most times, although Tim and Eric had occasionally managed to distract him with sex. Then again, Tim had compared Eric to a god more than once, so maybe that was the same thing.

He shook himself. He was obviously still drugged. "You two are… different around each other."

Eric winced, and Tim kicked himself silently. He hadn't meant to cause Eric to shut down.

"Let's just say we've come to a better understanding of each other over the past few days," Richard replied. He pressed a kiss to the side of

Eric's neck, drawing Tim's attention to a bruise there that Tim had assumed came from his captivity, but now he wondered. Richard never left marks where they'd be visible. They'd spent too many years hiding in plain sight to take that risk, even now when there was no chain of command to protest their homosexuality or to accuse them of fraternization.

"You can say that, but I'm going to need more detail, please. Talk to me, Eric."

Eric sent him a pleading look that almost made Tim relent, but if he did, this tension would keep festering and he'd be no closer to a solution. "When I left on the Syria op, you were still in the hands of a terrorist group, and Richard was still on a rampage the likes of which no one will forget anytime soon. I wake up a week later to the sight of the two of you kissing. Most beautiful thing I've seen in a long time, but not what I would have predicted even if I'd known the rescue op was a success. And then this morning while I was still worried about how you were coping with having gone through hell, you were worrying about Richard. I'm not complaining about the changes. I just need to catch up so I can play ball by the new rules."

"We both realized how much of the work we'd let you do in this relationship," Richard said. "We decided it was time we both started pulling our own weight."

"Oh, for fuck's sake, stop dancing around the subject and speak English."

Eric snickered and looked up at Richard. "You made Tim curse."

"Jesus Christ, you two are ridiculous," Tim said, but he couldn't stop the smile that spread at Eric's comment. "I was a sailor too, you know. I know as many swear words as Richard does."

"You just don't usually use them," Richard said. "Eric is right about that part. We aren't trying to hide anything from you, Dav. It's been a rough week. We both fucked up more than once, and it's not something we're eager to relive even in talking about it. As for new rules, it's nothing like that. Just Eric and me making an effort to take care of each other instead of always assuming you'll be the one to take care of whoever needs it. He had to tell me you always shaved him after a bad mission. I never knew. I don't ever want anything to happen to you, but I need to know how to help when you can't, and I need to know my help is welcome, even when you're around too. That's what's different."

"I didn't think Richard really wanted me," Eric picked up when Richard was finished. "I thought with you out of commission, I was a burden, nothing more. I need you both so much, but I didn't think the request would be appreciated, so I tried to manage on my own. I had such a bad panic attack that I nearly ran. I think I would have if I could have gotten my feet underneath me before Victoria found me. Richard and I had a long talk after that and cleared up some misconceptions on both our parts. Maybe he doesn't know everything you know yet, but he's paying attention."

"You always say we're strongest together," Richard said. "I know that's true, but any tripod will fall if one of its legs is weak. We didn't realize how weak our link was until it was tested."

Tim was pretty sure his fondest dreams had just come true.

CHAPTER 24

"COME BACK at dinnertime," Smithers ordered on Tuesday morning. "You've spent every waking hour here. You need a break. Both of you. He'll be in PT and then moving to a regular room."

Eric started to argue, but he wouldn't win. Reluctantly he followed Richard out of the hospital. "What are we supposed to do until dinner?"

"I should probably check in with Heikkinen," Richard said. "You're welcome to join me. You'll have to get used to working with her if you're going to take on some of Dav's responsibilities."

"No way," Eric said through his laughter. "Nobody wants that, including me. I can find something to do to keep myself busy. Maybe I'll go for a run. I don't know when I was last as lazy as I've been this week."

"It's not laziness when you're recovering from torture," Richard said.

"I have to start building back up my stamina," Eric insisted.

Richard parked the car in front of their temporary quarters. "Just don't push so hard you end up in a bed beside Dav. That won't help anyone."

Eric smiled and leaned over to kiss Richard before going inside for a bottle of water. He needed to get back in shape, but Richard was right that he wasn't helping anyone if he made himself sick in the process.

When he came back out, Richard had already gone. Eric brushed aside the tendril of unease that curled through his stomach. He'd been invited to go with Richard and had declined. Richard wasn't picking work over him.

He started out at an easy jog, letting his muscles warm up and get used to the motion again. He passed a few people as he ran and was passed by others. He tried to focus on the run and nothing else, but the thought of Richard giving him command duties wouldn't leave him alone. He knew nothing about command. Sure, he could look at a situation and see options for how to make the best of it, but that wasn't command. That was just… tactics.

He picked up the pace, hoping the increased exertion would distract him, but he couldn't outrun his own thoughts. Half of Strike Force Omega wouldn't work with him even under Tim's command. How did Richard expect him to take Tim's place? They'd laugh in his face, and then Richard or Tim would have to step in to keep everything from going to hell, and that wouldn't do anything for Eric's supposed authority. His pulse pounded in his ears as he imagined the reaction from Taylor and some of the team that had gone with Tim into Syria. Nobody had called him half-breed since Tim and Victoria had kicked a couple of people's asses, but that didn't mean they respected Eric, only that they kept their opinions to places they wouldn't be overheard.

It would be complete chaos, and now that everyone knew the three of them were lovers, it would ruin Richard's and Tim's authority too.

"Next time the voices start, think of this moment, right now, and remember what I tell you."

Eric clung to the memory of Richard's voice in his ear as he'd fucked Eric until he couldn't think, much less move. *"We want you. We love you. We need you."*

He had to trust Richard to know what he was doing. He was aware of Eric's problems. He knew the people on his team. He wouldn't set Eric up to fail. He'd send him out in command of people he could work with. *"You think I don't see you, Eric Newton, but I do. I'm not blind to your faults. You're still the best thing I've ever seen."*

Yes, Richard had said those things. He had to focus on Richard's words, not his own doubts. Richard believed in him. He had to believe in himself. He had to let go of the past and move forward. He had to be the man Richard saw when he looked at Eric.

He was so fucked.

"How LONG have you been here?" Richard asked when he finally tracked Eric down in the gym on base.

Eric finished a set of reps and wiped down the machine. "Since you went into your meeting. I went for a run, and then I came here to lift weights. I've got to get back into shape if you're going to foist Tim's command off on me."

That hadn't been Richard's intent when he told Eric his plans. "If you pull a muscle lifting weights your first day back, that's going to be a lot harder to recover from than a little weight loss."

"I haven't strained anything. I know my body's limits."

Richard refrained from pointing out that Eric's limits were different than usual, what with having been imprisoned for months. He didn't want to antagonize Eric, just convince him to take a break. "If you're done, I thought we could spend a couple of hours working on your bow. It looked like it was going to need more than just being restrung."

"The wood is old and weathered. It needs to be cleaned and oiled, probably sanded down a bit, and then I have to decide if I can leave the natural wood or if I need to varnish it. That would decrease its value as an antique but probably increase my ability to actually shoot it."

"Let's go find what you need and get started."

ERIC SET down the cloth he'd been using to spread mineral spirits on the bow. He couldn't decide if it was just filthy or if someone had stained or even painted it at some point, but either way, restoring it wasn't going to be a one-day process. His arms and back hurt. He'd told Richard he knew his limits, but he'd pushed hard today, and he was paying for it now.

"Done for now?" Richard asked as he set the beer he'd gone to find in front of Eric.

"Yeah. It won't hurt it to sit, and I need a break." He stretched his arms over his head and groaned at the pull of sore muscles.

"It sounds like you need more than just a break," Richard teased. "Are you stiff?"

"A little. It felt so good to work out, but I may have overdone it a little."

"I could give you a massage if you want," Richard offered. "Probably not as good as a professional one, but I've picked up a few things here and there over the years."

Richard's hands on his bare skin, rubbing him down, helping him relax.... "Sounds like heaven."

"Go lie down on the bed. Take off as much as you want. I'll find some lotion to use and meet you there in a minute."

Eric put the bow away carefully—it was an amazing specimen—and headed into the bedroom. He stripped his shirt off, groaning at the way his muscles pulled. He bent to undo his boots and groaned again. He'd focused on his upper body because those were the muscles he needed to draw his bow, but he'd apparently done a number on more than just his lats. In for a penny, in for a pound. He stripped off the rest of his clothes and stretched out on his stomach. Richard would undoubtedly have something to say about his bare ass when he came in, but it wasn't like he hadn't seen it before.

"Oh, is it going to be that kind of massage?" Richard said when he came in a few moments later.

"No, but it seemed silly to leave my shorts on for modesty's sake. Neither of us has any."

"True." Eric heard the squelch of a lotion pump and braced for the cold cream against his skin, but when Richard touched his shoulders, the lotion was warm from his hands. "If I use too much pressure, let me know. I want this to feel good, not to hurt."

Eric nodded into the pillow. He had a pretty high pain tolerance, so he didn't expect to have anything hurt, but he was still bruised in places and scabbed over in others. Richard smoothed his hand down Eric's back with enough pressure to cause his spine to crack in a couple of places. Each time it did, Eric relaxed a little more as the stiffness eased. He closed his eyes and concentrated on the feeling of Richard touching him, long, slow strokes of his hands, forearms, even his elbows digging sure and steady into his aching muscles. With each pass, the knots faded a little, lulling Eric into a state of blissed-out peace. He hadn't realized how sore he was, not just from the workout but in general, until the muscles started to unclench. Richard moved on to Eric's legs, giving them the same thorough attention, although using less pressure. Eric sighed and sank deeper into the bed, every muscle heavy now. He yelped when Richard hit a particularly sore spot on the side of his right thigh.

"Sciatic nerve. I'll be careful." Richard eased up on the pressure after that, although even the lighter pressure still sent sparks of pain down Eric's leg. He tensed in surprise when Richard moved up to his ass and pressed down on the thick muscle there. The pain spiked, then eased, leaving Eric gasping. "Where did you learn that?"

"A particularly good massage therapist in Thailand," Richard said. "But you have to trust your masseur enough to let him put his hands on your ass, and a lot of people don't have that kind of relationship with the person who does their body work."

Eric wouldn't know. He'd never had a regular masseur and had only rarely gotten massages at all. Although if Richard was offering, Eric would sure as hell take him up on it. Anything that got Richard's hands on his body was a good thing, as far as Eric was concerned. The fact that he was so much more relaxed was a bonus. Richard switched to the other side of Eric's body and worked the same spot on the opposite cheek. It wasn't nearly as sore, leaving Eric free to focus on the sensual slide of Richard's skin against his own. He shifted on the bed to make room for his awakening erection.

"I'm not hurting you, am I?" Richard asked.

"Not at all." Eric arched a little, inviting Richard's caress again. "Keep going."

Richard chuckled and swept his hands down the backs of Eric's thighs and then back up between them, grazing his balls in passing. Eric hissed with pleasure and waited to see what Richard would do next. He repeated the same caress several more times before growing bolder on the return stroke and sliding his fingers into Eric's crease. Eric spread his legs in silent invitation. The next time Richard slid his hands down only as far as the tops of Eric's thighs and made no pretense of continuing the massage when he drew his fingertips over Eric's entrance.

It would have been so easy to press up into those wandering fingers, draw them inside him, and let Richard make love to him again as he'd done over the past few days, but Richard's words from the day before echoed in his head. "Eric and me making the effort to take care of each other...." They'd been exactly what Eric needed to hear, but in the silence of his own heart, he knew he'd done a lot more taking than caring. He'd needed the reassurance of Richard holding him tight, pressing him into the mattress, driving into him. He'd needed to be wrapped up so tightly in a cocoon of Richard's love that he couldn't doubt his welcome, and after the false start, Richard had given him that and more.

Now it was his turn to give to Richard. He rolled onto his back.

"My turn?"

"I'm not the one who worked himself too hard in the gym today," Richard said.

"That's not what I meant." Eric hooked a hand around Richard's neck and pulled him down into a kiss. "Let me make love to you for a change?"

"Anytime you want."

"That's a dangerous offer," Eric teased as he propped himself up on an elbow. "You're a sexy bastard when you're giving a briefing."

"You can fuck me as soon as it's over," Richard said.

That thought finished what Richard's hands had started—Eric was hard as a rock. "I'm going to take you up on that. Just wait and see."

"I'm looking forward to it already."

Eric sat up the rest of the way and went to work on the buttons on Richard's shirt. Once he got that off, he pushed at Richard's shoulders, urging him to lie down. Richard went easily enough, his willingness to follow Eric's lead its own turn-on. God, he could sit here and stare at Richard all day. Acres and acres of smooth skin spread out over rock-hard muscle, all just waiting for him to enjoy. He could sit and stare, but touching and tasting would be even better. He stroked Richard's collarbone with one finger, watching goose bumps rise beneath his touch. Richard lay still, all coiled tension and pent-up need, and let Eric touch. His own blood ran hot from the massage and from Richard's eyes on him now. And judging from the bulge in Richard's pants, he wasn't far behind. He unbuckled Richard's belt quickly. "Lift up."

Richard lifted his hips so Eric could push his pants down to his knees. Eric grinned at the contrast of tight, white cotton against his skin and trailed a finger up the curve of Richard's cock. "That has to be uncomfortable."

"You could take it off," Richard retorted.

"I could. Or I could leave it on a little longer." He bent swiftly and sucked on the tip of Richard's erection through the cloth. If Tim were here, he'd accuse Eric of being a tease, but Eric wasn't teasing. He had every intention of following through, just in his own time. Richard threaded his fingers into Eric's hair, holding him in place, so Eric sucked a little harder. Richard moaned and tightened his fingers, a grip that a week ago might have sent Eric straight into a fight-or-flight mode. Now, it just drove him on.

He worked his hand beneath the placket to find silky skin. He could draw it out more, but he really wanted Richard's cock in his mouth and then his own cock in Richard's ass, and neither of those things would happen with clothing in the way. He sat up and finished pulling off Richard's clothes. "Where do you want me to suck you? Your dick or your ass? Or your nipples? What would make you feel the best?"

"You want me to make decisions?" Richard complained.

"I want you to feel good," Eric replied. "What do you want?"

"Anything you do will feel good."

"Richard." Eric's voice betrayed his exasperation, but he was determined to do this right, and that meant giving Richard what he wanted, not what Eric felt like doing.

"Surprise me."

That so wasn't helpful. Eric took a moment to think back over the times they'd had sex over the past few days and the things that had made Richard react the most strongly. The one thing he'd asked for specifically that first time was for Eric to rim him. And he'd gone absolutely wild when Eric played with his nipples. He couldn't do both at the same time, but he could warm up with one and then switch to the other. And he could definitely have a second go at Richard's nipples while he was inside him. "Roll over."

Richard rolled onto his stomach with his knees tucked under him so his beautiful bubble butt was in the air, right where Eric could get at it. "You're too good to me."

He buried his face in Richard's ass, reveling in the warmth of his skin and the smell of his musk. He wanted to just crawl inside Richard and stay there for a while. Given the impossibility of that desire, he'd settle for tasting instead. He licked across Richard's hole, loving the way Richard gasped and pushed into his touch. Yes, this was the right choice.

He licked and sucked and nibbled until Richard was dripping onto the bed below, and his own erection throbbed like a toothache. He lifted his head finally and rolled Richard onto his back again. "So I can see your face."

Richard lay back and stroked himself while Eric got a condom on and coated it in lube. "Are you stretched enough?"

"I guess we'll find out," Richard replied. Eric wasn't sure he liked that answer, but Richard was tugging on his hips insistently, so Eric moved between his thighs and lined up. Richard's muscle stretched around him as he pushed inside, hot and tight, but not resisting. He kept close watch on Richard's face for any sign that he was going too fast and hurting Richard. Eric could live with any number of things, but knowingly hurting Richard was not one of them.

Richard's face was the perfect picture of ecstasy.

When Eric was as deep inside Richard as he could go, he paused for a moment to give them both a chance to catch their breaths. Richard opened his eyes, his gaze dark with need. Eric grinned rakishly and reached over to tweak one of Richard's nipples.

"Fu-uck," Richard breathed brokenly. His muscles clenched around Eric's cock, sending a fresh wave of lust sparking along his nerves. He rocked his hips experimentally as he played with Richard's nipple. Richard's hips stuttered against his as a moan escaped Richard's mouth. Eric smiled. Damn, this was fun! Why hadn't he found this out sooner?

He settled in to play, thrusting just enough to keep them both on edge without pushing them over and alternating between Richard's nipples whenever one arm got tired of holding him up. Richard writhed on the bed beneath him, curses and pleas mixing together with Eric's name into a string of babble that pushed every one of Eric's buttons.

His own control nearing its end, he thrust harder, pulling back more each time until he was pounding into Richard with all his strength. Richard egged him on with each stroke. Eric fought back the climax bubbling up in his balls until he felt the spasms of Richard's orgasm start. He rode out the waves of their release and collapsed forward onto Richard's chest.

Richard wrapped his arms around Eric's shoulders and held on tight. Eric wanted to protest that he was supposed to be the one doing the holding, but he felt far too good to move.

CHAPTER 25

TIM SMILED as Eric walked into his hospital room the next morning. He had the same swagger as the day before, loose-limbed and sated, but the smile was different. Eric had two modes after an op—the clingy, postdisaster, "reassure-me" mode and the cocky, "I survived, let me prove it to the world" mode. Both modes led to spectacular sex, but one made him a greedy bottom and the other an insatiable top. He'd been in greedy-bottom mode when Tim had seen him last, still seeking reassurance that the world hadn't ended, but that had disappeared. Tim loved this look on him. It always—*always*—resulted in the kind of mind-emptying orgasm that left Tim boneless and unable to remember anything but Eric's name. He envied Richard. Tim was usually the one who benefited from Eric's world righting itself after his stress wore off.

"You look well rested," Tim said.

Eric grinned at him, an expression that had Tim squirming even in his half-drugged state. He'd had a very pointed conversation with the doctor, and she saw no reason why he would suffer any side effects other than the current limits on his movements. Tim was tempted to lure Eric closer and convince him to share a little of that smirk. He couldn't move his legs easily on his own yet, but his hands worked just fine.

The door opened again and Richard came in. Eric's grin widened as he turned to welcome Richard into the room. Tim watched for the telltale hitch in Richard's step. Yep, there it was. "Looks like somebody got lucky last night."

"Somebody might have," Eric agreed. "Depends on how you define lucky."

And wasn't that Eric to the core? He'd tell anyone who asked that he'd gotten fucked the night before, but he'd never talk about the nights he did the fucking. Tim had asked him about it one time. Eric had shrugged and said he didn't care what people thought of him, but he'd never give them a reason to question Tim or Richard's authority. Tim had replied that he didn't see how what they did in bed should have any effect on their authority, but Eric hadn't changed his ways.

"Richard?"

"He hasn't lost his touch." Richard's drawl was nearly as self-satisfied as Eric's grin. Tim hated him a little bit right at the moment. He shifted on the bed, trying to make room for his stirring cock and force his legs to move. He needed to go home. Now.

"Good to know. Now I just have to get well enough to take advantage of it again."

"What's the word from the doctor this morning?" Richard asked.

"The word from the physical therapist is that she wants me to be able to move my legs well enough on my own to move them on and off the bed and to be able to stand with support well enough to get in and out of a wheelchair. At that point I can go home, assuming we can make the place we're going accessible to the wheelchair."

"We'll have to measure the doors," Eric said. "The only problem I can see is the bathroom. We can put a stool in the tub for you to sit on, but getting in and out is going to be a bitch."

"Between the two of us, we can brace him and lift his legs," Richard said. "I know how strong you are. You can hold his weight."

Tim hated the idea of being that dependent on Richard and Eric, but it would be better than staying at the hospital until he could get in and out of a tub by himself or until he was well enough to fly home. He tried to remember how long it took after Eric's ACL surgery before he could climb in the tub, but the weeks blurred together in his memory. Even that wouldn't be more than a ballpark figure, given the additional injuries from the bullets.

"We could ask about getting a different house," Eric said. "Boling still owes you a favor or two."

"We'll make do with what we have," Tim said. "No reason to use a favor that could be important later just to save my pride. Besides, I like sharing a tub with the two of you."

Eric turned that smirk on Tim, making him shift again. At this rate, he'd get all his PT exercises done before noon. "You gonna be up for anything other than bathing that quickly?"

"The bullets hit my legs, not anything important." Tim retorted. "I might not be up for anything athletic, but I'm sure we can find ways around that."

Richard's gaze was as hot as Eric's, a weighted caress over Tim's skin as Eric advanced on him with predatory intent. Tim braced one arm on the railing of the hospital bed and caught Eric around the shoulders with the other. Their mouths collided in a deep, searching kiss. So fucking Richard last night hadn't settled Eric completely. Tim grinned into the kiss and stroked his thumb across the sensitive patch of skin behind Eric's earlobe. The shudder that ran through him only made Tim hungrier.

He released his grip on the bed rail when he felt Richard's hand on his and turned it so their palms touched. Richard twined their fingers together and squeezed gently. When Eric finally ended the kiss, panting a bit from the intensity of it, Tim looked at Richard. "He's not done yet."

Richard's eyes sparkled with an intoxicating mixture of love, lust, and amusement. "I should hope not. He only fucked me once last night."

"I was taking it easy on you," Eric said. "After all those complaints about being an old man."

Tim snorted. "Don't take it easy on him tonight. You need it, and he wants it." And Tim wouldn't be there to see it. Soon, but not tonight. It was his own damn fault for getting shot. He'd just have to exercise harder so he could go home soon.

"Come home and make sure we do it right," Eric replied.

"Don't think I won't." As much as he reveled in everything they did together, he was especially fond of the nights Eric and Richard gave in to his whims and let him tell them what to do to each other. His own personal live porn channel. And when they were done with each other and too wrung out to move, he'd slip behind one or the other and find his own release in their willing bodies. That might have to wait a little longer, but he could watch them together and direct their lovemaking and be involved that way.

"As soon as you're up to it, we're all yours," Richard said, his voice dark with promise.

"It's Tuesday?" Tim asked.

"Wednesday," Eric said. "You're still off by a day."

Tim frowned. He didn't like losing time. "By next Wednesday, I'm going home with you."

To his relief, neither of them contradicted him. But if he didn't get his mind off sex, he wasn't going to make it until next Wednesday, and while he was in a private room now, that only meant he didn't have a roommate. Nurses still barged in whenever they felt like it. He couldn't even ask for a hand job now for fear they'd come in during the middle of it.

"I looked over the dossier from Westin," Tim said. "We have a problem."

Richard's expression sobered. He grabbed the chairs that had been pushed back against the wall during Tim's PT session and brought them back to the bedside. He urged Eric into one of them and took the other for himself, an arm around Eric's shoulders. Tim almost regretted bringing it up as he watched all animation fade from Eric's face, but they had to get this taken care of.

"What did you find?" Richard asked.

"Hand me the folder." Richard passed it to him, and Tim flipped through it to the two pictures of the village where he'd been shot. "This is the picture we were given. It shows what appears clearly to be military installations. Weapons caches, oil drums, training grounds. This is what we used to decide to take the op, and this is what we used in planning it. This picture"—he pointed to the one that showed the women and children—"was not in any of our briefing materials. If we'd seen this, we might not have taken the mission at all, but even if he had, we certainly would have planned it differently. There's no time stamp on this photo, so we can't prove that Collins had it before we accepted the mission, but he almost certainly had it before we executed the mission because it doesn't show any of the damage I know we did to this building here." He tapped the photo to show them what he was talking about. "Most importantly, though, the first picture—the one we used to plan the mission—isn't accurate or complete. Even if we take out the question of the other photo with the women and children, which shows a different section of the compound, the first photo doesn't match what we found on the ground."

"Keep talking," Richard said.

"See this section?" Tim said, pointing to the row of oil drums. "That was in the village, but it wasn't next to these buildings. There's an open area—a village square of sorts—between the buildings and the fuel depot. And the training area, if it exists, wasn't anywhere near either of them. Honestly the villagers were smart to have the oil canisters separate from the buildings. If something happens to those drums, they won't take out the houses when they blow, but my concern is why we were given a doctored photo as the basis for all of our mission planning."

"It wasn't my fault," Eric murmured so softly Tim barely heard him.

"What?" Tim said. "I know you're used to taking flak for stuff in the field, but who in the hell suggested you were responsible for *this*?"

"His own fucked-up psyche," Richard muttered.

Eric elbowed him and looked up at Tim with a troubled stare. "The terrorists drugged me sometimes before they interrogated me, to the point that I don't know what I might have compromised because there are huge gaps in my memories. One of the things I do remember is how fixated they were on ops and information related to Syria. When I came back and found out you'd been shot on an op in Syria, I thought…."

"I told him he couldn't have been responsible because we didn't even have your op on our radar when he was captured, but that hasn't seemed to make it through his thick skull," Richard said.

"Do you believe it now?" Tim asked.

"If the op went south because what you found on the ground differed from what was in the mission briefing, then even if they managed to get something useful out of me, it doesn't matter because you went in with bad intel."

"We went in with bad intel," Tim confirmed.

"Eric, stay with Dav," Richard said as he stood. He held out his hand for the folder. "We need the undoctored photo. Westin got everything he could from his contacts. Let's see if Heikkinen has any better luck."

"You sure you want to go there?" Tim asked. "It's one thing to ask her to spy on other governments and groups. Do you really want to ask her to dig up dirt on our government?"

"Do you have a better idea? Whoever did this nearly got you killed. Maybe it wasn't Collins. Maybe someone fed him false information. But whoever it was, however it happened, it can't happen again. We have to find out what happened so we make sure it doesn't happen again. You might not be so lucky next time. Or Eric might not be. Or Amato or Westin or Sanders or any of the other people who trust us to make good decisions and take only the missions we believe we have a chance of coming home from."

"No, I don't have a better idea. Not if we want to keep going," Tim said.

"Are you suggesting we retire?" Richard asked.

Eric looked as shocked as Richard sounded.

"I don't know. Maybe I am," Tim said. "I'm not going to bounce back from this. I'll get better, yes, but if we were still in the Navy, they'd already be writing up my medical discharge papers, or if they didn't, they'd be looking at transferring me to an office somewhere. I'm never going to be field ready again."

"You don't know that," Eric said. "Even if you're not 100 percent of what you were, you'd still be far more deadly than most soldiers at their best."

"Maybe, maybe not." Eric's faith warmed Tim's heart, but it wouldn't make his legs heal any faster or make him any stronger at the end of the day. "We never had an exit strategy. I think we sort of figured we'd go down in a blaze of glory like all good warriors do, but I went down, and I'm still here, and I'm not seeing the appeal of it as much anymore. I'm not saying we toss in the towel and walk away right now, but maybe it's time to come up with that exit strategy. I'd kind of like to grow old with the two of you."

"That's all the more reason to find out the truth," Richard said. "If this is out there, hanging over our heads, even if we walked away, it could come back to bite us in the ass. If we deal with it, whether we retire now or ten years from now or never, we have the protection of proof."

Tim hated it when Richard was right. "Tell her not to get caught. I really don't want to end up in Leavenworth or somewhere worse."

"You won't. I won't let it come to that."

Tim didn't like the sound of that either, but he'd deal with that problem another day, if it became a problem. It was getting close to lunchtime, and nurses would be in with food, and then Jamie would be around to torture him some more.

"Go talk to her. We'll be here when you get back. Or if we're not, it's because my physical therapist is a sadistic bitch who delights in torturing me. I'm taking Eric with me for protection."

Richard barked out a sharp laugh and leaned over to kiss Tim. Tim didn't cling to him, no matter how much he wanted to. Richard knew what he was doing and knew the risks he was taking. They'd discuss it more later and put contingency plans in place. Heikkinen was good, but that didn't lessen the risk they were taking.

Richard broke the kiss and took a step back. Eric caught Richard's hand and held on. "Don't fuck it up."

"I won't," Richard swore. "I have too much riding on this."

CHAPTER 26

RICHARD DROVE back to the base and headed to the house. Heikkinen had said she would meet him there in about twenty minutes. His mind raced as he tried to distill what he needed to tell her into the most succinct pieces. She needed a complete enough picture to know what to search for, but Richard was still not completely sure he trusted her. She'd been part of all the briefings with Collins as well. Could she have been part of this? He supposed he'd find out. He parked the car and went inside to dig out his Glock 37. He slipped it into his belt at the small of his back where he could reach it if necessary but where it wouldn't immediately be obvious to Heikkinen beneath his jacket. She wouldn't be surprised to find him armed, but he wanted this conversation to end well, not in threats.

Precisely twenty minutes after her text, he heard a knock on the door. "You wanted to see me, Commander?"

"Come in, Heikkinen. Can I offer you a drink?"

"Is this a social visit, sir?"

"No, this is definitely business."

"Then I'll pass."

She took the chair Richard indicated, and he sat down across from her. "Somebody is fucking with us," he said without preamble as he passed her copies of the dossier. He would keep the originals for himself. "This is what Westin dug up, but while it proves that someone is jerking us around, it doesn't prove who."

"I'll read it later. What do you suspect?"

"Davenport went through the records last night. The surveillance for his op was incomplete, and one of the photos was tampered with, according to his memories of the site." Richard pulled out the photo Tim had shown him and outlined the issues.

She took it from him and studied it closely. "They're good, whoever did it. This isn't some hack job messing around with Photoshop."

That wasn't reassuring. "All of our intel on this op came from Collins and two of his aides. I'll get you their names. I don't know where they got it because it's never been an issue until now."

"They could be dupes in this as much as we were," Heikkinen agreed. "What are you asking me to do?"

"Whatever it takes. I need the original photo because while I trust Davenport's memories, that isn't going to stand up as proof, and I need proof of who did it. Can you do it?"

"Do you know what you're asking?"

He met her icy gaze without flinching. "Yes."

"If this goes bad, I'm not taking the fall alone."

"If this goes bad, we'll all be dead and it won't matter."

"I'll do it, but don't expect answers tomorrow. This could take months." Richard had been afraid of that. "Do what you have to do."

"And in the meantime?"

"In the meantime, we don't take any new ops from the Pentagon."

"That's going to hurt some people's pocketbooks."

"I'd rather hurt their pocketbooks than have them wind up dead. I'll make the announcement this afternoon to everyone who's here in Germany and get the word out to the rest after that's over."

She rose and took the folder. "I can't stand people who play dirty. You'd think all the years I spent as a spy would have cured me of that, but it only made me feel more strongly. I will find out who did this. Do you want me at the meeting?"

"It will be more telling that you're concerned enough to skip the meeting in favor of starting your search."

"Then I'll be on the next plane out. I can't do what I need to do from here. Their security isn't good enough. I'll be in touch."

He rose as well and offered his hand. "We'll keep you posted on our whereabouts through the usual channels. The house in the Caymans is open to you if you need it."

"Let's hope it doesn't come to that."

RICHARD SENT texts to everyone from Strike Force Omega currently on base, calling a meeting for two o'clock that afternoon. He started to text Eric to tell him not to come, that it was more important for him to stay with Dav, because Richard expected the meeting to be full of tension and anger, much of it directed at Eric. While Richard didn't blame him for anything he'd spilled while he was being tortured, not everyone was as accepting. But as much as he wanted to protect Eric, he couldn't take those decisions out of his hands. With a sigh, he dialed Eric's phone.

"Richard?"

"Heikkinen agreed. She's already on her way to see what she can find out. I've called the people who are local to meet at two. I expect it to be nasty as fuck. You don't have to attend. You know everything I'm going to say."

"And leave you to face the clusterfuck by yourself? I don't think so. I'm a big boy, Richard. I can face whatever they have to say about me. Whatever steps you put in place to protect people after I was captured, nothing changes the fact that they got intel from me. Not to mention the fact that we're not a secret anymore."

Richard had been afraid Eric would say that. "You don't have to, but thank you."

"You're welcome. I'll be there a little before two. Where are we meeting?"

"At the house. It's the only space I'm relatively sure is secure." He couldn't be completely sure Boling or someone higher up hadn't bugged the place, but he'd seen no sign of it. He should have asked Heikkinen to check before she left. Then again, she'd spoken openly with him, which was almost as reassuring.

ERIC ARRIVED at quarter 'til two. Richard pulled him into a tight embrace and kissed him thoroughly. When he finally released him, Eric looked as dazed as Richard felt. "They're going to come in with questions and concerns and maybe even accusations, and I'm going to pull the rug out from under them when I tell them what we've learned and what we've decided—for the short-term, at least. Until Heikkinen finds proof, we can't move beyond that. Don't defend me. Don't try to protect me. And don't get angry at anything they say."

"I have sat in tense briefings before," Eric said.

"There's never been a briefing like this one." He rested his forehead against Eric's. "Trust me to handle this. If I need more from you than silent support, I will ask for it. Until then, don't throw fuel on the fire."

"You don't know what you're asking."

"Yeah, I really do. I love you, Peaches."

"I love you too. For what it's worth, Tim gave me the same lecture before I left the hospital. He says you're a fool for not waiting until he was well enough to leave the hospital and that if you fuck this up, he's never sleeping with you again."

"He did not say that last part," Richard replied.

Eric grinned at him. "He really did."

"Fuck you." Richard's voice conveyed his amusement. Eric smirked at him.

"No, I'll be the one fucking you tonight, remember?"

Richard wasn't sure he'd be able to let go that way after the upcoming meeting, but he and Eric could negotiate that later.

The doorbell rang, interrupting their conversation. "Have a seat," Richard said. "I'll answer it."

He opened the door to find the rest of Eric's team on his doorstep. "We thought we'd get here early," Amato said. "In case Eric needed the support."

"Come in." He opened the door wider and stepped back so they could file in. They found places surrounding Eric. Richard caught his eye and smiled. Eric smiled back, but he looked more worried now than he had before. He was probably wondering what his team had heard from the others to make them feel like he needed the support. Richard hadn't spoken with any of them in a few days, but he knew how rumors made their rounds. By now, they were probably Godzilla sized.

At two o'clock exactly, the rest of Dav's team from Syria showed up. Richard reminded himself he owed these people Dav's life. No matter what they said, he would keep a lid on his temper.

"How's Davenport?" Li, the medic on Dav's team, asked before Richard had even closed the door.

"Awake," Richard replied. "I didn't thank you guys for pulling him out. I owe you his life."

"He wouldn't have left us behind. We weren't going to abandon him," Taylor, the sniper, replied. "We been hearing things, boss."

"That's why we're here," Richard said. "Have a seat and we'll get started."

Estrada and Jones, the two remaining members of the Syria team, nodded at him as they walked by. He felt the rise in tension in the room the minute they caught sight of Eric. He cursed under his breath and wondered if Dav was right. He was so much better at handling these kinds of things than Richard was.

"Where's Heikkinen?" Sanders asked. Eric elbowed him, but the words were out there now.

"Working," Richard said. "Or on her way to somewhere she can work."

"Alone?" Estrada asked sharply.

"Some ops are best performed alone."

"What kind of a solo op requires Heikkinen?" Taylor demanded.

"And when are we getting a new mission? I get antsy around so many soldiers all at once," Jones said.

"Who's going to lead the team until Davenport gets well?" Li asked, directing the question to Jones rather than to Richard, not that it made any difference. "We can't exactly go out without a team leader."

"You sure it's a good idea for *him* to be here?" Taylor added. "We don't know what they did to his brain. He could be a sleeper now for all we know."

Amato was on her feet and halfway across the room before Eric managed to stop her. Richard couldn't hear what he said to make her stand down, but she never would have done it without prompting.

"Enough!" Richard roared. "If you will all let me talk, I'll tell you what's going on and answer as many of your questions as I can, but you will all keep your comments about anyone else's loyalty to yourself. No one in this room is disloyal, or they wouldn't be here. Understood?"

Everyone settled down, although the anger hadn't cleared from Amato's face, and Taylor looked more sullen than ever.

"First, because Li asked and because I know what it means to face combat as a team, Davenport was downgraded to a regular room yesterday, so you'll be able to visit him now. He has a long recovery ahead of him, but the doctors expect him to be fine." He held up his hand to silence the question he could see forming on Li's face. "That's the good news. Now that we've got that out of the way, here's the rest."

He took a deep breath and met Eric's gaze, a lifeline thrown across the room full of strength and support and love.

"We knew the op in Syria went FUBAR. What we didn't know until today was why. Westin pulled some strings at the Pentagon and found evidence we were given incomplete information before the op. When Davenport looked over it, he found that it was not only incomplete but inaccurate. You asked where Heikkinen is? She's gone to find out who tried to fuck us over and why."

Richard paused to let his words sink in. "Until she has answers for us, we don't trust anyone not on our payroll. Not Boling, and especially not Collins."

"What about new ops?" Taylor asked.

"Until I can trust that I'm making decisions with the most complete and accurate information available so I can do everything in my power to ensure you all come home safely, we won't be taking any new ops," Richard said. "Honestly I wouldn't blame you if every one of you stood up right now and walked out. You trusted me, and I got conned."

"You can't take this on yourself," Eric protested. "This came from outside."

Richard shot him a quelling glare, but Eric didn't back down.

"He's right, Commander," Estrada said. "Maybe some of us have to leave because we gotta have money to live on, but you ain't the one jerking us around with bad intel. That be on those motherfuckers, whoever they are."

Richard appreciated the sentiment—and the fact that everyone in the room seemed to buy into it—but it would be a long time before he forgave himself for overlooking the doctored photo. "It will be some time before Davenport is able to travel. We'll stay here as long as he needs medical care, although I don't know how long Boling will continue to accept our presence on base, especially when I start turning down new missions. As soon as we're able, we'll relocate to the Caymans. If you choose to leave— temporarily or permanently—you can check in through the usual channels. If you intend to come back, make sure we know how to reach you."

"How long do you expect this to last?" Jones asked.

"I don't know," Richard said. "Heikkinen is the best in the business. If there's proof out there, she will find it, but it won't happen overnight. Whether it's a week or ten years, though, I have no way of guessing."

"So you just gonna sit around in the Caymans and drink rum and fuck your boy until then?" Estrada asked.

Richard grabbed Estrada by the collar and pulled him to his feet. "I am trying really hard right now to remember that I owe Davenport's life to you, but if you ever make a comment like that in my hearing again, I will forget everything I owe you and make you eat your words. Do you understand?"

"Sir," Estrada said shakily. Richard dropped him and stepped back to gather the rest of the room in with a single look. "If any of the rest of you feel that way, there's the door. What I do in my personal life is no one's business but mine and the people I do it with. Is that clear?"

"As long as personal attachments don't influence your professional decisions, I have no problem with it," Li said.

Richard wasn't sure that was any better, but Dav would shoot him if he came back with the news that he'd driven off half the organization. "I'd like to think Davenport and I have enough of a track record with each of you to give you the answer to that."

Li shrugged. "We didn't know you were sleeping with them before."

"Which means it didn't influence my decisions, did it? If I were playing favorites, someone would have noticed."

"As long as I don't have to work with Newton," Taylor muttered.

Richard let that one pass. Eric had a team, and a damn loyal one, already. Eric might take over some of Dav's field responsibilities, but he could do it in his own team first, maybe with a few handpicked people added until he had the same kind of track record that Dav did.

"He already has a team," Westin said, "and we don't need you."

That wasn't where Richard would have expected Eric's support to come from, but while Amato and Sanders wore the same mulish expressions, Westin had chosen to speak up. Interesting.

"Any other *relevant* questions?" Richard asked.

No one spoke up.

"Then get the hell out of my house."

Dav's team rose and filed out. Richard would have to ask Dav to reach out to them and smooth over the ruffled feathers. Then again, after hearing what they'd said about Eric, he might not want to. Eric's team didn't move.

"I thought I told you to leave."

"We will," Amato said, "but first we need to say this. We talked about it, and here's the deal. We're a team, Eric, Sanders, and me, and Westin's stuck his neck out for all of us enough in the past week for him to count too. We didn't know about you, but it doesn't matter. We talked about it, and in all the time we've been part of this organization, you've been as ruthlessly fair with us as with any other team. We get good ops and we get shitty ops and there's no playing favorites. I can't make the others change their minds, but whatever you need us for, we're here. Whether it's to run interference with Boling, to kick Estrada's sorry ass, or just to do milk runs to keep an eye on things while we're laying low. You name it, we'll do it."

Richard nodded, unused to that kind of personal loyalty anymore. He'd had it with the other SEALs before they retired from the Navy and set out on their own, but since then, he'd always been the one in charge, never the one in the field with the teams. They'd set it up that way because someone had to pull the strings, and Dav was better at blending in and appearing harmless than Richard was. The team's loyalty had always been to Dav, if it was to either of them, or within each team. Richard had accepted that as the price of command, but now that it was on offer, he'd take it. He shook Amato's hand, then Westin's and Sanders's in turn. "Thank you. It's good to know Eric has someone on his side."

Amato glanced over her shoulder at Eric. "You should come spar with me again. Your reflexes are rusty." She looked back at Richard. "You should come too. How long has it been since you were in a real fight?"

He and Dav sparred regularly to stay in shape when they were at home, but never where others could see them. Amato might be in for a little surprise if he took her up on her challenge. "Depends on what you call a real fight."

She laughed. "Come to the gym tomorrow with us. It's time to show us what you've got, Commander."

"We'll see," Richard replied. "It will depend on Dav and what the doctors say about when he can come home."

"Tomorrow," she repeated. "It'll be good for both of you. Ask Davenport if you don't believe me."

"Tomorrow afternoon, then," Richard said. "After we've gone by the hospital to check on Dav. We'll let you know what time."

"See you then, Commander. Eric."

She nodded at Richard, gave Eric a hug, and led the others out of the house.

"That went better than I expected," Richard said once he and Eric were alone again.

"That was better?" Eric asked.

"Nobody punched anyone and nobody quit on the spot," Richard replied. "At this point I'll take it." Adrenaline jittered through his system, leaving him twitchy. He needed to go for a run.

Eric gave him a slow, thorough once-over. "Fight, flight, or fuck?"

Richard grinned. "Definitely fuck."

CHAPTER 27

"YOUR RECOVERY has been impressive, Mr. Davenport," Smithers said the following Wednesday, just as Tim had predicted. "We'll release you shortly on the condition that you're going somewhere wheelchair accessible and with a handicap-accessible bathroom."

"We've measured all the doorways," Eric said. "The wheelchair will fit through all of them. We won't be able to get the wheelchair into the tub, but we can get it to the side and then lift him in. We found a shower chair for him to use so you don't have to worry about him slipping in the tub."

"You'll need help getting in and out of the wheelchair even for things like going to bed, for some time to come. Your physical therapist will be able to tell you when you're ready to switch to a walker and on from there."

"We've already talked about it," Tim said. "She expects another four to six weeks in the wheelchair. Beyond that, we'll just wait and see."

"Good." Smithers shook his hand. "I wish you all the best, Mr. Davenport. Try not to land back in my hospital bed again."

"No, ma'am," Tim said. "I don't plan on it."

She looked at him sadly. "No one ever does."

Tim couldn't argue with that.

"Ready?" he asked Richard and Eric after she left.

"Whenever you are," Richard replied.

The hospital orderlies wouldn't let Tim roll the wheelchair out of the hospital by himself, although Jamie had worked with him on how to steer it as part of their PT sessions. He would be far more dependent on Eric and Richard than he wanted to be as it was. Expecting them to push him around in the wheelchair was one step too far. When they got outside to the car, Tim pushed himself to his feet slowly, ignoring the hands outstretched to catch him if he fell. He wasn't going to fall. He was just going to turn a little and then sit down in the passenger seat. He braced himself on the car door and the roof as he turned and lowered himself into the seat. He had to lift his legs to get them into place. He and Jamie were working on that too, but his thigh muscles were heavily damaged by the bullets and would take time to recover.

Richard came around to the driver side, and Eric climbed into the seat behind him after putting the wheelchair in the trunk. "Do not coddle me," Tim said as soon as they pulled out of the parking lot. "I know I'll need help with certain things, but don't assume I need help with everything. I need to feel like myself again."

"As long as you promise not to overdo it," Eric said. "I've been where you are—sort of, anyway—so I understand how you feel, but I also remember what happened when I pushed too hard and nearly had to go back in for a second surgery."

Tim remembered it too. He would push because he had to get better to be ready for whatever came from Heikkinen's search, but he would let them help when he needed it.

"Are you hungry?" Richard asked. "Eric made curry last night so it would be ready for today."

"I could eat," Tim said. After more than a week of hospital food—and German hospital food at that—Tim would kill for something more than meat and potatoes. "But what I really want is a shower. Sponge baths just aren't the same. I want the smell of antiseptic gone."

"We have the bathroom set up," Eric said, "although that's definitely something you'll have to let us help with."

"I told you last week I wouldn't complain about sharing a tub with the two of you. As long as you get me clean, you can do whatever it takes." He stretched to turn around in his seat. The movement pulled on the tender scars on his chest, but he ignored it. "You're getting a little scruffy too, Eric. It might be time for another shave."

Richard hissed out a breath next to him, and Eric looked between the two of them eagerly. He ran his hand over his jaw. "One cheek for each of you."

Tim smiled and reached for Richard's hand. Richard squeezed back. They could do this. Finding the right balance was just a question of practice and the willingness to adapt. "Does that only apply to your face?"

"You're not getting a razor anywhere near my dick," Eric said immediately.

"I wasn't talking about shaving, only about sharing."

"You've never had trouble sharing my ass," Eric retorted.

Tim grinned. No, they hadn't. Eric was right about that. Tim couldn't wait until he was strong enough for Eric to ride him. As much as he wanted it, he didn't think his legs could handle the jostling that inevitably ensued at the moment. He'd find other things to enjoy in the meantime.

The house on base was fairly standard, but it was the most beautiful thing Tim had seen in a long time because once they were inside, it would be their sanctuary. He could shower, help Richard shave Eric, eat, and sleep in a bed with his lovers again.

Eric pushed the wheelchair up to the door of the car, but when he reached inside to give Tim a hand, Tim batted it away. "Hold the wheelchair. It getting knocked out from under me is going to hurt me far worse than standing on my own."

Eric grabbed the handles and held it steady. Richard hovered but didn't offer to help. Tim wanted to tell them both to go away, but that wasn't going to happen, so he'd settle for the best he could get. He reversed the process of getting into the car, although standing from the low seat was more of a challenge than he anticipated. "Richard, I need your hands."

Richard reached out immediately, giving Tim something to brace against as he pulled himself to his feet and turned to sit in the wheelchair. He maneuvered up the sidewalk with minimal difficulty, although the concrete dragged at the wheels more than the tile in the hospital had done. Eric got the door open, and Richard helped him over the threshold when the front wheels got stuck, and then they were inside. Tim let the wheelchair roll to a stop and simply sat there.

"You okay?" Eric asked.

"I will be. I just need a minute to breathe."

Richard looked like he wanted to question that, so Tim reached for both of them. "Come give me a kiss. A proper one this time. We don't have to worry about anyone walking in on us."

"Go ahead," Richard said when Eric glanced up at him. "There's more than enough to go around."

Tim might have protested being compared to a buffet, but he was too moved by the new awareness between them to complain too loudly. Eric bent to kiss him, but the angle was awkward. He dropped to his knees, putting himself at close to the perfect height for a kiss. Tim took his time, rediscovering every nook and cranny in Eric's mouth. Eric opened for him and sucked on his tongue teasingly. Tim stroked the patch of skin behind his ear in retaliation, only to find Richard already stroking the sensitive spot. He brushed across Richard's fingers and joined him in getting Eric all worked up.

"No fair ganging up on me," Eric said with a gasp.

Richard bent and pressed a kiss to the same spot. Tim shivered in sympathy, knowing all too well what Richard's goatee felt like against his erogenous zones. "Think of it as getting double your money."

Eric moaned and tilted his head.

Richard brushed his hair out of the way and licked over the spot. "Kiss Dav. Remember?"

Eric moaned again and turned back to Tim for another kiss, but Tim could already tell from his glassy stare that he'd take whatever Tim gave him but wouldn't have his wits about him to initiate anything. That was fine with Tim. After feeling out of control of everything since he realized the op in Syria had gone to hell, being in control of his lovers felt perfect.

When they'd reduced Eric to a gasping mess and he was swaying on his knees in front of Tim, Richard straightened and winked at Tim. Tim had that second to prepare for the onslaught of Richard's mouth against his. He might have succeeded in controlling Eric, but Richard was a long way from giving in. Then again, Tim hadn't asked yet. He'd save that for later, once they were all in bed.

Richard left him a gasping, mewling mess, but that was nothing new. He'd managed that at twenty-two, the first time they'd kissed. Experience had only made him more potent.

"I think it's time for that shower," Tim said huskily. He needed less clothing between them as soon as possible.

Eric led the way into the bathroom and settled on the toilet seat. "Shower first or shaving first?" he asked Tim.

As much as Tim wanted a shower, he knew how likely it was that shaving cream would end up in places other than on Eric's face. If they shaved him first, then they could all get clean in the shower after. "Shaving, but help me get undressed. I only have a few shirts here. I don't want to get this one all wet and covered in shaving cream."

Tim managed his shirt well enough, but when it came time to stand, he needed Eric's support. "You'll have to get my pants undone," he told Richard.

"I think after twenty years, I know how to get in your pants," Richard teased.

Tim rolled his eyes, amused to see Eric doing the same, and stood still while Richard unbuttoned his pants and pushed them down to his knees. Tim sat back down carefully and lifted his feet one at a time to get them free of the pants legs.

"Your turn," he said to Richard and Eric when he was down to his underwear. Richard stripped off his shirt but left his pants in place while Eric stripped all the way down to his skin. Tim took a minute to study Eric now that he could see him fully. He had definitely lost weight, and he'd acquired some new scars, but everything seemed healed other than a few bruises that had faded to greenish yellow almost hidden by his golden skin.

Richard handed him the canister of shaving cream and the razor, interrupting his perusal. "I got to shave him last time. You go first today."

Tim squirted a handful of foam into his palm and smeared it over Eric's left cheek. Eric leaned into his touch eagerly but without any of the glassy-eyed trance he sank into when he needed the comfort of the ritual. Tim suspected he needed the ritual more than Eric did at the moment, although Eric definitely had enough stubble to warrant a shave. He scraped the blade along Eric's cheekbone and worked down from there, slow even swipes of metal against skin until he reached the line of Eric's jaw. He wiped the foam away with a towel Richard had draped over the arm of the wheelchair and leaned in to kiss Eric again. Eric met him halfway this time, darting his tongue along Tim's lips and into his mouth. Tim wanted to move closer, to step between Eric's widespread knees and pull him into a tight hug, but he couldn't stand easily, and even if he did, he'd never manage the two steps to get closer.

As if sensing his problem, Eric scooted forward until his thighs bracketed Tim's knees, careful not to bump against Tim's injuries, and Tim could feel the heat from his skin. He reached between them and stroked Eric's slowly filling cock. "It's going to be a while until I can fuck you again, but I'm not waiting much longer to get my mouth on you."

Eric practically bounced to his feet. Richard's throaty laughter reminded Tim that they weren't alone with their ritual this time, although Richard didn't seem bothered by their routine. He glanced at Richard to check. Richard just smiled at him. "What are you waiting for? If he puts his dick in my face, I'm certainly not going to say no."

Just like that, the worry that had grown as he saw all the signs of the blooming relationship between Richard and Eric disappeared. They had always managed to make love to each other with no one feeling neglected. He had to stop worrying, or he'd end up creating problems where there were none.

Tim licked the tip of Eric's cock, letting the smell and taste of him reinforce that they were all home, safe and together. He'd feared he would never have this chance again, and now that he did, his own limitations kept him from doing everything he wanted. He pushed his frustration aside. He would heal, and as he did, Richard and Eric would be right there with him, and as soon as he could, he'd show them just how glad he was to have the three of them back together again. He licked and mouthed at Eric a little longer before sitting back in the wheelchair. Eric made an inarticulate protest—Tim's favorite kind—but Tim nudged him back onto the toilet lid. "We aren't done, but Richard hasn't shaved you yet."

Eric turned that heated focus onto Richard immediately. Tim started to roll back so Richard would have space, but Richard and Eric both stopped him. "Don't make him flinch—I don't want to cut him—but you should take advantage of all that bare skin."

Tim reached out to touch Eric's arm, but while he appreciated the chance to feel connected to them, he didn't want to interfere with the intimacy between them either. Instead he watched their expressions: the way Richard held his tongue between his teeth as he concentrated on keeping the razor steady, the way Eric tilted his head into Richard's steadying hand. He gripped Eric's arm more tightly, not to draw Eric's attention but to be a part of the incredible moment. Did Eric look at him that way? He must have, but Tim had gotten too used to the way things went between them to see it. He should be grateful to Richard for showing him what he'd forgotten how to see.

When Richard set the razor aside and wiped Eric's face clean, Tim leaned into him with the same aching need he could see on Eric's face. Eric turned back to Tim and kissed him desperately. Tim returned it in spades. Then he felt Richard's hand on his shoulder—it had to be Richard's, he was holding both of Eric's—and all the pent-up fear and frustration caught up with him. Tears welled up in his eyes and spilled over. Every muscle in his body hurt, and that wasn't going to change anytime soon unless he doped up on more and stronger medicines than he was comfortable taking. He could put on a brave face for the rest of the world, but Richard and Eric deserved more than that brittle façade.

They held him through his bout of self-pity, and he felt better when the tears were done.

"Ready for that shower now?" Richard asked.

"Yeah, that sounds about perfect." His voice sounded like he'd swallowed gravel, but his smile felt genuine for the first time in days. He was home, and everything was going to be okay.

CHAPTER 28

RICHARD STRIPPED the rest of the way and offered Tim his arms to brace himself when he stood. "Eric, get his briefs down. We can pull them off him once he's seated on the shower stool."

The words were functional, nothing more, but Richard's voice was warm, and Tim was turned on from shaving Eric and watching him and Richard together. Eric's hands near his dick did nothing to calm him down.

"I guess you're as glad to be home as we are to have you here," Eric said as he peeled Tim's underwear down to his knees.

"You better believe it."

Eric stepped into the bathtub and braced his arms around Tim's chest, careful to avoid his still tender scars. "Lean on me. I'll take your weight while Richard lifts your legs into the tub. Tell us if anything hurts."

Tim leaned trustingly against Eric's chest. He didn't have to be the strong one here like he did in the field. For all that he didn't want to be coddled unnecessarily, he could let Richard and Eric help him. Richard lifted his legs, and between the two of them, they got him onto the shower stool. Richard stepped into the tub in front of him and pulled Tim's underwear the rest of the way off. Then he turned to adjust the water, giving Tim one hell of a view.

"Makes you just want to take a bite out of it, doesn't it?" Eric murmured in his ear.

"Or else spread it wide and fuck it until he's screaming," Tim agreed.

"Let's start with a bite. We can discuss the rest later."

Tim kept hold of Eric's arm as he leaned forward so he wouldn't overbalance and slip off the stool and bit lightly into the lower curve of Richard's ass, right where it joined his thigh. He would have sworn Richard had heard his conversation with Eric, but he still jumped when Tim made contact with his teeth.

"You're supposed to be taking it easy," Richard scolded when he turned back around—easily as hard as Tim was, Tim noticed with some satisfaction.

"I just leaned forward a little," Tim said. "I didn't take a bullet to the gut. There's nothing wrong with my abs. And weren't you the one telling me to suck Eric because he was waving his dick in my face? What was I supposed to do when you put your ass there?"

"Exactly what you did," Eric interjected. "Is the water hot yet? The sooner we get Tim clean, the sooner we can get him fed and go to bed."

Richard grumbled but switched the stream of water to the shower nozzle and sprayed the water onto the tile wall to Tim's left. "Check the temperature. I don't want to burn you."

Tim checked the water, but the temperature was perfect. "Let me have that so I can get clean."

"And deprive us of the pleasure of taking care of you?" Richard asked. "I don't think so."

"Think of it as foreplay," Eric added. His words defused the tension that had started building in Tim's temples. If he weren't injured, he would jump at the chance to bathe and be bathed by his lovers. Maybe they were being extra solicitous because of his legs, but they would enjoy it as much as Tim would. He leaned back against Eric's warmth and gestured for Richard to get started.

Having all their attention focused on him as Eric washed his hair and Richard gently scrubbed his feet and up his legs was positively decadent. Richard was careful with the healing scars, no longer heavily bandaged but still very tender to the touch, while Eric took care to keep the shampoo out of his eyes. "You're spoiling me. I'm never going to want to take a bath any other way again."

Eric just hummed behind him and rinsed out his hair. When he was done, he passed the showerhead back to Richard to rinse Tim's legs and turned his attention to Tim's back and shoulders. "You're tense," he said as he ran soapy hands over Tim's back. "You should get Richard to give you a massage later."

"He does give good ones, doesn't he?" Tim said.

"Best I've ever had."

"He's just saying that because I let him fuck me when I was done with the massage. Happy ending and all that."

Tim tipped his head up so he could see Eric's face. "You had enough muscle control left after he was done with you to actually fuck him? I'm impressed."

"I didn't get to finish," Richard grumbled. "He distracted me."

"That makes it even more impressive. I've never managed to distract you like that."

"Yeah, well, he's too sexy for his own good."

Tim could hardly argue with that when he'd fallen in lust at first sight. The love had come later, strong and pure, but the first glimpse of Eric had been an unexpected punch in the gut. The only difference now was that he expected it.

"I'm right here, you know," Eric said.

"And your point would be?" Richard asked.

"Just shut up and kiss me."

Richard braced his arm on the wall and leaned over Tim to kiss Eric. Tim stroked Richard's hip and leaned more heavily against Eric's stomach. He had to get them in bed and soon. He could feel himself tiring, and he didn't want to collapse too quickly. He had *plans* for tonight.

They seemed to share his idea. They broke the kiss and finished washing Tim quickly.

"Ready to get out?" Richard asked.

"Yes."

Richard turned off the water while Eric dried Tim off as best he could. "If you stand up and hold on to Richard's shoulders, I can dry you off the rest of the way and then we can get you out of the tub and into bed."

"Food first," Tim said. "Once we get in bed, I don't want to have to get up until morning." He let Richard help him stand and hold him in place while Eric dried Tim's ass and the backs of his legs. Eric pushed the shower stool out of the way and stepped right up behind Tim, so close Tim could feel the heat of his erection. He sagged back against Eric so Richard could lift his feet clear of the tub and get him seated in the wheelchair. They helped him dress—just underwear and a shirt since they were going back to bed as soon as they finished eating—but Tim wouldn't let them push him into the kitchen to eat. "Get the food ready. I'll be out in a minute."

Eric went immediately, but Richard hovered in the bedroom.

"Don't be a mother hen," Tim said. "I won't do anything stupid. I just need a minute to rest."

"You could let us help."

"I could, but I wouldn't get stronger that way. I've moved more today than I have in the past week, and yet all I've done is come home and had a bath. I have to build my stamina back up."

"I heard from Heikkinen this morning," Richard said. "She has a lead, but she said it would take her at least a month to unravel it, probably longer. You have time. You can let yourself heal."

Richard's news wasn't as reassuring as he intended it to be. If Heikkinen had to work that hard to find their proof, someone had gone to great lengths to hide it. "You realize we may not like what she finds."

"She couldn't find anything I would like," Richard said. "But whatever she finds, we'll deal with it then. Until we have something concrete in our hands, all we can do is rest and recover and be ready to move when the time comes."

"Does Eric know?"

"I told him as soon as she called. I didn't bring it up at the hospital because there were too many people around, and we had other things to take care of when we got home."

That was okay, then. He didn't want to keep secrets from Eric or to worry that Eric would feel like they were keeping secrets even if they weren't trying to.

"Food's hot," Eric called from the kitchen.

Richard took a step toward the wheelchair but backed down at Tim's glare. "I'll do it myself." He rolled the wheelchair out to the table. "It smells delicious."

"It's nothing fancy. Just some sambar and rice. An easy first meal home."

"Your nothing fancy is still better than anything I've eaten in weeks," Tim said. He dug in as soon as Eric set the dish in front of him. The broth was highly flavorful without being overly spicy, and the vegetables were still firm. Exactly what Tim had been craving. They ate in near silence, only the sounds of their silverware against the cheap CorningWare punctuating their meal. When Tim couldn't eat another bite, he leaned back in the wheelchair and folded his hands over his stomach. "You keep feeding me like that and I'm going to gain fifty pounds."

"You'll burn it all off doing PT," Eric said. "You look done in."

Exhaustion was creeping in, but Tim held it at bay. "I need to brush my teeth, but then bed sounds good."

They followed him back into the bathroom, helped him brush his teeth and shift to the toilet and back, and then took care of their own nightly routines while Tim rolled back into the bedroom. If they wouldn't yell at him, he'd try to move to the bed by himself, but falling, possibly hurting himself, and making them angry didn't figure in his plans for the rest of the night.

They came back out of the bathroom in only their underwear. Tim almost told them to get rid of the rest of it too, but if he waited, he could have them tease each other through the cloth first. "Help me into bed?"

Richard held the wheelchair while Eric helped Tim shift onto the bed. Richard pushed the wheelchair out of the way and came around to the other side of the bed. Tim lay there for a moment, enjoying the heat of their bodies on either side of him. They snuggled close and gave every impression of expecting to fall asleep.

Really? They didn't know him any better than that?

"You know what would make me sleep especially well?" Tim asked.

"What?" Eric said.

"Watching you two get each other off."

"You're tired. You need to sleep," Richard said. "We'll do whatever you want tomorrow."

"Didn't you say you wouldn't turn down Eric's dick in your mouth?"

"If he waved it in my face," Richard reminded him. "He's not waving it anywhere at the moment."

"That can be fixed," Tim said, reaching toward the placket of Eric's boxers. "The two of you have put blowjobs on my mind. I want to see you suck each other off."

Eric batted halfheartedly at his hand. "You really should rest," he said. "Richard's right. Tomorrow morning, when we're all rested."

"I'm sore and grumpy and really want something to distract me," Tim snapped. "Eric, get your ass over here. I know you take orders better than this."

"Only from you," Eric said, but he sat up and looked at Tim expectantly. "Where do you want me?"

That was more like it. "Richard still needs convincing. I guess you'll have to wave your dick in his face after all. Lose the shorts."

Richard started to sit up, but Tim caught his shoulder. "Unless you're taking your own underwear off, don't move."

Richard subsided onto the bed with a mulish look on his face. That was okay. Tim knew how to fix that. Eric walked naked around the bed to Richard's side. Richard tracked his progress, much to Tim's delight. Richard might be pretending to sulk, but he wouldn't require much of a push. "Climb up here," Tim told Eric. "Give him a kiss to get him in the mood."

"Are you going to dictate the entire evening?" Richard asked.

"That depends on you. If you need it, yes. Otherwise I'll just lie back and watch."

"On one condition," Richard said. "You stay right where you are. No moving around, no trying to get a better view. You just watch."

Tim slid his hand down Richard's chest and tweaked a pert brown nipple. "No touching at all?"

Richard's voice was strangled as he replied, "No moving around to get involved. If you can reach without moving, that's fine, but the minute you shift so much as a millimeter, we stop."

"Fair enough," Tim said, although if all went according to plan, Richard would be far too caught up to notice if Tim moved a little bit.

Eric climbed on the bed and straddled Richard, his knee pressing against Tim's hip. Tim stroked his skin in silent welcome. Eric smiled at him and then leaned forward, almost close enough to kiss Richard. "Richard can grumble all he wants. I'm too happy to have you back with us to complain. If this is what will help you feel like you're home again, I'll do whatever you ask."

"It will," Tim said. "I can't do any of the things I want to do, but this way I can feel like I'm a part of it even if all I do is watch and direct."

Richard brushed his fingers against Tim's hand in silent apology. Tim took it and squeezed gently. He expected Richard to loosen his grip, but he held on. A second later, Eric joined in, three sets of fingers twined together.

"Go on, kiss him," Tim said.

Eric closed the gap between his mouth and Richard's. Tim could see how quickly the kiss deepened, although Eric kept just enough space between them for Tim to catch a glimpse of their tongues dueling in the space between their lips. He licked his own lips, wanting to join in, but not wanting to risk Richard's wrath by moving to reach them. Instead he reached across his body with his free hand and stroked Richard's cheek and then Eric's in turn. Eric broke the kiss to nip at Tim's finger. When he went back to the kiss, Tim played along the seam of their mouths, caressing lightly as they devoured each other. Richard bucked upward, grinding against Eric's ass, which rested on his groin.

"Get rid of his underwear," Tim told Eric.

He regretted the loss of Eric's fingers in theirs the moment he pulled away to strip Richard, but as soon as he'd tossed the underwear aside, he slipped back into their grip. "Before you get too settled, why don't you turn around? Suck each other off for me."

Eric spun around, hovering over Richard on all fours, his ass in perfect reach of Tim's hand and his mouth perfectly positioned over Richard's cock. He glanced back at Tim. "Like this?"

"Perfect."

"Almost," Eric said. He slid his hand back into theirs. "Now it's perfect."

Tim stroked his own erection a couple of times, but as good as it felt, he needed the connection with Richard and Eric more. He ran his hand over the curve of Eric's ass, reveling in the freedom to touch. Eric moaned and lowered his head to take Richard in his mouth. "That's it," Tim said. "Take him all the way in."

Richard moaned at that. Tim could imagine what he was feeling, how Eric's throat opened around him, all wet heat and velvet constriction. Eric could deep-throat like nobody's business. Tim turned his attention to Richard next. "Your turn. He's waving it in your face."

Richard huffed a little as he rolled his eyes, but he licked his way up Eric's cock and back down the other side. That was typical Richard, making you desperate enough to beg for it. Eric wouldn't be begging tonight with his mouth stuffed full, but Tim would move things along when he was ready. He had some tricks up his sleeve too.

They were so damn beautiful together that Tim could almost be satisfied with watching. They moved together with that same ease he'd never seen before Eric was captured, but Tim was getting used to it now. It was what he had always wanted, after all. He ran his blunt nails along Richard's scalp and watched him arch into the touch. From there he moved up the back of Eric's thigh to cup his balls and then delve into his crease. Eric shifted his legs wider to give Tim access, but without lube he couldn't do much more than tease. He was sure they had it somewhere, but he wasn't going to stop watching long enough to find it.

Eric bobbed his head rhythmically on Richard's cock, and Richard met every downward slide with a thrust of his own. Tim traced Richard's lips with his finger. "Go on. He's taking such good care of you. Let him fuck your mouth."

Richard and Eric both moaned at the suggestion. Tim waited a moment for them to get settled and then worked his hand between their bodies to find one of Richard's nipples.

He could slow things down and draw it out, but he could feel exhaustion dragging him down. He pinched Richard's chest just the way he liked it, a silent signal to move things along. Inspiration struck as he watched Eric's cock disappear into Richard's mouth. He slipped his finger alongside Eric's cock and let Richard's tongue coat it in saliva. It wasn't lube, but it would let him play with Eric. Eric opened beneath his fingers. Tim didn't try to delve deep, but he worked his finger in to the first knuckle, just enough to stretch Eric's guardian ring a little and give him the feeling of penetration. Eric shuddered and arched into his touch. It wouldn't take much more, Tim knew. He almost leaned forward to whisper encouragement to them, but he didn't want to take the chance of Richard calling it all off, not when they were so close.

He tightened his grip on their entwined fingers. "You're so gorgeous, everything good in my world all wrapped up together. I want to be where you are, either one of you, or snuggled tight between you. I want you in me, around me, in every way we can think of and a few that haven't been invented yet. Let me see you come. Let me see how good you're making each other feel."

His voice broke, but he barely noticed, too fixated on Eric and Richard to care. Eric's control shattered first, no real surprise. He arched his back sharply and came with a muffled shout. Richard took the whole load and kept right on sucking until Eric whimpered and pulled away. Tim transferred his attention back to Richard, sliding his hand back to Richard's nipples. It didn't take much for Richard to come, only a few well-placed rubs of his thumbnail combined with Eric's skilled mouth.

Tim lay back against the pillows, panting nearly as hard as Eric and Richard. He rubbed himself through his underwear, desperate for his own release so he could finally collapse into sleep.

"You've had your fun," Richard rumbled in his ear. "Now it's our turn." He kissed Tim deeply, letting Tim taste Eric's release on his tongue, while Eric worked his cock free of his underwear.

"I'm still hungry," Eric said, each word sending air eddying around Tim's feverish skin. "Got a load for me?"

Tim couldn't arch into the tease. It hurt to lie there. It would be agony to lift his hips, but he was almost desperate enough to try. "Don't tease him," Richard said. "We're supposed to be welcoming him home."

Tim cried out in relief when Eric enclosed the tip of his cock. Then Richard bent as well and licked the shaft from the base to where it disappeared in Eric's mouth. It was more than Tim's overheated senses could stand. He came with a shout, pleasure warring with pain as he lost the battle to stay still, but nothing could shatter the feeling of finally being home.

He collapsed onto the bed, only barely aware of Eric and Richard moving around him.

"Here," Richard said, holding a pill against his lips. "If you don't take this, you'll be too sore for PT tomorrow."

Tim accepted the pill docilely and swallowed it with the water Eric offered him. He could feel oblivion beckoning, but he couldn't let go yet. Not until Eric and Richard came back to bed.

A moment later they returned to the same positions as before they'd started making love, one on either side of him. Richard found his hand and held on tight. A second later, Eric closed his over both of theirs. Tim closed his eyes and stopped fighting the darkness.

He was home.

EPILOGUE

Six months later

TIM OPENED his e-mail to find an encrypted message from Heikkinen. "Richard, Eric, you'll want to see this," he called. They were only in the next room, but for all the progress he'd made since he'd gotten out of the hospital, he still needed a cane to walk more than a few steps on even ground. His physical therapist continued to point out progress and insist he had more to make, but calling them to him would probably always be faster.

Richard came in first, still rubbing a towel over his chest as he dried off from his shower after his morning run. Tim envied him the freedom to go down to the beach outside their house—he still had to take the walker if he wanted to walk the dunes. The months of rest had taken years off the visible stress on Richard's face. With each passing week, he looked more like the man Tim had first fallen in love with, and that was enough to curb all but the worst of Tim's frustrations. Richard had taken up scuba diving, of all things, and spent more time in and on the water than he did at home. The sun had darkened his skin to ebony, and the swimming had burned what little fat remained, leaving him chiseled and more gorgeous than ever. "What's up?"

"An e-mail from Heikkinen. Let's wait for Eric."

"He was putting his bow away. He won't be a minute."

Eric had spent the intervening months restoring the bow Richard had found and researching its possible origins. They'd probably never know for sure, but Eric's best guess dated it from the Hundred Years War and Edward's failed attempt to take the city of Reims, one of the few battles where their longbowmen hadn't given the English a huge advantage. He hadn't found records of other battles in the area where the bow was found that would have included the kind of weapon he had finally been able to shoot.

And hadn't that been a night? Eric, high as a kite from restoring the bow and getting his strength back to full force, had ordered Tim to be patient while he fucked Richard into oblivion, only to move on to Tim and do the same to him. Tim had never seen him as voracious as he was that night. He shifted in the chair and met Richard's gaze. From the heat in his expression, Richard was remembering the same night… with the same fond memories.

Eric came in a moment later and froze in his tracks at the looks Tim and Richard turned on him. "What? I didn't do anything."

"Just remembering," Tim said. "I can't see you with your new bow and not remember."

Eric's posture changed from one step to the next as he advanced on them. "Is that why you called us in here?"

It wouldn't be the first time, but it wasn't the reason today. "No, unfortunately. We have an e-mail from Heikkinen."

Like he'd flipped a switch, the seducer disappeared and Eric was all business again. Six months out of the field hadn't taken that from him. Tim wasn't sure anything ever would.

"What does she have to say?"

Tim clicked open the e-mail and skimmed down the text. "She left a 'delivery' for us."

"She might have given us a little more notice," Richard grumbled. "We might not have been working today."

"She didn't say she was here, just that a delivery was," Tim pointed out.

"She wouldn't trust this to anyone else. We may not see her, but she was here," Richard replied.

"I hope she got an eyeful," Eric replied. "Where would she have left a delivery?"

"Hell, it could be anywhere," Richard said.

"She wasn't sending us on a scavenger hunt. She knows the house is secure, so there's no reason to hide it once it's inside."

"I don't know if that makes it better or worse," Eric replied.

Tim shook his head at the two of them. For as well as they'd adapted to not having regular active missions, they were still touchy as a cat in a room full of rocking chairs. "She probably left it sitting on the kitchen table while you two were elsewhere. I did my morning PT and then came in here."

The other two continued to mutter, but the package was exactly where Tim had predicted, sitting on the middle of the table wrapped in brown butcher paper. Across the front, Heikkinen had written, *They're good. I'm better.*

Tim tore off the paper and flipped open the thick folder. At the top was an e-mail from Collins acknowledging receipt of the doctored photo from a CIA address he didn't recognize.

ERIC WALKED on one side of Tim, Richard on the other, carefully matching their strides to Tim's slower one. Next to them, he felt positively homely in his plain black suit, but his stint in the military had not ended as well as theirs had. No one would appreciate him showing up in uniform. Tim and Richard, on the other hand, wore their full dress whites with pride and dignity—Eric refused to feel guilty about wanting to get back to the hotel and strip them out of uniform as soon as this goddamn meeting was done. He still wasn't sure why they insisted he attend the meeting with them when he had never had any contact with Collins or his higher-ups at the Pentagon, but Eric hadn't fought them too hard. He loved watching them kick ass and take names, and he expected this to be a spectacular ass kicking, even if the men they were going to meet would have been their superior officers if they were still on active duty. As it was, they had nothing to lose. They'd proven they could adapt to life away from Strike Force Omega just fine over the past six months.

They reached the door to the briefing room where they would meet with Collins and whoever else Richard had managed to corral into the meeting. Eric hadn't paid much attention. One general was pretty much the same as another to him. Tim paused for a moment, his jaw setting as he propped the cane up next to the door.

"Dav, you don't have to do that."

Tim shook his head. "They understand strength."

"The fact that you're walking at all is more strength than they could even begin to comprehend."

"They won't see it that way, and you know it. It's a smooth floor. I can do this."

Eric wanted to take Richard's side and insist, but Tim was right. It was the reason they wore their uniforms—minus their sabers—with their chests adorned with the medals and pins of their service, their ranks proclaimed proudly on their shoulders. They were SEALs, scarred by what they'd endured both in the service and out of it, but unbroken.

Richard's expression grew grim, but Eric didn't falter the way he might have once. He wasn't the one about to feel the force of Richard's displeasure. "One more thing for them to answer for."

Richard raised his hand to knock on the door, but Eric caught his fist before it connected. He gave Richard his most encouraging smile. "This is it. Don't fuck it up."

Richard huffed, but he smiled as Eric had intended. Then he rapped sharply on the door but didn't wait for the call to enter. Eric understood. The Pentagon had called the shots for long enough. It was their turn now.

"Commander Horn, Lieutenant Commander Davenport," Collins said coldly when they walked in.

"Collins," Richard acknowledged. Eric swallowed the smile that rose to his face at the general's expression at the slight. "General Mays." Collins's face looked like he'd swallowed a lemon, but he didn't reply. "This is Mr. Newton, our operations officer."

Eric didn't blink at the new title. He might have washed out of the military because he couldn't follow stupid orders, but life had given him as perfect a poker face as any man in the room.

Mays nodded his acknowledgment. "You said you needed to speak with us?"

Tim handed Eric the copies they had made of Heikkinen's report. The originals were safely stowed away where they could be leaked if things went badly, today or in the future, but Richard didn't expect it to come to that. Eric hoped he was right. He set them on the desk in front of Mays and settled back to watch the show.

THE TENSION that had been growing in Richard since their plane landed in Washington, D.C., exploded in his gut. They had only walked a dozen steps into the briefing room and already Dav was nearing the limits of what he could do without limping or stumbling. He wouldn't have given the folder to Eric otherwise. Sure, it included him, but Dav wouldn't have done it for that reason alone. Eric knew where he stood with them. He didn't need a symbolic inclusion to prove it. He took a deep breath and fixed Mays with his most intimidating stare. The man hadn't gotten to be a general by being a pushover, but Richard was a SEAL. He could stare down the best of them.

"We have prided ourselves over the past ten years in working with your generals. We were the weapon you pointed at a problem and we solved it, whatever it took. The only thing we requested—the only thing, General—was the most complete and accurate intelligence you could provide about the missions you were giving us. Yes, we're a covert ops group. Yes, we agreed to take missions that the Armed Forces couldn't be seen to touch. We evaluated the risks, made decisions accordingly, and did our jobs." Richard took a step forward, not quite in Mays's face, but close. They had too much riding on this to risk Mays not understanding how deadly serious they were. "We did our fucking jobs, and we did them well."

"I'm aware of your track record," Mays said.

"Then you're aware that about a year ago, Collins requested the loan of a sniper on an Army mission in Turkmenistan. The Army team came back. My sniper didn't." Richard wouldn't discuss what that had done to them. It wouldn't serve any purpose to talk about how it had shredded him to the very core when Eric hadn't checked in.

"Casualties are a regrettable part of any mission," Collins blustered.

"Bullshit," Eric interrupted before Richard could tear him a new one. It was probably just as well. They were done with Collins no matter what, but they were still hoping to work with Mays beyond this meeting. "They left me there. I wasn't wounded. I wasn't compromised. I wasn't even surrounded. I was abandoned, and when I tried to make my way out on my own, I was captured by the very people we were there to take out. I'm good, General Mays. I may even be exceptional, but I can only fight so many at a time before they win by sheer numbers alone."

Hearing it laid out so plainly brought all the rage and helplessness Richard had felt back to the fore. Eric hadn't just been captured. He'd been abandoned. Maybe not deliberately set up, but deliberately left behind.

"You were the sniper Horn sent?" Mays verified.

"I was. I was rescued by Strike Force Omega operatives four months later. Collins received a full report on my debriefing, which included the details of my capture," Eric said.

Mays frowned. "I remember the Turkmenistan mission. I don't remember a debrief."

"Maybe you should ask Collins about that," Dav said. "The report is included in the folder in front of you, along with a printout of the e-mail showing when we sent it to him and his acknowledgment. As troubling as that is, however, our people are our responsibility. We accepted that when we left the Navy and created our own force. What we did not expect was to have our own government provide us with false information prior to a mission."

"That's a hefty accusation," Mays observed.

Of course it was. They wouldn't be here if it were anything less than that.

"Our intelligence officer brought us the contents of that folder after a series of missions went bad in suspicious fashion," Richard said. "Newton didn't return. Davenport led a mission in Syria on a military installation, only to find he was attacking a village with little, if any, military activity. If you'll look at the first page, you'll see Collins's acknowledgment of a photoshopped image of the village. The original image is included in the file as well. That clusterfuck nearly cost Davenport his life."

Mays opened the folder and leafed through the first few pages. "What is it you want, gentlemen?"

"That depends on you," Richard replied. "We will not work with Collins again. Davenport is my eyes and Newton my hands, and Collins's fuckery nearly cost me both of them." Collins spluttered, but Richard ignored him. "If you want to continue employing the services of Strike Force Omega, we have a few conditions. Otherwise, we can leave right now, and Collins can find some other patsy willing to take the fall for him."

"There are dozens of organizations that would jump at the chance to work with us, without your scruples," Collins snarled.

Richard arched an eyebrow, but it was Dav who answered. "As you wish, gentlemen. I'd say it's been a pleasure, but we'd all know I was lying." He pivoted, militarily precise, and started toward the door. Richard could see what that had cost him. He followed on Dav's heels, ready to offer his support if Dav faltered even a little. Eric matched him on Dav's other side.

"What conditions?" Mays said, drawing them back.

"As I said, we will not work with Collins again or accept any mission he is involved in, regardless of how peripherally." Richard turned back to face them as he spoke, but he didn't approach the desk again.

"He currently oversees the majority of the areas where we need teams of your caliber," Mays replied. Richard nearly snorted at the flattery. Like that was going to sway them.

"Then I suggest you find us someone trustworthy to work with," Dav said. "You know how to reach us."

"And if I replace Collins as your contact? I imagine your list of demands is longer than just that."

Richard's rage broke free of his control. He couldn't stand there a second longer and listen to Mays try to protect Collins and figure out a way to keep them at the same time. They had fucked with him one time too many. It had nearly cost Dav and Eric their lives, and Mays wasn't even acknowledging Collins's lies. "You know what? I've changed my mind.

I've dedicated my entire adult life to serving this country, either officially or unofficially, and in doing so, nearly lost everything. I think that's enough. Collins says he can find a dozen other groups to take our place? Good luck with that. But think long and hard before you let him double-cross anyone else. We chose to report it. Some of our less *scrupulous* colleagues might choose to retaliate instead."

The words were out of his mouth before he could consider them, even before he really knew he was going to say them, but a quick glimpse at Dav and Eric showed no doubt on their faces. Quitting might not have been their plan when they walked in the door, but they were right with him now.

"Is that a threat?"

"No, it was a warning," Richard said.

"If you walk out that door, there won't be any more contracts," Mays said.

Richard laughed, though there was no humor in the sound. "That's what I'm counting on." He took Dav's elbow to help him out of the room. Eric walked on Dav's other side, although he didn't reach out while they were in sight of Collins and Mays. The moment the door closed behind them, Eric let out a whoop.

"Did you really just tell them to go to hell?"

Richard snorted. "Did I fuck it up?" He didn't think he had, but Dav and Eric wouldn't contradict him in front of anyone else even if they disagreed.

"Strike Force Omega is your life," Eric said.

Richard shook his head. "You and Dav are my life."

"What happens now? Besides not having to talk in code anymore," Dav asked.

Richard didn't know. He hadn't gone in with an exit strategy, but they had enough money saved up that they didn't have to do anything immediately, and even when they did, they could decide what. Eric might like to teach medieval history somewhere. He'd be the best damn teacher any of those kids ever had. Dav still had some recovering to do before he'd be good for much beyond computer work, but there was money to be made in consulting. They could keep their hands in without putting themselves in the line of fire. All of that could wait until later, though. "Whatever the hell we want."

Eric grinned, all teeth and sparkling eyes. "You have no idea how much I want to fuck you right now."

Richard grinned back and winked at Dav. Dav cocked an eyebrow at him in amusement.

"You did tell him anytime, anyplace," Dav reminded him. Like there was any chance of him forgetting. "Our hotel room is waiting."

He was in for the best fuck of his life.

ERIC KEPT his hands to himself all the way back to the hotel and into their room. He even waited through Tim and Richard taking off and hanging up their dress uniforms. When Richard disappeared into the bathroom, Eric turned to Tim.

"I won't have the patience to stretch him enough for us to both fuck him, so we'll have to find another way to fuck his brains out. Heads or tails?"

Tim grinned at him, the manic light in his blue eyes a sure match for the restlessness under Eric's skin. "I can't give him the reaming he deserves with my knee the way it is. I'll take heads."

"You're already better than that one doctor said you'd ever be, and even the most optimistic of them said it would be at least a year to recover. You'll get back to being able to ream him. Just wait and see." He saw the way it ate at Tim how slowly his rehab was going, but Eric had listened to the doctors and physical therapists talk. Tim might see it as slow, but everyone else was amazed at his progress. Eric and Richard just had to remind him of it occasionally.

Richard came back out of the bathroom wearing nothing but his underwear. Eric wolf-whistled because he could. Richard flipped him off, but he was smiling as he did, so Eric advanced on him intently.

"Get comfortable," he told Tim as he crowded against Richard. Richard opened his arms in welcome, settling his hands on the swell of Eric's ass as Eric pulled his head down into a torrid kiss. Behind them he heard Tim finish getting undressed and settle on the bed. He pushed Richard's underwear down and felt him step out of it, leaving him the only one partially clothed. "Lie down next to Tim."

"You calling the shots tonight?" Richard asked, but he did as Eric had directed.

"Unless you have a better idea."

Richard shook his head. "Nope, just checking."

"I did say I wanted to fuck you."

"So you did." Richard stretched out next to Tim and tugged him into a kiss. Eric stood there for a moment, watching them together. They fit together, yin and yang, perfect complements to each other. Even now when he saw them like this, he wondered how they had found the space between them to include him. He didn't question that he belonged with them. They had driven those doubts from his mind completely. No, he only wondered occasionally what had made them look his way in the first place. He climbed onto the king-size bed at their feet, one hand on each of their ankles. As he'd predicted, they rolled apart to leave space between them for him if he wanted it, but for once he didn't dive in the middle. Richard would argue with him if he said it, but he understood the magnitude of what Richard had sacrificed when he walked out of Mays's office an hour ago. He intended to show Richard just how grateful he was for it.

"Stay right where you are. Tim's going to keep your front warm while I take care of your back." He glanced up at Tim. "Unless you want to do the honors of stretching him out for us?"

"Not sure I can wait long enough for you to stretch me that much," Richard admitted, bringing back memories of the night he and Tim had done that to Eric. He hadn't thought he could wait either, but it had been worth it when Richard had finally prepared him enough that he could take them both at once. This afternoon, though, he suspected none of them had the patience for it.

"We'll save that for tomorrow, then," Eric said. "Tim, you didn't answer my question. You want to play with his ass for a while before I fuck it, or do you want his chest and mouth?"

"I never say no to playing with either of your asses," Tim replied with a wink. Eric tossed him the lube, which he caught handily and set aside. "Roll over the other way, Richard."

Richard turned so his back faced Tim. Eric stretched out in front of Richard and slid a hand over his hip. Richard leaned into the touch and tipped his face toward Eric for a kiss. Eric met him eagerly and delved into his mouth, determined to use every trick in his arsenal to make Richard feel good. He heard Tim shift on the bed again, only barely stopping himself from breaking the kiss to check on him, and then Richard bucked against him. Curiosity got the better of Eric, and he broke the kiss to see what Tim had done to make Richard react so strongly.

He should have known. Tim had slid down the bed enough to get his mouth on Richard's ass. He had long suspected that Richard's appreciation of being rimmed owed a lot to Tim's fervor for doing it. It hadn't been Eric's favorite form of foreplay until Tim had shown him how good it could feel.

Eric pressed one leg between Richard's, spreading them enough to give Tim room to work. That it also pressed their cocks together so that Richard ground directly against him each time Tim hit a particularly sensitive spot was a side benefit. Eric reached between them to stroke Richard a few times until he was fully hard. That was a good start, but he wasn't thrashing and moaning yet, and Eric was determined he'd be there before they were done with him. To that end he nipped his way down Richard's neck to his nipples, already standing at attention. "Somebody's eager," he teased as he flicked his finger across one of them.

"Somebody needs to stop teasing and get on with it," Richard grumbled.

Eric flicked again. "I thought that's what Tim was doing."

Richard jerked against Eric suddenly. Eric looked over his body at Tim's grin. "Did you just bite him?"

"Somebody had to punish him for his insolence."

Eric laughed at the grumpy look on Richard's face and kissed him to ease the sting of their teasing. Richard never refused if Tim or Eric was in the mood to take charge, but he had enough of the commander in him to cede only slowly. The trust it required humbled Eric, a reminder of the truth of Richard's assertion that he and Tim needed Eric too, because it almost always took both of them to get him to relax and completely let go.

He'd learned the trick now, though, so Richard could be as grumpy as he wanted. He'd give in when Eric started sucking his nipples. He took a deep breath, letting the scent of Richard's cologne mingled with desire add to his own arousal. If he hadn't felt Richard growing tense beneath his hands, he might have stayed there longer, just enjoying the smell. Instead he leaned in and licked across one tight peak. Richard groaned and grabbed his head, pressing him closer. Eric sucked Richard's nipple into his mouth and held it between his teeth, not quite biting down. Richard dug his fingers into Eric's scalp, so Eric retaliated by flicking his tongue back and forth across the captive flesh. Richard bucked against him so hard Eric wondered for a second if they'd made him come already. He was flying high from his meeting. It wouldn't be the first time adrenaline had brought things to a faster conclusion between them than they expected. Richard was still hard, though, so Eric moved his mouth to the other nipple even as he continued to tweak the first one with his fingers.

"Fuck, you're killing me," Richard said. "If this isn't your end game, it's time to move on."

Eric released his hold on Richard's nipples and pushed up on one elbow to meet Tim's gaze. They could certainly do it this way, get Richard off and then take care of each other, but it wasn't what they'd talked about.

Tim rolled to his back with a grunt and sat up. "Not the end game, but you'll have to give me a minute."

Richard sat up immediately and offered Tim a hand so he could shift up to a sitting position against the headboard. "Hey, you used to not be able to shift positions at all once we got in bed," Richard reminded him when Tim grimaced at needing the help.

"You set?" Eric asked.

Tim nodded.

Eric nudged Richard's hip. "Up on your knees. You get fucked from both ends this way."

Richard fell on Tim's cock like a starving man, leaving his ass in the air just begging for Eric's attention. Eric met Tim's gaze over Richard's back as he grabbed a condom and rolled it on. Tim's blue eyes had already glazed over from Richard's mouth on him. Eric smiled at the sight as he slicked himself and probed Richard's entrance to make sure he was wet enough to take it. Tim must have stretched him as he was rimming him, because he was loose and wet, just waiting for Eric.

Tim grabbed Richard's head, holding him still while Eric pressed in. He'd intended to go slowly, but Richard rocked back hard, forcing Eric all the way inside him. Eric groaned.

"Don't you love it when he's too eager to wait?" Tim asked.

"God, yes." Eric rocked forward, pushing Richard toward Tim. Tim braced his hand next to his hip and thrust up into Richard's mouth as best he could. Maybe it wasn't as forceful or as graceful as he once would have been, but Richard certainly didn't seem to care as he groaned around Tim's cock and bobbed his head to meet each thrust. Eric timed his movements to Tim's so that he pushed Richard forward each time Tim lifted up, driving into Richard from both directions. His head swam with the intensity of Richard's tight heat around him and the thought of true freedom and what that would mean to all three of them now that they no longer had to worry about moving in the shadows. He'd been sucked into them before he was fifteen and had been convinced he'd die in them, right up until Richard and Tim had given him hope for something else, but even then, he'd spent more time there than out with all the missions they took. Now though….

"You know what today is, right?" he said as he thrust into Richard again. Richard couldn't answer, although he turned his head just enough to show he was listening.

"What?" Tim asked for them both.

"Our independence day," Eric said. "As of today, we don't take orders from anyone. We're free."

"Free," Tim repeated with a soft laugh that turned to a groan when Richard bobbed his head to take him deep again. "I like the sound of that."

Richard clenched around Eric, who could practically hear him grumbling, "More fucking, less talking." Richard had given them their freedom with his actions in the meeting today. He thrust harder, giving Richard what he was asking for now. He ran his hand up Richard's spine as he did. "You gave us that," he told Richard. "You went in there today to protect us, and you came out having gained us so much more than just protection."

He kept pummeling Richard as he spoke, past the point of trying to match his movements to Tim's. He looked up to check on Tim, only to find Tim watching him with such intensity that he nearly lost it.

"No more worrying that this will be the mission someone doesn't come back from," Tim said.

"No more playing politics with the Pentagon," Eric added.

"No more playing politics with the teams," Tim said. "Nothing but the three of us and whatever we want to do."

Eric stroked Tim's calf, needing some contact with him, and reached around Richard with his other hand to stroke his cock. "Make him come, and I'll make you come."

Richard groaned and hollowed his cheeks around Tim's erection. Tim let out a hoarse shout and bucked up into Richard's mouth. With his head thrown back and his eyes closed in ecstasy, he was utter perfection in Eric's eyes. He collapsed against the headboard, panting hard.

Eric pulled out long enough to flip Richard onto his back. He needed to see Richard's face too. The moment Richard was settled, Eric plunged back into his tight passage, throwing all his weight behind the thrust. "Fuck!" Richard gasped.

"That's exactly what he's doing," Tim said, deadpan.

Eric snorted despite the intensity of the moment and fucked Richard as hard as he could. "That way?" he teased.

Richard didn't answer, but Eric hadn't expected one, not with him pounding Richard's ass and Tim playing with Richard's nipples. Eric stroked Richard's cock a couple of times, and that was all it took. The spasms of his muscles set Eric off in turn, and his elbows gave out. He landed on top of Richard with a grunt, his brain shorting out from the pleasure.

He tipped his head into the caress of one of his lover's hands, Tim's probably given the angle and the fact that the hands on his hips almost had to be Richard's. He pressed a kiss to Richard's sternum and levered himself up on his elbows again.

"Where are you going?" Richard grumbled, not letting go of his grip on Eric's hips.

"Nowhere," Eric said. "Just getting rid of the condom." He dealt with it as quickly as he could and then settled back between Richard and Tim. They rolled onto their sides to surround him with their heat. He sighed happily. "Not going anywhere ever again."

When ARIEL TACHNA was twelve years old, she discovered two things: the French language and romance novels. Those two loves have defined her ever since. By the time she finished high school, she'd written four novels, none of which anyone would want to read now, featuring a young woman who was—you guessed it—bilingual. That girl was everything Ariel wanted to be at age twelve and wasn't.

She now lives on the outskirts of Houston with her husband (who also speaks French), her kids (who understand French even when they're too lazy to speak it back), and their two dogs (who steadfastly refuse to answer any French commands). The cat pretends they're all beneath her, no matter what language they're speaking.

Visit Ariel:
Website: www.arieltachna.com
Facebook: www.facebook.com/ArielTachna
E-mail: arieltachna@gmail.com

An At Your Service Novel

When Anthony Mercer walked into Au cœur du terroir, he was looking for good food and a pleasant evening spent with a friend. He never expected to meet—and sleep with—Paul Delescluse, a waiter at the restaurant. After spending a magical week together in Paris, Anthony must return to his life in North Carolina, while Paul remains in France.

Despite the distance and the lack of promises between them—Paul wants sex, not a relationship—Paul and Anthony forge a solid friendship. Then Anthony's job takes him back to Paris, this time to stay. Paul is thrilled to have him back, but Anthony has a harder choice: be another of Paul's conquests or fight for the relationship he knows they could have, if only Paul would believe it.

www.dreamspinnerpress.com

ARIEL TACHNA

SERVICE
WITH A
Smirk

An At Your Service Novel

Pascal Larocque, a waiter at a high-end Montréal restaurant, knows what it means to love—and he knows what it means to lose. He buried the man he expected to spend his life with years ago. He's perfectly happy with his solitude, or so he tells his friends. But a chance encounter in a neighborhood bar followed by a run-in at his apartment building turns his world upside down.

Mathias Perras is twenty-four, newly arrived in Montréal, and works two jobs so he can live on rue Sainte-Catherine in the heart of the gay district. During the day, he's on a fast track to management at the Banque de Montréal. At night, he waits tables at a gay bar down the street. He's burning the candle at both ends, but it will be worth it when his career takes off and he has the life he's always dreamed of. When he meets Pascal, one more piece of that dream slots into place. Pascal is everything he wants in a lover: older, self-assured, established in his life and his career. But Pascal doesn't look at him twice. What's a boy have to do to get a little action?

www.dreamspinnerpress.com

DREAMSPUN DESIRES

Ariel Tachna

UNSTABLE STUD

Lexington Lovers

Horses were his passion, until he laid eyes on his boss.

Lexington Lovers

Horses were his passion, until he laid eyes on his boss.

Eighteen months ago, tragedy struck Bywater Farm when a riding accident killed Clay Hunter's lover and traumatized his prize horse, King of Hearts. Clay and King lingered in limbo, surviving but not really living, until a breath of fresh air in the form of Luke Davis, a new groom in the stud barn, revives them both.

When a fall from King's back sends Luke to the emergency room, Clay watches the shaky foundation of their budding relationship tumble down. Can Clay really love a jockey again, or will his fear of losing another man he loves keep them apart for good?

www.dreamspinnerpress.com

DREAMSPUN
DESIRES

A MATCHLESS
MAN

Ariel Tachna

Lexington
Lovers

None of the matches
caught his eye as much
as the matchmaker himself.

Lexington Lovers

None of the matches caught his eye as much as the matchmaker himself.

Growing up poorer than poor didn't leave Navashen Bhattathiri many options for life outside of school. All of his concentration was on keeping his scholarships. Sixteen years later, he's fulfilled his dream and become a doctor. Now he's returning home to Lexington and is ready to prove himself to the world. In doing so, he reconnects with Brent Carpenter—high school classmate, real estate agent, all-around great guy… and closet matchmaker.

Brent makes it his mission to help Navashen develop a social life and meet available, interesting men. Unfortunately Navashen's schedule is unpredictable, and few of those available, interesting men value his dedication like Brent does. Brent's unfailing friendship and support convince Navashen he's the one, but can he capture Brent's heart when the matchmaker is focused on finding Navashen another man?

www.dreamspinnerpress.com

CHECKMATE

Nicki Bennett
and
Ariel Tachna

All for Love: Book One

When sword-for-hire Teodoro Ciéza de Vivar accepts a commission to "rescue" Lord Christian Blackwood from unsuitable influences, he has no idea he's landed himself in the middle of a plot to assassinate King Philip IV of Spain and blame the English ambassador for the deed. Nor does he expect the spoiled child he's sent to retrieve to be a handsome, engaging young man.

As Teodoro and Christian face down enemies at every turn, they fall more and more in love, an emotion they can't safely indulge with the threat of the Inquisition looming over them. It will take all their combined guile and influence to outmaneuver the powerful men who would see them separated… or even killed.

www.dreamspinnerpress.com